PRAISE FOR WILIAM H. LOVEJOY:

"An ultracool, swiftly paced tale of cyberspace chicanery."
—*Kirkus Reviews* on BACK\SLASH

"Lovejoy knows his computers inside-out. Fascinating."
—*Publishers Weekly* on *BACK\SLASH*

"A nice blend of high-tech corporate espionage, subterfuge, and sabotage. Tightly plotted, well-written and thoroughly engaging." —Nelson DeMille on CHINA DOME

". . . a crisp sabotage thriller . . . like Craig Thomas's, Clive Cussler's and Tom Clancy's works. Hard, tight action sequences."
—*Colorado Reporter-Herald* on CHINA DOME

"An exciting aerial thriller. Buckle your seat belts!"
—Joe Weber on DELTA GREEN

"Lovejoy writes in afterburner . . . leaves you dry-lipped, moist-palmed and hungry for more."
—M.E. Morris on ALPHA KAT

"High-tech . . . red-hot . . . thriller fans are going to enjoy this one!" —Stephen Coonts on ALPHA KAT

"Lovejoy has proven himself a master storyteller . . . solidly entertaining." —Clive Cussler on ULTRA DEEP

This story is dedicated to some strong and selfless people:

Commissioners George Douglas, Pat Goodson, Ed Jolovich, Lorraine Quarberg, Judy Vasey, Linda Vosika, and Don Warfield,

And to the talented people who support them:

Steve Butler, Tully Holmes, Deborah Iverson, Joe Moreland, Carol Narva, Rachel Riles, and Terry Steege.

PINNACLE BOOKS are published by

Kensington Publishing Corp.
850 Third Avenue
New York, NY 10022

First Pinnacle Printing: January, 1999
10 9 8 7 6 5 4 3 2 1

Printed in the United States of America

PARADISE

One

If it were not for the man in the rear compartment who was trying stoically to control the pain in his gut, Kelly Koehler would have worried less and enjoyed himself more.

From the helicopter three thousand feet above it, the sea was as flat and smooth as azure ice. Eight miles away, the jungle of the coast was a greenish smudge riding the horizon and wavering in the humid heat. In the west, towering stratocumulus clouds, pristine against the brassy blue of the sky, promised their daily deluge.

A seventy-foot Shell International platform tender cut a slice out of the blue ice dead ahead, her bows tossing a white curl to either side as she lumbered along at twenty knots. She was headed toward Lumut.

A couple miles to the east, the magnificent sight of a Chinese junk under full sail caught Koehler's attention and imagination. In the hurry-up 1990s, most junks were converted to diesel power, and seeing one rigged with the square lugsails was a rarity.

Koehler had an affection for almost anything well-aged, well-maintained, and seaworthy. His wife, Sherry, complained that his mistresses of the sea were overly alluring even though they were sexually inactive. Still, Sherry enjoyed having control of the helm as much as he did.

As the chopper passed over Shell's tender, a few sailors on the deck threw casual waves their way.

Frank Morris, the helicopter's usual pilot, returned the greeting through his side window, then said, "You saw the junk?"

"Couldn't miss it, Frank. You know my personal radar homes in on anything with sails."

"That one's local, right?"

"The Chinese chief of mission lives aboard, I heard. Someday, I'm going to ask him for a tour."

"You're going to be down there tomorrow, aren't you, boss?"

Koehler glanced at the man in the left seat of the Aèrospatiale Dauphin and said, "Tomorrow's Saturday, Frank. Where else would I be?"

"I was told you exec types were supposed to put in all your overtime on Saturdays. I wish you'd live up to it."

Koehler laughed. He was the Field Manager and ranking local executive for GlobeTech Explorations, but he was also a diehard weekend sailor. There wasn't much that could keep him out of the cockpit of the forty-foot ketch that he moored in Brunei's principal harbor at Muara. He and Sherry devoted their Saturdays and/or Sundays to sailing some of the most beautiful waters he had ever encountered. He'd been doing it for nineteen months, and though it meant some long days and nights during the week, he tried his best to keep his weekends clear.

"You don't know what you're missing, Frank. You want to go out with us tomorrow? We're going to spend two days sailing north toward the southern end of the Sulu Sea."

"I get seasick, Kelly."

"Not in these seas, you won't."

Frank Morris shook his head. "I've got to overdose on Dramamine before I get in the bathtub."

The assertion was hard to believe. Morris was a hard-bodied forty-one-year-old, though the body was constructed along the lines of a fire hydrant. The squint lines at the corners of his eyes and the silver-faced sunglasses told the world he was a pilot. The red bandanna sweatband and the stubble on his cheeks suggested he might be a tough one. He'd flown Army Apache attack choppers in the Gulf War and racked up enough flight hours in other rotary aircraft types to warrant his position as Koehler's chief pilot in Brunei. He headed the four-pilot, two-helicopter air force that supported the GlobeTech offshore drilling operations.

Koehler had first met Morris in the Gulf when Kelly was on active duty with his naval reserve unit, flying Sikorsky Sea King search-and-rescue helicopters off the *Roosevelt* during the hundred-day war.

When Koehler wanted to bring his flight time up to date, Morris went to the left seat, and his copilot, Andy Jenkins, went to the back. Jenkins was in the rear compartment now, tending to a roughneck they'd just lifted off GT Bravo and who was in the early stages of an appendicitis attack. The roughneck's name was Pete, but Kelly couldn't recall his last name. His weather- and sun-beaten face was pale and twitched now and then, and he'd let everyone in earshot know he wasn't happy about his forthcoming surgery.

Having the sick man aboard kept Koehler from really

enjoying himself, skimming a few wave tops or cutting some high-G maneuvers, but he was happy to have a cyclic and a collective in his hands once again. Morris, who was responsible for the chopper according to the corporate organization, was just as happy to have him flying on the straight and level, no doubt.

"If you change your mind by five in the morning, let me know."

"That's another thing," Morris said. "Sailors get up too early."

"Makes us fearless."

"Fearless? Hey, Kelly, the word you're searching for is 'foolhardy.' "

"You Army guys just don't get it, do you?"

"We don't get wet on purpose."

Koehler maintained his southwest heading toward Bandar Seri Begawan, the capital city, and kept an eye peeled for other air traffic. There wasn't much of it. A Brunei Shell helicopter was outbound from the coast for one of the platforms now several miles behind him. Another helo, an Air Services Sikorsky S-61, announced it was just taking off from Conoco Crystal. A Gulfstream corporate jet coming out of Singapore was somewhere in the vicinity, headed for the airport at Bandar Seri Begawan. Koehler hadn't seen it, but he heard the Brunei air controller talking to its pilot.

His secondary radio was tuned to UHF 243.0, the international distress channel which, in the Navy, he'd referred to as Guard. There was rarely any traffic on the channel, so he was half shocked when he heard:

"Anyone! Anyone on this channel!"

He stabbed the transmit switch on the stick and spoke into the microphone cantilevered in front of his mouth from the headset.

"This is GT Zero-Two on two-four-three. Am I responding to an emergency call, over?"

"Yes! Yes! This is BS Albatross. There has been an explosion!"

The man on the radio wasn't the normal operator, Koehler thought.

He looked left and saw that Morris was already checking the chart for the location of the platform.

"What kind of explosion? How bad?"

"A very big explosion, mister. There are many dead and injured, and we cannot reach many of the lifeboats. The platform is on fire! Please to help us?"

The controller broke in to say that other helicopters were on the way.

The Shell International platform tender that they had passed over earlier also replied in the affirmative. So did a half dozen other boats running around in the offshore oil field. The emergency channel became chaotic with overriding transmissions.

Koehler glanced over his shoulder into the rear compartment. On the intercom, he asked, "What about Pete?"

Jenkins, with a headset clamped over his ears, was telling the stricken and white-faced roughneck about the problem. He had to yell over the roar of the twin turboshaft engines.

The driller, in obvious pain, said, "Ah, shit, I can hold on. Go for it!"

If it were Pete on a burning rig, he'd want the same reaction from anyone with a hand to lend.

Jenkins looked up at him, and Koehler nodded. He put the Dauphin into a right bank and picked up speed.

"Brunei Air," he said over the air, "GT Zero-Two is responding to the emergency at Albatross."

"We want two-six-five, Kelly," Morris said.

"Going to two-six-five."

"I wonder what the hell happened," Morris said.

Friday, March 7, 1:49 P.M.

"Excuse me, Captain."

The master of the Ultra Large Crude Carrier (ULCC) *Maru Hokkaido* turned from his study of the eastern seas and gave his attention to the junior communications officer.

"Apparently one of the platforms is on fire, sir. There is a great deal of traffic on the emergency frequency."

"Injuries?"

"Yes, sir. Fatalities, also, from the early reports."

The first law of the sea was to respond to others in distress, but the *Hokkaido* was not a ship with the ability to cruise through oil fields; she was far too huge. This was an emergency he could do nothing about.

It was also an emergency that raised inexplicable little tingles in his mind. His palms itched.

Captain Maki Hirosiuta spun on his heel and crossed the busy bridge to the port-wing windows. His officers magically cleared a path for him.

The ULCC was moored at the pumping station with her stern aimed southward, toward the coast of Brunei, though the shoreline was not visible. At six hundred meters of length, the supertanker dwarfed her sisters resting nearby. Seven crude oil carriers were nuzzling from the man-made islands of the pumping stations, and another eleven rode at anchor several kilometers away, awaiting their turns. On the other side of this station, a Very Large Crude Carrier (VLCC) was pumping off seawater ballast as she started taking on the more precious liquid.

The bridge, located high on the stern superstructure,

was seven stories above the surface, and Hirosiuta had a clear view over the VLCC toward the oil field to the southwest. Oil rigs dotted the horizon like a sparse forest. The smudge of black rising on the far side of the field seemed insignificant at this distance, but he knew that it was not.

He had a connection with it.

The undersea pipelines, resting on the floor of the ocean, connected all of the drilling platforms with the pumping stations. Hirosiuta knew there was no danger for his ship; fire could not traverse the pipelines—for lack of oxygen, and in any event, the valves to the stricken rig would have been closed immediately. He also felt a connection with the men aboard the platform. Fellow sea travellers, almost. He hoped none of them were injured.

An eerie chill slithered down his spine. He thought that Brunei was a place he would rather not be.

Dismissing the communications officer, he took three steps to the forward windscreen and stared down at the deck. The bow was a third of a kilometer away; in severe storms at sea, it would disappear from the view of the bridge. On the main deck, with its checkerboard of large hatches and maze of piping and pumps, half of his 120-man crew scurried about, shunting the flow of oil from one tank to another, securing hatches, preparing for the deluge to be spilled into empty tanks. Five half-meter diameter hoses, suspended from the cables of amidships and forward cranes, connected the pumping station to the receptacles on the ship. As he watched, a crew of four disconnected one of the hoses, and the crane operator swung it away from the deck, back toward its rightful place on the station. Another crew armed with brooms and high-pressure water hoses began immediately to scrub the deck of oil spillage. Hirosiuta demanded that his ship be maintained in first-class order. Scum and rust were not allowed to accumulate.

Without taking his eyes from their perusal of the deck, he asked, "Load status, First Officer?"

Yaguchi, who stood near a computer monitor placed below the windscreen, responded immediately. "Another six thousand barrels, Captain, and we will be fully loaded."

"Time?"

"Within the hour, sir."

"Alert the engineering officer and prepare to retrieve lines. We will get under way as soon as the last hose is disconnected."

"Yes, sir."

The captain waited for the complaint.

"Uh, sir?"

"Yes?"

"Sir, the men . . . well, I believe they were anticipating a few hours of free time ashore."

"I know, First Officer Yaguchi, and I sympathize fully. However, my instinct suggests our interests will be far better served the sooner we are at sea."

Hirosiuta knew it was difficult to argue with the captain's instincts.

Two

Friday, March 7, 1:52 P.M.

Standing at the cluttered counter in the pharmacy, she said, "Good afternoon, Mr. Zhou."

He gave her the shadow of a smile, but did not really look into her eyes. "Good morning, Mrs. Koehler. How may I help you?"

"I need a bottle of aspirin. The one-hundred count, I think."

He stepped back to a shelf and found the box, and she asked, "How is your new granddaughter?"

"She is fine."

"I'll bet she's a beautiful baby. I'd love to see her sometime."

"Yes."

He placed the bottle in a small sack, took her Brunei dollars, and counted out her change without saying another word.

It was strange; he was usually so talkative. His wife, normally out in front, was nowhere to be seen. Well, maybe she was with the daughter and the new baby.

She bid him goodbye and walked a half block to the market where she bought tea, Coca-Cola, bread, butter, and potatoes. Kelly had told her he was sick of rice. In all of the exotic places they'd lived, he'd adapted to the prevalent cuisine, but at heart he was a Sunday-roast-beef-and-potatoes guy.

At the market, she again sensed a reservation in the Chinese woman who operated it with her husband. There was a resistance to meeting her eyes.

Sheryl Koehler thought the difference in attitude from just two days before was remarkable.

She taught English three mornings a week in the Chinese elementary school three blocks from her house. Malay was the official language of the country, but Chinese and English were mainstays also, and the schools were always looking for a little help from native speakers. On Tuesdays she assisted in another elementary school where the predominant language was Malay and the religion was Islam. It was closed on Fridays, naturally.

She enjoyed working with the children immensely, and the jobs also gave her an excuse to not spend every day with the wives of foreign workers—primarily administrators in the oil game and governmental bureaucrats—who dedicated a great deal of their lives to tennis and bridge. A few, she was certain, would have dedicated themselves to daily appointments with martinis if alcohol were not banned in Brunei. And a few others found solace in evaluating their prospects with the husbands of their tennis partners.

The majority of the foreign community was housed in Kuala Belait or Seria, the towns sixty kilometers to the west which served the oil fields. The seventy thousand toolpushers, roughnecks, roustabouts, engineers, chemists, cooks, clerks, and divers were quartered in neat little rows of prefabricated housing. In Bandar Seri Begawan, the managers and some of the technical people for a dozen oil companies mixed with the few representatives of the diplomatic corps. Brunei Shell Petroleum, a fifty-fifty partnership of Shell International and the Brunei government, was by far the largest entity, but other smaller companies had similar arrangements with the government. GlobeTech was one of them, and the contract was the reason she and Kelly were living in paradise.

Carrying her umbrella, Sherry strolled the tree-shaded street toward the center of town. With a population of around seventy thousand people, the capital was not an overwhelming metropolis. In fact, it had all the character of any Malay town, complete with open sewage canals, which made the air less than aromatic. The exceptions in the capital were a few high-rise government buildings, the Winston Churchill Museum, and several hotels. Tourism was not promoted at all, and there were only nine hotels in the entire country.

As she wandered back toward the four-room house on the river that she and Kelly had rented, she paused frequently to speak to the people—many of whom she knew by name—whose friendships she had fostered since their arrival in-country. Usually, they were interesting conversations, conducted in a melange of English and Chinese. Over time, she had accumulated bits and pieces of Malay and Chinese, but she was by no means fluent in either language.

By the time she had picked up her cleaning and had her arms full of packages, Koehler was certain that something was wrong. It was nothing overt, merely an undercurrent of change in the people she thought she had come

to know. They were reticent to talk to her; they knew
something she did not know.

It was unnerving.

She hoped Kelly got home early so she could discuss it
with him.

She didn't like feeling spooky.

Or spooked.

Friday, March 7, 2:11 P.M.

Headed west at 150 knots air speed, Koehler soon saw
the thicker, blacker column of smoke rising on the far side
of the field of offshore platforms, about thirty miles away.
The drilling rigs stretched across the horizon ahead, reaching from the shores of Brunei out beyond the twelve-mile
limit on his right. The separation between platforms was
anywhere from a half mile to a mile. It was one of the
richest reserves in the world, and no one wanted it to last
any longer than necessary. By the year 2010, there wouldn't
be anything left.

"Shades of Kuwait," Kelly said.

"Gotta be bad," Morris told him, "if we can see it from
here."

Almost every offshore platform was burning its excess
gas in a bright flame and thin trickle of white smoke from
their vertical flare towers, the high points on the rigs.
Simply by the inky color of the smoke ahead of them,
it was apparent that Brunei Shell Albatross was in deep
trouble.

"It's especially bad if they can't reach the lifeboats,
Frank."

Lifeboat stations tended to be scattered at different levels
and on all four sides of the platforms. For a typical plat-

form, there could be as many as 250 men working at various tasks on seven or eight decks.

"Andy," Koehler said on the intercom, "you want to deploy the hoist?"

"Will do."

He didn't know whether he'd need it or not, but he wanted to be prepared. Koehler hoped it didn't come to pulling one man at a time from the platform or the water.

A blast of air sent dust and a few papers swirling around the cabin as Jenkins slid the side door open and reached outside to swing the stubby arm of the hoist from its flight position folded above the door. Koehler took a quick look back to make certain Jenkins was wearing a lifeline. He was.

"How's Pete holding up?" he asked.

"He says he's all right," Jenkins said.

Morris switched the primary radio to the UHF channel used by Brunei Shell and a cacophony of overriding transmissions assaulted their ears. It sounded as if the MSV *Malay Princess* out of Kuala Belait was under way. Besides providing diving services, the Multifunction Service Vessel (MSV) was a floating firefighter. It would also take her at least an hour to reach the scene. Platforms near the damaged rig attempted to call in reports, but only served to confuse the communications. They couldn't react to the emergency anyway, beyond sending their guard boats. Additional choppers were reported taking off from Kuala Belait and Seria.

"Did you catch that report, Kelly?" Morris asked.

"Yeah. Seven dead. This isn't a good start."

A few minutes later, he was into the field, losing altitude to 500 feet AGL (Above Ground Level) as he passed between the first platforms—a Brunei Shell rig and one belonging to Exxon. The wakes of small boats were interspersed among the platforms, all aimed in the direction

of BS Albatross. Each rig was supposed to have a guard
boat attending it at all times, and some of them were
abandoning their current tasks to assist Albatross.

The smoke boiling off the rig was prominent now, thick
and black and churning in the air as it stretched for the
sky. It was an obviously oil-fed fire. Beyond the column,
he saw that rain clouds were approaching from the west.
Well, they'd need all the help they could get.

"How many wells, you think?" Morris asked him.

An offshore installation was far too expensive to be
devoted to drilling one well. Most platforms drilled multi-
ple wells on different angles. All three of the platforms
Koehler was responsible for would eventually complete
forty-eight wells each.

"She's been there awhile, Frank, and though she's
smaller than most, I'd bet we're talking around thirty holes
in production."

Koehler knew a little something about most of the installations in the field. It was part of his job, and he was good
at it. He'd been working oil fields since he was seventeen
in Oklahoma, earning weekend gas money as a roustabout.
Now, at forty-one, he had a petroleum-engineering degree
from the Colorado School of Mines and twenty years' experience with three corporations, seven with GlobeTech. The
years in harsh environments had kept him hard, and maybe
a little hard-edged. The sun had bleached his chestnut
hair several shades lighter, and a few crises had added
dashes of gray to it. His face was lean, weather-tanned,
rugged with crow's feet and laugh and worry lines, and
from it, his gray eyes smiled or drilled, fierce as any diamond-
tipped drilling bit.

Many of the installations reached to his altitude, and
Koehler kept the Dauphin far away from them. The platforms in the Brunei field ranged from 500 to 800 feet in
total height, though about half their length was below the

surface. That still left three or four hundred feet projecting from the surface of the sea. With decks that were the equivalent of ten to thirty stories above the ocean, one didn't casually step off into space. From those heights, the landing surface might as well have been concrete. Abandoning ship was not as easy as it sounded.

Koehler bled off more altitude as they got closer and assessed the surface. Pretty calm, a two-foot sea running. A bit of a breeze preceded the storm clouds coming out of the southwest. Would have been a good day for sailing.

He should call Sherry, let her know what was going on. Maybe a little later, after he'd assessed how long it might take.

"Half mile," Morris said.

"Jesus!" Jenkins exclaimed from the back, where he was hanging halfway out the side door.

"Drilling deck and module deck are totally engulfed," Koehler said, then said it again on the radio when he realized that no one had been making reports to the air controller.

"Thank you, GT Zero-Two. What more can you tell me?"

Kelly figured a bunch of bureaucrats were gathered around radios, listening in. They'd be worried.

"The lower two decks of the seven-deck platform are a maelstrom of red and yellow flames. On the western side, flames are crawling the full height of the rig, and the chopper pad is hidden in smoke." He circled the rig counterclockwise. "Six of the lifeboat stations are accessed from those decks, and all six boats are still hanging in their davits Hold on! Now, five boats! We just lost one."

While he watched, the sixth boat lost its tethers to fingers of fire and tumbled in flames 150 feet to the sea.

There were already other lifeboats launched, and they were struggling to get clear of the three massive legs of the installation. The guard boat, a fifty-foot trawler moonlighting from its fishing duties, was attempting to gather the lifeboats, as well as pick up a few swimmers. They had either jumped and survived or, since one of the two cranes had its cable extended to the surface, slid down the cable. The crane operator might well have made his last load a cargo net full of drillers, welders, and painters. Some men might have gone down the lifeboat lines suspended from davits.

He quickly briefed the controller on those aspects, then said, "Brunei Air, I'm about to go in."

"Copy, GT Zero-Two."

Koehler raised the nose a little, gained a few feet of altitude.

"Watch the two-twelve, Kelly."

"I see it."

The Brunei Shell helicopter was a Bell 212. It was hovering just off the top deck, trying to maintain stability in the broiling smoke and heated air currents rolling off the hot metal of the steel structure, while eager hands in the rear compartment pulled oil workers aboard. The 212 could handle fourteen passengers.

The helicopter pad, perched on steel beams and trusses fifty feet above the top deck on the northwest corner, and identified by a yellow circle with a large white "H" in the center of it, was useless. It was surrounded by flame and smoke, and Koehler could see where the deck had buckled from heat.

The Bell shot away.

"GT Zero-Two's in next," Kelly called on the radio.

"Go," someone said back. He didn't know who it was, but certainly not an air controller.

Koehler zoomed in to take the Bell's place. His vision was hampered by the roiling smoke, and while the rotors blasted it away, he was limited to about fifty feet of visibility. Coming out of that hellish cloud were dozens of men, choking, clamping wet towels and shirts to their heads. They were blinded by the smoke and searching for any angel. They were surprisingly in control, he thought, many of them helping their injured fellows.

The hot, roiling air made the approach tricky. His hands on the cyclic and the collective were poised for instant reversal.

"C'mon, a little more, five feet . . . four. . . ."

Andy Jenkins's voice sounded in his earphones as Koehler inched the Dauphin sideways toward the deck. Morris lowered the landing gear. The acrid tang of burnt oil assaulted his nostrils. The roaring bellow of flames could be heard above the whine of his engines. The fires sucked up oxygen fast, leaving little for men to breathe. Suffocation or smoke inhalation might be preferable to death by burning, he thought. Some of these images he had seen before, in Kuwait and southern Iraq. Koehler didn't like them a bit, but he wasn't about to shy away from them. If he could help, he'd do it.

A steel module for some use was hung from a tower over the side of the platform directly in front of him. Kelly watched it closely because his rotors were spinning less than four feet from it.

"You want me to do this, Kelly?" Morris asked.

He knew Frank was gently reminding him that the Army pilot had more recent flight hours, and many more of them, than the Field Manager.

"You Apache types shoot 'em down. I pick 'em up. I know how to do it." Koehler immediately regretted his snappish tone. "Sorry, Frank. I've got it."

"Sure thing."

The Dauphin slid sideways, bucking in the air.

"Down a tad, boss!" Jenkins shouted from the rear compartment.

Koehler, glancing through his side window, saw that a

tad was two feet. He eased off and the right-side main gear touched down, more or less. It was straddling the three-foot-high steel barrier protecting the edge of the deck. The left-side gear hung in space.

"C'mon, you guys!" Jenkins yelled. "I can take eight!"

A group at the front of the pack broke away and ran for the chopper, pushing injured men first, scrambling up the railing, then over the threshold of the doorway. Jenkins hauled them in.

They got nine, Kelly adding power as the payload on the chopper increased. Piling on weight while not sitting on a pad was tricky.

"Go!" Jenkins shouted.

He lifted a little to clear the gear from the railing, then sailed off to the left.

A glance in the back showed him confusion. The Aèrospatiale was rigged with eight seats, and they tended to get in the way of rescue operations. He saw two men with burned hands. They sat in their seats, staring at the backs of their raw and bleeding hands.

The Sikorsky, which could load thirty souls, was right behind him and warned him of its presence on the radio.

"Copy that, Air Services," he replied, then said on the intercom, "Pick me a place, Frank."

"The Bell's dumping on the trawler. There's another one coming, two o'clock."

He looked ahead to the right and saw the boat. It was a power cruiser, also probably working as a platform guard boat, and Koehler headed for it.

The captain figured out right away what he was up to and killed his throttles. As the cruiser died in the water, Koehler swung around to its stern, and watching his rotors for clearance near the boat's flying bridge, settled until Jenkins's open door was about six feet above the upholstered seat spanning the stern well deck. A deckhand appeared and tried to catch people as roughnecks and roustabouts rained down on him.

"All clear," Morris said.

"Let's do it again," Koehler told him.

He noticed the sea was picking up a little, as was the wind, and took a look to the west. Twenty minutes and they'd have their standard afternoon shower.

It looked like it was going to be a long afternoon.

When he got turned around to face the platform again, he saw that the Sikorsky was still in place, loading. The civilian helicopter was the same type he'd flown for the Navy, which called it a Sea King. The Bell 212 was hovering behind it, waiting for another chance.

Koehler drifted off to the left, to check the other side of the installation. The problem there was that the derrick and an unmanned crane with its boom lowered to horizontal prevented a chopper from getting close enough to the deck to make a pickup.

On this side, the flaring tower interfered with the arc of the rotors, and on the other side, a wall of flame wasn't going to allow anyone through.

Two more helicopters arrived from the shore, both Bells, but they were constricted by the available route for approaching the platform. He saw that some enterprising souls had thrown ropes over from the fourth deck, and five or six men had actually slid through and past the flames on the lowest decks and almost reached the sea before the ropes burned through.

"That takes some guts," Kelly noted.

"I hope to hell they made it," Morris said.

"The trawler's going after them."

An air controller came on the air, gathering up all of the choppers on the Brunei Shell channel, telling them to go to his UHF channel, and Morris switched them over.

With a few brief questions, the controller assessed the situation with the aircraft, then took over their guidance.

"Air Services Three-Five has a full load and is away," the Sikorsky pilot reported. "I've got injured, and I'm going right for the hospital at Kuala Belait."

"BS Six-Six, you're in," the controller said. "GT Zero-Two, you're next."

"Zero-Two, roger," Morris replied.

"Frank," Koehler asked, "you think we could sit on a crane?"

Morris scanned the platform, spotting the crane lowered on the opposite side.

"If there's a risky way to do something, that's the way you want to do it, isn't it, Kelly?"

"Better than wasting our fuel."

"Hell, let's give it a try. It either works or it doesn't."

"Brunei Air, Zero-Two."

"Go ahead, Zero-Two."

"We're going to try an approach from the south side. If some of these guys can crawl out on the crane boom, we can take them off."

"Approved, Zero-Two." The controller warned the other choppers of Koehler's movement, then said, "Let us get the waiting helicopters in close and try to clear the smoke from the platform."

The controller, who was over fifty miles away in Bandar Seri Begawan, was thinking clearly, Kelly decided. Make breathing a little easier for those on the installation. He saw the top deck was getting crowded as more men climbed to it from the lower decks. The upper level was so crowded with machinery, piping, and steel storage sheds they didn't have much room in which to assemble.

Koehler rolled to the left, then moved forward at a walking speed, easing up to the crane boom. When the operator had abandoned it, the boom was left in a nearly level position, aimed slightly away from the platform. It was perhaps ninety feet long, the tip about fifty feet from the side of the installation. The two tensioned guy wires that raised and lowered it were angled from the tip upward to supporting posts at the back of the operator's cab.

"We can set down about ten feet from the end," Morris said, "and still clear the side of the platform and give the rotors clearance over the vertical-lift cables."

Their rotors, along with those of the arriving Bells, blew smoke from the upper decks, and a few of the trapped men saw his approach and figured out what he was trying to do. They broke out of the mob and ran for the crane, climbing the ladder to the operator's cab.

He walked the Dauphin forward.

"Pull the gear, Frank."

"Coming up."

Morris raised the gear, understanding that Koehler didn't want to get a wheel caught in the guy wires.

Men were already scrambling out from the cab, crouching as they walked the lattice work of the boom, their hands gripping the cables.

Koehler felt the fuselage rubbing the crane's tension wires. He hoped the whole damned thing didn't just collapse.

Andy Jenkins yelled, "I can take eight at a time!"

It took them a little longer to load this way. Straight down was a two-hundred-foot drop to the sea, and the evacuees weren't high-steel workers. It was a scary walk, then crawl for the last twenty feet to the chopper, but less frightening than staying aboard the Albatross.

When he had his load, Koehler lifted away, and one of the Bells slithered in to replace him.

The air controller announced a Chinook on the way. The dual-rotored heavy-lift helicopter could accommodate forty-four passengers.

"About time the big guys got involved," Morris said.
"Amen."

The afternoon looked a little shorter, now.

Rain started to fall by the time they transferred their refugees to the power cruiser.

Jenkins checked on their appendicitis patient, but Pete wasn't ready to abandon the rescue efforts.

And UHF 243.0 sounded off again:

"This is Chevron Mirador. We are reporting a Code Blue emergency."

Friday, March 7, 2:43 P.M.

Benjamin Shaikh's headquarters was located in Kuala Belait. Half of his battalion was quartered in the barracks there, while the balance was divided between Seria and Lumut, where the liquified natural-gas refinery—one of the largest and most modern in the world—was situated.

Shaikh was Nepalese and a major in one of the foremost military forces of history, the Gurkhas. Equivalent to America's Special Forces or Britain's Special Air Services, the Gurkhas had been serving the British Army since 1815.

Benjamin Shaikh was thirty-eight years old, tall for a Nepalese, with a spine as rigid as an ironing board, and named by a father who had also served in the Gurkhas and who admired Disraeli. The coffee-colored skin of his face was smooth and unmarked by the stress of command. His dark brown eyes could issue an order with a steel-edged glance. He wore the standard British combat uniform in camouflage pattern, though his creases and the starch behind them were evident. The Gurkhas were equipped as any British unit, except for the special addition of the *kukri*, a curved knife that had inspired many stories of horror from Germans, Japanese, and Argentineans. The stories went well with the reputation for ferocity that the Gurkhas enjoyed.

At the moment Shaikh stood in his orderly room with his sergeant major and his battalion clerk, who was switching the radio between the Brunei Shell and the Brunei air controller channels. The three of them had been listening to the rescue efforts at BS Albatross.

Shaikh looked sideways at Sergeant Major Suraj Irra, ten years his senior, and every year crammed with hard experience.

Both of them thought this incident an accidental occurrence.

"The patrol boat is en route, Major," Irra said.

He had no more than made the statement when the Chevron platform announced its emergency.

Irra came to attention, his head turned slightly as he focused his ear on the radio's speaker.

"We have a condition blue emergency," the radio operator at Mirador said, "and the OIM has ordered the installation abandoned. A large detonation ignited flammables on the derrick deck, and the fire is spreading from there. Lifeboats are currently deploying, and we request assistance in evacuating our personnel."

The OIM was the Offshore Installation Manager, the captain of the ship, as it were. There were three levels of caution—yellow, red, and blue, the highest. The OIM did not give up his control of a platform that could cost anywhere from sixty to a hundred million dollars unless the circumstances were dire, indeed.

"Sergeant Major, alert the other boats, and get us a helicopter."

"Sir!" The grizzled veteran donned his green beret with the gold flash, spun on his heel, and left the orderly room.

"Corporal, we want a level-two alert issued to all forces.

Recall any troops now on rest and recuperation. Full strength by 1600 hours.''

The corporal picked up his telephone.

Neither God nor Mother Nature had meant for there to be coincidences, Major Shaikh believed, and certainly, explosions on two platforms in the same day, within forty-five minutes of each other, were not to be perceived as coincidence.

He was under attack.

Three

The three mounting, then receding, wails of the sirens brought Li Sen to the door of his shop. He stood under the canvas awning stretched over the sidewalk and looked to the skies while the rain splattered in the street. There was nothing to be seen but the low, light gray overcast; there was no red-tinged warning of fire racing through the city. Since so many of the city's structures were constructed of wood and other flammables, and were situated so closely together, fire was a concern.

There was not even the smell of smoke, except for cooking fires. Ozone was in the air.

Across the street, his friend Mr. Luang, who operated a bicycle store, also stood in his doorway, his eyes searching the skies. The shopkeepers waved to each other, but did not cross the street. Why get wet?

A Fiat sedan came racing up the street, splashing water

from its tires, and pulled to the curb. Two young men, both Bruneians of Malay extraction, got out of the car and ran to get under the awning. They wore high-topped running shoes, pants of sail cloth, which ballooned around their legs but were pegged tightly to their ankles, and gold studs in their ears. They were of the new generation, and Li Sen was able to withhold his admiration.

"Good afternoon, gentlemen," Li said.

"What of the siren?" the shortest man with the orange-dyed hair asked.

"I believe it is an alert, to call the firemen to their stations."

"Ah. I am glad I am not a fireman."

He was unlikely to be anything, in Li's esteemed opinion. Today's youth could not conceive of an issue of importance beyond the wail of amplified guitars. Perhaps that could change with better guidance.

The taller man asked, "Do you have portable CD players?"

"Of course. Either by Sony or by Sharp. My assistant will be happy to assist you."

The men entered the store of Li Sen. It featured electronics of all kinds, from CD players to personal computers. Li's business was quite profitable and supported his family extremely well. His three sons worked in the store and did not dye their hair.

At the moment, however, he was more interested in the sirens, which were now silent. Certainly, something momentous was occurring, and he thought he might know what it could be.

He kept his smile to himself.

When he pulled away from the crane boom with his third load—mostly burn casualties this time, Koehler hit the transmit button. "Brunei Air, GT Zero-Two."

It was a moment before he got a response. "Zero-Two, Brunei."

"I've got burn victims and a pending appendectomy. Request clearance to the beach this trip."

"Zero-Two, you are cleared to the aid station at Kuala Belait. Maintain one thousand meters altitude. Be aware of outbound aircraft flying at two thousand meters."

"Roger that, Brunei. Zero-Two out."

Koehler's last look into the rear compartment had caught the grimace of pain on his roughneck's face, and he'd decided medical attention for the man had risen on his priority list. On top of which, BS Albatross was now swamped with helicopters. A few had already been diverted to whatever was happening at Mirador.

"Want a breather?" Morris asked.

"All yours, Frank."

Koehler waited until he felt Morris's hands jittering the controls, then released them. He stretched his fingers and worked his shoulders, felt the tension drain away. Hell, he could have let Morris do some of the flying earlier. What was he trying to prove? That he still had what it takes at age forty-one? He didn't think he was old enough to worry about losing it, just yet. If he were required to be honest with himself, however, he'd also have to admit that his training was not current with what he'd been doing.

"Hey, Army guy?"

"Yo, Navy?"

"The next time I take away your job at a crucial time, kick my ass out the door, will you?"

"You did all right, Kelly."

"I'm five years out of training for this stuff. It's your job, and you're aircraft commander."

Morris glanced over at him. "I did think we were paying you too damned much for what we were getting out of you."

Koehler grinned at him.

From the back he could hear the screams of one man over the roar of the turboshafts, and Kelly looked back. The screamer was nearly naked, his skin torched across his belly, chest, and arms. Jenkins didn't have one damned thing in the first-aid kit to ease his pain. The copilot looked at Koehler, face screwed up as if he were feeling the pain himself. He was frustrated by his inability to help.

On the radio he heard the air controller diverting yet more aircraft to Mirador. The Chevron installation was eleven miles out, in four hundred feet of water, and it was a big one at 950 feet and 230,000 tons of weight. The Eiffel Tower wasn't much taller.

The rain really opened up then, splattering the plexiglass of the windshield. Visibility wasn't too bad, though. Silver cloud cover at maybe four thousand feet and at least five miles visibility. He could see the coast from here.

As he aimed the Aèrospatiale for the shore, Morris's face was grim. He said, "Twice just doesn't happen, Kelly."

"Think so?"

"Know so."

"You're right, of course."

Koehler punched in the digital numbers for the company channel on the radio. His office in Bandar Seri Begawan, the shoreside office in Kuala Belait, and the administration offices on the three platforms—GT Alpha, GT Bravo, and GT Charley—all monitored the channel.

"All GlobeTech personnel, this is Koehler. Who've I got?"

"Monica, here, Kelly." Monica Davis managed the head

office, and sometimes Koehler. The two of them comprised the whole headquarters staff.

"Slim Avery in Kuala."

"Alpha's here."

"Charley accounted for, Kelly. This is Jim Meara."

"GT Bravo."

"Find all the OIMs for me, please."

While he waited, Koehler spoke to the Kuala Belait manager, Slim Avery. The shoreside facility primarily managed logistics and maintained an inventory of material and supplies. Avery also provided transport for the personnel who worked the offshore platforms aboard the helicopters and the GlobeTech fleet of tenders.

"Slim, where's the other chopper?"

"Right here, Kelly. I've got the word out for Foster and Pease. I expect them to show up soon."

"Good. Put them in the air right away. Brunei Air will probably send them to Mirador. And stand by for us. After we offload at the clinic, we'll drop in for some juice."

"Got it. What about the boats?"

GlobeTech had three sixty-foot seagoing ships. Two were used for crew transfers and supplying the rigs, and one as a workboat. For guard boats, Koehler contracted with nine fishing boats that shared round-the-clock shifts at all three installations.

"If you can find enough crew, Slim, send them out."

"Will do."

"Monica," Koehler said, "will you call Sherry and tell her I'm going to be late?"

"Sure thing, boss."

By the time he had those items off his mental checklist, the offshore installation managers—Driscoll, Irving, and Starquist—checked in.

"All right. For all OIMs. We're going to assume the events today are not fate. That leaves sabotage, and we want to prevent or prepare for it. Let's not release the guard boats. Mirador's going to have plenty of help soon. I want you to go to condition yellow immediately and suspend normal operations for the time being. Put everyone to searching the platforms for anything that doesn't look like it should be there."

That was a hell of a chore, he knew. Any outsider would assume that half the equipment on a platform appeared as if it didn't belong. And there were so many nooks and crannies, a search could take days. Still, they had 240 searchers on each rig.

The managers all understood his concern, and none of the three questioned his orders.

Jake Driscoll, OIM on GT Alpha, said, "Kelly, what about the legs?"

"Yeah, send some teams down."

"I mean the outside."

"Hell, Jake, you're right. Where's the ROV?"

Slim Avery broke in, "On board *Saturn*, Kelly."

That was the workboat.

"Send her to Alpha first, then to the others, Slim. We want a good look at the legs and tanks."

"Roger that, boss."

The Remotely Operated Vehicle (ROV) with its video camera and small propellers swam around in the depths where only high-saturation divers could go. The images captured by the camera were transferred via fiber-optic cable to monitors on the surface. Koehler didn't want to wait until he could contract some divers before he had a look at the exterior of the legs.

"Questions, anyone?"

There were none, and he said, "Okay, let's go to it. Call me if you run into anything strange. And be careful, guys."

Morris slowed the Dauphin to 100 knots as they crossed over the piers at Kuala Belait. The Sikorsky was just lifting off the chopper pad at the hospital, and Morris gave it some room before slipping in and settling on the concrete. Seven nurses and interns ran out through what was now a downpour to meet them, pushing a couple of gurneys.

This wasn't a full-service hospital. It was meant to handle emergencies, but it did have about ninety beds. Soon, if Mirador was as bad as it was beginning to sound on the radio, they'd be diverting to the small facility at Seria or to the major hospital at Bandar Seri Begawan.

They were offloaded in five minutes, Koehler giving Pete a thumbs-up as he settled into a wheelchair to be pushed from under the rotor blades, and Morris took off for the short hop to the GlobeTech compound a mile away.

It was located five blocks in from the coast, and it looked like any oil patch support facility in the world. A large yard was encircled by chain-link fencing, and steel buildings were spotted around the perimeter. Equipment ranging from flatbed semi-trucks to generators, pumps, stacks of drilling pipe, and steel casing were parked in seemingly haphazard fashion. Naturally, the rain was turning the dirt compound into a muddy mire.

Near the smaller steel building that served as the office were a couple of pickups and a rectangle of concrete. Morris landed on it, next to the other Dauphin. He killed the twin 700-horsepower Turbomeca turboshaft engines.

Eddie Foster and Chuck Pease, the aircrew of the other chopper, were working on it, pulling the seats out of the rear compartment, pushing them out to men who were supposed to be off-duty, but who had shown up to help. They carried the extra seats off to stack in a corrugated-steel shed. It gave them more room for injured, as well as a weight saving that allowed a couple more passengers to be crammed on board.

Andy Jenkins started pulling the seats on Zero-Two, as

two other men unreeled a fuel hose and dragged it toward the helicopter.

Koehler and Morris unfastened their harnesses and slid out of their seats to run through the rain to the office. Slim Avery pulled open the steel door as they reached it.

Avery matched his nickname. Six six and a hundred and seventy pounds, he disappeared when he turned sideways. He was close to sixty years old—forty of them spent in oil fields of one kind or another—balding, and hawk-nosed. He was also a genius when it came to keeping supplies flowing.

He had three mugs of coffee waiting for them.

"Where's Andy?" he asked, speaking loud enough to overcome the drumbeat of rain on the metal roof.

"Be in, in a minute, Slim," Kelly told him.

He took his mug and sipped hot, 100-octane coffee as he leaned against the chest-high counter that divided the office in half. A couple beat-up sofas took up this half, and behind the counter were four desks, a wall of filing cabinets, and computer terminals. The radio was muted but alive with transmissions. There had never been a woman in the building, and Avery took that to mean he could paste *Playboy* centerfolds on the walls, which he did. Fortunately, there had never been a visitor from the Islamic government, either. Someday, Koehler was going to have to tell him to take them down.

"Anything new on the radio, Slim?"

"I listened in on some of the other company channels. Most of 'em seem to be thinking like you. They're searching their platforms for explosives. Brunei Shell moved all their platforms to condition yellow."

They stopped talking for a few minutes while the whine of ignition and then the beat of rotors signalled Foster's takeoff. Jenkins came in, water dripping from the bill of his baseball cap. Avery handed him a steaming mug.

"This is weird shit," Jenkins said. "It doesn't happen in Brunei."

Kelly had been thinking the same thing. He had never heard of any group, or any individual for that matter, with a grudge against the government or the oil companies.

"And, Jesus!" Jenkins went on. "That poor bastard was burned bad, Kelly. I'm going to hear those screams for a long time."

Koehler wasn't looking forward to the next few trips. He said, "Slim, you have anything around for burns? We weren't very well prepared."

"The guys are throwing a medical kit aboard for you, Kelly. Got some salve in it, but that's the best I can do. If it's really bad, there's a couple morphine ampules."

"Okay, let's get back in harness." Koehler downed the rest of his coffee and led the way back to the chopper.

The rain was still coming down but starting to lose some of its momentum. Rain in Brunei, he was accustomed to. The coast got around a hundred inches a year while the interior soaked up as much as two hundred inches.

At Morris's raised eyebrow, Koehler shrugged and went around to the left side. He'd let the chief pilot be the pilot.

They ran through the checklist, fired the turboshaft engines, and Morris whipped in pitch and sprang them from the ground. He put the nose down and headed toward the sea while Koehler checked in with Brunei Air. Andy Jenkins, with no seats in the rear compartment, hung onto the backs of both their seats.

They were needed at Mirador, so Morris put them on a course for the eastern side of the oil field.

And they were just over the docks when two holes magically appeared in the windshield right in front of Koehler. The plexiglass starred and went nearly opaque.

Koehler was stunned.

But it was Jenkins who screamed.

Friday, March 7, 3:51 P.M.

Major Benjamin Shaikh's entire air support group consisted of six Black Hawk helicopters, one of which was disassembled and undergoing an overhaul. He had always argued that the air group was insufficient for his needs in an emergency, but his arguments disappeared in the heat of budget battles. Only sixty-six soldiers of the battalion could be airlifted at one time, and not even that many at the moment. Since all of his men were required to be air cavalry trained, including continual parachute and rappel training, the helicopters were in constant usage, and just as frequently in need of maintenance.

He and Sergeant Major Irra had boarded the aircraft code named Tiger Three and were six kilometers off the coast, headed toward BS Albatross. They stood upright in the rear compartment, hanging onto straps from the roof and wearing headsets. They also wore the bulky life vests required by regulation of passengers over the sea. Shaikh rarely ignored regulation, and his subordinates risked his wrath if they attempted to skirt the rules.

Below, he saw the Multifunction Service Vessel *Malay Princess* moving slowly in the same direction. The MSV did not look like a ship. It appeared to be a smaller version of one of the offshore platforms. There was no attempt at streamlining, and her two decks were squared off, with numerous strange boxes, sheds, and modules attached to them. Two cranes were mounted to one side. There was a helicopter landing pad. There were two pressurization chambers for maintaining or changing the environments of the deep-sea divers. Her four legs disappeared below the surface, but Shaikh knew they were firmly attached to two submarines that operated in parallel. The submarines gave her propulsion and the ability to raise and lower in the water.

As his pilot took them alongside, Shaikh saw that she was testing her firefighting apparatus in preparation for engagement at Albatross. One side of the MSV was liberally fitted with water nozzles and monitors, all of them remotely controlled by an operator on board. She could deliver twenty streams of water at high pressure over distances of hundreds of feet.

The pilot of the Sikorsky Black Hawk stayed well clear of the MSV as the starboard side erupted in fountains and sprays that turned the air into almost solid liquid. Shaikh watched for the several seconds it took to bypass the MSV.

A few minutes later, they reached the base of the first column of smoke. Several miles to the northeast, another column streaked into the rain-washed sky.

From where they stood in the opened port doorway of the helicopter, Sergeant Major Irra pointed downward and to the west. One of Shaikh's armed patrol boats was standing by, her crew tending to several bodies stretched out on the deck.

At least a dozen other boats and small ships circled the damaged installation. Several were already headed toward shore, filled to capacity with victims and survivors.

Six helicopters orbited, awaiting instructions.

As far as Shaikh could tell, the installation was now fully abandoned. The fires still raged over the lower decks, and it appeared as if the rainfall had done nothing to quench them.

A new voice came onto the radio, announcing itself as the offshore installation manager for Albatross. He was apparently on board one of the circling helicopters.

"I have a preliminary report, gathered from witnesses. There were three detonations, one on the derrick deck, one on the module deck, and one near the well head. We assume several Christmas trees were destroyed, allowing oil and gas to flow freely. The fire spread rapidly, and could not be controlled by the sprinkler systems. Two of the major firefighting systems were damaged in the initial explosions.

"The only numbers I presently have are these: There are at least sixteen dead and seventy-two injured. One hundred and forty-one others are accounted for, and six men are missing.

"Gentlemen, I thank you all for your assistance. Without you, the numbers would be far worse."

Irra said, "Major, we are not going to examine that installation for quite some time."

"I think you are correct," Shaikh replied, then spoke to the pilot. "Lieutenant, we will go to Mirador."

"Yes, sir."

The helicopter heeled to the right and picked up speed. It could fly at 180 miles per hour, and it did not take them long to reach Chevron Mirador.

This was a larger platform with forty-four wells. Sergeant Major Irra had verified the information.

The Black Hawk circled the installation, staying high and away from other aircraft. Here, they were able to use the helicopter pad, and the larger Sikorskys and a Chinook had evacuated most of the men. Shaikh counted seven lifeboats in the water, four of them tied together and in tow behind a trawler.

Bright sheets of yellow and red flame licked at the upper decks from the first three decks. In the jumble of conversations on the radio, he thought he heard someone say there had been four explosions. Already, Shaikh dreaded the coming paperwork—interviewing witnesses, developing reports.

The number of dead was unknown at the moment. In the normal course of an emergency, workers aboard the platforms would report to assigned assembly points and pick up cardboard strips with their names on them. The strips that were not retrieved helped administrators account for those who were missing or injured. This emergency, however, had occurred so rapidly, with fire blocking off many of the assembly points, that the system had fallen apart.

There were over forty injured, but that count was going to be increased. Helicopters with injured aboard were now being directed to Seria.

"The well casings have been damaged," Irra said. "Do you see the slick forming?"

"I do. Please alert the containment section."

The forty-four wells drilled deep into the crust of the earth rose from the seabed to the platform through casings up to thirty-six inches in diameter called conductors. Some of them were damaged and oil was seeping directly into the sea from beneath the surface. The oil field was prepared for such incidents, and several ships loaded with containment booms were always on call.

The oil field was not, Shaikh knew, prepared for more than one or possibly two incidents at the same time. Though some of the company workboats had pumps and hoses for small conflagrations, there was only one major firefighting vessel, the *Malay Princess*. It might be weeks before the fires were controlled and the wells sealed.

He moved away from the doorway and tapped the copilot on the shoulder, then asked for the telephone. The man passed it back to him.

Reluctantly, he keyed in the number for the interior minister's office. That official, Mohammed Hassanal, was one of the royal family, as well as the man to whom Shaikh reported.

He instantly responded to the telephone call, and Shaikh knew that the man had been aware of events, probably hanging over the telephone, but chose not to nag or interfere until Shaikh had something to report. The minister was a good man to work for.

"What is the situation, Major?"

Shaikh provided the numbers as he had heard them, reinforcing the notion that they were preliminary.

"Minister, these were not accidents."

"I am afraid that I must agree with you. Why would anyone want to sabotage the wells?"

"I cannot answer that, sir. My intelligence sources have detected absolutely no hints of dissidence."

"Dissidence? Are you suggesting this is a revolution, Major?"

"At the moment I would hesitate to suggest anything," Shaikh said. "However, the methods and the targets carry the rotten odor of rebellion."

"But why?" The minister was truly puzzled.

"Why, indeed, Minister?"

Friday, March 7, 3:59 P.M.

At his small convenience store in Seria, Shafruddin bin Anwar listened with trepidation to the radio reports of the fires in the oil field.

This would not be good for business.

He relied heavily on the wants and needs of the oilmen who populated the town, and the loss of sixty or seventy customers with unique needs would harshly impact his cash flow.

Brunei was truly a paradise in the sense of climate and the prosperity of its citizens, but for many of the oil field workers, it could be a hardship posting. While the salaries were large and went untaxed by either Brunei or their native governments, the men and women working the field had very few places to spend their money.

Anwar attempted to assist them in any way he could. His shelves were stocked with Twinkies and Coca-Cola and Kleenex. One wall held a massive selection of videotapes for rental. He had bins of audiocassettes and CDs.

And below the flooring, in his storage room, which was all but invisible, he had ample stocks of Jim Beam and Johnnie Walker, of Coors and Budweiser, of videos produced in Los Angeles and Amsterdam, and of picture books published in Germany and Sweden.

He accepted special orders.

There was a demand, and he supplied the demand.

In another four years, Anwar expected to be a millionaire.

He was worrying about the extension of his personal goal when the front door opened.

He smiled at the four Bruneian men who entered. They would not be interested in his more exotic wares, but he was certain they would want *something*.

They smiled back at him, then raised their arms, revealing very wicked assault rifles.

Shafruddin bin Anwar had seen many things on his videos, but he had never seen weapons such as these in person.

He refrained from showing his fear, and said, "Do you men wish to have my money? You may have it all."

Approximately six hundred Bruneian dollars.

None of them answered.

Instead, they all fired their weapons at once.

It was unthinkable.

And as he smashed against the wall behind the counter, he realized for a split second that it hurt.

Four

Omar Padang was Chief of the Royal Brunei Police, and his job was not a difficult one. There was very little serious crime in the sultanate. The rare murder was almost always a result of passion, and an emotionally charged family member could usually be singled out and quickly arrested. The unsolved felony crimes on his desk could be counted on less than ten fingers.

Traffic offenses were far more numerous, especially since there was one automobile for every two persons in the country. The 1,100 kilometers of highway that traversed Brunei produced most of his headaches in the forms of torn metal and mangled bodies.

Padang was a diminutive man, except for the paunch that stretched his waistband and forced him to wear suspenders under his typical white suit coats. He wore his authority as if it were his due, and his temperament was often described by foreigners as "feisty." With long black hair swept back from his forehead and over his ears, Padang's face was unlined and clear, though often puffy, as if he were inclined to retain water. He wanted his deep-set eyes to be penetrating, and when he was angry, they were.

Often in his years, Padang had felt he did not have enough to be angry about, not in an overt way. The use of his full range of skills was severely restricted in the current environment. How could he demonstrate his capability by chasing traffic violators?

Now, though, his potential might well be tested. In fact, he was certain of it.

His aide, Captain Awg Nazir, had focused Padang's attention on the blossoming problems in the oil field, and he strode down to the communications center to listen to the barrage of radio reports being monitored by his staff. He fired off orders as the situation appeared to become more and more critical: "Alert the minister's office ... call Shaikh's headquarters ... get Haji in here ... alert Lieutenant Hashim and the rapid response team...."

Lieutenant Ali Haji arrived on the run, his fat belly shivering under his stretched uniform shirt. Haji was considerably fatter than Padang, and his three chins quivered as he brought himself to attention. He did not like Padang in the least. Omar Padang knew this, but unfortunately, Haji was a second cousin of the interior minister, Mohammed Hassanal.

Haji had entered the police department as a lieutenant, with no formal training and no experience, which was not entirely unheard of, of course. The police department was one department that provided jobs as a way of channelling government revenues into the economy. Padang had many men, and many divisions, which contributed little to real police work. Of course, he also had divisions that he considered highly trained, and of which he was very proud.

Padang had given Haji command of the city traffic division to keep him busy, confused, and out of the way.

Padang resented the intrusive power of the royal family, foisting off unemployable relatives on him. Padang had himself worked his way through the ranks; he knew every facet of police work from experience. His insights regarding competencies for a career in law enforcement were for naught when it came to Ali Haji, however. Worse, Haji had a loyal following among the men of his command, men who hoped their association with Haji, and by extension, the royal family, would gain them favor in some near future.

The lieutenant stood on the polished linoleum floor, his eyes shifting around the room, attempting to make sense of the radio babble and the general confusion. "Yes, Chief Padang?"

"Take thirty of your command, find trucks, and go to Kuala Belait."

Haji's eyes squinted his disbelief. "But, Chief Pa—"

"Major Shaikh may need your assistance. I want you there."

"That is three-fourths of my division, Chief Padang. Who will—"

"I will have the investigative division and the response team cover in your absence."

"But, Chief—"

"Now!" Padang almost called him a fool in front of the communications staff, but halted himself in time.

Haji rotated on his heel, almost tripping over himself, and departed the center, again on the run. His leather heels slapped on the floor of the corridor.

A fax machine at the side of the room began to hum,

and Nazir looked down at it. "Chief! You will want to see this."

Padang crossed the room and read the first sheet of paper as it emerged from the machine:

A PROCLAMATION OF
THE FRONT FOR DEMOCRATIC REFORM

"What in the devil is the Front for Democratic Reform?" a nearby radio operator asked.

"No doubt, we will soon know," Padang told him.

Friday, March 7, 4:19 P.M.

Frank Morris had reacted by instinct instantly—he had taken hits before. When the first bullet holes appeared, he rolled hard into a diving right turn, accelerating away from the area of danger. Fifty feet off the water, he banked left, levelled, and shot away from the coast.

Koehler trusted Morris's instinct. He had taken one look at the sea, then shoved his headset aside, released the snaps on his harness, and struggled out of his seat. Jenkins was crumpled on the cargo deck, a bright red stain spreading across the rubber anti-skid decking beneath his legs.

Koehler went to his knees next to the pilot, searching for damage. Jenkins was conscious, but barely so. His glazed eyes sought Koehler's. Shock was taking hold quickly. Koehler ripped buttons, peeling away the bloodied work shirt. Major hole in the lower left chest. Bubbling wound. A glance at the man's face found crimson bubbles forming on his lips. His mouth was drawn into a tight line of pain. Lung wound.

Also a wound in the thigh, and from the angle of the

leg, the bone was broken. The blood was gushing forth. Artery.

Koehler scrambled over the man to the back bulkhead, where the medical kit had been lashed. He ripped the Velcro fasteners apart, pulled the box forward, unsnapped the lid, and went to work on the leg first, wrapping a tourniquet above the wound and cranking it tight, to slow the flow of blood. Then he found a compress, packed it over the chest wound, and held it in place. Rolling Jenkins slightly, he checked his back for an exit wound, but found none. The slug had lost most of its momentum plowing through the floor.

Without a headset, Koehler's ears were assaulted by the roar of the turboshafts, and it took him a moment to realize that Morris was shouting at him.

"How bad, Kelly?"

"Head for the clinic!"

"Gone!"

Morris worked the controls and the radio, making a wide circle to approach the coast a few miles west of the attack zone and alerting the medical personnel. They were waiting at the pad when Morris set it down. He killed the engines, and both he and Koehler followed the intern and nurse who took possession of Jenkins.

Forty minutes later, they were still standing around in the small waiting room, looking up every time a door opened. No word, yet. There were no seats available. Less injured men from the platforms crammed the room, awaiting the eyes of a doctor. They talked to each other in subdued tones reflecting both a need to whisper in hospitals and their relief at being off the burning platforms.

Finally a young Malay nurse approached him, but she didn't have any news. "Sir, would you like to wash?"

Koehler looked at his hands. They were covered with

Jenkins's blood. The knees of his jeans were also caked with dried brown blood. He'd been so worried, he hadn't even realized it.

"Uh, yes, thank you."

He followed her down a corridor to a rest room, scrubbed his hands and forearms, and even the left side of his face where blood had splashed. When he got back to the reception room, Morris was standing at the window watching another chopper landing.

"Black Hawk, Kelly. The cavalry has arrived."

Koehler knew the Gurkhas were responsible for oil field security, and that they flew Black Hawks, but he'd never had contact with any of them before. He watched two men in battle dress utilities emerge from the rear compartment and cross the grass toward the door. It had stopped raining, and a brilliant sun was beginning to appear on the horizon.

By the time they reached the door, he had identified the insignia—a major and a sergeant major. They entered and stood just inside the glass doors, looking around the crowded space. The major's eyes caught his own, held for a moment, then he made his decision. He crossed the room to Koehler, the ramrod-stiff NCO trailing behind.

"Sir," the major said in British-accented English, "you would not be GT-Zero-Two, would you?"

Koehler held out his hand. "Kelly Koehler, GlobeTech field manager. This is Frank Morris, chief pilot."

"Major Benjamin Shaikh. Sergeant Major Suraj Irra."

Everyone shook hands, but in the Brunei manner—touching hands lightly, then drawing them back to their chests.

"You heard what happened, Major?"

"The air controller informed me, Mr. Koehler. His report was not well detailed, however."

"I don't know that I'll be any more help," Koehler said. "I think we took a half dozen hits, a couple in the windshield, more in the floor." He told the officer they were waiting for word on Andy Jenkins.

Shaikh looked to Morris.

"I saw some holes, then got the hell out of Dodge," Frank said. "Sorry I can't be more helpful."

"Would you recall approximately where the attack originated?"

"I've got a general idea," Koehler said.

"Perhaps, if you could show us. . . ."

Koehler turned to look toward the nurses' station.

"Go ahead, Kelly," Morris said. "I'll stick close here."

He was reluctant to leave, but finally nodded and followed the two professional soldiers back out to the helicopter pad. Shaikh and Irra paused to look over the damage to the Dauphin. There were more holes in the floor than he had remembered—at least a dozen in the rear compartment, three between the seats Morris and Koehler had been strapped into.

"I guess I lost count of the hits," Koehler said.

"You were quite lucky," Shaikh said.

"I wish Jenkins had the same luck. What's going on here, Major?"

"If I could tell you, Mr. Koehler, I certainly would. We have not had incidents like this before."

They climbed into the Black Hawk's rear compartment and were soon in the air, headed for the beach. Irra got on the radio to someone, probably ordering up ground troops, but the language wasn't one Kelly had control over.

Over the headset he had been provided, Koehler directed the pilot to fly northeast over the GlobeTech storage yard, following the flight path Morris had taken. He saw Slim Avery and a half dozen men standing outside the office, looking up as they went over.

The pilot brought his ship to a hover as they crossed over the highway and neared the docks. The facilities along here were primarily in support of drilling and pumping operations. The sultanate was attempting to rebuild an ebbing fishing enterprise—in anticipation of the time when the oil was depleted—and new trawlers appeared all the time. There were few boats based in Kuala Belait, though, and their operations were located about a mile to the east. Here, there were a dozen piers, most of them devoted to freight. In addition to both concrete and older wooden-framed docks, a melange of buildings, warehouses, storage lots, and travelling cranes created a maze. Trucks and laborers milled around in organized confusion.

Koehler stared through the windscreen. He hadn't been paying much attention at the time of the attack. Finally he pointed ahead. "There, Major. We passed almost directly over the middle Shell dock. The attack came from below or to the left. Automatic weapon. Seven-point-six-two, at least."

"Land here, Lieutenant," Shaikh said to the pilot.

The chopper sailed over a chain-link fence and put down in a parking lot. By the time they were on the ground, three jeep loads of Gurkhas screeched off the road and into the lot.

Irra went to meet them, barking orders, and the men spread out in teams of two and began to advance toward the warehouses lining the shore.

The Black Hawk shut down, and the rotors slowed.

"The chances of finding them are pretty slim, Major."

"Perhaps we will find the gun. It was large caliber, an M-60 or something similar. I do not like automatic weapons, unless they are in my control."

"A very good point," Koehler conceded.

They stood around near the helicopter as the search got under way. Irra retrieved a portable radio from inside the chopper and took occasional reports from his patrols.

Kelly sat down on the floor of the Black Hawk.

Shaikh found a canteen of water, took a swig, and offered it to Koehler. He hadn't realized how dry his mouth was, and he accepted it gratefully. The water was warm.

"Excuse me, Mr. Koehler," the major said. "I have the impression you have been under fire before."

"I flew Sea Kings for the Navy. In the Gulf."

"Ah! You are no longer in your navy?"

"I'm in the reserves. Lieutenant commander."

"As a pilot?"

"Regrettably, no. Because my job has taken me places—Saudi Arabia, Scotland—where I can't keep my flying time current, they sent me to a two-week school, then transferred me to intelligence."

"Are you a good intelligence officer?"

Kelly grinned. "My talents have never been tested, Major."

They made small talk for twenty minutes while Irra took reports on his portable radio—all negative. Then Koehler asked, "Sergeant Major, is there a way I could talk to the hospital over your radio?"

"Certainly, sir. We will use the helicopter's radio."

A few minutes later, Koehler was patched through to Morris.

"Anything, Frank?"

"Andy's out of danger, but they've still got him on a critical list. He hasn't come around yet, and the doc says it'll be a couple hours. I'm going to hop the bird over to the yard and check for damage."

"Okay. I'll catch up with you there."

He gave the microphone back to the copilot and turned around just as gunfire erupted somewhere to the west.

Irra's radio sounded off, chattering in that same language Kelly didn't know, and the sergeant major looked to Shaikh.

For a brief instant, the commander's face turned quizzical, as if he couldn't really understand what was taking place. Then he recovered and said, "One of my patrols has engaged persons unknown, as they say. I should not take you along, Mr. Koehler."

"That's all right. I'll walk back."

He watched the Black Hawk take off, then looked for a way to get around the parking lot's fence.

Friday, March 7, 5:55 P.M.

Li Sen's eldest son closed out the cash register and began to total the day's receipts while Li placed the "Closed" sign on the glass door and set the locks. His two younger sons appeared from the storage room in the back carrying large sheets of plywood.

The plywood had already been cut to size, and the young men quickly fit it into place behind the front windows and began to nail it in place. The youngest son, Li Yat, cast furtive glances toward Li as he worked. His face remained stoic, but Li knew that his mind was in turmoil. He did not understand, and Li supposed that he did not approve. Many of the younger generation would not, for they did not understand the history or the tradition. He would not, naturally, show disrespect to his father by questioning him.

Across the street, Li saw similar plywood going up behind the windows of Mr. Luang's store. Along the street only one other shop was taking the same precautions. Most had received the warning, but most were being foolish. Perhaps they did not think their merchandise was as valuable as Li considered his own. And perhaps it was he who was being foolish, fearing broken windows.

He stepped back as wood was fitted to the door. The interior began to darken as the daylight was shut out. He examined the barriers fitted to the windows on the right and pointed out places where an additional nail would add strength. Yat went to the task, his mouth full of nails.

Li supposed his sons thought him an old man, but at sixty-one, he had much of his life ahead of him, and he thought it was to be the important part of his life. He had much to give, and his wisdom had been tempered and nurtured by all of his years.

When the task was complete, the four of them went through the storage room to the back door, his oldest son carrying the receipts, and the middle son throwing the handle on the electrical box that cut off all electricity in the shop. The display televisions and stereos died.

They stepped outside, and Li used his key to secure the three deadbolt locks on the steel door.

"You will now go to the house and stay with your mother and sister until I call you."

"Yes, Father," came in unison

The boys drove away in the old Renault he allowed them to share, and Li got into the five-year-old Chevrolet sedan for which he had paid $12,000 American a year before. He started it, reversed away from the back of the store, and drove around to the street where he braked to a stop. He took a few minutes to survey the commercial stores arranged along it.

His neighboring shopkeepers might not heed the warning to protect their businesses, but they were otherwise prudent. The street and sidewalks were bereft of people, as he had rarely seen them before at this time of the day. No one desired to test the predictions too far.

Engaging first gear, he released the clutch and turned left onto the street. After driving west for four blocks, he turned the Chevrolet left again, leaving the highway that followed the coast, and drove along the road leading into the jungle. It was a short drive. Only fifteen kilometers separated him from the headquarters of the Front for Democratic Reform.

Friday, March 7, 6:04 P.M.

Lumut, on the coast near the center of the country, was not very exotic for a village in paradise. It served primarily as a living center for those working at the refinery.

The liquid natural-gas (LNG) refinery was one of the finest and largest in the world, in addition to being the most modern. The maze of buildings, piping, towers, tanks, and marine transfer facilities were complex and mostly incomprehensible to those outside petroleum engineering. Brunei Liquified Natural Gas, the name of the company, was divided in ownership by thirds between Shell, Mitsubishi, and the government.

Pushpa Shong Tong, a senior manager at the plant, signed in a few minutes after six and began his normal evening tour. Already the lights were beginning to come on, and by dark the refinery would appear much like an amusement park, a shining metropolis that could be seen far out to sea.

He started in the chemistry laboratory and took his time examining the workers there, making certain that only those who belonged to this shift were present. When he was satisfied—and had noted two unexplained absences, he left the building and walked the concrete sidewalk toward the main plant. He would examine it on his way back, but bypass it for now and make the nightly trek around the massive tank farm. This was where the LNG was stored until specially built tankers moored themselves to the pumping station offshore and transferred the liquid to their pressurized tanks.

He was strolling just inside the eastern chain-link fence,

studying the rows of massive tanks, when a sudden sharp clicking sound caught his attention.

He drew to a stop and switched his attention outside the fence.

Rolling terrain spotted with clumps of foliage was predominant, and the low sun created strange shadows across the dunelike landscape. It seemed empty.

And then he saw a figure emerge from a shallow ditch two hundred meters away. Without his glasses—which he only used for driving, he could barely make it out.

It raised its arms.

Funny.

And then spit little spits of flame from a stick.

Clicking sounds.

But the dirt outside the fence suddenly erupted in tiny fountains, one fountain after another.

And Tong realized what was happening.

And immediately considered all of that volatile fuel arranged so neatly in tanks behind him.

He turned and ran for the chemistry building as fast as he could go.

Friday, March 7, 6:20 P.M.

In his spacious office Interior Minister Mohammed Hassanal replaced the telephone on his desk thoughtfully, then returned to the conference table in the far corner. His cousin Hamzah bin Suliaman, the defense minister, and several of their aides sat around it. Coffee cups, a large map with red plastic beans resting on it, and four telephones littered its top.

One of the assistants replaced a phone. "One of Major Shaikh's patrols has killed two men and recovered weapons."

"Identification?" Suliaman asked.

"None, Minister. Both were Chinese. The Gurkhas are currently under fire by two additional groups, numbers and weapons undetermined as yet."

Suliaman grimaced. He was a handsome man, dark eyes and white, even teeth typically gleaming from his tanned face. There was no smile as he looked up at Hassanal.

The interior minister sagged into his chair, as if he were a man considerably heavier and more exhausted than he was. "The Sultan directs us to give no quarter. He insists the people cannot be dissatisfied with his rule."

Hassanal glanced down at the copy of the manifesto on the table. It demanded the Sultan's abdication, the inauguration of universal suffrage supporting a democratic government, increased citizenship among the Chinese population, the dispersal of wealth accumulated from oil revenues, and a reduction in the rate of oil production. The Front for Democratic Reform (FDR) could not ask for much more. Citizens already had free health services and free education. The government and the military spilled over with unnecessary jobs, created to provide avenues for channelling funds into the economy. The per capita annual income for Bruneian citizens was $19,800 American, the highest in Southeast Asia.

"Until today, I would have agreed with him," Suliaman said. "Are we going to send word of this damnable group out to the army, Mohammed? Should we notify Shaikh?"

"I think," Hassanal said, "that we will keep it to ourselves for the time being. This Front . . . this FDR can promote themselves without our help."

"That is what I am afraid of," Suliaman said.

"What word from Padang?" Hassanal asked his aide.

"There are no reports of trouble within the capital, Minister." He pointed to where a red chip had been placed on the map. "A Brunei Shell facility has been attacked at Seria, with one killed and four wounded."

Eleven red chips now dotted the map, identifying the locations of incidents along the coast as well as at the two oil platforms.

"The police chief has sent thirty men to Kuala Belait, to assist Major Shaikh," the assistant added.

Hassanal frowned, then looked to his cousin.

"The unrest appears to be centered in the west, at the oil towns," Suliaman said. "I suppose I should deploy another company of infantry. Colonel Bakir has them standing by at their barracks, and the helicopters can have them there in twenty minutes."

The Brunei Army currently had a strength of nearly 9,000 men, its sole mission one of defense. It was supported by the Royal Brunei Malay Regiment Air Wing, commanded by a British Royal Air Force officer seconded to the sultanate. The air wing was completely a helicopter force consisting of ten Bell 212s, 205s, and JetRangers. The Royal Navy was not much stronger, floating on a melange of gunboats, cutters, and small vessels retrofitted after being acquired from other governments. Most of the ships were already in the oil field. The destroyer *Bulkiah* was moored in the harbor at Muara.

Hassanal thought for a moment—he had less confidence in the state of military readiness. Finally he nodded his concurrence. "It will be more like two hours, Hamzah, but yes, you should send them. Call your generals."

Suliaman frowned. "They're not available."

That was mildly disturbing, but nothing Hassanal wanted to worry about at the moment.

He asked, "Why?"

"I am going to find out, believe me. Shamin Bakir's the only one I've been able to reach."

"Then call Bakir."

Suliaman glanced at his aide, an army lieutenant colonel, who picked up a telephone to relay the order.

The interior minister swept another phone from its cradle and stabbed the buttons.

"Chief Padang."

"Why have you sent policemen away from the city, Omar?"

"Minister? Why, I thought it a prudent maneuver to bolster the Gurkhas. The problems—"

"You did not check with me."

"I have much experience, Minister. I think—"

"Perhaps you will not have more experience, Omar. When a question of strategy or tactics is involved, you will consult with me. Is that clear?"

"Uh . . . yes. It is clear."

"Recall the policemen."

"I . . . I am not certain I can contact them right away."

"Then find a way. Concentrate on that, Omar." Hassanal slammed the phone down.

Another telephone buzzed, and Hassanal grabbed it.

"Hassanal."

"Minister, this is Major Shaikh."

"Yes, Major?"

"The refinery at Lumut has come under attack."

Hassanal closed his eyes as he envisioned two hundred million dollars' worth of plant erupting in flames.

"Status?" he asked.

"The guard contingent is holding them in place for the moment, but it appears that the rebel force is receiving reinforcements. I am bringing in an additional two platoons."

Shaikh's was the first mention of a "rebel" force. Hassanal did not appreciate hearing it, but could think of no better substitute.

"Where is the army company?"

"I have not seen it, Minister."

Ridiculous. They were probably lost, and how could anyone become lost in Brunei?

"How close are these . . . these rebels to the refinery?"

"Close enough for rockets, Minister."

"Keep me informed, Major."

He hung up and told Suliaman, "You had better send two companies, Hamzah."

Friday, March 7, 6:46 P.M.

Morris landed at Bandar Seri Begawan International Airport, one of five airports in the country, but the only one with paved runways over 3,000 meters long. Koehler unbuckled his harness and shoved the door open.

"You stick close to a phone, Frank."

Morris nodded. "Either the hospital or Avery's shack."

Koehler slipped out of the Dauphin and walked toward the chain-link fence as the Aèrospatiale gathered power and lifted off. A policeman stood near the gate and eyed him speculatively as he approached. Kelly bade him good evening, and the man opened the gate for him. No smiles tonight.

He found his company Ford Explorer in the lot and unlocked it, then crawled in and started it. He was conscious of the lack of civilian traffic as he left the airport grounds. There were quite a few cops around, and a few oil types, but standard airline passengers seemed to be in short supply. He wondered if regular airline flights had been cancelled.

The streets of Bandar Seri Begawan were similar to the airport, as if martial law had been declared, or a curfew set, and he had missed the announcement. A few cars cruised, headed for somewhere, overseen by an occasional police vehicle. On the sidewalks, very few pedestrians hustled with unaccustomed rapidity toward their destinations. Probably home, where they could bar the door.

He noted that a few stores had boarded their windows, and that did not bode well.

Despite the lack of crowds, there was a tension in the air. Koehler tapped the radio buttons, scanning the four AM and four FM stations that served the country, but the voices he could understand and the music sounded normal.

It was the fastest trip through town he had ever made, and Koehler felt uncomfortable about it. He parked the truck in a slot near the shore and got out to walk a quarter block to the entrance to his section.

Kampong Ayer, meaning "water village," was home to 27,000 Brunei Malays, and the traditional wooden houses built on stilts extended far into the bay. He walked up a gangway, then followed the dock for a hundred feet until he reached his rented house. Sherry was waiting for him, watching for him, because she jerked the door open just as he reached for the handle.

"Hey, doll!"

"Are you all right, Kelly?" She grabbed his arm and pulled him inside.

"I'm fine, hon. But what about you?"

"Something strange is going on," she insisted.

Koehler pushed the door shut and locked it, for all the good it did. All of the shutters on the big windows were open to allow errant breezes through the screens. He looked around the small living room. Bamboo furniture with bright blue and yellow cushions and a woven rug on a polished teak floor. There was one bedroom and a bathroom down a short hallway, and a kitchen/dining area. The big ceiling fan in the living room rotated with indifference.

"What have you heard?"

"Not a thing. I've been listening to the English-language station, but the news is as bland as ever."

She backed away a couple steps to look him over, and he knew he wasn't in the best of shape.

"Is that blood?"

"Let's sit down," he suggested.

Koehler would have liked a drink. He kept a couple bottles of Chivas and some beer on the ketch, hidden in a chain locker, but he never indulged unless he was outside the territorial limit. He firmly believed in respecting the local law and customs.

When they were side by side on the couch, he told her the story of his afternoon.

"Andy Jenkins!"

"We think he's going to be all right. Frank is staying close, and he'll let me know."

"My God, Kelly! This is terrible."

Sherry Koehler was no stranger to the rough edges of life. She'd been with him in Saudi Arabia and in Aberdeen, Scotland, when he worked the North Sea fields, and she knew the kind of people who played the oil game. They tended to be hardened and tough men, and their women matched them.

In that stormy sea of pirates and brigands, Sherry was his beautiful island. She was four years younger than Kelly at thirty-seven, petite at five four, with slim, almost boyish lines, a halo of platinum-blond hair reaching almost to her shoulders, and an oval face with touches of the angelic in it. Mary Tyler Moore smile. Sailing tan. Green eyes that occasionally sparkled with devilment, and arched eyebrows reflecting her deep curiosity about people. Better, she had an intellectual bent that he admired. It was nice to come home and talk about art and architecture, music and litera-ture, after a day with men whose conversational tastes ran to oil, brawls, and fast-paced women. Tonight was going to lack culture, he thought.

She told him about the feelings of dread she had experienced while shopping that afternoon. "Something is very wrong, Kelly."

"I know. But I don't know what."

She jumped to her feet. "You haven't eaten!"

"A sandwich would be fine."

He followed her to the kitchen and poured Coke over a glass of ice. "Want one?"

"Not now."

She made him a thick sandwich of fresh bread, slabs of roast beef, and mustard. They sat at the small dining table while he ate.

"There was nothing on the radio about the platform fires, Kelly."

"I imagine the boys at the palace didn't want to frighten the citizens. They've probably got a tight rein on the native media." There was only one local television station, but satellite downlinks connected Brunei to the rest of the world. For a tiny nation, Brunei was technologically quite advanced.

If, however, the rest of the world didn't know about oil rigs going up in flames, the news wasn't coming over any downlinks.

"You know what I think?" she asked. "It's the Chinese."

"Why?"

"Two things. First, it was the Chinese merchants who were acting withdrawn. Second, you have to look at the history. The Chinese have had ties with Brunei for centuries."

"Until eighty-four."

"Right. With independence, British-protected citizens lost their status and became stateless. Only five percent of the Chinese have citizenship. That second-class rank has been festering."

"Maybe," he said, and while finishing his sandwich, got up and went to the door opening on the veranda. The back side of the house had a full-width covered veranda overlooking the water. On the negative side, it faced a similar porch twenty feet away on the house across the waterway. Privacy was not a general feature of the Kampong Ayer community.

He stepped outside and crossed the eight-foot deck to the railing. His Malay neighbor was out on his own deck and waved at him. Koehler waved back, careful of his hand. Gestures were important in Brunei and one did not, for example, point with the index finger. For pointing, the thumb was used.

He looked down. Tied to the base of a ladder was his small dinghy, ten-horsepower Evinrude attached to its transom. It was his transport to the twin-masted *Serendipity* moored in the bay near Muara.

Sherry followed him outside.

"It's still there. I checked earlier."

"Okay." He turned and leaned against the railing. The shadows were getting longer, night falling. It was still warm, but there was enough of a breeze to keep the mosquitoes away. Lights were starting to come on all over the village. Smudge pots were fired to drive off the insects. "I called Monica on the flight back and had her issue a company-wide order."

"What kind of order?"

"I want to keep our people off the streets, so everyone's confined to quarters. Only essential transport personnel are going to be out and about for the next few days."

"I'm worried about the families," Sherry said.

"So am I." About twenty percent of GlobeTech's workers had their families with them, sharing the small prefabricated housing unit located in a compound in Kuala Belait.

"I'm also worried about you. I think, in the morning we'll put you on a plane for Singapore. You can catch up on your shopping."

"No damned way."

In the dim light he saw the green fire rise in her eyes. She could be stubborn, a trait he had noted in her Peoria, Illinois, parents.

"It's safest, hon."

"If you're worried about safety, you'll go with me, then."

"I've got two thousand other—"

"I'm not going. I—"

"I may have to leave soon, go back to Kuala Belait. I don't want to worry about you, Sherry."

"I'll stay in the house."

"Promise?"

"Promise."

He sighed. But she was a competent sailor, in fair weather and bad. "If it turns ugly, and I call you, I want you to get Monica, then go out to *Serendipity* and sail straight north."

"Not if—"

"I can always catch up with you."

She moved up close to him and put her arms around his waist. "I'm sticking with you, guy."

He shook his head, but kissed her on the nose.

"Want to stick with me through a shower?"

"Uh-huh."

"Then we'll pack a couple bags, just in case."

"Maybe later," she said, then took his hand and led him back inside.

Sometimes her schedules were not the same as his own.

Friday, March 7, 7:21 P.M.

Captain Rajpal Singh, a ferocious-looking Nepalese with a jagged knife scar marring his right cheek, slid through the weeds, down the side of the ditch, and crawled over to where Benjamin Shaikh rested against the embankment.

To either side of him were eight of his Gurkha troops. They were in full combat gear, but not a single piece of metal clanked as they moved about. If he hadn't known they were there, they would have blended with the darkness afforded by the ditch.

Shaikh looked over the rim of the ditch, in the direction from which Singh had come. The refinery was ablaze with lights. Flaring towers, floodlamps, structure lighting made the huge plant look like a small city. With nightfall, it had become a tremendous hazard, backlighting his fighters so they could not raise their heads without offering excellent targets for the snipers at the road ninety meters in front of them.

As soon as he learned of the attacks against the refinery, Shaikh had left Irra in charge of the soldiers ferreting out renegades in the Kuala Belait dock area and flown directly to the refinery. His helicopter now rested in a parking lot inside the refinery fences. Shaikh did not have so many helicopters that he could risk them. He now had forty men defining a leaky perimeter sixty meters outside the fences of the refinery, but he was beginning to believe it might not be enough.

At first it was a small band of attackers, but as soon as counterfire was returned, another small band popped up on the other side of the refinery. The same was true on the docks, Irra had reported. The Gurkha troops would capture or kill a two- or three-man team of rebels, only to come under fire from another group of bandits.

"Captain?"

"They will shut off the lights soon, Major. They have to first shut down their operations."

"Someone may halt their operations for them, if they do not hurry."

"The manager says that the obvious target is the tank farm on the northern side of the plant."

Shaikh knew where it was. Dozens of huge tanks filled with liquified gas under pressure were protected by the refinery on the south and by the sea on the north. To the east and west, however. . . .

"Take your third platoon, Captain. Establish a defense on the east and west sides of the farm."

"Defense, sir?"

"If you see a worthy target, destroy it."

"Sir."

The captain slithered away, calling to his sergeant.

The man next to Shaikh dug his knees and elbows into the muddy earth of the ditch—not over a meter deep—and clambered forward. He was rewarded with the immediate stuttering of an automatic rifle. Kalashnikov, by the sound of it, Shaikh thought. Probably manufactured by the Chinese under Russian license. Three green tracers zipped overhead, and the man slid back down.

"Do not take unnecessary chances, Private."

"I am trying to pinpoint them, Major."

"Wait for darkness."

The rebels also had rocket-propelled grenades. Several had been aimed their way. As yet, they had not utilized heavy machine guns or antitank weapons, and Shaikh hoped they did not have them. An antitank rocket would raise havoc with the tank farm.

The lights of the refinery began to flicker and die. Sheets of blackness swept from one end of the plant to the other. Some of the flaring towers remained in ignition, but there was nothing to be done about that, he supposed.

He would allow ten minutes for night vision to be restored, then he would find out how truly fierce these supposed rebels were.

As soon as the allotted time had dripped slowly from his wristwatch, Shaikh said to the men on either side of him, "Stay low. They will be in the ditch on the other side of the highway. Make your first objective the shoulder of the road. Spread out. On my command."

He rolled onto his stomach, then rose to his knees.

"Now!"

He launched himself upward, over the rim of the ditch, his nine-millimeter semiautomatic pistol held out in front of him. He pounded forward, aware that his men were keeping pace with him.

Ahead, he could see little in the darkness. To the right, a kilometer away, were the lighted windows of some building. To the left, coming from the east, he saw three sets of headlights.

Seventy meters. . . .

Heart beginning to pound a little.

Eighty meters. . . .

Unbelievable. They had not yet taken fire.

Ninety meters. The drainage ditch along the highway came up, and Shaikh slid into it, went to his belly, and crawled up to peer across the crown of the highway.

Nothing.

They had evaporated, whisked away like ghosts into the night.

He heard firing from the other side of the refinery.

"Corporal!"

"Sir!"

"Keep two men here. Send two back to where we were. The rest should circle to the west."

"Immediately, sir. What of the trucks?"

"I will warn them."

Shaikh stood up cautiously, then walked across the highway to look into the ditch. No one was present. He went back to the center of the road and unclipped the flashlight from his belt.

Turning it on, he began to wave it back and forth in the direction of the oncoming trucks.

They did not dim their lights, and he squinted his eyes against the illumination. He heard them slowing, going down through the gears. When they reached him, they were down to a crawl.

He stepped to the side, and the first truck stopped next to him. The door opened and a bulbous figure descended. The figure had its own flashlight, and it momentarily blinded Shaikh.

"Put that down, you fool!"

"Oh! I'm sorry, Major Shaikh. I did not know who you were."

"Do I know you?" Shaikh could not make out the man's features.

The man shone his own light on his face. His many chins picked up many shadows. His eyes appeared washed out and feeble.

"Ah, yes. Lieutenant . . . Ali Haji. What are you doing here, Lieutenant?"

"I was told to come in your support, Major."

Shaikh did not need support from bumbling policemen. What was Omar Padang thinking of?

He quickly flashed his light at the sides of the trucks. They were small—weapons carriers—and the beds were loaded with men. No helmets. Not even riot gear. Then again, the Sultan had never experienced a riot.

"I have thirty with me, Major."

"How are you armed?"

"Sidearms and shotguns."

Against assault rifles and grenade launchers?

Still, Haji's policemen could free up Gurkhas for more important chores.

"All right, Lieutenant. There are at least four groups of rebels attempting to reach the refinery."

"Rebels!"

"For want of a better term. I do not know who they are. You will report to Captain Singh, and he will disperse your men around the tank farm and the refinery. If you encounter gunfire, keep your heads down."

"At once, Major."

Haji struggled back into the truck, a major feat for a man of his bulk, and Shaikh used his portable radio to call Singh and warn him.

"Police?" Singh replied in disgust.

"They are armed bodies. Use them."

"Sir."

He called his pilot and ordered him to pick him up on the highway, and as he waited, he watched the trucks pull off the road, dip through the ditch, and drive toward the refinery, now lighted with only sporadic flares.

He hoped it was there in the morning.

Friday, March 7, 8:40 P.M.

Omar Padang was in his communications room. The reports came in steadily from Kuala Belait, Lumut, Seria, all far from the capital.

The rebel teams were flushed out steadily, captured or executed, but for every team that fell, two more sprang up to take its place. Police, army, and Gurkha units complained of steadily increasing incidents of harassing fire.

One of the radio operators said, "Lieutenant Haji just called in. His division is being emplaced at Lumut, around the refinery."

"That is an excellent place for him," Padang said. The refinery was not meant to fall.

He crossed the room and sat in a chair next to Captain Awg Nazir.

"The regiment?" he asked.

"Minister Suliaman has sent three companies west. Two are in Kuala Belait, the other in Seria."

"And the air wing?"

"The two helicopters we worry about are in Seria."

"Good. Navy?"

"All questionable vessels are now patrolling the oil field. I have already received the code word from the *Bulkiah*."

"Excellent. The television station? The radio stations?"

"The rapid response teams are in place. They await a signal."

"Send it."

Padang stood up and went to the door of the communications room. Two policemen dressed in the camouflage uniforms of the rapid response force stood in the corridor. He motioned them inside.

They entered, unslinging their M-16 rifles and snapping loaded magazines into place. The loud clicks caused the four communications technicians to look up.

The policemen stepped to either side of the doorway and lowered the muzzles of the rifles, aiming at the operators.

Padang said, "Communications will now cease. Secure your consoles."

Four mouths dropped in amazement.

"I will be at the palace, Nazir."

"Of course, Minister Padang."

Omar Padang had just secured his new title.

Five

The interior minister had often asked Padang why he spent so much money on training and equipping a rapid response team that would never be needed. Now Hassanal would know.

Forty-five members of Padang's elite police corps were waiting for him when he arrived at the palace, which was alight with several thousand lamps. The pure ostentation of the structure represented everything Padang found repulsive about the Sultan and his entourage. The multi-millions of dollars torn out of the natural resources of his country and poured into the comfort of the Sultan was obscene. Whenever he looked at it, he was reminded of every slight he had ever suffered at the hands of an elitist family which assumed that birthright provided them with intelligence or insight, or both. Their logic was fallacious.

Omar Padang knew many envied him his position as the

chief of police, but none knew the indignity he suffered to hold it. He had never married, though even if he had, he was certain he would not have bared his innermost thoughts to a mate. How can one describe the rape of a soul?

His introspection was interrupted by the buzz of his cellular telephone, and he unclipped it from his belt.

"Padang."

"This is Awg Nazir. One of the patrol boats informs me that a Japanese supertanker departed the pumping station earlier without clearing customs. The patrol boat, number one-two-two, is following the tanker."

"Detain it, Captain. That is our oil."

"Minister, it is in international waters."

"With our oil."

"Should I check with President Li?"

"Of course not!"

He snapped the switch to cut Nazir off.

He quickly surveyed his force, kneeling in rows to either side of the road. Half were Chinese—a membership Mohammed Hassanal had questioned and decried, but which Padang had managed to keep in place. A substantial number of Bruneian Chinese in his department was a requirement of his own, but not one levied by the royal family.

They were dressed in camouflage, helmeted in black, and armed with Uzi machine pistols and rocket-propelled grenade launchers. Stun grenades hung from their web gear. They were extremely well-trained for this operation, a floor plan of the nearly 1,800-room palace ingrained in their minds, and Padang knew he did not have to lead this charge.

He raised a thumb toward the palace, and both lines of men came to their feet immediately and advanced at a run. In the soft and manicured grass off the road, their passage was not notable. Padang stayed at the edge of the road and walked after them.

There were twenty-seven members of the immediate royal family in the country at the moment, and they were protected within the palace and while travelling by a hand-picked detachment of thirty bodyguards. At this time of night, two-thirds of that group would be off-duty, residing in their own quarters in the palace. Padang expected the resistance to be fierce, but short-lived.

Unfortunately, entrance to the palace was not to be gained silently, as he had hoped. A sudden burst of gunfire was answered by several staccato responses, then it was quiet again. By the time he reached the grand entrance, skipped his bulk through the doors, and stood in the mar-ble-floored foyer, his police had disappeared into the bow-els of the building. Two uniformed guards lay on the floor, swimming in their own blood.

Padang walked over and looked down at them. One was obviously dead, but the other twitched and moaned and looked up at him, his eyes recognizing the police chief, beseeching.

Padang withdrew his Glock semiautomatic pistol and shot the man between the eyes. Someone had been care-less, leaving a live guard behind, and he would chastise them later.

With his pistol hanging in his hand at his side, Padang moved down the echoing corridor, eyeing the priceless paintings hung on the walls—he recognized none of the artists' names—and the treasured bric-a-brac displayed in glass cases and on pedestals. He would have shattered glass and swept vases, statuettes, and bronze busts to the floor, crushed them under his boots, mangled them with kicks, but he had agreed to keep the damage to a minimum.

The object was to send the artwork back into the world marketplace and recover the nation's gold. Members of the primary committee had argued strenuously for this, pointing out that much of the Sultan's treasure had been in the family for centuries and had appreciated considerably. The sale of the collections would bring them millions. Perhaps a billion dollars.

Padang had given in, and therefore, his troops were armed with stun grenades, rather than fragmentation grenades.

He now heard them detonating. The booming concussions rushed down the hallways from all directions in the palace. Automatic weapons opened up. From a lower floor, he heard sustained gunfire. The bodyguards had been located and would now be dying in their sumptuous quarters.

At the end of the corridor, he turned left, followed that long hallway for fifty meters, then walked into one of the great rooms. Four of his men were already there and trained their weapons on six of the royal family standing before a huge window. Two of them were small children, trying hard not to cry. Three of the adults were women—wives, probably in shock, their faces displaying their indignation at the affront to their personal well-being. The last was a young man, not yet twenty-one. Someone's son. A future pariah.

Padang knew none of them.

The young man knew him. "Chief Padang. Thank God you are here. Arrest these men."

"Be quiet or you will be shot."

The young man started forward. "Chief!"

Padang raised his gun hand, and the man retreated quickly, to be wrapped in the arms of one of the women. The young man's eyes suddenly showed less wrath and more fear.

Excellent. Reality would shape his education now, at least for the next few weeks.

The rattle of gunfire was beginning to die away. The palace was so extensive that some of the battles sounded as if they might be in another country, or at least another town. Breezes created by the air-conditioning carried the acrid tang of spent gunpowder. A mist of smoke hung in the air. It might pollute the fine furnishings scattered about the room—silk-clad sofas and easy chairs, spindly-legged tables, ornate and gilded credenzas. The oil paintings and brocaded draperies would have another patina layered upon them.

Within five minutes, other members of the family began to appear, forcefully moved into the room by the muzzles of assault weapons. They were lined up along the window wall.

Here at last was the Sultan. Sultan and Prime Minister His Majesty Paduka Seri Baginda Sultan Haji Hassanal Bulkiah Mu'izzaddin. The name Bulkiah came from the fifth sultan and dated to the fifteenth century.

An old man, though carefully pampered and nurtured. He had assumed the throne in October 1967 when his father abdicated in his favor, allowing the establishment of the constitutional monarchy. When he looked at the man, Padang did not see hundreds of years of lineage and tradition. He saw a man who exploited his people for his own gain, just as his predecessors had.

The Sultan said, "Padang, this is outrageous."

Padang smiled. "Your outrage will be short-lived. I will schedule your trial to be the first."

"What! There will be no trial but your own, Padang. No matter how long it takes."

He let all of the years of anger show in his eyes and face. "One week! That is all there is of your future!"

"You are delirious!"

"Ha! To tell you just how demented, oh Sultan of the past, on March twelfth, you will be tried, then executed."

"World condemnation will forestall that plan, Padang."

"The world cannot react in a week. We have seen that in the Persian Gulf, in Bosnia, everywhere. On March twelfth, you meet your maker."

"Never!"

"Well," Padang conceded with a grin, "if not, then the international community will have yet another surprise. It really doesn't matter to me. Get in line!"

"You haven't the authority to—"

"If you do not want to be muzzled like the dog you are, you will keep your mouth shut," Padang told him.

The Sultan's eyes turned murderous, but he backed into the line of his blood and kin. And very quickly, Padang thought, the fight and the spirit went out of him. His shoulders slumped, his eyes sought answers in some far-away place that only he could see.

Padang scanned the line of people cowering in front of the window, and he wanted to order his men to erase them from the earth. Accomplished in one long barrage of fire.

In this, too, he had compromised with the committee. Until the coup was firmly established, the family was to be kept alive, though not in such splendor as they were accustomed to finding. They were simply to be bargaining chips, if needed. Once the administration was on a firm foundation, he had been promised, then the trials would begin. And after the trials, the executions. Every man, woman, and child with a claim to the name Bulkiah. Except for those—seven of them—who were now abroad. They were travelling, attending universities, playing.

Li Sen, Lim Siddiqui, and Peng Ziyang did not know of the March 14 deadline Padang had set for himself, of course. Omar Padang had considered this very carefully. Speed was essential to counteract any international response, and even if a token complaint was raised, he had the perfect deterrent. He had considered that very carefully, also.

He could not help but be impressed with his planning.

A rapid response team lieutenant stuck his head in the doorway, spotted Padang, and trotted over.

"Lieutenant Hashim?"

The man smiled. He had a streak of soot across his nose. "The operation is almost complete, sir."

A few gunshots echoed through the halls.

Padang raised an eyebrow.

"The defense and interior ministers are still holding out. It should not be much longer."

Some of the women hostages were now crying, despair taking hold.

"The security contingent?"

"There were no survivors, sir."

"Very good."

"And the servants have been turned into the street. We are conducting our room by room sweep presently."

In a house this large, that could take awhile.

An additional six members of the royal family were ushered into the room, forced to the far wall. Padang counted twenty-five of them, now. He had eleven of his men covering them, and each man, he was certain, wanted to open fire as badly as Padang wanted them to do so.

Perhaps they would hold off.

"Lieutenant, do you have the restraints?"

"Right here, sir." Hashim held up a bundle of plastic handcuffs.

"Let us begin."

The gun battle sounds ceased. The war was all but over.

Padang watched as two of his men began to cuff the prisoners. Neither of the policemen attempted to be gentle, and Omar Padang did not bother to admonish them.

At last, Hassanal and Suliaman appeared at the doorway, prodded by gun barrels.

Suliaman had been wounded. Blood seeped through the fabric of his jacket, along the length of his right arm. The defense minister appeared much less the international playboy he was reputed to be.

At the other wall, Suliaman's wife erupted into wails and tears.

"Padang! What in God's name are you doing?" Hassanal sprang forward, and two policemen leaped to grab his arms and pull him back.

"In fact, I *do* act in God's name, Mohammed." Padang had waited eight years to call the man by his first name, all he should have ever been entitled to. Now, there were no artificial titles to hide behind.

"Traitor! Pig!"

Padang smiled. "Add them to our collection."

He turned to follow their progress across the room, and as Suliaman passed in front of him, the ousted defense minister suddenly threw off the man holding his uninjured arm and launched himself at Padang.

The chief absorbed the brunt of the attack with his big stomach, but was knocked off balance, tripped backward over a glass-topped table that crumbled under his weight and shattered. He landed on his back, his face coated with blood from Suliaman's wounded arm.

Suliaman looked down at him and said, "That's where you belong, you son of a whore."

Padang pulled the Glock from its holster, and barely sighting it, fired. The bullet slammed into Suliaman's knee-cap, and he yelped and went down like a slaughtered steer.

The man's wife screamed, raced across the room, and fell by his side on her stomach, her arms fastened behind her.

Lieutenant Tan Hashim rushed to help Padang up, his

face no mask for his concern. He knew of the restrictions regarding the family.

Padang regained his feet and now looked down on Suliaman, their roles satisfyingly reversed.

"We will have to take that leg off, and you will no longer be any trouble."

"But, Chief . . . ," Hashim whispered in his ear.

"So? There are accidents just waiting to happen."

Friday, March 7, 10:07 P.M.

When the radio and television stations went off the air, Hua Enlai, the Chinese government's envoy in Brunei, had not been immediately concerned.

Of course, Hua had never been accustomed to being overly alarmed by any occurrence in his thirty-three years. His father was Minister of Commerce for the People's Republic, an ardent communist, and very close to the Premier. Hua Enlai's life had been cushioned from the realities of socialist life in many ways. He had memories of a comfortable childhood, no anxiety about admission to a university, and no concern for achieving a reputable position in the government.

He had devoted eight years to posts of increasing importance in the bureaucracy, and then gladly accepted appointment in Brunei. His family made the rigor of foreign posting most agreeable by providing him with the junk now moored in Muara as his official residence.

The building in which the mission in Bandar Seri Begawan was housed was not particularly grandiose, but then, he had very little to do but oversee various negotiations related to commerce. Usually his responsibilities revolved around the social events conducted by the diplomatic community. They involved a minor sort of spying, attempting to gather tidbits of information that might eventually lead to knowledge of some importance.

Tonight he was hosting the diplomats from the French and Italian consulates, and the dinner had gone quite well, even past the time one of his subordinates notified him that the broadcast stations had become silent.

As they left the table and accepted after-dinner liqueurs from waiters with silver trays, his assistant again slipped through the door and moved to his side.

"What is it now?"

"Sir," the man whispered, "I have just learned that our own communications are inoperative."

"What! That is impossible."

The secret radios, with their special encryption circuits, transmitted and received their signals from antennas mounted on the roof of the mission. They were impervious to outside interference.

"Apparently, it is not impossible, honored sir. All of the antennas are damaged beyond repair. We do not know when this happened."

"Call the police! They are supposed to protect us."

"I did just that, sir, and they said they would be here soon. I also attempted to call Beijing, to notify them of the problem, but the long-distance telephone circuits are out of order."

Hua was about to express his indignation over this affront when his deputy in charge of protocol entered the dining room.

"Sir, there are policemen at the door."

"Yes. We called them."

"These men say we must leave with them."

Hua was now irritated. He brushed past the protocol deputy, went into the foyer, and marched to the doors where two of his security men were holding back a contingent of a half dozen men dressed in Brunei police uniforms.

The security men stepped aside as he approached.

"Sergeant, what *is* the problem?"

The policeman was Chinese, but he did not defer greatly to his ethnic brother.

"There appears to be some revolutionary activity taking place. My orders are to move you to a hotel where we can more effectively see to your protection."

"Revolution! In Brunei?"

"I am not aware of the details. Come, we must go."

"Absolutely not. I am entertaining tonight."

The man had the gall to unsnap the cover over his holstered pistol. The security agents immediately bristled.

"You and your staff are to come with me. The Minister of the Interior demands it."

"Hassanal?"

"We do not have time to waste, Envoy Hua."

The policemen behind the sergeant began to spread out on the wide portico.

Hua did not want a war to be started on his doorstep.

"How long is this to last?"

"Very likely only for the night," the policeman suggested.

"And the mission? Who sees to its protection? We have valuable documents here."

"We will leave the normally posted guard."

"I would prefer to go to my junk."

"That is not possible."

"Ridiculous!"

"Sir?"

"Oh, very well. Let me notify my guests."

Before he returned to the dining room, though, Hua

gave instructions for securing sensitive documents in the vault, along with the secret radios.

Perhaps one day they would once again work.

Friday, March 7, 11:14 P.M.

Benjamin Shaikh had arrived back at his headquarters an hour before. He could no longer act the commander in the field. There were so many skirmishes taking place from Seria to Kuala Belait that he had to assume the role of commander at his headquarters.

His orderly room was jammed with subordinates responding to his orders. The primary radio and portable radios kept him in contact with the teams engaged with the rebels. Captain Rajpal Singh was in command of the Gurkhas and the police at Lumut, and Lieutenant Pant had assumed control of the diversified forces in Kuala Belait. His adjutant, Captain Shrestha, stayed near the base radio and directed the efforts of two platoons fighting seven separate battles in Seria. Near Putong, another group of rebels had attacked an army barracks.

Though it was not quite within his power to do so, Shaikh had declared martial law in three towns several hours earlier, using the radio stations to warn residents and urge them to stay in their quarters. He had been just in time, apparently, for the radio stations had now ceased to broadcast, and he wondered who had ordered that action.

His role, in fact, was confused. The oil fields were his province, not resistance to a rebellion. He was content for the moment to assume that the attacks were directed at oil field personnel and equipment. He had not taken his request to Minister Hassanal, judging time to be of the essence. No doubt, Hassanal would berate him for the omission. But that would come later.

Right now, his intelligence team was attempting to make sense of the disorder. He was not aware of any proclamations, and he had no feeling at all for the quality or quantity of his adversary. Reports now coming in on the military radio net identified dead or captured enemy as both Malay and Chinese. So much for his earlier thoughts of a Chinese rebellion.

There was no single thread to follow toward an identification of the hostiles or their leadership. It was a definite disadvantage.

A corporal waved at him, and Shaikh dodged around a desk and went to take the man's portable radio.

"Lion One," he said. They had taken up their pre-planned emergency code names a few hours before.

"Lion Three." That was Suraj Irra.

"Go ahead, Three."

"Lieutenant Pant has been killed. I have assumed command here."

"Very well. Confirmed. One out."

Shaikh lamented the letters he would have to write. Pant was a good man, a gentle man, and he would miss him. And he was the eleventh to die.

He stopped by the desk of a sergeant who was monitoring the aircraft.

"Status?"

"Major, I have allowed one of the three helicopters patrolling the oil field to return here for refuelling. One Black Hawk is carrying ammunition and rations to the siege at Lumut. Your helicopter is on standby."

"Thank you, Sergeant."

"Major Shaikh! If you would?"

He joined Captain Shrestha at the radio console, and the operator punched the play button on a tape recorder.

"I was monitoring the local marine channel," the corporal explained.

Over the hiss of radio static, Shaikh plainly heard, ". . . all tanker captains. This is the Brunei Navy cutter *Saifudden*. All tankers are ordered to remain in place at their moorings or at the pumping stations. No ship is allowed movement without the express consent of the Navy. Repeating. . . ."

He looked at Shrestha, who shook his head in amazement.

He noted the absence of the term "Royal." Normally, the ship's captain would have said, "Royal Brunei Navy." Still, he did not know what to make of it.

Shaikh ordered his sergeant to detach a Black Hawk to the pumping stations, and a few minutes later, the report came back: "Lion, Tiger Four. We circled the tanker mooring and identified three ships of the navy standing off the mooring. They appear to have all deck guns manned."

"Have him return to patrol," Shaikh told the sergeant.

"This does not sound good," Shrestha said.

"No, it does not."

Shaikh picked up a telephone and dialled the interior minister's office. There was no answer. And there should have been a night-duty officer present.

He tried the defense minister's number with the same result.

The police headquarters was not answering its telephone, either.

"Are you beginning to get a sense of it?" he asked Shrestha.

"I am, Major."

"We are hamstrung. We need information badly."

Friday, March 7, 11:52 P.M.

The bow wave thrown up by the brusque bow of the *Maru Hokkaido* crested at eight meters. Bow-on, observers tended to see the tanker as a city block of skyscrapers approaching. Small things in her path, like power yachts or sailboats, would be tossed aside like a child's bathtub toys. With 1.1 million tons of crude oil walled into her double-hulled structure, her displacement was such that her momentum was difficult to overcome.

Should Captain Hirosiuta want her to stop, he would have to plan the maneuver well in advance. It had required twenty kilometers and nearly two hours at full power to bring her to her cruising speed of twenty-eight knots. An emergency signal to stop would demand four or five kilometers, with the massive twin screws howling a protest in reverse. The supertanker would not turn on a dime, barely in a space the size of Oahu.

She was so huge that the vagaries of the sea seemed to have less effect on her than she had on the sea. Walking her decks was similar to walking the solid concreteness of downtown Tokyo. Squalls did not affect her passage or her stability. Typhoons of medium intensity could make her heel by a few degrees.

Maki Hirosiuta enjoyed walking her decks; he was proud of her, and he was proud to have been selected to command her. The captain had not enjoyed a full night's sleep in a long time, however. He was wont to arise several times during the night, to dress in an immaculate uniform, and to wander without warning through unexpected spaces. The engineering spaces. The dormitories. The many recreation rooms where off-duty personnel pursued card games, chess, mah-jongg, movies, and video games. Without fail, he always stopped by the bridge to check on the current watch.

Occasionally, and despite the fierce winds created by her passage, he walked the open-deck catwalks to the bow and peered into the forecastle quarters assigned to deck crew. Once, he had discovered a bow watchman asleep at his post, though he was connected by a communications headset to the bridge. Both the watchman and the third officer in command of the watch discovered they had made their last voyage aboard a supertanker.

Tonight he walked the carpeted subdeck—below the main deck—that housed crewmen in twelve-man compartments. He pushed open doors and looked in on his sleeping charges. Though he was constrained by the need to maintain the aloofness of command, Hirosiuta frequently felt very much the father. His responsibility insisted that he examine the children's rooms and chase away ogres lurking under beds or calm a bad dream.

He found neither tonight, and he eventually returned to the elevator and took it up eight decks to the bridge.

With the hyperactivity of loading oil behind them, the bridge was now a calm sanctuary. It was lighted only by the myriad blue, green, and amber output of light-emitting diodes and digital readouts in the instrument panels below the windscreen. The light of the compass ahead of the helm cast the helmsman's face as ghostly. A boatswain's mate seated near the entrance called out, "Captain's on the bridge!"

"Remain at ease," he said and advanced to where First Officer Yaguchi stood to the left of, and behind, the helm.

Through the windscreen, the night was utterly black. Above, a million stars sparkled crisply through a pristine atmosphere. The phosphorescence created by excited plankton disturbed by the bow cutting through their waters gave off a dim glow outlining the gunwales. An ideal night, the captain thought.

"Good morning, sir."

"It is that, First Officer. Are we expecting a change?"

"There is nothing dramatic, sir. We will encounter a low-pressure system around ten o'clock in the morning."

"Traffic?"

"None ahead of us, Captain. Radar reports a small ship astern that has steadily closed on us."

"Following our track?"

"Yes, sir."

"I will look."

He turned and went aft, bypassing the high-mounted captain's chair and the navigation table, to the radar room at the back of the bridge. Pushing through the curtain that kept the compartment at its required level of semidarkness, Hirosiuta found the operator perched on the edge of his chair in front of the radar screen.

The man looked up and started to his feet.

Hirosiuta waved him back to his chair and came up behind him to study the screen.

Every time the scan passed the quadrant to the *Maru Hokkaido*'s southeast, it left a large blip blinking on the screen.

"Distance?" he asked.

"Twenty-one hundred meters, Captain."

"Do you know what it is?"

"I think a fourteen- or fifteen-meter-long boat, sir. It has been holding thirty-six knots for the past two hours. I worried at first, because they followed in our wake, but now they have altered course to pass us to the starboard."

Hirosiuta studied the scope for several more minutes, did not see any alteration in the boat's course, then said, "Thank you."

He went back to the bridge, picked up binoculars from a clip on his chair, then crossed the bridge to the starboard-wing door. Pulling the door open, he stepped out onto the wing.

The night was heated, moist, balmy, but the warmth was destroyed by the strong wind pouring over the bows. He slipped his uniform hat from his head and tucked it beneath his left arm, then leaned against the shielded railing and held the binoculars to his eyes.

The boat was illuminated by its red and green running lights, and he quickly picked up the image in the field of the binoculars. The darkness of night, however, kept him from any further identification. There were no interior lights, so he could not construct an image of its superstructure. The seas were calm, with long, long swells perhaps a meter in height running to the south. The boat rose and fell smoothly.

He lowered the binoculars and returned to the bridge.

"Captain?" Yaguchi asked.

"I do not know. I think I will wait here for a while."

Half an hour later, the boat overtook them on the starboard side, giving them a one-kilometer berth, which was safe enough. Another scan with the binoculars was inconclusive. It could have been a power yacht with an enclosed flying bridge.

If so, it was a yacht he was uncomfortable with. He did not know why, except that the feeling was similar to the one that had urged him to leave Bruneian waters quickly.

"First Officer, come ten degrees to port."

Yaguchi passed the order to the helmsman, but it would be several minutes before the tanker began to even respond to the change in steering.

Hirosiuta wanted to give the smaller boat even more clearance than its captain thought prudent.

Ten minutes later, with the bow responding and the monster ship beginning to turn slightly to the west, the small boat was about even with the bridge. The captain examined her once again through the binoculars.

"She is turning on us, Captain," Yaguchi said.

"Yes." He kept the glasses trained on her as she came closer.

Soon, he could discern the numbers on her bow: 122.

And then, streaming in the wind, the yellow flag with white and black diagonals. He could not make out the overlaid red emblem, but it was the Brunei flag.

The intercom buzzed, "Bridge, Communications. Is the captain available?"

Hirosiuta stepped to the intercom and pressed the lever. "Bridge. This is the captain."

"Sir, the boat calls us."

"Relay it."

He lifted the microphone next to the intercom and spoke into it. "This is Captain Hirosiuta of the *Maru Hokkaido*."

"Captain Hirosiuta, I am Captain Dyg Thambipillai, Patrol Craft one-two-two of the Royal Brunei Navy."

"What may I do for you, Captain?"

"Sir, it is a matter of your manifest. The export office of Shell Brunei wishes a confirmation."

Irregular.

Hirosiuta looked down on the boat, now forty meters off the starboard side. It was positively puny next to the ULCC.

"It is difficult to stop," he said.

"Unnecessary, Captain. We can transfer the examiners while under way."

The captain sighed. "Very well."

Turning to Yaguchi, he said, "Lower the landing stage."

"Sir."

Yaguchi issued the orders, and as Hirosiuta watched the main deck, a party of seamen appeared, activated the midships starboard crane, and lowered the landing stage and stairway over the side. Within ten minutes, the patrol boat came alongside, and shortly, three men dressed in the uniform of the Royal Brunei Navy appeared at the gap in the starboard rail. One of them carried an attaché case. One of his seamen led them back toward the superstructure.

Hirosiuta pressed the intercom button. "Communications, this is the captain. Immediately send a message on the company frequency to our headquarters. As follows: Brunei naval unit boarding our vessel to examine manifest. Signed Hirosiuta, and add our current position."

"Yes, sir."

"Sir?" Yaguchi asked.

"Yes, First Officer?"

"I should like to examine Lifeboat Station One."

"Very well. I have the conn."

The boatswain's mate echoed the change in command, and Yaguchi left the bridge, headed for the elevator bank.

A few minutes later, a seaman from the deck crew ushered the visitors onto the bridge.

The first man saluted, and Hirosiuta returned it, then introduced himself.

"I am Captain Thambipillai," the man said, "and in the name of the Republic of Brunei, I am assuming command of this vessel."

As he spoke, one of his men opened the attaché case, removed three small machine guns, dropped the case to the deck, and passed the guns to his compatriots.

Hirosiuta was astounded, and he was heartsick. There was absolutely nothing he could do. The surge of hatred that welled in him like bile rising in his throat turned his mouth acidic, but had nowhere else to be vented. There was not one weapon on board with which he could defend himself or his prized ship.

The boatswain's mate leaped toward one of the Bruneians before Hirosiuta could utter a warning.

The burst of fire was loud in the enclosed space of

the bridge. Port-side glass shattered, and the boatswain's mate's face erupted blood. The impact of the bullets knocked him backward, slammed him to the deck on his back. He did not move.

The helmsman fell to the deck, but Hirosiuta did not think he had been hit. Junior officers and technicians burst from the communications and radar compartments at the back of the bridge. They slid to a halt when they saw the guns.

"We can do this my way, or the bloody way," Thambipillai said.

"This is piracy."

The man swung his gun toward the navigator.

"What do you wish?"

"First, we will stop this tanker."

"That will take a long time."

"We are in no hurry."

"Helmsman."

The man clambered to his feet and regained his position at the wheel. "Sir?"

"Order engines ahead slow."

Saturday, March 8, 12:09 A.M.

The jarring ring of the telephone startled Koehler and brought him hopping out of bed.

Sherry said, "What the hell? It's the middle of the night, Kelly!"

In the dark, he banged his shoulder on the door frame of the bedroom as he searched for the hallway. It was a short hallway, and in the living room, moonlight let him find the telephone on the coffee table.

Koehler glanced at his wristwatch. He had talked to Slim Avery a half hour before, learning of firefights all over

Kuala Belait, but none seeming to affect any GlobeTech personnel. They were secure on the rigs or holed up in their quarters. A dozen men were staying at the supply compound, supposedly to protect it and the helicopters, though no one had a weapon larger than a penknife.

"Koehler."

"Mr. Koehler, this is Benjamin Shaikh."

Koehler didn't know whether to be surprised or scared. Both, he decided.

"Is there a problem, Major?"

"There may be, sir. I hope you were not bragging when you told me you were an intelligence officer."

"It's not something to brag about, Major."

A restrained laugh on the other end. "Can you tell me if there appears to be any unrest in the city?"

Puzzled, Kelly carried the phone on its long cord toward the front window. Sherry had gotten up and was standing naked in the hallway, watching him. A pale and very attractive wraith. He was also bare-assed and thought he'd rather go back to bed.

Pulling the bamboo shade aside, Koehler looked out on the dock, then sideways toward the city. It was dark and calm. There were very few lights on in any of the houses within his own suburb of Kampong Ayer. He could hear water lapping at the stilts of the house.

He told Shaikh as much.

"Mr. Koehler, none of the ministry offices are responding to telephone calls. The police headquarters is not responding, either. I have tried telephone and radio contacts with the regiment, with the air wing, and with the navy. Again, no one in command is available."

"Jesus! This is a takeover of the government?"

"I fear so. And I am amazed that the telephone system is still operating, though international calls are not going through."

Shaikh told him about the radio transmissions aimed at the tanker captains, telling them to remain in place.

He told the Gurkha commander about the sense of desolation in Bandar Seri Begawan that afternoon—the boarded windows he had seen, the restraint among the Chinese that Sherry had encountered.

"Sherry is your wife?"

"Yes."

"I would get her out of the country if it is still possible, Mr. Koehler."

"Look, call me Kelly. I'll try the airport."

"I wonder if . . . on your way to the airport, you could perhaps reconnoiter the city, then let me know. . . ."

"I'll do my best, Major."

"Benjamin."

"Benjamin. Who's behind this?"

"That is a puzzle. We have encountered both Malay and Chinese rebels. I would have best guessed a plot of noncitizen Chinese, I suppose. They have been denied full participation for a long time."

"I'll get back to you as soon as I can."

Shaikh gave him several telephone numbers and radio frequencies, and Koehler scrambled to find a pen and notepad. He hung up and ripped the page of numbers from the pad.

"Kelly?"

"Doesn't look good, hon. Though you do."

She gave him a halfhearted grin. "Tell me."

He told her as they dressed in the bedroom in the dark. For some reason, he didn't want to turn the lights on.

He hooked her bra for her, then stopped her as she pulled a white T-shirt over her head.

"Pick something dark, Sherry."

"Dark? Oh."

She found a navy-blue shirt as a substitute.

Koehler decided on blue jeans, black running shoes, and a black T-shirt. When they were dressed, he rummaged in the dresser drawer for all of the Bruneian dollars he could find and stuffed them in his pockets. He picked up the two suitcases they had packed before falling into bed. Falling into bed the second time.

Carrying them to the living room, he asked, "Suppose there's any more money around the house?"

"Maybe the kitchen."

She banged some drawers and came back. "Forty bucks, Bruneian."

"Put it in your purse."

On impulse, Kelly picked up the telephone and dialled GlobeTech's home office in Houston.

He got a chime and a message in three languages. In English, it was: "We are so sorry, but all international circuits are busy at this time. Please place your call later."

"About what I thought," he said to himself.

"What?"

"International calls are blocked. Where's the phone book?"

She found it in an end table, and Koehler carried it to the window to use the moonlight. He called the airport.

It rang. And rang. And rang.

"No friendly skies this morning, Sherry."

"I wasn't leaving, anyway."

"The hell you weren't."

"Not without you. What about Monica?"

Monica Davis, his office manager, had a house a few blocks away.

He keyed in the numbers, and the phone rang six times before a sleepy voice answered.

"Monica, wake up."

"Kelly? That you?"

"You pack a bag. And only one bag. I'll pick you up in ten minutes."

"What! Kelly! What in the world?"

"I'll tell you later. Get a move on!"

He hung up.

"As soon as we pick her up, I'll run you out to *Serendipity*."

"Kelly. . . ."

"I need you to protect her for me, Sherry."

"Only if you . . ."

"We'll see." He hoped that, if she felt some responsibility for someone else, she'd worry less about him.

And there were others.

From his hip pocket, he pulled his small address book and found the number for the local Phillips man.

"Hey, it's the middle of the damned night!"

"Jim, Kelly Koehler."

"Oh. What's up, Kelly?"

"You know what's going on west of here?"

"Too damned aware. I've got all my people digging holes in the sand."

"I think the Sultan's tumbled."

"Shit!"

"Communications are hog-tied, Jim, except for the local phones. I'm starting a calling tree. You call two others."

"Gotcha. Thanks, Kelly."

Koehler called the Exxon rep and gave him the same message.

"Kelly?" Sherry said.

"I made my two calls. Let's get out of here."

He carried the bags out to the truck, unlocked the hatch window, and tossed them in the back. The city didn't have many streetlights, but he decided to drive without headlights, anyway. It would be slower, but less attention-getting. As they pulled away from Kampong Ayer, he searched for alien shadows moving in the alleys and the streets, but saw none. It was entirely eerie. The capital, with its Muslim traditions, was usually bereft of nightlife. Visitors or foreign workers had to adore rental videos.

Nothing moved on the streets. He thought he saw eyes peering from darkened windows, but it was probably his imagination.

But not Sherry's. "I think everyone's awake. Except the foreigners, maybe."

"Think so?"

"Can't you feel them looking at us?"

"Well . . . maybe."

They drove past the palace.

It was blazing with lights.

Unconsciously, he pressed the accelerator and picked up speed. Passing the main entrance road, he looked up its length and saw several vehicles parked at the end of it, gathered near the grand entrance. A few of them were covered trucks, and Koehler thought that ominous.

He was relieved to turn off the main thoroughfare, drive a block, and pull up near Monica's rented house. She was waiting on the sidewalk, and he got out to get the luggage.

Two suitcases.

"Monica."

"I just couldn't help it."

He sighed and threw them in the truck. They were heavy as hell.

"You taking gold out of the country?" he asked.

"Out of the country? Are we leaving?"

"Damned sure. Let's go."

Sherry brought her up to date while Koehler selected another route back toward the river. He didn't want to go anywhere near the palace.

He took odd little streets, cramped with run-down housing that he'd never travelled before, driving slowly, circumnavigating the man-made lagoon surrounding the Omar Ali Saifuddin Mosque, a magnificent structure honoring a former sultan. Its facade, domes, and minarets were brightly lit by floodlights, as was the ceremonial stone barge in front of it. Religion wasn't going to be dimmed, even if the government went down.

As he crossed an intersection, a pair of headlights flashed on down the side street, catching the Explorer in their beams. He tromped the pedal and raced to the next corner, turned right.

Glanced back. White Jeep skidding around the corner a block away. Probably police, but he didn't think he trusted the police any longer.

Two blocks later, on the deserted street, he was holding fifty, but the Jeep's lights swung around the corner, and it was hot on his trail.

Damn! He was heading away from the river.

The women were silent, and a quick glance around showed him white faces.

He swung the wheel hard to the left, ignoring a stop sign, and found to his regret that he was on Jalan Pemancha, a major street that passed by the Brunei Hotel. It was an international class and expensive hotel, and he wondered if it might be a haven this time of night. He kept the pedal down.

Saw the hotel coming up.

And shit! There were a half dozen police cars parked around the entrance.

He slammed on the brakes, spun the wheel, and shot down another side street.

Three blocks ahead, he saw more headlights.

Grabbed the next right.

"Kelly?"

"I think they're on the radio with each other."

"But why?" He could hear the tremble in Sherry's voice.

"Probably want to quarantine foreigners."

"To hell with their quarantine," Monica Davis yelled.

"Sherry?"

"I'm with you, Lone Ranger."

"They're blocking us from the river. We'll never reach the ketch."

"Let's go west," Sherry told him.

"Bullets out that way."

"There may be some here, too."

Koehler whipped a right at the next corner, just as a Jeep swung around the corner a block back. He took another left at the next intersection, and found the four-lane boulevard all to himself.

For about one minute.

He was doing eighty, his eyes frantically watching the intersections for potential crash victims, when three sets of headlights suddenly filled his rearview mirror.

Saturday, March 8, 12:43 A.M.

Mohammed Hassanal was sick at heart. He was deeply worried about his wife, Serena, and his twelve-year-old son, Jahan. They had been forced into the back of another truck, and he lost sight of them when the canvas was pulled down.

His son squealed in fright.

A gun prodded him in the back.

He whirled around. "You will regret this for all of eternity, Hashim."

The man, brazenly adorned with police lieutenant's insignia, laughed at him. "If regret is the same as laughter, yes, I think that is true. Get in the truck!"

"Where are you taking us? I demand to know."

"Demand all you wish, former minister. Perhaps a cruise.

Would you not like a cruise just now? You may get away from your troubles?"

Hassanal's hands were bound behind him with the plastic handcuffs, but his legs were free.

"Slime!" he yelled and kicked out with his right foot.

Hashim dodged the kick easily, and swung his Uzi in a rapid arc that connected with Hassanal's nose. His head was knocked backward, he stumbled into the back of the truck, and blood gushed down his face.

He shook his head trying to clear it, spattering blood to either side. Padang had set an example for their treatment, he realized. He suspected that they were not to be killed, but anything short of death might be tolerated. They had left Hamzah bin Suliaman trussed on the floor of the room, his shattered knee creating pain that echoed in the expression of his face.

"If he dies before we get back to him, it is God's will," Padang had said.

Padang! The damnable man Hassanal had trusted for eight years. Why had he not seen the treachery in the man's eyes? Hassanal had already made his vow. Omar Padang would die a dog's death, and a very slow one.

"In the truck, now! Or you will join your cousin."

He tried to bend over the lip of the bed, but his tied hands allowed him no leverage, and two policemen grabbed his legs and threw him upward, sprawling face first on the splintered wooden floor. Conscious of his undignified position, Hassanal rolled sideways, pulled his knees up, then rolled onto them. He stood upright.

"Sit down!"

There were wooden slat benches along each side, and Hassanal settled onto one of them.

The Sultan was on the other side, near the front, his arms pulled tightly behind him, and he stared wordlessly into some infinity. The pigs had no right to treat a wise and elderly man in such a fashion. How much the Sultan had done for his people! Did no one recognize that?

Hassanal realized he was sitting next to Naomi, Suliaman's wife. Her face was streaked with tears. She wore a shapeless, dark blue shift, an expectation of Muslim women, but he knew her to be a beautiful woman. At the moment, her chest heaved with suppressed cries, and he did not think she was even aware of her daughter, sitting next to her and also crying.

He leaned closer to her. "Hush, Naomi. This will be avenged."

She looked up at him, her dark eyes brimming with moisture. "But Hamzah! He is dreadfully wounded!"

"They cannot let him die. It would lead to the supreme punishment when this is over."

"It is true?"

Hassanal fervently hoped so.

Saturday, March 8, 4:20 A.M.

In the tiny hut hidden in the rain forest, Li Sen and the other two committee men waited anxiously. They were surrounded by eight armed men, intended for their protection, but ominous in their bearing. They sported an odd accumulation of weapons, none of which Li recognized. Half of the protective unit was Chinese and the other half Malay.

Li Sen was not a violent man. He abhorred the thought of what might be taking place in the city, but he also knew it was inevitable and necessary. While he was a citizen, so many of his brothers were not, and when they had come to him, nearly five years ago, he had agreed to take up their cause.

Their cause was simply to obtain citizenship in the nation

in which they and untold numbers of their ancestors had been born. For five years, Li had petitioned the palace ministries, the Sultan himself!, and all to no avail. The frustration was enormous, and it was at a peak when he had been approached by Omar Padang.

The police chief knew of his activities, of course, and had even located this secret headquarters. Padang's proposition was simple. He needed to form a coalition, to obtain Chinese support for his project. There were Chinese in the military and in key communications positions.

The secret negotiations—taking place late at night in a dozen hideaways—lasted eight months, and this was the result. Li waited with his colleagues, a noncitizen Chinese named Peng Ziyang and a Malay businessman called Lim Siddiqui, while their militant arm performed his chores. No doubt with glee, Li Sen thought. Omar Padang frequently frightened him.

It was Padang, however, who suggested that the future government remain in hiding at this juncture, safely away from harm. Li had possibly been too quick to agree, and he felt as if he were being cowardly. A leader should lead from the front. Now, it was too late, and he hoped he had not set a wrong example.

The hut was illuminated with two propane lanterns hanging from an overhead beam, and the bright flares cast dark shadows behind the single table and dozen chairs filling the room. Half of the bodyguards slept upright in their chairs. Food cartons were tossed in a cardboard box in the corner. There was no telephone, but there was a battery-powered two-way radio, provided by Li Sen, and from time to time, one or another of them paused to look at it.

One of their bodyguards had fiddled with it earlier in the night, and they had listened to radio transmissions made by the army, the air wing, and the Gurkha battalion. Most of it was incomprehensible to Li since he did not profess to be a military man. He saw himself simply as a diplomat. It was he who would save the emerging democracy, protect it from the hungry wolves snapping at their international door.

At long last he heard the code words come over the radio's speaker: "Peace be with you."

Li scrambled out of his chair and knelt before the radio on its wooden crate. He pulled the microphone from its hook and pressed the transmit button.

"Omar, is that you?"

"I am Fox. Remember that."

"Yes. Yes. Dragon is here."

"All is clear," Padang said. "The city awaits its first Provisional President of the Republic of Brunei."

"I am coming," Li said.

His anxiety dissipated, and his heart soared.

Saturday, March 8, 5:17 A.M.

Tokyo was coming alive, her streets jamming with men and women and their automobiles intent upon arriving early for an extra day of work in order to get an edge on their fellow workers, who were also arriving early on a Saturday.

Meoshi Kyoto surpassed them all. He had been called at one-thirty in the morning, and he had been in his office twenty minutes later. Three hours after that, his uniform was still crisp, but his eyes sagged with the weight of the previous night's late hours—an involved argument with his wife over the future course of his career—and his mouth felt dry and gritty after a half night of telephone dialogue.

At forty-eight, Kyoto had streaks of gray in his short-cropped black hair and an intricate system of wrinkles at the corners of his eyes, but his body still fit well within his uniforms, as it should for a colonel of the Japanese Defense Forces.

It was his military status that was the source of his problems. Kyoto longed to get back to his regiment, to become immersed in the discipline of the infantry he loved. Unfortunately, one of the traits repetitively praised by his superior officers was his diplomacy, and Kyoto had been assigned to the Foreign Ministry nineteen months before as Liaison Officer. In fact, he was further assigned to the Deputy Minister for Marine Affairs, Kato Asume.

And that personage had, for the second time, evaluated him with a superior rating, with glowing recommendations, following up with an offer of employment in a civilian capacity. Kyoto had been disheartened. He detested his job as boring, ineffective, and pointless. Kim Kyoto thought he should resign his commission and accept the job in the ministry. She thought he had excellent prospects as a state official.

But now, for the first time, he was faced with a crisis that had sharpened his interest, as well as his anger.

His desk was littered with his handwritten notes, accumulated during the course of his many telephone calls, and he did not have them organized when Asume finally burst through his doorway. Kyoto had called his superior as soon as he knew of the problem with the *Maru Hokkaido*, but apparently the deputy minister had gone back to sleep for a few more hours.

Kyoto rose to his feet behind his desk.

"Colonel! What is the latest news?"

"Ah, Minister, I could be prepared to brief you in ten

minutes.'' He gestured toward the heap of notes on his desk.

"Nonsense. Let us do it now. I have ordered coffee for us.''

Asume sat in the chair at the side of the desk, and Kyoto resumed his position. He was about to speak when an aide appeared with coffee, and he waited while it was poured.

"As I told you earlier, Minister, the *Hokkaido*'s captain notified his company headquarters he was being boarded by someone from the Brunei Navy. Shortly thereafter, someone calling himself the *Maru Hokkaido*'s first officer contacted a French container ship named *Herault Transporter*. He said he was calling from a lifeboat radio, which restricted his range. He reported hearing gunfire on the bridge, and that the tanker was slowing in the water.''

"Yes, yes! I know all of that.''

"The *Herault Transporter* reached the scene at three-forty-six, an hour and a half ago. They . . .''

"There are rumors running through the hallways, Meoshi. A slaughter!''

"There is no confirmation of that, Minister. The French ship reports that the tanker is almost dead in the water, and that a Brunei gunboat is standing by. When the *Herault Transporter* attempted to close, she was warned off, and a rocket was fired across her bow. Currently, she is forty kilometers away, over the horizon from the tanker.''

"That is all?''

"I understand that a crewman on the container ship captured part of the confrontation on a camcorder, and I have requested a copy of the videotape. I also understand that he has already sold the tape to CNN.''

There were many times when Kyoto lamented the invention of the video camera.

"There is no word from the tanker?''

"None. She is not responding to her radios. Nor is the Brunei boat."

"Crew?"

"Apparently, there is supposed to be a crew of one hundred and twenty-one. The ship's owner will be sending us a roster."

"Nationalities?"

"Mostly Japanese, they think."

"The perpetrators?"

"Unknown. We have only the identification of the gunboat. The next development is alarming, also. All communications, telephonic and radio, with Brunei are unsuccessful. We cannot determine if the gunboat is legal."

"Sum the risks."

"At this point, a supertanker worth one hundred and sixty million U.S. dollars, one-point-one million tons of high-grade crude oil, and most important, probably one hundred and twenty-one lives. Probably all Japanese citizens."

"And piracy on the high seas."

"Yes, Minister."

"All right. Make yourself an expert on this event, Meoshi. I will be needing you."

"Yes, sir."

"I have already spent an hour with the Foreign Minister, and he is now meeting with the Prime Minister . . ."

Perhaps Kyoto had underestimated Asume and his penchant for sleep. But then, like all bureaucrats anywhere, he would be well-practiced in protecting his backside.

". . . and they will be discussing the episode with the United Nations ambassador in"—he glanced at his watch—"one half hour. If you have better information confirmed by then, let me know immediately."

"We will seek UN assistance?"

"That is my understanding," Asume said.

"I foresee problems," Kyoto could not help saying.

"See? You are very good at what you do, Meoshi. We will get you out of that uniform yet."

Six

Four floors below Christian Drieser's office window, 23rd Street was a mess. The sun was shining and the temperature had climbed to almost 35 degrees, but the remnants of yesterdays' snowstorm was piled along the sidewalks, and the cars swooshed through the slush without regard for their neighbors. Sheets of grimy, icy sludge arced from under tires to splash against other cars, buses, trees, and unfortunate pedestrians. Taxicabs looked like they were made of streaked marble. A total lack of courtesy prevailed among every driver.

Not unlike his own world. Drieser was an Undersecretary of State, but without a specific charge. He was sometimes described as a troubleshooter, sometimes as a high-level gofer for his good buddy, the Secretary. He and Douglas Chambers had attended Harvard Law together. With a law degree and a background as a Supreme Court clerk, a

Securities Exchange Commission investigator, a Central Intelligence Agency analyst, and a State Department researcher—read spy, he had a varied set of experiences that served him well in his present position. The Secretary of State had selected him as the ideal man to take care of odds and ends.

At eight inches over six feet, and three pounds over three hundred, he was not a typical spy who disappeared into any group of pedestrians. Sandy-haired, with thick glasses and a florid face, he stood out in crowds, and he drew attention wherever he went. Drieser didn't let it worry him. This was the age of communications technology, and most of his snooping was accomplished over telephone lines and satellite links. Wild Bill Donovan, the scion of the Office of Strategic Services, would have been astounded by what could be accomplished in 1990s American intelligence-gathering.

Drieser was standing at the window, dictating memos to Judy Blalock, and contemplating the random mayhem perpetrated by Washington drivers upon their fellows when Blalock said, "Chris, look at this!"

He turned and followed her pointing finger toward the three television monitors in a console at the sidewall. The center screen, tuned to CNN, held a murky picture, but clearly one that was going to be important.

As he watched, Blalock grabbed the remote and turned up the volume. Drieser slipped behind his desk and picked up the phone from its console, pressed a speed dialling button.

"Tell the Secretary to turn on CNN."

Another button.

"Research."

The research functionaries of the department did not report to Drieser, but they were too afraid of him—and his position—to ever deny him.

"This is Drieser. Get someone at the FBI in Atlanta to hit up CNN for a copy of the tape."

"What tape, sir?"

"It's being aired now. Then, call the National Security Agency and find out if they've got any satellite surveillance of the event."

The man clearly didn't know what event had become so paramount, but he'd figure it out. "Yes, sir. Right away."

Drieser went around his desk and sat down in a visitor chair next to Blalock. His bulk towered over her diminutive figure.

". . . again, this video was shot by a crew member of the French ship which first reached the scene, about two hundred miles south of Amboyna Cay in the South China Sea. The *Maru Hokkaido*, a Japanese supertanker, which you can barely make out on the left of your screen, was en route to Japan."

The video had obviously been captured at night, but the nearby seas were lit by floodlights from the ship. The surface of the ocean mildly rose and fell within the scope of the light. The camera panned to the right, and the running lights of a much smaller vessel appeared.

Abruptly, a streak of white light launched itself from the small boat, appeared to home in on the video lens, then passed to the left. The suddenness of it made Drieser jump in his seat. The videographer jumped, too, because the image went wild and wobbly for a moment.

"At this point," the commentator said, "once she had been fired on, the French ship, the *Herault Transporter* turned away as she had been ordered and sailed from the scene.

"For those of you just joining us, we have dramatic video images of an incident taking place in the South China Sea. Apparently, a Japanese supertanker has been hijacked at sea by a patrol boat flying a Brunei flag. At this time, Brunei officials are not responding, and communications with the tanker have been cut off. A French ship that was contacted . . ."

The phone rang, and he reached behind him to snatch it, not taking his eyes from the screen.

"Chris, this is Doug."

"Mr. Secretary."

"This is dynamite."

"I'm afraid so. I've got people looking for evidence and confirmations. I'll have more for you later."

"I'm going to ask the President to convene the National Security Council, and I'll want you there. The Japanese will most likely go to the UN with this, and we need to be ready."

Drieser thought about that for a moment. "They'll get a chilly reception."

"I imagine so."

Saturday, March 8, 4:34 A.M.

Koehler's night drive along the coast of Brunei had not been without incident. His anxiety level had topped the meter a number of times.

As soon as he was certain the three vehicles behind him were intent upon stopping the Explorer, he pulled on the headlights and floored the pedal. Somebody behind him radioed ahead for assistance because, near the western reaches of the city, a white sedan suddenly pulled onto the highway, then went broadside across both lanes.

"Eek!" Monica screeched.

Kelly kept the pedal down.

Two men in civilian clothing scrambled out of the car, took one look at the oncoming truck, and raced for the shoulder of the road.

Koehler went after them, veering toward the curb, not aiming for them, but hoping to clear the car in the middle of the street. The tires went off the pavement, bounced over the curb, rumbled. He missed the car on the left, and a palm tree on the right, but only by inches. At eighty miles an hour, the obstacles shot by him in seconds.

His armpits were damp, and it wasn't the heat.

The pursuing vehicles were forced to slow to bypass the barrier, and one of them stopped. A few minutes later, the remaining two were again closing on him. One of them thought to turn on its emergency strobes. He couldn't hear a siren. No one was shooting. He thought it was possible that the police had broadcast some rather strict standing orders regarding foreigners. Let us have no international incidents.

The streetlights ended, and shortly, the road narrowed to two lanes. It was a pretty decent highway, and he got his speed up to around a hundred, the body swaying as he took the shallow curves. The engine screamed. The cars behind stayed with him, but couldn't, or wouldn't, close on him. Maybe those standing orders didn't apply to foreigners involved in car accidents.

On his right, he saw the lights of a few ships off the coast. The stars shone down.

"Nice night for a drive," he said.

"Be careful, Kelly," Sherry cautioned.

He reached across, found her leg. It was trembling. He kneaded her leg above the knee, and she gripped his hand, then pushed it away.

"I can't believe we're running from cops," Monica said from the backseat. "This is unreal."

He thought it was, too. Maybe he was doing the wrong thing.

Glancing in the rearview mirror, Koehler checked his backseat passenger. Davis was strapped in. He should have checked for seat belts earlier. All he needed to do was miscalculate one of the mild curves of the highway, run off the side of the road, and roll it a few times. Three foreigners accounted for.

He released the wheel again, reached across and checked the belt on Sherry. She grabbed his hand, held it for a second.

"If they start shooting, I'm stopping," he said.

"They wouldn't shoot at us," Monica said. "Would they?"

"I don't think so," Sherry answered for him.

Twenty kilometers later, approaching the village of Tutong, he ran into another roadblock.

Literally.

Coming around a shallow curve of the highway, he saw it almost too late. A pickup and a car nosed toward each other across the road. No lights, no warning signals. By the lack of warning or other signs, he couldn't have known whether it was a government or a rebel blockade.

"Get down! Hold on!"

He wasn't going around on the shoulder for this one. There was no shoulder, and the loose soil would have created spectacular events for the speeding truck. Tiny lights blinked at him, and he knew what they were. He'd seen them before. These guys thought flying lead would stop him.

He went sideways in his seat, pulling his shoulders and head down until he could barely see over the dashboard. Sherry was stretched as low as her shoulder harness would allow, her head pressed against his hip.

Rhythmic thuds hitting the truck. The windshield starred on Sherry's side. The women screamed.

His side window shattered, glass flying.

The Ford smashed into both of the parked vehicles in the middle of the highway with loud, successive bangs, one slightly after the other, and the truck lurched from one side to the other, tilted up on two wheels. The smashing, tearing metal was loud in his ears. Both blockade vehicles spun away, their front ends mashed by the momentum of the truck.

Instant blackness.

He lost both headlights.

Koehler gripped the wheel with whitened knuckles. It came back, landing on all four wheels, and he was still in the center of the road, but blind. He eased off the gas and sat up, his eyes searching the outside mirrors. They were gone, too. The interior mirror still worked. He hadn't seen even one of the men at the roadblock, couldn't identify them as friend or foe.

"Everyone all right?"

He looked to Sherry, saw her straightening up, shaking her head. Her blond hair was in disarray, a gleam in the darkness. She clutched her hands to her face, but nodded at him.

"Okay back here," Monica said, "except for this puddle on the seat."

"Maybe that's the only roadblock."

"I hope so. This wasn't in my job description," Davis complained.

The truck seemed to be handling all right, except for the fact that he no longer had headlights. He scanned the instruments, worried about the radiator, but the temperature was holding.

"On the bright side, my lovelies, our pursuers have turned back."

In the mirror he saw an exchange of muzzle flashes, most of them from the roadblock, and the pursuit cars rolling to a halt. They backed-and-filled, scrambling to get turned around.

He still didn't know who was who. Rebels at the road-block? Rebels in the cop cars?

Kelly slowed until he was holding forty miles an hour, the black gleam of the pavement barely revealed by the moonlight. The truck continued to run, and he was thankful for that.

At Lumut, he encountered another roadblock. This time, however, he recognized the boxy silhouettes of military vehicles, and he was relatively assured that he was in Gurkha territory. On top of that, he saw no way in hell he was going to get around this one.

A bright spotlight was turned on him, nearly blinding him and making him aware of the two bullet holes in the windshield on the passenger side. The starred glass was held together by its inner layer of plastic, but the spotlight caught the cracks, refracted light, and made the windshield almost opaque. The light blinked at him three times, and he rolled to a stop.

He didn't have to roll down his window; it was gone. Slivers of glass littered the floor, the seat, his clothing.

A dark shape materialized alongside, looked through the broken window at the three of them, then asked, "Do you have identification, sir?"

"Kelly Koehler. I'm with GlobeTech Explorations. Who are you?"

"Captain Singh. I am of the Gurkha Battalion."

"Good. Can you reach Major Shaikh?"

"I can. For what purpose?"

"He wanted me to get him some information."

The Nepalese stepped back and passed his flashlight over the truck. "At some cost, I think."

"I ran a roadblock at Tutong. I didn't know whose side they were on."

The captain pulled a portable radio from his web belt, reported in to someone, then handed the radio to Koehler.

"Mr. Koehler . . . Kelly, this is Benjamin Shaikh."

He pressed the transmit stud. "Keep in mind that I'm an amateur, Benjamin, but I can tell you the city doesn't look good." He related what he had seen of military trucks at the palace, police cars at the Brunei Hotel, deserted streets, and pursuing police cars.

"And these police cars abandoned the chase at the Tutong roadblock?"

"Yes, and since I don't know who was operating the roadblock, I still don't know who the good guys are."

"It is very confusing," Shaikh agreed. "The rebels are now disappearing, and we have only one engagement in progress at the moment. Even where you are, near the refinery, the revolutionaries have apparently given up the assault. You said that you have your wife with you?"

"I do. As well as my office manager. The airport sounded closed, so we didn't even try it. Another thing, Benjamin, the international phone circuits haven't been opened again."

"Yes. I have tried to call my headquarters in Britain several times."

"You don't have a satellite link?"

"Not on my budget, Kelly."

"Me either."

"Where will you go?"

"If your captain will let me through, I'll go to the GlobeTech supply compound in Kuala Belait. I've got to figure out what to do with my people."

"Very well, then. I will talk to you later, and Kelly, thank you for your information."

"I'm not sure it's much use to you, Major. Good luck."

Koehler gave the radio back to the captain, and after a truck was pulled back, they were allowed through.

"I'm glad you know some friendly people," Sherry said.

"Until yesterday, hon, everyone was friendly."

He limped the Explorer into Slim Avery's compound an hour later and parked under the building's green-shaded light.

Avery and Morris came out of the office to meet them.

"Jesus Christ!" Avery exploded. "What did you do to my truck?"

Morris spotted his passengers. "Hey, Sherry, Monica. We moving the whole headquarters?"

"Hi, Frank," she said, her voice a little stronger than it was an hour before. "I hope we're moving something somewhere."

Morris helped the women out of the truck, giving Davis an extra squeeze. Koehler had long thought something was going on there, but he wasn't given to snooping.

Avery hustled them all inside his bailiwick and offered coffee. The overhead fluorescent lights bathed everything and everyone in a harsh glare. Kelly thought his passengers looked extremely pale in the early morning hours. He felt pale, himself. Outrunning pursuit and crashing roadblocks were not a part of his world, and he still couldn't quite believe he had accomplished it.

Monica Davis—on her first trip into Slim Avery's world—wandered around the walls, studying the *Playboy* centerfolds. "Slim, you don't have my picture up here."

"I'd sure like it," he told her.

She grinned at him. "Not in my current condition. My hands are still shaking, see? I didn't know the boss could drive like he does."

Avery pointed through the front window. "You call that driving? I can get from here to Bandar Seri Begawan with only a minor dent."

Morris raised an eyebrow, and Koehler brought them up to date. While he spoke, Sherry accepted a cup of coffee and wrapped her free hand around his upper arm. She hugged her close to her.

He got his arm free and wrapped it around her and squeezed. God, he could have killed them all.

"The major problem," Kelly said, "is we don't know what the hell's really going on, or who's in charge."

"But a contingency plan is definitely called for," Morris said. His cheeks were coated with whiskers, and his eyes were red. He hadn't slept much, and Koehler thought the looks Monica gave him spoke of a very personal concern.

"How's Andy?"

"Out of the woods, I think, but still unconscious. Pete got his appendectomy, and he's doing fine. Bitching about the food."

"Okay, good. Yeah, a contingency plan. Monica, what's our current manpower strength?"

She knew the numbers by heart. "On this rotation, we've got seven hundred and forty-six on the platforms."

They ran a four-day on, three-day off, rotation, but the rotation days differed from platform to platform.

"And ashore?"

"Currently, seven fifty-one on the drilling crews. With the pilots, boat crews, and Slim's cadre, there's another fifty-four."

"Dependents?"

She closed her eyes and pursed her lips into a round oval. "Ronnie Baxter just brought his wife and baby over last week, so now there's three hundred and eighty-four dependents."

More than nineteen hundred people. All of them at risk, and all of them on Kelly's responsibility chart.

"What's the transport situation, Slim?" he asked.

Avery came to the counter and rested his elbows on it. He had to bend down to reach it.

"The two choppers. Three workboats. I've got five flat-bed semis, eight two-ton trucks, seven pickups, three Jeeps, and the junk heap you drove in."

"Not much, is it? The helicopters wouldn't make a big dent. We've maybe got the nine trawlers we contract as guard boats, though." The contract required that a guard boat be in attendance at each drilling rig twenty-four hours a day. "Those captains would take a bonus."

"If you had it in cash," Morris said. "They may balk at IOUs."

"Worse, where you gonna go?" Avery asked.

Morris said, "There are trails that pass for roads, westward into Sarawak, and I think we could even get the semis over the main ruts, if we can beat the rain. But, what have we got on the other end? Miri Marudi or Kampong Sibuti don't even qualify as villages."

"Five thousand population at Marudi," Sherry reminded him. She'd been doing her studying.

"Okay, yeah. But how are they going to deal with an influx of two thousand people?"

"We aren't the only ones, Frank," Koehler said. "Phillips, Exxon, Shell will be trying to get their people on boats, choppers, and trucks, too. Sixty, seventy thousand people."

"Shit. Kuching"—the capital of Sarawak—"is over four hundred miles away, Kelly. We'd have to haul our own gas for refuelling, and I'd bet you it's a twenty-hour trip, if not more."

"Okay, let's get the OIMs involved in this," Kelly said.

Avery went to turn up the radio, and Koehler refilled his mug with Avery's toxic coffee.

After a whispered conference, Monica and Sherry went to the walls and started pulling tacks, then taking down pictures.

"Hey!" Avery yelled.

"You want to take them with you, right?" Monica asked.

"Uh, yeah, guess so."

"Besides, we don't want to offend visitors, if we get visitors."

"What's so damned offensive?" Avery asked between radio calls.

By four thirty, the centerfolds were in a neat stack on Avery's desk, Avery had contacted his drivers and ordered every vehicle back to the compound, and Driscoll, Irving, and Starquist had all checked in. Koehler told them what he knew, which seemed like very little.

"We haven't located anything particularly lethal in our searches as yet," Driscoll said.

"But we aren't done yet," Starquist added.

"My communications technician says there's a bunch of radio traffic, starting a couple hours ago," Driscoll said. "A lot of these companies are closing down operations."

That's what he got for waking up his competitors in the middle of the night, Kelly thought. "I think we should do the same. Secure all drilling and pumping, seal off the wellheads."

"Irving, here. And then?"

"And then everyone comes ashore."

"Jesus, Kelly," Starquist said. "Not even a watchdog crew?"

"Not a soul. If we have to scoot, it's going to be more controllable from a single location. Avery's going to contact our trawler captains"—he looked up and Avery nodded—"and see if we can't augment our transport. The minute I get word that the situation is turning to mush— more than it is now, I'll give the signal, and we'll ship out the workboats and trawlers with as many as we can get aboard. Dependents first, and their destination will be Kuching. We can fly them out of Kuching to Singapore, if we need to."

"That's only six, seven hundred people," Morris said, leaning forward so his voice carried over the microphone.

"Another three hundred go overland. Then we turn the boats and trucks around and come back for the rest."

"In fact," Avery said, "since I'm the logistics guy, we just truck everyone we can't get on a boat over the border to Miri Marudi in about four trips. It's maybe ten miles of bad road. That gets everyone out of the country a hell of a lot faster, and then we can start making the long hauls to Kuching from there."

"Good, Slim," Koehler said. "Much better. We could have everyone out of Brunei in six or eight hours. Let's plan it that way. Questions?"

He answered a couple, then backed away from the radio.

Sherry Koehler said, "I hope you don't think I'm a dependent."

Saturday, March 8, 5:45 A.M.

Omar Padang completed the last of four circuits of the city and parked his Land Rover in front of police headquarters. The way he was rushing around, he was certain he had lost at least five pounds during the night.

He felt good about himself and about the progress of the revolution.

Pushing through the front door, he entered a wide corridor that was awash in activity. Men rushed from office to office, but all were smiling. They grinned hugely when they saw him. They felt good about themselves, also.

He took his time going down the hall, accepting congratulations as they were offered, and asked a sergeant to find Awg Nazir for him. At the end of the hallway, he entered his office to find Li Sen, Peng Ziyang, and Lim Siddiqui waiting. The three men had demonstrated the epitome of depression and doom for the last eight months, but now the exuberance afloat in the headquarters building had proven contagious: All three men were grinning broadly.

Li Sen was sitting behind Padang's desk, but Padang ignored that slight for the moment. Let the man assume his own importance for the next week. It would be short-lived enough.

All four of them, the primary committee of the Front for Democratic Reform, shared congratulatory exclamations, and Padang settled on the couch next to Siddiqui. A moment later, a hand rapped at the door, and Captain Nazir entered. He, too, was in an excellent mood, for he knew that within a few days, he would become the new police chief.

Nazir carried a clipboard of notes, and he sat in the remaining guest chair, alongside Peng Ziyang.

"You have been out in the city, Omar?" Li asked.

"I have. For the most part, it is very quiet. Most citizens will be staying indoors today, I think. All has gone according to plan, with the city and the district of Tembur-ong already secured. Captain Nazir will brief us on the details."

Padang had been listening to the police frequencies as he toured, so he knew most of the details. At least, he knew those pertaining to the police.

"First," Nazir said, holding up a long computer listing, "there are the foreign nationals—"

"Wait!" Li interrupted. "What of the Sultan?"

Nazir looked up from his listing to Li. "He and the royal family are all aboard the destroyer *Bulkiah*, as scheduled."

"None were killed?"

Nazir glanced at Padang, who said, "Hamzah bin Sulia-man attempted to live up to his image and offered resis-tance. He was wounded, but by now his injuries have been tended to, and he should also be aboard the destroyer. There were no other mishaps."

Padang did not mention the execution of the royal body-guard members. And he did not repeat his own conviction that the family should have joined the bodyguard in saluting Mohammed. The Chinese faction had demanded safety for the royal family, making the point that they might be required as hostages at a later point in time.

"Very well," Li said. "Go on, Captain."

"The foreign nationals are almost all accounted for, and they have been transported to hotels, where we can better watch them. The diplomats and their staffs have been placed at the Sheraton Utama Hotel and the Jubilee Hotel. The foreign businessmen and their families are at the Brunei Hotel, as well as the Riverview."

"You did not violate the consulates or missions?"

"Of course not. The diplomats were invited to the hotels."

"You said 'almost all,' " Lim Siddiqui said.

"There are a few gaps in my roster. Some Exxon, Phillips, and GlobeTech officials have not yet been accounted for. It can be assumed that they were out of the city, perhaps at the oil field, at the time we approached their houses."

When Li Sen nodded, Nazir went on. "The foreigners have been told their relocation is temporary, and that it is required for their safety. As stability is achieved, they will be encouraged to return to their daily lives as if nothing had changed."

"Keep them well-fed, and they will not complain," Padang said. "Not one of them will risk the loss of the money they steal from us."

"Next, the police. The major non-loyal unit"—non-loyal to Padang—"was ordered out of the city before the palace was taken. Any other non-loyal personnel have disappeared—slipped into the jungle—or have been imprisoned. We have twenty-seven former policemen in custody.

"The army. Two of the most questionable companies

were among the three sent to Kuala Belait by Suliaman, and that made it easier for Colonel Bakir. He immediately disbanded two companies, leaving him with five companies of loyalists. There were some disagreements, as expected, and forty-one were killed, approximately two hundred wounded. Another three hundred have been detained. The loyal companies are now assembled on the coast road with trucks and personnel carriers, awaiting your orders, President Li.''

Li beamed at the recognition, possibly missing the details of dead and wounded, and Padang hoped he enjoyed it for as long as he had it. Li waved his hand in acknowledgement, and Nazir went on.

"The air wing. Four helicopters returned to Bandar Seri Begawan against orders of army commanders in the west. The other six helicopters are somewhere in the west, and we do not yet know their allegiance.

"The navy. Here again, there was some resistance. The early figures suggest nearly two hundred fatalities were suffered, as well as some four hundred casualties. However, every vessel is now subject to our ... to the committee's command. The results this night have far surpassed our expectations, gentlemen.''

"I am dismayed at the deaths,'' Li said.

He would be.

"That is all? That is the sum?'' Peng asked. "What about the tankers?''

"Well,'' Nazir conceded, "there was one incident. Those tankers moored at or near the pumping stations have been placed in quarantine. However, at the time of the first detonations at the wells, a Japanese tanker managed to slip away. By the time we had vessels in our control, it was well at sea.''

Li appeared relieved. "So? We lost one.''

"No, sir. Chief Padang sent a gunboat after it. The tanker has been captured and is under our control."

"What! In international waters?"

Padang said, "The oil belongs to the Republic of Brunei, Sen. It is not likely that Japan would have paid us for it, not without a new agreement in place, and I certainly was not going to give them free oil."

"Oh, my!" Peng said.

Li's face paled, and his breath came in short gasps. Perhaps he would have a heart attack, and save Padang additional trouble later.

"It is of no consequence," Padang said. "No one will pay attention, and as soon as Japan pays us, we will send their oil on to them."

Li stared at him.

"We will now secure the west," Padang said. "I anticipate that by noon, the entire country will be secured."

He had already learned that loyalist army soldiers had set up a line of defense at Tutong. He thought Bakir's forces would make short work of that obstacle.

"There is to be no violence," Li cautioned. "We must offer to negotiate for surrenders first."

"Of course. Now, if you will excuse me, I must tell Colonel Bakir it is time for him to move ahead. With negotiations, Sen."

M-16s and M-60 machine guns made negotiations very simple.

Saturday, March 8, 7:10 A.M.

Sergeant Major Suraj Irra entered the orderly room, two Gurkha privates trailing after him. The privates appeared much the worse for wear. They were in dress uniforms, but the uniforms were filthy, encrusted with dirt and mud.

The faces of the two enlisted men were not in much better condition than their uniforms.

"Major, these men have information for you."

Shaikh studied them silently for a moment. If they had misbehaved in some way, or missed a formation, or been late to a duty assignment, Irra would have taken care of it in his own manner, in his own time.

"Tell me."

· Both came to rigid attention, and the closest man said, "Sir, we were on leave, staying in a . . . a boardinghouse in Muara."

In a Muslim country, a boarding house could have many connotations.

"Proceed."

"When we became aware that . . . that something was wrong, we tried to find transportation back to our barracks."

"Very good. But you could not find transportation?"

"No, sir. Two policemen attempted to arrest us, and I am afraid we resisted."

"Were they hurt badly?"

"I do not know, sir. We ran. We walked all the way from Muara to Bandar Seri Begawan, and then here, and we were afraid to use the road."

Shaikh might well place letters of commendation in their dossiers. "Do not worry about the policemen. What else?"

The private described the port city and the capital much as Kelly Koehler had, but added, "We saw foreigners, Americans, French, Chinese, German, I think, being taken from their homes and placed in police cars. That is why we assaulted the policemen."

"Understandable. Is there anything else?"

"Yes, sir. I . . . we saw the Sultan. He and others were under heavy guard, being taken by launch to a destroyer moored off Muara. We were not close, trying to get around the port, and at the time, we assumed the guards were the Sultan's, but later, I began to question that conclusion."

"And it is well you did, Private. Excellent. I am proud of you both."

They smiled, but weakly.

"Now, you must get cleaned up, get something to eat, then sleep for a few hours before reporting to your platoon. Dismissed."

The men saluted, turned, and left the orderly room.

"I hope it is our teaching that has instilled some of this initiative, Sergeant Major."

"I should like to think so, Major, but perhaps it is inborn. Either way, the omens are just as unfavorable."

Irra was not one to complain, so Shaikh assumed the man was almost as worried as he himself.

"Let us go in my office," Shaikh said. "Captain Shrestha! Would you join us?"

When the three of them had taken the three available chairs in Shaikh's tiny office, he said, "Let me synthesize the current situation.

"One. Our charge, and our only charge, is the protection of the oil field. Captain?"

Shrestha said, "Presently, the containment booms have been deployed around the oil slick at Mirador. That is now stable, and oil-consuming bacteria agents have been sprayed on the slick. The fires at Mirador and Albatross continue to rage, and the firefighting ship is working the Albatross fire. Divers are working below the surface, attempting to cut off the flow of fuels. Several ships with pumping capability are fighting the fire at Mirador."

"And my orders of oh-six-hundred hours?"

"I issued a radio directive to shut down all platforms and onshore pumping sites. At that time, many offshore installation managers and field managers had already begun to shut down wells. Brunei Shell field maintenance crews are currently closing down the onshore wells.

"As of fifteen minutes ago, we have three helicopters and eleven patrol craft on stations around the field."

"Thank you, Captain. Now, number two. We are out of contact with our regimental headquarters. For the moment, we will assume they do not yet know of our situation. The battalion is seconded to the Sultan, and he may be in hostile hands. We do not have direction from a superior authority.

"Three. I am commander in the field, and soon I will have to make a decision relative to our position. Technically, we cannot abandon our charge and change our mission to one of fighting rebels, whoever they may be. Have you made contact with the army, Captain?"

"Yes, sir. A company commander is due at any moment to talk with you."

"Good. Sergeant Major, what is your assessment of the tactical situation?"

Irra straightened up in his chair. "The explosions on the platforms, all of the small firefights, the assault at Lumut were only diversionary. They were intended to direct attention away from the capital while the coup was taking place. Also, I would assume the diversion allowed the deployment away from the city of loyalist units, like the army companies and the police who appeared at Lumut. That is a large assumption, and far from proven, on my part, Major."

"Nevertheless, I agree with you. Captain?"

"I agree, also."

"Now, the rebel units creating the diversion have withdrawn," Irra continued. "That makes me think that Bandar Seri Begawan is secure in rebel hands. I will go so far as to say that Temburong is also lost to government forces."

The nation was divided into four districts—Belait, Brunei and Muara, Tutong, and Temburong. Geographically, the country was also divided into two pieces, with Temburong—an elongated oval about forty kilometers long and fifteen wide—jutting to the south from the western end of Brunei Bay. Temburong was separated from the rest of the country by the Limbang River valley, leading to Brunei Bay, and owned by Sarawak.

If the rebels held Temburong, along with Bandar Seri Begawan and the port of Muara on the west end of Brunei Bay, they held about a third of the national territory.

"And the next move by the revolutionaries?" Shaikh asked.

"Will be to secure the west, along with the oil fields. They do not want to lose the fields or the refinery, sir. They will march west along the coast road. The interior of the country is all but impassable with rain forest."

"Absolutely," Shaikh agreed. "We will send my helicopter to reconnoiter the coastal road and see what the future might hold."

"I might suggest," the adjutant said, "that a part of our responsibility is the oil-field work force. I would think the rebels want to keep that intact. Without workers, there will be no production, and without production, whatever government is in power will not have revenues."

"Excellent point," Shaikh said. "I will set aside time to worry about it. Evacuation would be a nightmare."

"Not impossible," Irra said, "but certainly nothing the oil companies have ever considered."

"I think I am hearing a suggestion that, even if we do not take an offensive position against the rebels, we might well set up a perimeter around the foreign workers' residences and defend them. Cutting off production and revenues?"

"It is only a suggestion," Shrestha said. "We have already stopped production, and we have the authority of our mission behind us."

"I will think about—"

"Sir! A telephone call."

He looked to the man in the doorway. "Take a message, Corporal."

"It is Police Chief Padang, sir."

Shaikh picked up his telephone. "Yes, Chief Padang. What is the situation in the city, sir?"

"Major Shaikh, I am calling to inform you that the government is now subject to the direction of the primary committee of the Front for Democratic Reform. Until the first election, the chief executive is Provisional President Li Sen. I am Minister of Security, which includes both internal and external concerns. You will now report to me, Major Shaikh."

"Impossible, sir."

"Impossible! Certainly not."

"I would need orders signed by my regimental commander, by the British Minister of Defense, and by the Prime Minister. Until I receive them, there will be no change in my mission or my chain of command. Where is the Sultan?"

"Major Shaikh! I am ordering you to lay down your arms and surrender to Colonel Bakir when he arrives."

"Chief Padang, the Gurkhas have never surrendered their weapons or their allegiance. We will not start now."

"The consequences will be dire!"

"I trust, sir, that you can live with them." Shaikh slammed the telephone down.

"Major?" Irra asked.

"I believe I have made my decision."

Saturday, March 8, 9:30 A.M.

Li Sen was nervous. The lights were so hot. A trickle of perspiration ran down his left temple, and he dabbed at it with a handkerchief.

He was uncomfortable in the Western suit, and it did not fit him properly. It was too large, and the jacket bulged in the back. Li had wanted to wear a traditional Chinese tunic, but Padang had prevailed—this telecast could be rebroadcast internationally, and he should appear to fit in more readily with international expectations.

For now, the telecast was aimed only at Bruneian citizens, and he sat in the chair provided for him, under the blazing studio lights. A cluster of microphones was on a stand before him. The audio portion of the message would be simultaneously broadcast over the four radio stations.

"Five seconds, Mr. President."

He clutched the handkerchief in his right hand, hoping it was out of the camera's view. In his left, he held the final draft of the paper he had so laboriously developed over four years.

The red light on the camera came on, and the director nodded vigorously at him.

Attempting to not clear the giant frog that was suddenly born in his throat, Li began:

"My fellow citizens, I am Li Sen, Provisional President of the Republic of Brunei. I hold this office as representative of your Front for Democratic Reform, and I hold it only until the people speak in elections to be called in the near future.

"I know you are hungry for information, so let me tell you what has occurred in the past few hours. First of all, the Sultan has elected to abdicate his responsibilities to the nation, and he and the royal family have fled to the refuge of the sea. Secondly, upon learning of this startling development, the Front for Democratic Reform moved quickly to maintain order and to fill the vacuum created by the dissolution of government. Our immediate purpose is to protect life and property.

"I will also tell you what the future holds. Periodically over the next few days, you will be provided reports of the reforms taking place in the government. Many of those will seem mundane to you, but they are important in the establishment of a democratic government. Immediately, Police Chief Omar Padang has been appointed Provisional Minister of Security. His concern is for the safety of citizens and visitors within our borders. I implore you to cooperate with Minister Padang and representatives of his office.

"This temporary administration is dedicated to open disclosure, and I do not hesitate to tell you that several units of the regiment and the regimental air wing do not understand the course our nation is taking and are in open rebellion. I hope the men of those units are listening to me. Please, for the sake of your relatives, lay down your arms. Bloodshed is unnecessary and personally repellent to me.

"Understand, also, that the protection of the oil fields by the Gurkha Battalion, while a long and honorable tradition, has been deemed redundant. It is a task that may be easily accomplished by citizens of Brunei, and the Gurkha Battalion is formally discharged from its responsibilities. As soon as transport can be arranged, the Battalion will depart Brunei.

"Now, citizens! To the important points of my message. When I call you citizens, I am a man of my word. No longer will certain segments of our society be denied full participation in society or government. As of today, all residents of Brunei meeting certain criteria of longevity or birth are accorded full citizenship. And, nine months to a year from now, when the first elections are scheduled, *all* citizens will choose their representation. In that process . . ."

All traces of his nervousness had disappeared, though he still dabbed at beads of perspiration, and Li Sen warmed to his topic. It was a long one, and he hoped to accomplish it within an hour.

Saturday, March 8, 9:43 A.M.

The old man droned on and on, as if he were a disciple of Thomas Jefferson, with a little Karl Marx thrown in from time to time, just to provide variety. And protect those free education and health benefits. Koehler appreciated the appeal to the people in regard to the distribution of profits from the oil field to all Bruneians, though he wondered how the FDR was going to calculate profits. A lot of crap could be charged to overhead costs. He also appreciated Li's desire to curtail production, so as to extend the life of the oil field. As an oilman, however, he understood a different set of economics. If GlobeTech were ordered to reduce its output by sixty-six percent—which Li was proposing—the company wouldn't draw down enough revenue to support its manpower, much less a reasonable profit.

Shell, Exxon, Phillips, Conoco, and the others would be having the same reaction. If Li thought he was making conversions with his little speech, he was sadly mistaken.

The supply compound office didn't have a television, but as soon as Li got under way, Avery had been inundated with telephone calls from the residential compound three blocks away, and Morris found the broadcast on one of the radio stations.

Li's recounting of the peaceful takeover sounded too good to be true, so Koehler called Shaikh.

"Yes, Kelly, I am listening, also."

"Anything you don't believe?"

"Very little of what Li says is plausible," the major said. "For one thing, neither the Sultan nor members of his family would leave the country by ship. He has a personal fleet of jumbo aircraft, which is quite luxurious. For another, there is a pitched battle between loyal soldiers and rebel soldiers under the leadership of a man, a colonel, named Bakir. The battle line is currently four kilometers west of Tutong, and the army unit that was here has been ordered to assist the loyalists. I make the assumption that you drove through a loyalist roadblock."

"Will the loyalists hold out?"

"I doubt it, Kelly. My reconnaissance an hour ago suggested that Bakir has a two-to-one advantage."

"What are the Gurkhas going to do?"

"Mr. Koehler!"

"Sorry. I know better than that. How about philosophically? So I know where I stand."

"Hmmm. We will do our duty. I am currently deploying platoons so as to protect the residential compounds of the work force. As you probably know, most companies have ordered their personnel ashore."

"In the last four hours, Benjamin, I've gotten almost everyone off the platforms. We should be finished in the next half hour."

"That is probably wise, but I am not certain that I can assure their safety. We are a small unit, and we are talking about seventy thousand people, including families."

Kelly noted that Shaikh did not reveal numbers when he spoke. The numbers of men, equipment, or weapons he had at his disposal. That was a proper attitude, and Koehler thought the major was quite capable. He was probably also cleaning out his warehouses of rations, ammunition, and other materiel.

Koehler told him, "I'm ready to ship my people out if it's necessary. I've looted my commissary and spread it among the personnel. We've depleted our stores of gasoline and oil, loaded it on trucks. We're taking avgas, also. Would you have any advice, Benjamin?"

"You would go west? It is a difficult trek, and one fraught with the possibility of confusion."

"It's the only one open. If every company goes at once, we'll turn that path into a highway."

"Kelly, the fewer people I am responsible for protecting, the greater my freedom of movement and my chances for success."

Koehler wondered if Shaikh's idea of success included eradicating a few rebels. He wouldn't ask.

"Thanks, Benjamin. You need anything, let me know."

"I thank you. Go with God."

Koehler hung up and turned to Avery. "Move 'em out, Slim."

Avery looked down at the clipboard, on which he was keeping track of numbers. "The three workboats and four trawlers are at the dock. We'll load dependents. The last four trawlers"—they hadn't convinced the ninth captain—"are making the last run to Bravo and Charlie. I'll have them head west directly from there. The trucks are ready to go."

"Good man." Koehler turned toward Sherry and prepared for an argument, but the radio interrupted.

"Kelly," Jake Driscoll said over the radio, "I think you'd better get out here."

The OIM didn't make silly suggestions, so Koehler grabbed the mike and said, "On my way, Jake."

Frank Morris bolted out of the tilted-back chair in which he'd been trying to catnap. Sherry stood up from her chair.

"Frank, you can sleep."

"Easy for you to say."

"And Sherry, we may have to bring back a full load."

"I don't want you out of my sight," she said.

"Only take an hour."

"I'm not leaving here until you're back."

"Ditto," Monica Davis said. "Somewhere it's written that the bosses have to go down with the ship."

"That's only the captain, Monica."

"Well, I'm the captain when you're out of the office."

At least, Kelly thought, he'd worry less about Sherry in Slim Avery's care than if she were still in Bandar Seri Begawan. He shook his head and followed Morris outside to the chopper pad.

Only GT-Zero-Two was present. Foster and Pease were using the other helicopter to lift gasoline bladders from the ground to the beds of the flatbed semis. Over the border, in Miri Marudi and points to the west, GT-Zero-One would meet the convoy and offload the bladders. That would give the vehicles and helicopters refuelling points along the way. A few roughnecks assigned to each refuelling station would assure that the fuel remained GlobeTech's.

They strapped in, Morris in the pilot's seat, and went quickly through the checklist. Koehler noticed the three holes still visible in the floor and shuddered. The plexiglass windscreen had been replaced with their last spare.

There was no asking for permissions. Brunei Air Control had been off the air for hours. Company helicopters filled the sky, seemingly in search of haphazard objectives. It called for greater awareness, and Koehler was half-surprised that no midairs had been reported.

He saw an Air Services Chinook headed west. Kelly had tried to charter some of their aircraft earlier in the morning, but they were booked solid. Brunei Shell had bought out every seat, and since the Chinooks couldn't reach

Kuching, Koehler suspected Shell was doing the same thing he was, just getting people over the border, first.

Morris fed in power, then pitch, and lifted off. They gained altitude heading for the coast, and Koehler tried to assimilate the apparent confusion on the ground. Hundreds of trucks were gathering around the residential compounds. Some of them were tankers. Everyone was taking a supply of fuel along. Gurkha two-and-a-half-ton trucks were deployed in several locations, the soldiers building sandbag emplacements on the perimeter of the compound, between apartment buildings and single-family units.

He looked to the west. Kuala Belait was right on the border of Sarawak, so it wouldn't take a long time to get out of the country. But the roads climbing the hills through the jungle left something to be desired.

Morris saw where he was looking.

"It's going to be a damned nightmare, Kelly."

"Sure as hell. That's a one-lane path, Frank. The trucks trying to come back are going to have a hell of a time getting around the ones headed out."

"And sure as shootin', Kelly, we'll get an afternoon downpour. That road is going to be mud and guts."

"We get back, Frank, I want you to load this hummer with every bit of medical gear we've got left. Stop by the clinic and get Andy and Pete, then haul them over to Miri Marudi."

"Got you covered, boss. Eddie Foster's got that chore, when he goes over to offload bladders."

"I'm glad I've got sharp guys working for me. I'm afraid I'm going to blow some of the details."

"It's no more than I'd expect from the executive corps, especially when they're ex-Army. Happens everywhere I go."

"Love you, too."

Morris angled the nose of the Dauphin down and they shot through the oil field at two thousand feet of altitude. The whole field was a madhouse. Trawlers, workboats, tenders, and smaller craft were swarming, dashing back and forth. Passing a Shell Brunei platform, Kelly saw an elevator descending to sea level with a dozen men aboard. An inflatable Zodiak boat powered by a fifty-horse outboard waited for them.

"Li Sen gets control of this field," Morris said, "and he won't have much. I'll bet there aren't a hundred Bruneians capable of operating a platform."

"If that many," Koehler agreed.

He used the radio to call GT-Bravo and GT-Charlie, but didn't get a response. He hoped that meant that Irving and Starquist had evacuated with the last of the men to board the trawlers.

Switching the radio to the marine band, he tried several channels, fought the high volume of traffic, and finally located Starquist on his trawler. The platforms now had no guard boats, but then they didn't have anyone to tend to in an emergency, either.

"Starquist."

"Koehler. You see Irving?"

"About a mile ahead of us, Kelly."

"Get him on the radio, or catch up with him. I want him to go ashore with some foremen once he's past the border, and hike into Miri Marudi. He's to take charge of the way station we're setting up there. It's going to be a mess, with several hundred vehicles coming in. Have him set up a temporary compound for GlobeTech people."

"Will do."

"Next, you go on to Kuching and buy a hotel or two if you have to. You're the receiving station for GlobeTech's personnel as they arrive. Keep everyone comfortable, and we'll plan on staying a week. If nothing is resolved by then, we'll talk about scheduling flights out of Singapore to get people home."

"Talk about buying—"

"Use the Bank of Singapore credit line. You may have to put five, six people in a room, and if the overflow is too great, send some on to Singapore."

"Roger that, Kelly. When are you coming?"

"With the last load. I want everyone else out, first."

"Luck."

By the time Kelly had the far end of the evacuation organized, Morris was setting the bird down on GT-Alpha's pad. Two men, both supervisors, ran out to secure the tie-down straps, and Morris shut down the turboshafts. They slid out of their seats onto the pad and were met with a stiff breeze that blew hot off the steel deck.

He and Morris took an open cage elevator down to D Deck, where the administration office was located, and found Jake Driscoll.

"All but six of us are off, Kelly, but I thought you should see this."

Following Driscoll, they walked to the edge of the deck where a portable console was set up. It was two halves of a large aluminum suitcase, each connected to the other by cables, and each standing on its own collapsible legs. From one unit, a quarter-inch-thick fiber-optic cable trailed to the edge of the deck, then disappeared over the edge and into the sea below. It was the control unit for an ROV.

"We've been exploring the tanks and legs," Driscoll said.

The platform's three ten-foot-diameter legs were driven into the seabed 412 feet down, and each leg was surrounded at the base by large storage tanks. The tanks held oil in reserve until the platform was given permission to discharge the oil into the pipeline resting on the seafloor.

Inspectors could traverse the inside of the legs, using long, long ladders. The exterior of the legs were inspected periodically by deep-diving divers hired from the *MSV Malay Princess* and by the ROVs.

One of the supervisors was at the controls, two joysticks by which he could direct the ROV to dive, turn, stop. Set into the other case was a video screen which displayed the images captured by the ROV's camera.

On the screen was a platform leg. The ROV was positioned about twenty feet back from the leg, and with the aid of the robot's high-output halogen lights, Koehler could see the tops of the tanks secured to the base of the leg, so he figured the depth at about 350 feet.

"Okay, I'm oriented," he said.

The controller eased the throttle stick forward and the robot swam forward, diving downward a little, the orange paint-coated steel of the leg growing on the screen.

He spotted it before Driscoll had to tell him. In the triangular-shaped gap between two tanks and the leg, a large black box was adhered to the leg. It was just a black box. Eighteen inches by twenty-four by ten, he judged. A long black wire hung from the bottom of it, disappearing down between the tanks. That would be an antenna.

"I see it."

"Bad news," Morris said.

Koehler looked up and scanned the horizon. For as far as he could see, the platforms sprouted from the sea. He wondered how many of them were in the same condition as his own. The dry wind whipped at his shirtsleeves.

His flagship, Alpha.

"You want us to take the robot over to Bravo and Charlie and check them?" Driscoll asked.

"I don't think so, Jake. We're running out of time. Did you get that on videotape?"

"I did, sir," the operator said. He punched a button, and the videotape popped up from the console.

Koehler took it from him and said, "All right, guys. Shut off the lights and climb in the car. Frank'll drive us back."

"Don't forget the cat," Morris said.

Friday, March 7, 11:10 P.M.

The President was off on some important chore in California, probably political, and the Vice President had assumed the gavel. He looked around the table at the representatives of Defense, Intelligence, Treasury, and State. The National Security Advisor sat next to him, and everyone appeared as disenchanted with the late-night meeting as Drieser was. Additionally, by special invitation, the United States Ambassador to the United Nations was in attendance.

The Vice President swivelled his head toward the Secretary of State. "Your show, Mr. Secretary."

Douglas Chambers nodded at him, and Drieser stood up at his chair. It was located at the side of the room since he didn't have the rank to sit at the table.

"Gentlemen and Madame Ambassador, I'm sure you've all seen some of this, but let's look one more time."

Judy Blalock was seated at the side of the room, dressed in a teal-and-blue print pantsuit which defined her tiny but voluptuous figure. She had complained to him about being ordered to the White House without a chance to change clothes, and he had told her, "They're only interested in your mind, Judy." She had a voluptuous mind, too.

She flicked a button on her remote, and the videotape began to turn. The 48-inch monitor at the side of the room displayed the amateur videographer's efforts. The tape, obtained from CNN, had not been edited for short-attention-span consumer consumption, and this version was longer. It was still as serene, but for the violent launch of the rocket.

As it ran, he said, "The *Maru Hokkaido*, fully loaded with over one million tons of crude oil, was detained around noon, our time, today. Eleven hours ago. In the best judgement of the captain of the *Herault Transporter*, all, or most, of the crew are safe, but under control of the boarders."

Before anyone could ask, he said, "According to the company, the oil originated in Brunei, and it was bound for Japan."

He signalled Blalock, and she switched to another video recorder. The image now was blue. Almost totally blue. Along the left side was a brown-green smudge, and a few black specks were present in the lower right-hand corner.

"This image was captured a few hours ago by a National Security Agency satellite on routine track. The satellite is primarily concerned with activity in Southeast Asia." Drieser stepped over to the screen and used his finger to point. He didn't believe in Yuppie collapsible pointers. "Along this side of the screen, up here, you're seeing Vietnam, as seen through a thin overcast. Down here, this is a small island called Amboyna Cay. And farther down, almost off the screen, these are five ships now near the scene of the hijacking. They are all commercial vessels, standing by in case they can be helpful."

Again, Blalock switched recording machines, and another image appeared. It was almost totally black, but for swatches of red, burnt orange, and blue.

"This also comes from the NSA, an infrared image captured at night shortly after the boarding. Once again, the target of the satellite was not this incident, and so the action is almost off the screen. The darker red here is the tanker, and she was at speed, her engines putting off more heat, at the time the image was captured. This smaller dot is the assault boat."

"You've got the whole thing on tape!"

"I'm afraid not, Mr. Vice President. The satellite went out of range shortly after this. And we don't have anything earlier, at the time the boarding took place."

"So we have nothing?" the UN Ambassador asked.

"On direct evidence, no, ma'am. However, the NSA's primary goal is to intercept and interpret electronic communications, and so we went back over their recordings from that part of the world for the last twenty-four hours. We used key words—like 'oil,' and 'war,' and 'battle,' and 'Brunei'—since the assault craft was flying that flag, and had the computer search the tapes for conversations utilizing those words. We were inundated with copies of radio and telephonic communications in which those words appeared. All were non-encrypted, by the way, but we suspect some kind of revolution is taking place within the country.

"While we were at it, we learned that international communications with the state of Brunei have been cut off, from the Brunei end."

"Oh, no!" the Ambassador said. "Not another Kuwait."

"I hasten to say that we don't know what we have at this point. The State Department has been in communication with the government of Sarawak, but Kuching hasn't been able to clarify much for us. At least, so far."

The Vice President gestured to the Intelligence representative, the Executive Director of Central Intelligence, sitting in for the DCI. "What have you got, Ben?"

"We've been cooperating with State, sir. Undersecretary Drieser is showing you what we have."

The Secretary of Defense added, "Mr. Drieser called us just before five, and we sent out queries. We have a naval task force cruising the South China Sea, but they haven't been running recon in that direction. We're trying to get more information now, Mr. Vice President.''

"The composition of the task force?''

"An aircraft carrier with seven support vessels. We've turned them south, just in case they're needed.''

The Vice President turned back to Drieser. "Are you drawing conclusions at this point, Chris?''

"Nothing concrete, sir. As speculation, I would venture to say that the hijacking of the *Maru Hokkaido* is related to whatever is taking place in Brunei. If I want to project beyond that, I'd say the Japanese are going to blame, let's call him Mr. X, in Brunei. I believe they will want the UN to intervene.''

"No way,'' the ambassador said.

"We did it for Kuwait,'' the VP countered.

"We had international consensus in regard to Saddam's aggression,'' she said. "And look how long it took to get it.''

Shit, Drieser thought, let's get up-front about it, people: We did it for oil.

Seven

The newspapers and television were playing the story for all its worth, which was considerable. In Tokyo and Osaka, there had already been demonstrations in the streets, decrying the barbarism on the high seas. Giant posters of Captain Maki Hirosiuta's face were paraded through the streets, and the man was now a hero, whether he was or not. A wave of anger was curling across the islands.

The administration was feeling the pressure. Students with strident voices, and perhaps not enough to do, always seemed to generate unreasonable fear in political men and women. Of course, Meoshi Kyoto knew, former administrations had tumbled for less than an inability to protect Japanese citizens and property in international waters.

On the one hand, there was one group, backslapped across the face as it might have been, the loudest voices, who clearly did not understand the situation, demanding the strongest military intervention. You must send the navy and rescue our brave men.

On the other hand, palms upward, small groups of environmentalists were getting into the act, urging peaceful approaches and calm. They forecast a scenario of enraged Bruneians scuttling the *Maru Hokkaido*, disgorging her million tons of oil into the sea, befouling the water fowl, poisoning the fish, smearing the shores of tiny islands, and the western coast of Palawan in the Philippines. The Philippine government was not happy with that prospect and had said as much in official communiqués.

The Foreign Minister, quite appropriately, preferred a diplomatic solution. Meoshi Kyoto, as befit his position, supported both the Minister and the Deputy Minister for Marine Affairs. Privately, in concert with the strident voices and opposing his better sense, Kyoto thought a flight of four fighter-bombers launched from an aircraft carrier in the predawn hours might offer a rapid resolution, as well as suitable justice.

He could not help empathizing with the captive crew of the supertanker. No one should have to suffer the indignities imposed on hostages. The fact that they were countrymen elevated his anger and his imagination. As a soldier, he felt helpless, but his mind devised missions for Mitsubishi F-1 fighters.

There was another aspect. The Prime Minister had received a communication from some body identifying itself as the Front for Democratic Reform, signed by Provisional President Li Sen, demanding payment for the *Hokkaido*'s cargo to secure her release from official detention. The payment was to be made by electronic transfer, and went far outside the normal accounting procedures. The payment demanded was also two dollars per barrel higher than the current world market for high-grade crude.

The Prime Minister had ranted about extortion, blackmail, ransom, and other black crimes, not to mention the lack of a trading agreement with the newly arisen Front for Democratic Reform. The PM was quite willing to pay the Sultan, at prevailing rates, naturally, but no one knew where the Sultan was.

Kyoto was pacing his office fuming over and musing these issues when Kato Asume burst in. The man never walked through doorways; he always burst through them. His unconfined energy made other people tire easily.

Kyoto stopped his pacing. "Minister?"

Asume was positively bubbling with excitement. In his whole career, he had probably never faced such a crisis. "The diplomats have prevailed."

Kyoto was mildly disappointed.

"The United Nations ambassador is meeting with the Secretary General soon, to request a special session of the Security Council."

Kyoto hoped the ambassador was carrying a checkbook.

"Notwithstanding that approach," Asume said, "the Self-Defense Forces have rerouted the *Akagi* aircraft carrier group to the south."

"For Brunei?"

"No, Colonel, for the *Hokkaido*. You must now go home and pack your duffel bag, or whatever it is you pack. You are going to sea."

"Minister! I am an infantryman!"

Asume smiled. "You are also the government's envoy, at my request. An aircraft will be waiting to fly you to the carrier. These are your credentials."

The deputy minister handed him a buff-colored envelope, and Kyoto opened the unsealed flap to find a letter on official stationery. Signed by no less than the Prime Minister.

"Your task is to serve as liaison between the naval group

and the foreign ministry, Meoshi. Do not let the admirals explode.''

When dealing with admirals, Kyoto's colonelcy was about as adequate as the insignia of private soldier. He did not think the Prime Minister's letter would overcome the difference.

"Do not let them send us into war," Asume pleaded.

With Brunei, Kyoto thought it would be a very short war, but he said, "Of course not, Minister."

At the least, he would be out of the confinement of this office for an extended stay, and he would avoid the arguments with Kim at home. At the very, very least, he was placed in a quandry. Kyoto, a dedicated military man, was to persuade other military men that words were mightier than action.

He did not know whether he was up to the chore.

Saturday, March 8, 3:27 P.M.

Dorrie Alhambra clutched the single small suitcase she had been allowed in one hand and cradled her three-year-old daughter in the crook of her other arm. Sean, her five-year-old, carried his dump truck and threatened to wander off the side of the pier, simply by his inattention to where he was going. Dorrie tried to herd him back into the line with her knee.

It was raining fiercely. Everyone was drenched.

She had no idea where Kenneth was, though she understood that the platforms were being evacuated, also, and she prayed he was aboard the boat coming in. Maybe he would get here before . . .

A huge helicopter swooped in over one of the warehouses, shot alongside the pier, and landed on the end of it.

"Come on! Come on! Move forward!" The Shell Oil foreman controlling the line urged them onward.

The line surged ahead, and Dorrie prodded Sean, but he had started to cry. He didn't like loud noises.

Dorrie wanted to cry, also. She did not like confusion, and she wished they were back in Aberdeen, Scotland, where it was harder on Kenneth, but where she was closer to her friends and family.

"Sean! Darling, come along!"

A young woman she did not know stepped out of line and picked the boy up. He shrieked.

Dorrie smiled her appreciation.

The line was moving swiftly now, and when they reached the end of it, two men helped them all into the helicopter. It seemed badly overcrowded, but there were several vacant seats, and she dropped the suitcase on the floor and kicked it under one seat, then slumped into it gratefully, settling Tina on her lap. The young woman sat next to her, still holding Sean. Her wet clothing felt squishy on the Naugahyde fabric of the seat.

The engines bellowed, and over them, she called, "I can take him!"

"That's all right," the woman said. "He's fine with me."

Another helicopter raced by, its shadow making a rapid dark patch on the window next to her.

And then the door slammed, and almost immediately, she felt the seat sway under her as the helicopter took off. Dorrie did not like airplanes.

They rose higher in the air as they flew westward along the coast. Through the window she could see many boats headed in the same direction, their shapes vague in the rainfall. There were other helicopters, also. It was very frightening; she did not know what lay ahead.

Only minutes later she looked down to see a larger gray boat tossing on the rough seas, and she thought it was firing its guns. Little puffs of smoke erupted from it. They closed on it, but angled away to the left as they did.

The men on the boat became more discernible. They *were* firing their guns—at the boats coming toward them.

And then, aghast, she saw one of the men look up at them, then swivel his gun toward them. It flashed.

The water was so blue, so clear. The engines screamed. Sean yelled his fear.

And little holes appeared everywhere. Popping sounds. Sean's screech went to high pitch.

And Dorrie turned toward him, reaching out for him.

And saw that the young woman was slumped over, bright blood gushing down her blouse.

Saturday, March 8, 3:51 P.M.

The new Brunei navy didn't think highly of the evacuation of the oil field workers.

As soon as they heard the radio reports of "Guns fired!" and "Chopper down! Chopper down!", Koehler and Morris bolted out of the supply office, headed for the Dauphin.

Kelly barely heard Sherry's scream, "Don't you dare go!"

He saw her standing outside the office in the downpour as Morris lifted off, and he waved to her.

She turned her back, spun around, and pushed through the door.

"What the hell are we doing, Kelly?"

"Damned if I know, Frank. Instinct?"

"Must be. I can't resist a call for help."

"I'd feel better if we had just one little Minigun," Koehler said.

"Or even a slingshot."

The rain pelted the windscreen, splattering, running off

to the sides in thick rivulets. It had been raining for forty minutes, and the deluge seemed to be picking up steam. It was like flying through minestrone. Visibility was down to a half mile, and under normal operations, they wouldn't be flying unless it was an emergency. The shapes of the buildings around the docks were vague as the Aèrospatiale passed over them.

Morris immediately banked to the left and sped along the coast, a few hundred feet off it, and a thousand feet above the water's surface.

The radio was alive with discordant transmissions, but it wasn't clear whether the helicopter had been shot down or had crashed. The pilot had autorotated and gotten it down on the beach. He was reporting one dead and several injured.

Koehler kept himself busy scanning the skies around them, warning Morris when he saw another chopper. And there were plenty of them, most headed west. Out to sea in the field, he saw armadas of ships and boats forming.

Eight minutes later, on the Sarawak side of the border, they found the downed bird, pancaked into the sand of the beach. She was broken up, but she hadn't caught fire.

"Shit! An S-61," Morris said.

"I hope she wasn't fully loaded," Koehler muttered over the intercom, but knew that she would have been. Two Bells had landed next to the wreckage, and three other helicopters were circling. Morris stayed offshore, clear of them. The jungled hills crowded the beach.

Through the rain the image wasn't clear, but Koehler thought he saw a few bodies lined up in a row above the tidemark. Dead or injured. Men ran around, loading helicopters, searching the wreckage, helping casualties.

"Twenty-nine accounted for," someone said on the radio. "Two dead, six injured, two of them kids. This son of a bitch was shot down!"

Morris swore, then said, "What now, Kelly?"

"Let's go offshore aways and see what's happening. They've got enough help here."

Morris turned toward the sea, lost a little altitude, and picked up speed. He angled back toward Bruneian waters.

They passed over several ships—trawlers, cruisers, a platform tender—headed west and loaded to the gunwales with men, women, and children huddling under ponchos and pieces of canvas. The rain poured down. They also dodged a half dozen helicopters aimed in the same direction. Morris stayed low, passing under them.

And then they ran into the problem.

Seven Brunei navy ships—one small destroyer escort, a frigate, and five patrol boats—had set up a blockade, preventing the oil workers from escaping, though a few had broken through or beaten the blockade. Someone important in Bandar Seri Begawan knew they needed the work force. Koehler hoped his boats had gotten through earlier.

The ships were strung out in a ragged line, ranged from the coast out to a couple miles offshore.

Opposing them were Gurkha patrol boats. Koehler counted ten of them as the Dauphin crossed over their lines. Bunched up behind the Gurkhas was the fleet of evacuee shipping. A rusted-out freighter, trawlers, workboats, even several sailboats under auxiliary power. Kelly got a rough count at forty boats and ships pitching lightly in the chop of the sea. Most of the passengers were exposed to the rain, and everyone appeared sodden.

As he watched, a forty-foot power cruiser made an attempt to pass through the Gurkha line, then the Bruneian. She was kicking up a fair bow wave as she aimed between the Bruneian destroyer and a gunboat, but the destroyer opened up with a deck gun, placing a couple high-explosive rounds a hundred yards ahead of the cruiser. Great geysers of water erupted from the surface.

The cruiser faltered, drained off speed, and turned back.

"Christ! Did we plan on this, Kelly?"

"I sure as hell didn't. Watch the platform."

"See it."

Morris circled the rig and headed back. Another helicopter, a Conoco Bell, blinked its navigation lights at them.

"Looks like a stalemate of sorts. Li Sen, or whoever is running this operation, has told the navy to be cautious. He doesn't want an international incident, blowing a few Frenchmen or Germans out of the water."

"Hell, look there, Kelly! That Gurkha is going to test the assumption."

Morris brought the Dauphin to a hover, and they watched the patrol boat ease out of line and advance toward a rebel gunboat. Five men on the deck, two of them manning the pair of fifty-caliber machine guns mounted to either side of the deckhouse. Two men hovered over the bow-mounted 20-millimeter cannon. To Koehler, it looked like a pitiful set of armament. The navy boat was carrying a twin 30-millimeter cannon mount and four heavy machine guns.

The Gurkha boat hadn't advanced fifty yards before the rebel boat opened up, spitting 30-millimeter shells. A dozen splashed around the patrol craft before another dozen tore her apart. Fiberglass and armor plate flew even as the Gurkhas tried to return fire. Seconds later, a massive explosion ripped the side out of the hull, and a tower of flame rose from her stern.

"Goddamn it!" Kelly shouted.

"They aren't afraid to shoot Gurkhas," Morris said.

The confrontation had occured a quarter mile away to their left, but Morris still backed off, moving the Dauphin farther out to sea.

Until Koehler saw arms flailing the water. Three of the Gurkhas had cleared the wreckage and were bobbing in the waves, trying to get back to safety. The burning boat was settling low in the water.

"Kelly?"

"Go."

While Morris dipped the nose and accelerated, Koehler shed his harness and clambered into the back compartment, replugging his headset into a receptacle closer to the side door.

"If these assholes don't kill me," Morris said, "Sherry will do it for taking you in there."

"What have you been doing with my office manager?"

"This is a change of topic?"

"Just asking?"

"We're friends."

Koehler slid the door open, and the wind whipped at him. He leaned out to see ahead, raindrops stinging his face. The Dauphin was four feet off the surface, whitecaps reaching futilely for the fuselage. Morris was doing at least a hundred miles an hour, taking rain head-on below the rotor arc, the rotor downdraft kicking up more spray. The sea passed beneath in a blur.

He couldn't see a damned thing with the moisture in his eyes. Tasted salt.

The helicopter began to slow, and his vision started to clear. Then Morris was walking it forward, ever lower, the wave tops lashing at the skin. He saw one hand raised toward him, rising as the man rode upward on a swell.

"Go right, Frank!"

"I see him."

Four hundred yards away, he saw the gunboat. One man stood near the windshield, aiming at them with an assault rifle. With the shifting deck, he wouldn't be much of a marksman. Kelly hoped. And then didn't worry about it.

On his knees at the door now, reaching out, he wrapped his fingers around the man's wrist, saw the Nepalese face grinning up at him. He hauled back, brought the man close, then got both hands under the man's armpits and heaved upward. Though he was slight of stature, the man was heavy in his wet camouflage utilities and a full load of web gear. He came out of the water, hit the doorjamb at waist level, then jackknifed forward and scrambled until he had his feet on board.

"Thank you, sir!" he yelled.

Kelly gave him a thumbs-up. "That's one, Frank."

"Next one coming up."

The helicopter bounced, struck by a wave from the bottom, then there was another beseeching hand raised. The soldier beside him spun around, and the two of them soon had the second man on board.

Then the third.

Morris circled the burning boat, now only moments from sinking, but they didn't find any more survivors. They did find one body floating on its back, its chest peppered with shrapnel, and before Koehler could stop him, the first soldier dropped his web belt to the floor and leaped back into the sea. He swam frantically toward the corpse, got it in tow, and turned back. Morris met him halfway, and Koehler with his two new assistants levered the body from the sea, then recovered the rescuer. Koehler looked everyone over, searching for wounds, but found only scratches and bruises.

The Dauphin climbed to safer altitude while Koehler went back to the left seat. His shirt and jeans were drenched from the rain and the seawater transferred from the soldiers.

"Come ninety degrees, Frank."

Still in a hover, Morris turned the chopper.

Koehler looked through his side window at a laden workboat a hundred yards away. The name was on each side of the bow. *Peerless Fosdick.*

Looking back, he motioned one of the soldiers forward, a sergeant. The man rolled to his knees and crawled forward to grip the seats and look expectantly to Koehler.

Yelling over the roar of the turboshafts, Koehler told him, "Contact your boats! Have them withdraw!"

"Sir, I cannot!"

"Please! For ten minutes!"

The sergeant considered a moment, then nodded and gave Kelly the marine-band frequency. Koehler dialled it in and handed the man his headset.

A few minutes later, the Gurkha patrol craft started turning away from the line of confrontation. Koehler took the headset back and tried several marine frequencies before he raised the workboat.

"*Peerless Fosdick.*"

"GT-Zero-Two. I'm the chopper off your bow. Follow me."

"Zero-Two, I ain't flying nowhere, and I sure don't want to take a cannon round."

"They're not going to sink you," Kelly insisted.

On the intercom, Morris said, "They did take some potshots at us, Navy."

"With a twenty-two. Hell, Frank, they're under orders not to shoot up the foreigners."

"As evidenced by that Sikorsky on the beach."

"Some hothead who didn't get the word."

"Shit. Well, we'll give it a try."

Morris turned the Dauphin west, and staying fifty feet off the water, started forward slowly.

A hundred yards.

Two hundred.

Koehler craned his neck to look backward. The workboat was under way, following them.

Another hundred yards.

A few more boats fell into the wake of the workboat, picking up speed. The larger ships got under way.

Morris aimed into the gap between the gunboat and the destroyer, which was a quarter mile away.

Another hundred yards.

The destroyer fired.

Water erupted in a geyser from the surface two hundred feet off their starboard quarter.

"Am I steadfast, or do I tuck my tail?" Morris asked.

"Steady as she goes, Army."

Creeping along, twenty miles per, another fifty yards.

Another explosion, a little closer. Koehler heard the whistle of its arrival and the deep whump of its detonation. Salt water from the detonation may have hit them, but who could tell in the downpour?

"I know. Steady," Morris said.

The three Gurkha soldiers stood in the cabin doorway, staring out at the destroyer.

Behind them, more boats had pulled in to follow the *Peerless Fosdick*. A small tramp steamer was getting under way.

Then the destroyer was directly north of them, the gunboat two hundred yards away on the south. The deckhands on the gunboat stared at them, but left their guns alone. The destroyer decided against another shelling.

"I'll be damned," Koehler said. "We may have called their bluff."

"I'm damned glad you don't play poker, Navy guy."

Morris raced the Dauphin ahead for a half mile, then slowed, turned, and hovered.

"I'm relatively certain we're in Sarawak territorial waters," he said.

"Feels good to me," Koehler told him.

"The breach has been gapped, or vice versa."

The *Peerless Fosdick* was leading a mounting exodus. The workboat was making at least twenty-five knots now, and an ever-widening fan of watercraft spread out from her stern. The Bruneian destroyer and gunboat were backpedalling, letting the gap widen.

"They're not going to stop them now," Koehler said. "Hey, Sarge!"

The Gurkha sergeant trundled forward and grabbed the back of Kelly's seat. "Sir?"

"You guys want to be dropped on one of your boats or go back to your barracks?"

The man looked back at the body laid out against the rear bulkhead.

"The barracks, I think, sir. If it is not a problem."

"Not a problem."

On the intercom Morris asked, "You want to take the scenic route back, over Miri Marudi?"

"Yeah, we'd better."

On the shoreward trip, Slim Avery called Koehler on the company frequency, and Kelly assured him, and therefore Sherry, that they were fine.

"How we doing on the evac, Slim?"

"The last trawler's at the dock now. I'm waiting for trucks to come back, and I've got just over seven hundred people still here. All dependents are gone. Except for."

Koehler knew who the except for was.

"Put Sherry and Monica on that trawler. I'll catch up with them by chopper later."

"Ain't making no promises, boss."

Which was about the best Kelly could hope for, he supposed.

The Dauphin crossed the coast and headed inland, following a narrow stream, climbing to clear the hills. The jungle was thick here, double-canopied, and green as all of Ireland. The leaves shimmered under the onslaught of rain.

Following the river from the coast, the village was about eight miles inland, ten miles from Kuala Belait over the twisting, angry trail through the jungle. And when they got there, it was a madhouse.

In the clearings surrounding the thatched roof, stilted village, makeshift shelters had gone up—tents, squares of canvas, anything to protect people from the rain. Villagers stood around in amazement, watching their lives being inundated by unwanted tourists. A dozen helicopters were on the ground, shoved back under the jungle canopy to get them out of the way. Trucks and jeeps were everywhere, many of them up to their axles in mud. One of the companies had had the presence of mind to send a couple bulldozers, and they were frantically attempting to clear more space from the jungle. Another, more orderly, convoy was snaking its way out of Miri Marudi to the west, en route for Kuching, but Koehler could see it was having trouble on the water-slickened mud of the trail. At the speed they were making, Kuching was days away.

Vehicles on the road to Kuala Belait were at a near standstill. Koehler could see about a mile up that road, but nothing was moving very fast. The village was gridlocked, for one thing, leaving little space for arrivals, but trucks on the trail had mired down in gunk or slid off the road. He saw two Jeeps chained together attempting to pull a fully loaded semi out of a ditch to the side of the road. Worse, empty trucks headed back to the coast and Kuala Belait were finding it impossible to pass the oncoming horde on the single-lane road. One at a time, they were leapfrogging ahead, passing vehicles that pulled to the side for them, but then got bogged down.

Water-saturated men and women slogged through the

mud, trying to push their vehicles forward. Koehler thought more people were on the ground than riding.

"Jesus!" Morris said. "This isn't a plan at all. It's a goddamned circus."

"Looks about like Washington, D.C."

"The streets or the Congress?"

"Both. Over there, Frank. Zero-One."

Morris floated them toward the western edge of the village. The other Dauphin was on the ground, parked next to two semi-trucks and a couple Jeeps. Fuel bladders were lined up alongside one of the semis, and Koehler could see people packed together beneath the flatbed trailers, seeking protection from the rain. Twelve men were struggling with a tent and its poles.

"No place to put down, Kelly."

"We'll wait here." He got on the radio, "GT-Zero-One, Two here."

"One," Foster came right back to him.

"Why are those trucks sitting there, Eddie?"

"Some guy from Brunei Shell is trying to direct traffic, and Lord knows, someone needs to do it. He's passing out numbers, and it's going to be a while before we can get them back in line."

"Gas those up, Eddie, and give 'em a bladder of extra fuel, then send them on to Kuching. Let's try to clear out some of the traffic jam in the village."

"Gotcha, Kelly. Will do. Hey, what about Pete and Andy? I've got them in the back here, and Andy don't look so good."

Morris looked over at him.

Koehler only thought about it for a moment. "Put some avgas on one of the trucks, then refuel your bird. You fly as far west as you can, then put down and wait for your fuel to catch up. Soon as you get it, head for the hospital in Kuching."

"Roger that, Kelly. See you in Kuching."

"Hey, Eddie! See if you can't find Irving and have him talk someone into using those bulldozers to widen the road instead of building a city. These people don't want to stay here that long."

Koehler pointed to the east, and Morris pulled in pitch.

Saturday, March 8, 5:13 P.M.

"A Brunei Shell helicopter coming from Bandar Seri Begawan was just shot down, sir."

Benjamin Shaikh acknowledged the radio operator with a nod. His mouth was full of overcooked rice and shrimp, liberally soaked with curry sauce. It was his first meal in . . . he couldn't remember how long.

Sergeant Major Irra, also eating, asked the radioman, "Where did this take place, Corporal?"

"Near Tutong, Sergeant Major."

Shaikh swallowed. "Either Colonel Bakir has lost control of his command, or the range of targets has been expanded."

Irra shrugged. "Does it matter, sir?"

"Probably, it does not. The Tutong line will not hold for much longer, anyway, and then Bakir will come here and make new decisions about his targets."

Shaikh and a small contingent of his headquarters staff were camped in the living room of a residential unit he had commandeered. Captain Shrestha and a detail of men were collecting the last of the supplies from the barracks and loading them aboard a truck. Shaikh had ordered Captain Singh to withdraw his men from Lumut, and they were on the way back. He was relatively certain the rebel forces would leave the refinery alone. It was too valuable a resource.

He was concentrating his forces around the oil companies' compounds for two reasons. First, there was still over forty thousand people here, people he considered under the shield of his protection. Mostly, the evacuation was bedlam. The road to Miri Marudi was jammed tight, and trucks were stacked up throughout the compounds, waiting their turns to make the trek. He had talked to a Brunei Shell engineer, and the man had promised to send road-graders and land-scrapers up to the road and try to make it more passable.

His second reason for moving his headquarters was a matter of self-preservation for the battalion. He thought Colonel Bakir would have strong reservations about firing heavy caliber ammunition into the compounds, putting the foreigners at risk.

Shaik hoped it was so.

"All of the patrol boats are now at the dock," a sergeant reported.

"Good." Shaik was leaving the oil field unprotected for the moment, and he had recalled the boats and the helicopters. His rationale was the same as with Lumut. The rebels needed the oil. And he needed to mass his forces.

He heard the beat of rotors and stood up, carrying his plate, and went to the window. An Aèrospatiale Dauphin with GlobeTech markings was landing on the street in front of the tiny house. It settled next to his Black Hawk, and in line with two other Black Hawks. The rest of his air wing was refuelling and loading spare parts.

The Dauphin's rotors slowed, and he watched three of his men spill out of the back, then lift the body of their comrade from the deck of the compartment. They carried the body toward a truck in the dwindling rain.

Koehler and his pilot, the man named Morris, emerged and stepped to the ground.

He went to the door and opened it.

When Koehler came up the walk, Shaikh said, "I see now that it was you performing foolhardy stunts in the face of the enemy."

Koehler grinned, "I hope you won't spread it around, Benjamin. My wife doesn't want to know."

Shaikh returned the smile. "Thank you for retrieving my men."

"Frank and I try to side with the good guys."

He waved them inside. "Would you like food? The corporal burns what he can, but some of it is edible."

Morris said, "I could eat hot charcoal."

"Then you will enjoy this, Mr. Morris."

Shaikh signalled the corporal, and the man filled two plates in the kitchen, then brought them to Koehler and Morris. They sat around the coffee table on the sofa and chairs.

"Sergeant Major," Koehler said to Irra, "how do you manage to keep starch in your uniform? I look like I've been water-skiing in a marsh full of crocodiles."

"It is simple Mr. Koehler. One must change every half hour."

"I knew there was a secret," Koehler said, forking a heap of rice into his mouth. After he chewed, he asked, "Does this place have a videotape player?"

"In the cabinet under the television," Shaikh said.

Koehler unbuttoned his shirt, reached in, and withdrew a cassette. "You might want to look at that."

Irra took it and went to insert it in the machine. He turned the TV on, and they soon had an underwater picture.

Shaikh had seen similar footage of robot-generated video inspections as part of his normal duties. When the camera focused on the black box attached to the leg, he knew what it was.

"It is one of your platforms, Kelly?"

"Alpha. I don't know about the other two."

"Do you know how long the antenna is?"

"No. I suspect it's long enough to pick up ultra-low frequency signals, if the transmitter is fairly close. Maybe a couple miles."

"Remote-controlled explosive charge. The other legs?"

"I didn't have time to check, but hell, it doesn't matter. If one leg goes, the whole platform tumbles."

"And if that happens?"

"It's going to break a hell of a lot of important connections," Koehler said. "The seabed conductors, the storage tanks, probably the links to the undersea pipeline. We'll have oil all over hell."

"How much oil?"

"Difficult to tell, Benjamin, and I haven't had time to calculate it. Some of those wells are self-pressurized. They'll ooze oil on their own. Some are pumped. Some are water-injected."

Shaikh understood that concept. Water was pumped below the igneous rock containing the oil, increasing pressures from below that forced the oil to the surface.

"And do you suspect that your Alpha platform is not the only one fitted with such an appliance?"

"That'd be my best guess."

Morris went to the kitchen to get a refill of his plate, then came back and sat down.

"I must admit that your news is distressing," Shaik said.

"Distresses the hell out of me, too. If I could get word to my CEO and the board of directors, they could share my distress."

"In fact," Morris said, "it might create a wave of heart attacks."

Shaikh was not certain what he could do about mined oil platforms. He did not have deep-diving expertise in his realm. The *Malay Princess* had the divers, but was engaged at Mirador, and in any event, he could not ask them to assume the risk of removing the explosives. For all he knew, the black boxes were booby-trapped and would explode if an attempt was made to remove them.

"I suppose," he said, "it is the work of Omar Padang."

"Who's Padang?"

"He is—was—the police chief. Now, he calls himself Minister of Security."

"I thought this guy Li Sen was in charge."

"Perhaps that is true. However, I talked to Padang." He told Koehler and Morris about the telephone call.

"Pure crap," Morris said.

"They're probably all would-be tyrants. Maybe they'll kill themselves off fighting for the top spot. What word do you have about the other companies?" Koehler asked.

Shaikh had to refocus his thoughts from images of an oil field—his protectorate!—alive with flames and plunging oil platforms. "The field is practically clear. About two thousand men have volunteered to stay behind, and they are assisting in fighting the fires and containing the oil slick. They will live aboard whatever platforms they choose, I imagine."

"Ours are well-stocked, if they need food," Koehler offered. "I guess I wouldn't advise them to spend the night, given the tumor on the leg."

"As for the workers ashore, you have seen the chaos?"

"I have. It's going to take awhile."

"When will you go, Kelly?"

"After the last GlobeTech employee is clear."

"That'll be me," Morris said.

Koehler stood up. "Thanks for the dinner, Major. I hope we cross paths again."

"I am sure we will."

Shaikh and Irra followed them to the door, then watched as the Aèrospatiale fired its engines and took off.

"A resourceful man," Irra said.

"Yes, but he places additional worries on my head."

Saturday, March 8, 5:27 P.M.

Omar Padang was extremely angry. His naval forces had been unable to contain the foreign workers, and about half of them had escaped to the west. More were attempting to leave by land, and now that the rains had stopped, the road could well improve for them. An army helicopter sent out on reconnaissance had reported as much. Fortunately, there were so many helicopters flying about that an additional one did not create notice.

Reports had been made that Shamin Bakir was forcefully acquiring helicopters for military use from the many owned by the oil and service companies. As such, they flew in fine disguise around the country.

Padang stood on the bridge of the destroyer *Bulkiah* as she plowed slowly into the oil field and scanned the field with his binoculars. Off to the right, out to sea, he could see the fire at Mirador. Three small ships surrounded the platform, pouring water on the flames. Padang did not know how such fires were fought, but suspected they were attempting to suppress the flames sufficiently so that someone, or some robot, could approach close enough to cut off the flow of fuel.

Two additional ships were in attendance near Mirador, and he could not see what they were doing. Perhaps managing the circle of containment booms surrounding the oil slick.

The destroyer continued to pound ahead while Padang sought out a perfect hiding place.

"Minister, a radio call for you."

Omar Padang smiled. He could have gone the rest of

his natural life as a police chief. Now, he was a minister, all at his own initiative. Soon, he would carry more exalted titles.

He turned from his surveillance of the oil field and went to the side of the bridge to pick up a microphone.

"This is Omar Padang."

"Colonel Bakir."

"What is your situation, Colonel?"

"It should not be much longer. We have just captured eleven personnel carriers, and the opposition is beginning to crumble."

"Time?"

"To Kuala Belait? Two hours at the most."

Padang thought Bakir optimistic, but did not say so.

"Your first objective, Colonel, when your force reaches Kuala Belait, is to terminate the evacuation."

"Without killing a few foreigners? How am I to do that?"

Padang was beginning to find some credibility in Li Sen's insistence upon protecting the foreigners. Li forecast intervention by foreign governments if their citizens were murdered. Padang was certain he could stave off intervention, though he had yet to tell Li of his plan. He might never tell the man.

"You simply block the road with personnel carriers, Colonel. As many as are necessary. I doubt anyone will drive over them."

"We will try your method, first," Bakir said, doubt in in his tone. "Then, I will do it my way."

"No. If you, or if one of your men—accident or not, kill one foreigner, then you will stand alone and meet the incoming fighter-bombers. Do you understand me, Colonel?"

"The Gurhkas are included?"

"Of course not."

Several moments passed before an obviously reluctant Shamin Bakir said, "I understand."

He did not, of course. Some in the military had achieved their stations by running roughshod over anything in their paths. They gave no thought to other forces at work in the world around them. Padang, by virtue of his association with the Sultan and the family for many years, did understand that some actions created adverse reactions. He also knew he was susceptible to forgetting what he had learned, and it took a Li Sen to remind him.

Padang replaced the microphone and went back to the front of the bridge. Once again, he swept his binoculars along the horizon, then stopped and adjusted the focus.

"Captain," he said to the naval uniformed man standing next to him, "what is that platform?"

It appeared to be entirely deserted, but then most of them were. Padang had never spent a great deal of time in the field, but the current absence of helicopter and marine traffic gave the impression of a phantom community.

The captain consulted a chart. "That is GlobeTech Bravo, Minister."

Padang searched his mind for another chart. GlobeTech Bravo. GT-Bravo. Yes.

"We will utilize that platform."

"Of course, Minister." The captain ordered a change in course.

Half an hour later, the *Bulkiah* was holding station off the drilling rig, with her landing stage lowered, and Lieutenant Hashim and his men started escorting the captives down the stairway and into a small boat. Padang stood on the port-side wing and watched them.

Mohammed Hassanal twisted away from the policeman holding his arm and stopped to glare upward at Padang. His hands were bound behind him, and he was no longer the fearsome figure he had once been. Padang smiled at him.

The boat made three trips to the platform's elevator, and the only difficulty Padang observed was in the transfer of Hamzah bin Suliaman. Four of the rapid response team were required to handle the stretcher on which the man was secured, and they nearly lost it, spilling Suliaman into the sea, as they stepped from the landing stage to the boat. The loss would not have bothered Padang, but it would have annoyed Li Sen, and for the moment, he did not want Li Sen irritated.

Before the final journey of the captain's gig, carrying the balance of Hashim's security detail and his store of equipment, Hashim climbed the ladder to the bridge. Already, Padang could detect a hardening in the lines of the young lieutenant's face. He was gaining experience quickly.

"You have found everything to be satisfactory, Lieutenant?"

"Very much so, Chie . . . Minister. The food and water supplies are ample. There is no electrical power, and one of my men is attempting to discover how it was shut off. We are placing the men in one dormitory room, the women and children in another. There are steel doors, and they make excellent prisons. Soon, we will have the air-conditioning operating."

"Do not worry about air-conditioning. The family has had air-conditioning for far too long. We will not cater to their habits. Is there anything else?"

"One of the men discovered . . . ah, forbidden materials in a dormitory."

It was to be expected that the foreigners would have pornography.

"Confiscate it and destroy it. I see no reason to pollute the minds of our young men."

"Yes, sir."

"They did not destroy their communications equipment?"

"They did not."

"Very well. Do not use it unless there is an emergency. We want to continue the farce that this is an abandoned platform. Should helicopters or ships approach, stay out of sight."

"Yes, sir."

"Go, then, Lieutenant."

As soon as the last load of policemen had been deposited on the platform and the boat returned to the destroyer, Padang said, "We will now return to Muara, Captain."

"At once, sir."

Padang felt better. He had lost some of the work force, certainly, but he suspected many of them were family members, and women and children were only impediments. When Bakir reached Kuala Belait and ended the evacuation, Padang expected he would still have half the labor force. That should be sufficient to achieve the production levels he desired.

Within a week, Brunei would be as stable as it had ever been, and he could contemplate the next steps in his campaign.

Saturday, March 8, 6:40 A.M.

Christian Drieser emerged from the bathroom that was almost incapable of accommodating his bulk. He rubbed a hand over his cheeks, searching for any spot that his razor might have missed, and didn't find one. From his bottom desk drawer, he retrieved a fresh white shirt, pulled it on, and began to button it.

Drieser had spent the night in his office, an event that

happened occasionally, and one he always hated. The small sofa was terrible for sleeping, not designed for three hundred pounds, and hard on his back. It made him miss the extra, extra firm mattress of the king-size bed in his town house.

He had his pants undone and his shirt partially tucked in when his personal line buzzed. Though she had offered to stay, he had sent Blalock home after the security council meeting, and there was no one to answer the office lines except himself. Hanging on to his waistband with one hand so he didn't lose his pants, he picked up the receiver with the other.

"Chris, this is Doug. Anything new?"

"Not much more than in the message I sent you a couple hours ago. We're picking up a little ham radio traffic now, and a few aircraft have reached Kuching. They're all oil workers or their dependents. Mostly dependents. NSA's repositioning a satellite, and we'll have more in a few hours. At the moment there appears to be a pitched battle near Tutong between units of the army. To help matters, we don't know which side is which. Bandar Seri Begawan is quiet, and the ham radio operator thought that the hotels were full of foreign personnel. There's a massive migration headed west by road and sea. An Indonesian air force pilot reported that. How about your end?"

"It's been a long damned night," the Secretary said. "The Security Council executive committee met with the Japanese ambassador and his staff most of the night, and they were fishtailing all over the diplomatic highway. Until we know more about what's going on in Brunei, no one's going to take a stance. For now, and probably the future, it's an internal problem for the Sultan."

"And the *Maru Hokkaido*?"

"A horse of another color, yes. But the Council is taking the position that Japan owes the UN about two hundred million it pledged for the Gulf War and never paid. Essentially, the response is 'take a hike.' "

"Japan won't want to move unilaterally, especially if they have to contend with an unknown administration in Brunei. They'll want international support."

"Wanting and getting are two different concepts, Chris."

"Hell. I guess I'll go home and take a nap."

"Might as well. I'm going to do the same."

Drieser replaced the phone, zipped up, and buckled his belt.

He didn't like the way the scenario was playing out. If the Japanese got too aggressive with the supertanker, and she went down, they could well take a poke at Brunei. And if that happened, anything was possible. Brunei's buddies in the south—Indonesia, Malaysia, Singapore, maybe the Philippines—might hop in. And Brunei had long-standing ties to Britain, which hadn't failed to make the long march to the Falklands when needed.

This could get very messy.

A lot of it depended upon who was in charge in Brunei, and the only solid piece of evidence he had was a copy of the message the Japanese had received demanding payment for the *Hokkaido*'s oil.

The Front for Democratic Reform. No one at State, at Defense, or at CIA had ever heard of it. None of the agencies had any intelligence assets in Brunei. Who needed spies in paradise?

The Chief of Mission for the United States was Ambassador Nicholas Brent, but the embassy on the third floor of a building in Teck Guan Plaza in the capital was out of contact. State hadn't been able to reach them by international telephone or by the mission's own satellite system all day.

So. What if this FDR was somewhat legitimate in its aims to oust one of the richest men in the world from his hold on Brunei oil? It could very well be a popular uprising, and it could gain popular international support. No one liked a sultan in these enlightened times.

Japan could run into a buzz saw.

Drieser had no particular love for Japan. He liked his Sony TV, but he didn't like the way they manipulated trade to enlarge their own treasuries. Sell everything under the rising sun to U.S. consumers, but restrict sales of American products in Japan. Price their import cars to U.S. dealers in a way that kept profit and taxes in Japan and avoided paying American taxes on profits. Bunch of bullshit.

But Drieser disliked war more.

He decided against going home for that nap. Instead, he needed to learn more about Brunei and its supposed savior, the Front for Democratic Reform. He needed to learn a lot.

Picking up the phone, he punched in Blalock's voice-mail number.

"Judy, as soon as you get in, fire up your trusty computer and delve into the State data banks. We want to know the names of American citizens with a passport and a visa for Brunei. I think there's about seventy thousand noncitizens in the country, and hell, not more than half of them could be American, right? Then, run those names against DOD's personnel data bank. We could come up with a couple thousand roughnecks who once served in the Marines or something. That's the list I want to see."

Drieser wasn't quite sure what he'd do with it, but he needed intelligence badly, and he was ready to take any route he could.

Before a whole hell of a lot of people got killed.

Saturday, March 8, 7:45 P.M.

Koehler went over to the residential compound and talked to his people who were still waiting for transportation out. Three trucks had gotten back from Miri Marudi, refuelled, and loaded more workers aboard, but they were still waiting in line for the return trip.

A few Caterpillar road-graders and land-scrapers were widening the road on this end, the ground had dried out some, and the drivers were cooperating better with each other, but the pace hadn't increased by much. Some of the oilmen had decided to not wait for a ride and were walking to Miri Marudi. There was a long file of hikers loaded up with backpacks and suitcases also clogging the road now. Koehler still had around six hundred people in-country, and he worried about them.

Worse, he could now hear distant gunfire in the east. It was sporadic, but it only proved that the rebels were getting closer.

After he had passed out as many reassurances as he could, he walked back to the supply compound. He passed a Gurkha bunker made of sandbags, and he thought the soldiers didn't look as nervous as they should. Kelly was nervous.

The skies were uncharacteristically quiet. The helicopter fleets were on the ground or out of the country. He suspected that the rebels had gained control over a number of aircraft caught on the ground at the airports.

Walking through the main gate, Koehler thought the place looked like a ghost town. All of the vehicles were gone except for his battered Explorer parked near the office. The Dauphin sat forlornly on one of the chopper pads. The commissary building had its door open, swinging lightly in the breeze, but it had been cleaned out, and there was nothing left to steal. Only the lights in the office were on.

He crossed the yard to Avery's shack and pulled the door open. Everyone inside looked up expectantly.

Morris said, "Oh. It's only you."

"You were expecting rebels?"

"Yeah, I was. You hear guns?"

There weren't many of them left. Avery and two of his supply specialists who had volunteered to stay behind and help. Morris. Two women he couldn't force onto a boat or truck for love or money, or both.

Sherry and Monica were sitting around Avery's sole table, playing cards. Sherry looked up and asked, "How are they holding up?"

"You know men. When the pressure's on, the jokes only get raunchier."

"Tell us the jokes," Davis said.

"I never remember the punch lines."

"Sure you do. You just don't want to tell us."

"Anything happening?" he asked Avery, who was tending the radio.

"Eddie Foster found himself a clearing and put down to wait for fuel."

"Andy Jenkins?"

"Doing all right, boss. Eddie found some gal—a Conoco dependent—who used to be a nurse and took her along. And I got hold of *Gloucester*"—the GlobeTech platform tender—"and they say they're a couple hours out of Kuching. They'll be on the way back by midnight at the latest."

He walked around the counter, crossed to the table, and came up behind Sherry. Resting his hands on her shoulders, he kneaded her neck muscles. They were taut, revealing the tension she wasn't showing otherwise.

"I need that," she said.

"You need to talk to your mother, ask her why she didn't teach you to mind your man."

"*My* mother?"

"Oh. That's right. She doesn't listen to your father, does she?"

"Or anyone else."

She rotated her head back against his hands. Her hair felt silky. And he worried about her.

But not too much. When the time came, they'd all crawl aboard the Aèrospatiale and head pell-mell for Kuching. Or as far as the fuel load would carry them.

He lost focus on Sherry's muscles as he thought about what Avery'd just told him.

"Slim, can you still raise the *Gloucester?*"

"I can try."

He gave Sherry a pat on the shoulder, then went over to sit next to Avery. When the man contacted the tender after a few tries, he handed the microphone to Kelly. There was a great deal of static, and Kelly had to listen closely and speak clearly.

"*Gloucester*, this is Koehler. Can you get a tape going?"

"Roger. Hold on . . . there. Tape's running."

Composing as he spoke, Koehler dated and timed his report, then directed it to his immediate superior, the vice president for operations. He provided an overview of conditions in Brunei as he knew them, clearly distinguishing between what he had seen and what he surmised. He named the names he knew or had heard—Li, Padang, Bakir. Kelly confessed he had no clue as to the whereabouts or fate of the Sultan. He gave a rundown of the status of the platforms, the current location of GlobeTech employees, and the methods he was using to evacuate them. After considering it for a moment, he decided against reporting the explosives on the leg of Alpha. He was broadcasting in the clear, and he didn't want to alarm anyone except the right people. And he wasn't sure who the right people were.

When he was done, he ordered the tape shut off. "Now, *Gloucester*, contact anyone you can—Kuching or another ship—and have that forwarded to headquarters in Houston."

"Will do, Mr. Koehler."

"While I think about it, provide a copy to the American consulate in Kuching or in Singapore. They may not yet know what's going on."

"Roger."

Sherry came to stand beside him. "Will that get through?"

"I hope so. Radio operators are pretty accommodating."

"It seems primitive."

Koehler swung his chair around to face the room. "Doesn't it? I'm pretty damned used to picking up a phone, or sending a fax or e-mail."

"I'd bet most of the embassies and consulates have satellite links," Morris said. "You suppose they were cut off?"

"Either that, or this guy Padang has the honchos confined somewhere. Still, it's been about thirty hours. I'll bet the word's leaked out somewhere."

"But we won't see any Marines landing," Morris said.

"Doubt it. Not for some insignificant little revolution."

"It's pretty damned significant to me," Davis said. "I liked living in Bandar Seri Begawan."

"Maybe you will again," Kelly told her. "As soon as this settles down, we'll be back. GlobeTech's not going to write off its investment, and the other companies won't, either."

"So many people have been killed," Davis said.

Koehler didn't know the final count or the nationalities of the workers killed on Mirador or Albatross, but he was pretty certain that the two dead on the Sikorsky that was shot down weren't Brunei citizens. "There's probably a dozen among the oil community. That will raise some international hell.''

"But not Bruneians?'' Sherry asked.

"The world doesn't care about Bru—''

Everyone heard it at the same time.

The roar of engines, and the rumble of machinery.

"Kill the lights,'' Koehler said as he came out of his chair.

One of the supply techs leaped to the door, found the switch, and the room went dark.

Koehler raced to the window.

The highway beyond the gate started to come alive with headlights, one set after another. Streaming along at better than forty miles an hour.

"Personnel carriers, APCs,'' Morris said as he moved up beside Koehler.

He looked back up the highway, and for as far as he could see, it was packed. The boxy silhouettes were in both lanes, coming in double file. "What, forty of them, Frank?''

"At least. And each will be armed with a minimum of an M-60 machine gun. Ten, twelve troops each.''

As he watched, the lead vehicles went on by the supply yard, then peeled off to the left, their treads clattering as they left the asphalt for a dirt road.

"They're going around the residential compounds, Frank.''

"Yeah. They want to cut off the border. Methinks its time to crank engines, Navy.''

"I can't—''

Everyone in the office was crowded around the window, and Morris grabbed his arm and towed him around the counter to the far corner of the room.

Whispering, Morris said, "Let's get the women, Slim, and the other guys over the border. Then, you want to come back, I'm with you.''

"But—"

"You aren't going to accomplish shit if you're penned up in the residences, Navy."

"Okay. You're right." Koehler turned around and called out, "Get whatever you're getting, boys and girls. We're heading for the hills."

Koehler heard the beat of rotors passing over, and he had to believe that the choppers belonged to the rebel army. The Regimental Air Wing had some old Bell 205s—Vietnam-era Hueys—and a few later model 212s. All of them would be armed with machine guns or rockets. They were going to have to play a little hide-and-seek getting out.

But it was only a couple miles.

"Come on!" he urged.

Everyone grabbed duffel bags or suitcases and crowded around the counter.

Koehler pulled the door open.

Looked up to see a Huey hovering in the middle of the yard, thirty feet off the ground.

Sudden white flashes at its side.

Door-mounted M-60.

The 7.62-millimeter slugs arced across the yard, guided by green tracer rounds.

And found the Dauphin.

She exploded in flames.

The concussion knocked Koehler backward into Sherry.

Shrapnel whistled by in a dozen directions.

WORLD

Eight

Sunday, March 9, 2:15 A.M.

As an infantryman, even one accustomed to leaping from helicopters in his air cavalry training, Colonel Meoshi Kyoto preferred having solid ground under his feet, and he knew that he did not want to ever again accept a ride with the navy.

The flight south had been smooth enough, but as the pilot began conversing with some air controller and Kyoto knew they were nearing the carrier, the tension in his back began to mount. By some inexplicable twist of fate and electronic magic, the pilot actually found the carrier in the darkness of the night and sea, and as soon as the man pointed out the lights of the floating behemoth—the *Akagi* displaced 30,000 tons and carried 32 aircraft—Kyoto's back muscles tightened up until he was rigid in his seat.

Night launches and night landings did not thrill him as much as they apparently thrilled the pilot, who related anecdotes of near misses and near dunkings. By the time they were in their final approach, Kyoto knew everything there was to know about flunking the test of landing, but absolutely nothing of successful landings.

He wanted to close his eyes, but was afraid to do so. When the power came off, he thought they were going to fall into the sea or crash into the stern of the carrier. The tail sagged a little, so he could no longer see the lights of the flight deck over the pilot's shoulder.

They were not flying; they were falling.

And bang, they were stopped. He was flung forward in his harness, then the airplane slammed down to the deck, and the arresting wire dragged them back a few meters. He thought he would have bruises all over his body.

As the canopy rose to let in the blessed sea air, the pilot told him over the intercom, "You see, Colonel? Absolutely exhilarating."

Kyoto did not know how he was getting off this carrier, but it was not to be by way of an airplane flung into the sky by a steam-driven catapult.

For some reason he was surprised by the wind blowing across the huge deck, but then realized that the *Akagi* would be making her best speed of 35 knots. One of the many men wearing variously colored vests helped him from the rear seat of the aircraft and down a ladder, and another led him into the superstructure.

The maze of corridors and passageways was absolutely appalling. He would have been lost in a minute, but his guide showed him first to a stateroom where he rid himself of the pressure suit, helmet, and his duffel bag. Then they climbed several decks and he was shown the mess—where he was to eat; the Combat Information Center—where he was to touch nothing; the Communications Center— where he could make contact with Kato Asume; the bridge—where he met the captain; and the flag plot—

where he was introduced to Admiral Saburo Yakama. He assumed the rest of the ship was off-limits to him. And wondered if he would ever find a bathroom—which he had needed for the past hour.

He came to attention and saluted the admiral. The salute was returned.

"Please make yourself comfortable, Colonel. Do you have your orders?"

"I do, sir." Kyoto retrieved the hastily written orders and the envelope from his inside tunic pocket.

The admiral read them closely, donning a pair of half glasses to do so. He was a slight man, his face furrowed with experience and the harshness of the sea. His hair was thin and gray. His uniform was white and immaculate.

Yakama handed the paperwork back to him and smiled. "You seem to be in a precarious position, Colonel."

Kyoto could not help returning the smile. "You have interpreted my assignment accurately, Admiral."

Outside the admiral's window, high over the flight deck, the night was disturbed by the passage of lights. A highly pitched scream suggested a jet aircraft taking off.

"Let us make it easier for both of us," Yakama said. "I will readily share with you the intelligence I gather. I expect you to help me understand the machinations taking place in the Diet and the ministries. In the end we will both do what we are told to do by the bureaucrats. Please sit down."

They spent over an hour together going over the information currently available. Kyoto related the attempts to be made for a solution through the United Nations. Yakama said it would be some time before his airplanes could overfly the supertanker.

Kyoto then left to seek aid in finding a bathroom, then had a bowl of very good soup in the mess, then fell into the bunk in his stateroom.

Where he was aroused twenty minutes later and sent to

the communications center. The technician seated him at a console and gave him a telephone.

"Yes, Minister?"

Asume's voice *sounded* as if it were as full of energy as his walk. "The Security Council said no!"

"I assume that negotiations are ongoing."

"Yes. No doubt, we will come to some understanding. For the moment, though, Meoshi, the task of freeing the *Maru Hokkaido* is to be given to the military."

And rightly so, Kyoto thought. He was impressed by the little he had seen of the carrier.

"The Prime Minister," Asume went on, "has sent a message to this Front for Democratic Reform saying that Japan will not bow to hooliganism, that payment for the oil will be made to an escrow account in the name of Brunei Shell, and that the tanker is to be released immediately."

"And there is no response yet?"

"None."

"Very well, sir. We are currently thirty-nine hours from the *Hokkaido*. Admiral Yakama expects to send reconnaissance flights by tomorrow morning. He also tells me that an American carrier task force is steaming in the same direction, though it is several hundred nautical miles from us."

"That is interesting, Meoshi. The Americans may be more concerned than they express."

"There are Americans in Brunei. Perhaps that is their destination."

"Perhaps. And perhaps it is a race to see who can defuse this situation first."

Kyoto did not want it to be a race. Now that he was here, he wanted the Japanese Navy to prove itself capable of protecting Japanese citizens.

Without bloodshed, hopefully, but should it be necessary, why, that was what his country had trained him to accomplish.

Sunday, March 9, 3:41 A.M.

Colonel Bakir's traitorous army was not to be deterred by the presence of foreigners.

About an hour after the border was sealed by a row of armored personnel carriers, and a covered Jeep was seen to arrive from the east, Benjamin Shaikh had walked away from his temporary headquarters and out to the highway. The army soldiers resting on two personnel carriers parked along the highway eyed him speculatively, but did nothing.

The streetlights cast yellowish light on the highway and the soldiers. They appeared sickly.

He stood at the edge of the highway, and presently the Jeep returned and drew to a stop near him. Shamin Bakir got out and walked over to him. He was a scrawny little man, puffed up by his own ego. His combat helmet appeared entirely too large for his head, a bucket resting on a skinny tree stump. His eyes were dark and shifty, and they sagged from many hours of no sleep. Or perhaps Shaikh had a new impression of the man.

"Major Shaikh."

"Colonel Bakir."

"You are not at your barracks."

"I perform my duty."

"All of us perform our duty this night, Major. What do you perceive yours to be?"

"To protect the oil field and its personnel. It is in my charter."

"The primary committee has relieved you of your duties."

"Not until I have confirmation from my commander.

And he cannot confirm while you have blocked the communications lines."

"Neither the oil field nor the workers are threatened by anyone. You have no task."

Shaikh gestured toward the personnel carriers. "You do not consider that a threat?"

"The Army of the Republic of Brunei now assumes the obligation for protection of the field. The oil company employees are in safe hands. How many of them are there?"

Shaikh did not answer. He assumed about twenty-five thousand had been unable to get out. The streets of the residential compounds—a small city of houses, dormitories, and apartment buildings that had once housed seventy thousand—now seemed all but deserted.

"You are to order your men aboard your trucks. You will drive to the port of Muara where sea transport will be arranged to return you to Britain. Your arms and equipment are to be left behind."

"My materiel is not the property of Brunei."

"It is now."

"Until I have legitimate orders from my government or from the Sultan, I cannot recognize instructions from an administration that has no legitimacy in the eyes of the world."

Bakir patted the holster clipped to his web belt. It contained an old Army Colt .45, far too large for the man's hands. "I have all of the authority I need."

"It is the authority of cowards and traitors."

Bakir's dark eyes blazed, but Shaikh turned his back and walked away, down the slight slope from the highway, back between the two houses from which he had emerged. In his peripheral vision, he saw two of his own soldiers, behind a row of sandbags, raise their rifles.

He stopped and turned back.

Bakir stood on the verge, his heavy Colt aimed at Shaikh. "As I said, cowards."

He spun around and continued walking. Bakir did not fire, but Shaikh had no illusions. The man was not constrained by honor, but by the awareness of a dozen rifles trained on him.

In the next hours, until one o'clock in the morning, an uneasy truce had prevailed. More of Bakir's troops had arrived from the east to join the encircling siege. Shaikh had moved the oil field employees to the innermost houses and dormitories of the compounds, and his Gurkhas faced the enemy from bunkers constructed between structures on the perimeter.

By two-thirty, he estimated the Brunei strength at nearly a thousand men. Shaikh's battalion had had a strength of 362, but was now at 331. He had suffered twelve dead and nineteen wounded in yesterday's skirmishes, with twelve of the wounded now at the clinic, and seven walking well enough to carry their Armalite AR-18 assault rifles.

The oil company trucks and other vehicles were lined up two streets over, aimed to the west, and ready to move should the border open up. The road to Miri Marudi was now wide open, and the last radio reports stated that there were nearly fifteen thousand people now waiting in that village for further transport west.

The Gurkha battalion vehicles and five Black Hawk helicopters were parked on the first street inside the outer row of buildings.

At two-forty-five in the morning, as he, Shrestha, Singh, and Irra sat around the coffee table in the small living room, the fusillade began. Sporadic shots escalated into a thunder of machine-gun and assault-rifle fire.

Captain Singh raced out of the house. Irra grabbed a portable radio. The radio operator began taking reports, and passing them verbally to the adjutant. Shaikh reluctantly issued orders to return fire, but methodically, without wasting ammunition.

In minutes, they had an assessment, passed to him over the portable radios from the platoon commanders.

Sergeant Major Irra said, "They have positioned themselves so as to fire on our fortifications at oblique angles. They hope that stray rounds will not penetrate to the interior, hitting foreigners."

Casualty reports were already coming in.

"In all of our planning, Sergeant Major, why did we not anticipate a siege of the residential compounds?"

"I suppose, Major, because it is such a ludicrous thought. We know it will never happen."

"That is true. We will not hold for long."

"I think not, sir."

Most of their weaponry was of the .223 caliber AR-18 variety, with a few 7.62-millimeter M-60 machine guns. There were a half dozen antitank rockets available, as well as rocket-propelled grenade launchers. Bakir's forces had heavy machine guns mounted on the personnel carriers, and his assault weapons were the older M-16s firing NATO 7.62-millimeter bullets.

By three-thirty in the morning, the toll was mounting. Two armed Huey helicopters had joined the Brunei assault and were circling the perimeter, firing on his positions.

Shrestha came across the room and sat down beside him. "Thirty-seven killed, Major. I have moved fifty-eight wounded to a dormitory."

A fourth of his command out of action.

"What we need," Irra said, "are some armored personnel carriers. I propose that we acquire the seven blocking the road to Miri Marudi."

"An excellent suggestion," Shaikh commended, and they spent ten minutes outlining their course of action.

At three-forty, Shaikh sent runners to notify all positions, as well as the foremen among the foreign oil workers. He would not risk the radio, in the event that Bakir was monitoring the frequencies.

Sergeant Major Irra and a handpicked squad of twenty men, stripped to only essential gear and the antitank rockets, disappeared into the shadows, running westward between the darkened buildings. A minute later, the pilots and their crews appeared from the house next door, crossed the yard, and climbed into their helicopters, where they would wait for his signal.

Two minutes after that, one pilot ran up to where Shaikh waited beside the front door and told him, "The machine is damaged by fire, sir."

"Abandon it. Disperse your crew in the other helicopters."

"Yes, sir."

The waiting was excruciating. He thought of all that would go wrong in order to get it out of his mind quickly. Despite his cautions, the oil workers could not move in silence. Under the steady resonance of gunfire, he heard them yelling to each other in the next street, their diesel and gas-engined trucks starting ahead of schedule. He would be leaving nearly twenty-one thousand behind, but he did not have transport for more, and Bakir had demonstrated for the past hour that he would avoid harming them if he could.

He held a portable radio to his ear, waiting for word.

It came.

"Cobra."

Irra and his squad were through the Brunei line at the border, hopefully without being seen.

Six minutes later, "Cobra Two."

An unfortunate number of Bruneians had succumbed to the *kukri*, their throats opened from ear to ear. The

Gurkha Battalion now owned six or seven personnel carriers.

Switching to another frequency, Shaikh spoke into the radio, "Execute Waltzing Mathilda. Now."

The General Electric turboshafts of the Black Hawks began to whine. His headquarters staff dashed out of the door beside him, carrying records and radio equipment; Captain Shrestha the last to exit. They ran for their assigned seats on the helicopters.

Down the street behind the helicopters, two-and-a-half-ton trucks, tankers, jeeps, and weapons carriers roared to life.

His soldiers suddenly emerged from the shadows between houses, running for the trucks, burdened by their equipment.

Shaikh crossed the yard and climbed into Tiger Three, dodging under the barrel of the M-60 machine gun manned by one of the door gunners. He tossed his cap aside and pulled on a headset.

At the far west end of the compound, there was a change in the cacophony of the night. Two . . . three . . . four, five . . . six distinct detonations, followed by a series of spine-jarring explosions. Irra's antitank rockets had found targets in Bruneian personnel carriers. From behind. There would be shock among Bruneian troops. The whole sense of the battle shifted westward. There was a gap in Bakir's perimeter.

"Now!" he called to the pilot.

Tiger Three lifted off, followed quickly by the remaining three helicopters.

As they cleared the roofs of the houses surrounding them, they were met with a barrage of fire from the ground. The metal skin pinged with hits.

The door gunners opened up. The throaty roar of the

M-60s stung his eardrums. Spent cartridges clattered against the deck.

A Huey zoomed in from the north, its guns blazing whitely. The gunner to Shaikh's left swung his weapon toward it, green tracers ripping the night apart.

Behind them, Tiger Two erupted in flame and spun away, crashing into the roof of an apartment building.

The Huey blossomed in orange-yellow, the concussion of the explosion rolling across the earth. Nose down, it dove straight into the street they had just vacated, broke apart like an eggshell, and ejected fragments of aluminum and chunks of rotors into the nearby buildings.

Then they were clear, circling around to the south, the door gunners pouring molten heat down on Bakir's personnel carriers and dispersed troops.

Shaikh bent forward over his copilot's shoulder, searching through the windscreen.

The oil company trucks were on the move on the second street, slowly gaining momentum. On the near street, his own vehicles were starting to move, already turning into side streets, crossing the block to join with the oil trucks. They would infiltrate the column, spacing themselves among the foreign workers. Bakir would not fire on them.

Seconds later, the Black Hawks—now thoroughly separated for improved safety—reached the west end of the compound at two thousand feet of altitude. Looking down, he could see Irra's seven . . . no, six personnel carriers slicing up the Bruneian lines, opening the road to the west. They wheeled left and right, lighting the darkness with the ferocious fire of their machine guns. Backed, turned, raced ahead, cutting formations into ragged pieces. Grenade explosions peppered the lines. At least twelve rebel vehicles were in flames. Bruneian soldiers were running in fear, dropping their weapons, intent upon escaping the hell that Irra had created.

The first of the oil trucks, a flatbed semi-truck with nearly two hundred men clinging to the bed and to each other, flashed on its headlights and sped out of the compound, gaining the road, climbing into the jungle. On its heels came a dump truck, also packed with men. Then a weapons carrier loaded with Gurkhas who fired their assault rifles to either side. More followed, picking up speed, clearing the compound.

Almost fifty vehicles.

Shaikh silently urged them to greater speed.

"Huey!" shouted the pilot, dipping the Black Hawk so suddenly that Shaikh went to his knees.

Streaks of tracer fire went over their heads as the Sikorsky dove, twisting into a tight turn. Shaikh was thrown off-balance and smashed into the legs of the door gunner. Though the gunner was firmly restrained by his harness, Shaikh automatically grabbed him around the legs, to keep him from being tossed out of the helicopter.

As he scrambled to regain his feet, he heard the pilot calling, "Tiger Six! Tiger Six!"

"We have him, Three."

Shaikh looked out the side door to see another Black Hawk, defined against the night sky by its exhaust and muzzle flashes, screaming into a wide turn, facing off against the Huey.

Which decided valor lay in turning away, and it did.

But too late. Lances of fire found its vitals and it exploded brightly in the sky, then tumbled, spinning end over end across the border to crash in the jungle.

"Very nice, Six," his pilot radioed.

The three Black Hawks, now alone in the skies over Kuala Belait, orbited the west end, delivering withering fire on Bakir's forces, coordinating with Irra's ground attack. They were careful to avoid the center of the compound, where twenty thousand workers were congregated, and Bakir's soldiers were in disarray, retreating to the east as rapidly as their legs and their damaged vehicles would allow.

It took eleven minutes. When the last truck had crossed the border, Shaikh tapped the copilot on the shoulder and was handed the microphone.

"Lion Six, Lion One."

"Six."

"Execute Tango."

"Done."

With the Black Hawks flying cover, Irra's vehicles, now only five, raced eastward on the highway, creating consternation in Bakir's units, but essentially ignoring them. Irra bypassed the compounds, his camouflage-decorated personnel carriers speeding along at forty-five kilometers per hour, and just short of the GlobeTech supply compound, turned south on a dirt road that led past the hospital.

And then into the rain forest.

The Black Hawks followed along.

Sunday, March 9, 4:15 A.M.

The ship was dead in the water, or nearly so. Only mild propulsion was allowed so that the *Maru Hokkaido* could maintain her headway.

Maki Hirosiuta did not think the tanker had drifted more than a couple kilometers in the twenty-eight hours she had been hostage to the thugs who reigned over his bridge.

He completed his morning ritual of shaving and cleaning, then stepped out of his bathroom into the cabin. As he donned a fresh uniform, he walked aft to look through the stern porthole. The naval gunboat tethered to the tanker by a long line still trailed behind. He thought there were only three crewmen aboard her.

There were at least fifteen of them on board the tanker. His engineering officer had managed to convey the message that two remained in the engine room, watching over the few men allowed to work there. The rest of the crew was confined to their dormitory rooms, and the officers to the wardroom or their staterooms. Armed guards stood watch over them.

Setting his uniform hat squarely on his head, he opened the door to his cabin and stepped into the corridor. One of his captors, his face swarthy with whiskers and his naval uniform filthy with perspiration and grime, sat in a chair against the far wall, tilted back against the wall. Hirosiuta ignored him and crossed the corridor to enter the first officer's cabin.

Yaguchi was in his bunk, and at the sound of the door, his eyes glanced quickly toward Hirosiuta, then relaxed. The man's leg was encased in plaster, set by the ship's doctor. The left arm, broken at the forearm, was in a similar cast. The fingers of his right hand were trapped by a fiberglass splint. His face wore the bluish-black bruises inflicted by the men who had located him—and the radio—in the lifeboat. His jaw was wired shut by the doctor, broken in two places by gun butts.

Hirosiuta picked up the jug of ice water and replenished the glass with the bent straw.

"You are comfortable?"

The first officer nodded. He would not admit to discomfort, anyway.

Bending over the bed, Hirosiuta helped to raise the man's head, slipped one of the pain capsules between his lips, and held the glass for him as he sipped through the straw.

"It should not be much longer, First Officer. I imagine negotiations are well along."

Another nod, but the eyes did not believe him.

The captain gently lowered his head to the pillow and said, "I will be back to see you a little later."

He left the cabin and walked forward to the bridge. Hirosiuta was allowed a limited range of free movement simply because he assumed it as his right. The guards watched him closely but did not interfere with his circuit of his cabin, Yaguchi's cabin, or the bridge.

He entered it to find Captain Dyg Thambipillai sitting in Hirosiuta's chair, and an armed guard standing near the port-wing door. The Brunei captain was dressed in faded, wrinkled, and creased khakis, the armpits darkened. He could see the sun-stained spots on the man's collar, where an ensign's insignia had once been placed. A lieutenant's bars now tried to cover the evidence, but were pinned inexpertly. Thambipillai had promoted himself, possibly after killing his lieutenant.

The man's face was coated with whiskers and a drip line of dirt trapped in perspiration crossed his brow. He set a fine example of morale for his men.

Hirosiuta ignored him and stopped briefly over the bloodstains darkened on the antiskid surface of the deck. He prayed to his ancestors for the soul of the boatswain's mate.

Then he scanned the instrument clusters along the forward bulkhead, then the lightening horizon. There were no navigation lights in sight. He went aft to the radar room, which was uninhabited, but which still had an active radar, the scan moving slowly around the screen. He counted seven ships, all of unknown classification or tonnage, lying motionless beyond sight, about forty kilometers away. The radar was set to the 120-kilometer scan, and he saw no other vessels in the vicinity.

The waiting ships were there, either to help or to salvage the remains, though crude oil was notoriously difficult to salvage.

When he turned back, the pirate Thambipillai was standing in the curtained doorway.

"I am going below."

"What for?"

"To see that my men receive their breakfasts. You would do well to do the same, Captain. On your own boat."

Thambipillai grinned, revealing a blackened tooth. "You should just relax, Captain Hirosiuta. It will be another long day, I think."

Hirosiuta had been given no clue as to the reason for their detention. He assumed there were problems in Brunei, initiated with the explosions on the two platforms, but Thambipillai refused to say what role the *Maru Hokkaido* played in those events, and radio and television sets throughout the ship had been confiscated or destroyed.

The only certainty—he prayed that it was a certainty—was that Yaguchi's emergency message transmitted from the lifeboat had gotten out, or the company had received his own message reporting the boarding, and that the government was now working for their release. The idle ships waiting over the horizon suggested that the outside world knew a little of their predicament. Until something happened, however, Maki Hirosiuta's only course was to watch over his crew's and his ship's safety.

Despite the pig who blocked the doorway.

Hirosiuta advanced on him, and the man backed out of the doorway and let him through.

Given enough time, Hirosiuta thought it possible that he could eventually cow this devil's dog.

Sunday, March 9, 6:17 A.M.

By dawn, the temperature in the cramped room of two dozen bunkbeds was already rising. With the steel bulkheads, the heat was going to be oppressive later in the day.

The men imprisoned within the room had access to a bathroom, and therefore, water, but not much else. There was light from overhead bulbs, though no windows to allow vision or a breeze.

Mohammed Hassanal went to the steel door, which was locked from the outside, and banged on it with his fist. The reverberations ran around the room. Every movement on the platform seemed to result in a clank or a clink.

Ten minutes went by before the door pulled open and Tan Hashim stood in it, holding his semiautomatic pistol at the ready.

"I want food delivered here immediately," Hassanal said.

"You will get food when I am ready to give it," Hashim said. His eyes would not meet Hassanal's.

"And I want to see the women."

"You may never see your women again, if you do not cease making demands. I am not your slave."

"But you will be my prisoner. I will execute you personally."

The man would still not look him in the eyes, not as Padang would. Hassanal took that as a sign that the total of the man's courage rested in the Beretta pistol.

"You will also go to the infirmary and bring me a medical kit. The defense minister is in pain, and his fever is high. Should he die, you will follow."

"That—"

"Either at my command or Padang's. It is up to you."

Hashim stepped back and the door slammed in his face.

He walked over to the bunk where Suliaman had been

placed and looked down on his cousin and his friend. He was afraid the wound of the knee had been dressed inexpertly. It no longer bled, but it was trapped in a splint that held his leg immobile. Hassanal did not know about things medical, but feared that a great deal of reconstruction would be necessary.

"Hold on, Cousin. They will bring something."

"Certainly they will," Suliaman said. "It is your charm that is so endearing."

Hassanal smiled, and Suliaman tried to smile. His skin was hot to the touch, though, and the pain was revealed in his eyes. So much that he had once enjoyed of life would be no more.

Hassanal called to one of the boys to replace the wet cloth that was draped over Hamzah's forehead. He looked over to the Sultan, who was still in his bed, suffering a great depression. He barely spoke.

Gritting his teeth, Suliaman said, "It is not knowing that is so difficult."

Inclining his head in agreement, Hassanal asked, "I have spent the night wondering just who would align himself with Padang. Your generals?"

"I think not. It would be Bakir, a thief of some talent."

"You knew of this?"

"Suspected. I should have fired the man."

"Possibly. If Bakir is a conspirator, he will have met his match in Benjamin Shaikh."

"Can Shaikh do anything? Given his charge?"

"If pushed far enough, he will. Then, there are the foreigners."

He was interrupted by the banging of the door. A cardboard box was shoved inside, and the door was slammed shut again.

Crossing to pick it up, he pawed through the box. Someone had dumped what looked appropriate in the infirmary into the box. Bandages, Pepto-Bismol, aspirin, sulfa powder. Nothing antibacterial, nothing even approaching the power of morphine.

Kneeling on the floor next to Suliaman, he said, "My best offer is aspirin."

"I will take four."

When they had been administered, Suliaman said, "You spoke of the foreigners."

"Yes. If we are to hope for international assistance, we must also hope that many were killed."

"True. I will pray that it is so."

Sunday, March 9, 6:58 A.M.

The country is ours!" Shamin Bakir declared over the radio.

Li Sen listened closely, his pleasure displayed on his face, he thought.

Omar Padang, who was operating the radio in the police communications room, asked, "The Gurkhas?"

"They fled over the border."

"Casualties?"

Li Sen was most interested in casualties. From the beginning, his greatest reservations arose over the need for violence.

"Among the Gurkhas, I do not know," Bakir said. "They took their wounded with them. We have located about thirty killed in the action."

Li winced.

"And your own?" Padang asked.

"I do not yet know the numbers. A few."

"What of the foreigners?"

"Several have injuries, but not incurred from the battle. Not one was killed, Omar. As I predicted."

Padang did not react to the successful forecast. "How many foreigners are still here?"

"That is difficult to tell, there are so many. I judge forty or forty-five thousand."

Padang smiled at him, and Li was pleased. Enough to operate the oil field at reduced production, which was the objective.

Also in the room were Peng Ziyang and Lim Siddiqui, and their faces were also wreathed in triumph.

"Send me one of your helicopters immediately," Padang ordered. "I want to see for myself."

"That is not possible."

"Why not?"

"Of the ten assigned to the air wing, two fled to the west yesterday. Two are out of service for lack of parts, two are momentarily grounded, and four have been lost in action."

Padang frowned. "You captured the Gurkha helicopters?"

"Two were destroyed," Bakir said with great fervor, "one is not operational, and three escaped."

Padang's frown deepened, raising Li's level of concern.

"What is your deployment?"

"I have left a guard detail at the border, set a dozen roving patrols, and ordered the balance to return to the barracks. The foreigners will see little of us, and their confidence will soon be restored."

"I will talk to you later," Padang said and pushed the microphone away.

"Exactly what we hoped for," Li said. "Now, we must release the foreigners at the hotels. We will explain that life goes on as before."

"Not just yet," the new minister of security argued. "I will go to the airport and commandeer one of the Sultan's aircraft. I want to see Kuala Belait for myself."

"You do not trust Bakir?"

"He came to us, did he not?"

Sunday, March 9, 7:44 A.M.

When the Dauphin had begun to burn in earnest, and the Huey had slipped away over the western fence, Koehler shoved himself off of Sherry, stood up, and reached down to pull her to her feet.

"Hon?"

"I'm all right. Scared to death."

"Everyone else?"

There were no injuries among his six charges.

Morris looked out at the burning hulk and said, "Those shits! I loved that chopper."

"Jesus Christ!" Monica Davis said. "That was our way out."

"Let's not give up too early." He turned to a supply tech. "Can you crawl up on the roof and find out what you can see?"

"Sure thing, boss."

The man slipped past Koehler and went out the door.

He was back eight minutes later. "Difficult to tell in the dark, but I think they're surrounding the residences. I bet my left . . . that is, I'm sure they cut off the border."

That's what Koehler would have done in Bakir's place.

"Okay, we're taking Interstate Ten."

"Where's that?" Avery asked.

"I don't know, but it doesn't follow the coast." Kelly issued a rapid set of orders.

There was some debate when it came to the suitcases. Monica finally agreed to discard one of hers. Sherry repacked hers and Kelly's into one case. The rest of the

men were already down to what they had with them. Their
belongings were still in their apartments.

"Food. Everything edible we can find. Food takes prece-
dence over anything else. Water. Gas. See how many jerry
cans we can rustle up. We want the radio, Slim, along with
the antenna. Batteries. Let's go, everyone."

They loaded the roof of the Explorer. The techs drilled
holes in the skin to attach bungee cords holding the bag-
gage, cans, boxes, and a few tarpaulins in place. In the back,
Avery carefully packed the radio and two spare automobile
batteries. Sacks and boxes of foodstuffs were jammed everywhere.

Koehler sent one of the techs off with a pair of wire
cutters to open a passage in the back fence. He grabbed
a hammer and walked around the Ford smashing the tail-
lights, the license-plate light, and the single remaining
parking light in front. He removed the courtesy lights from
the interior.

If he couldn't have headlights, anyway, he didn't want
to have any observer spot them by virtue of stepping on
the brakes or opening a door. The Explorer was a dark
blue, and that was helpful.

Avery went back inside and came out with his centerfolds.

"Hell, Slim," Morris told him. "I have to leave my toys
behind."

"I don't."

Koehler checked the tires, then they crawled in, a feat
in social engineering. There were six of them, three in
front and three in the backseat.

The engine cranked on the first try, and none of the
idiot lights warned him of dire circumstances. Dropping
the gearshift into drive, he started across the yard. It was
difficult to see once he got out of the range of light from
the smoldering helicopter.

"I wish to hell we had some firepower," Morris said. He was in the right bucket seat, on the other side of Sherry, because he was so large.

Koehler didn't necessarily want anything that might draw fire toward Sherry and Monica, but he said, "We may run into something along the way. Hold on, everyone!"

He drove slowly through the gap in the fence, and the front of the truck dropped into the drainage ditch that surrounded the compound. Kicking in the four-wheel drive, he bucked on through the ditch, then was running free across a weed-choked field.

Through his broken side window, he heard a few shots fired. Token resistance from someone.

"Sinkhole," Morris called out. He was leaning forward, his hands on the dash, trying to see through the lacework of the windshield.

Koehler skirted the hole on the right, then found a road. They passed the hospital, which was fully lighted. Dozens of people stood outside, looking toward the coast, wondering what the hell was going on. He decided against stopping to tell them.

Past the hospital, he turned left onto a road that headed south into the jungle. He had never taken it and didn't know what lay ahead, except that it was better than what was behind them.

"I sure wish one of you guys had had enough foresight to bring a map," Kelly said.

"Got the best damned little map you ever wanted locked in my memory," Morris said.

"How's your memory?"

"Not so hot, lately."

The instant he penetrated the jungle, the world turned blacker than Avery's coffee. He couldn't see five feet beyond the hood. He let the truck growl along in low gear.

"Way I see it," Kelly told them, "we're about a mile from the border, going parallel with it."

"But the border curves to the southeast," Sherry said.

"True. So does the road."

"And we get farther and farther away from Miri Marudi as we go," Avery added from the backseat.

"We'll get down the road aways, curl up for the night, then see if we can't find a trail through the jungle that heads somewhere in the direction of Sarawak."

"Fine idea," Morris said, as if he didn't believe it was fine at all.

In fact, they quit going down the road. A grade of about ten percent suddenly appeared, and Koehler shoved the accelerator down to take it.

The road abruptly turned left, and he ran off of it into a tree.

"This ain't working so hot," Avery said.

Koehler shoved the shift into park and got out. Morris found a flashlight on the floor and got out with him.

On the left front, they found the dangling parking light, and with a penknife, he got the lens off, retrieved the bulb, then took it to the left side and inserted it in the socket of the light he had broken out.

When he switched the light switch on, he had one dim parking light on the front.

"Looks like a million damned candlepower to me," Morris said.

They got under way again, and now he had enough light to keep the truck on the road.

For all that was worth.

It narrowed. The center disappeared, leaving two ruts that saw traffic once in every two blue moons. Tendrils of vines hanging from the trees overhead reached for the windshield, scraped over the cargo loaded on top. Branches along the sides grabbed for the mirrors. Their passage alarmed the birds. Parrots cackled. Monkeys chirped.

Sherry wasn't successful in stifling a cry when the right front fender caromed off a tree, and a green snake dropped on the hood from above. It was about four feet long and four inches in diameter, and was just as surprised to be on the warm hood as Koehler was to have it there.

He slammed on the brakes, the snake slid forward off the hood, and he hit the gas, hoping he ran over it.

"Friendly cuss, wasn't he?" Morris said.

"I'm not getting out of this truck," Davis said, "until we reach Paris."

"Paris?"

"Or wherever."

"Monica," Avery told her, "you need to attend the Slim Avery School of Geography."

Four hours later, after midnight, they were twenty-two miles back into the jungle, according to the odometer, which was still working. What they found was the remains of a village, deserted for who knew how long, and almost reclaimed by the forest. It had been four families big, with the remnants of four thatched huts, one still partially standing.

"What do you think?" Kelly asked anyone.

"Not Hilton, but at least Holiday Inn," Morris said. "I'll vote in favor."

"I'm not getting out of the truck until there aren't any snakes in a mile," Sherry said.

There were probably a few thousand snakes *per* mile, but he parked the truck up against the hut, and the men crawled out with flashlights. Morris found a stick and rattled the soft walls of the hut, and damned if a couple snakes didn't slither away into the dark. He quickly shifted his light away from a glistening, shimmery body so the women wouldn't see.

Koehler appreciated that.

Avery restored a few stones to an ancient fire pit and soon had a fire going. With a couple tarps thrown on the ground inside the open doorway of the hut, the women finally ventured forth.

"I don't like this a damned bit," Monica said.

"Nonsense," Avery told her. "Listen to the sounds of nature."

"That's particularly what I don't like."

There were some big cats on the island of Borneo— leopards—but Koehler didn't know if they ranged this far north. Orangutans and gibbons stayed back in the darkness of the jungle and called out their outrage. The birds and insects made a constant chittering moan.

"Think about other things," Koehler suggested.

"Or staying busy," Sherry said. "Frank, bring your light."

Morris opened the tailgate for her and held the light while she and Monica made up sandwiches. They would have to use up the bologna and roast beef in the cooler soon, because what little ice they had had already melted.

The less-than-cheery group sat around in the hut and drank warm root beer and ate their sandwiches.

By two o'clock in the morning, everyone was sleeping except Koehler and Morris. Morris had offered to stand guard, and Koehler was too keyed up to sleep. He worried about his people trapped in Kuala Belait.

He went out and opened the back door of the Ford and sat down on the seat. Morris was sitting sideways in the front, with the door open.

"I used to think, Kelly, that Kuwait was not the most promising place to be in. This has got it all beat to hell."

"Couple days, we'll drive down to the capital and find the sunshine and the Sultan smiling on us."

"Your optimism has to reach an end soon."

"Got a flashlight up there?"

Morris passed him a six-cell job, and Koehler stood up and explored the edges of the clearing around the village. The jungle was so tangled it was impenetrable. And it was advancing. He felt like a fly in a Venus flytrap.

The road they had come in on, and which was now aimed almost due east, continued on through the village, and he followed it for a while, climbing a steep slope, working the light from side to side, to scare back into the jungle whatever might need scaring.

And a hundred yards up the ruts, he found an intersection. The little-used road T-ed into a slightly wider, slightly more travelled pair of ruts. He aimed the flashlight north and saw that, within a few yards, the road again turned east, after it got around a huge boulder blocking the way dead ahead of him.

To the right, it descended a shallow slope toward the south, toward Sarawak, and he turned that way and followed it for a while.

Something growled.

It was nothing he was familiar with, and he stopped dead still and waited.

Whatever it was didn't repeat the invitation, and Koehler went on.

Another couple hundred feet, the road curving west, he found a large clearing. Someone had once tried to grow something there. Maybe something illicit. Now, though, it was abandoned and overgrown with ground cover.

He moved the light slowly around the perimeter. Caught a few pairs of eyes in the trees and hoped they were birds.

He turned around and walked back, thinking about the possibilities of following this road in the morning and maybe ending up somewhere in Sarawak. As soon as he could get Sherry and Monica to safety, he and Frank could locate Foster's chopper—if he had made it to Kuching and back—and scoot back to Kuala Belait and check on the GlobeTech people.

He reached the Explorer to find Morris nodding.

"Go catch a couple hours, Frank."

"I was just trying to get your sympathy."

"You got it."

Morris stood, stepped around the open door, and sprawled out on the rear seat. Koehler took his place behind the wheel.

By four o'clock in the morning, he had pretty much hashed over his options, which were few, and was aware that the clearing was getting a bit lighter. He looked up to see a quarter-moon shining through the small gap in the three-tiered jungle canopy.

By four-ten, he was aware of turboshafts humming and rotors thropping. They were getting closer. He picked up the flashlight and stepped out of his seat.

Morris awoke at the sound, a military habit, and slid out of the truck to stand next to him.

"You don't think these guys would want us bad enough to hunt us down, do you, Navy?"

"Nah. Those sound like Hueys to you?"

Morris cocked his head. "Nope. Black Hawks, I'll bet you."

They were. The first silhouette crossed the sliver of moon, and Koehler immediately raised the flashlight and began to blink it. Morse code for G-U-R-K-H-A.

The first helicopter missed it, but the second went into a hover.

Koehler tapped out, W-A-I-T.

He started running up the road.

"Where the hell—" Morris called after him.

"Wait here."

At the intersection, he slipped as he made a running turn, regained his feet, and ran down to the clearing. He stood in the middle of it, and raised his light to the sky again.

A minute later, the nose of a Black Hawk advanced over the edge of the canopy, and its landing lights snicked on, all but blinding Koehler.

He backed away to the edge of the clearing and watched the first chopper settle in tentatively. It lowered through the hole in the canopy, slipped sideways to within a few feet of rotor clearance at one side, then eased toward the ground. Its engine wound down as the second helicopter appeared over the edge of the jungle and repeated the performance.

When the third aircraft was on the ground, a magical feat given the slim clearances available for it, and its rotors were dying, Koehler stepped forward into the nearly dark clearing and turned his light on himself.

Personal ID, in case they hadn't identified him in the landing lights.

"Good morning, Kelly," Benjamin Shaikh said, coming out of the dark. He carried a flashlight, too, and he turned it on, aimed at the ground.

"This is a hell of a coincidence, Major."

"Not really. We knew the clearing was here. It would have taken longer to find it without your help."

Koehler looked at the shadows of men slipping from the helicopters and coming up behind the major.

"This is all you've got left?"

"Except for Sergeant Major Irra, who should be arriving shortly."

"What the hell happened?"

"I will tell you, but the short story is that the country is lost."

"Lost?"

"Though not for long. We will take it back."

"With what? A couple dozen men?"

"More than enough, I assure you."

"I wish you luck. I just want to get my people to Miri Marudi."

"In the morning, we will fly you there."

Koehler felt a great weight lifted off his shoulders. And his heart.

Saturday, March 8, 9:36 P.M.

Christian Drieser had been pleasantly surprised by the gift the guy in research had sent him in midmorning. It was a transcribed version of a long radio message picked up by the State Department communications expert in Kuching. Directed to an oil company based in Houston by their field manager, Koehler, it nicely detailed some of what was happening in Brunei. Drieser liked the fact that Koehler had the presence of mind to copy the Embassy.

Parts of it were indecipherable as a result of radio static at some point in its transmission or in the relay of the tape, and there were quite a few bracketed blanks: [INDECIPHERABLE]. Still, it provided confirmation on several points with information already captured from ham radio and other sources.

In fact, Koehler's message had already had an impact. With confirmation from at least three sources relative to the deaths of foreign nationals during the uprising, the Secretary had gone to the UN Ambassador and the President, and a special meeting of the UN Security Council at three o'clock had produced a resolution condemning the manner in which the Front for Democratic Reform had accomplished its coup.

No big deal, really, but it might put the FDR on notice that they were being watched. If they got the message.

Communications with the country had not yet been reestablished, but they had opened a line long enough to get off a message to Japan, and maybe someone was watching a TV. They were also being bombarded by messages, as yet unanswered, by every government with a diplomatic mission in the country. No embassy or consulate had been heard from since the start of the revolt.

The other thing he had gotten from Koehler was names. Li Sen, matching the Japanese letter of demand as the Provisional President. Omar Padang. Army Colonel Bakir, with no first name.

Calls to DOD and CIA had produced slim dossiers on Omar Padang and Shamin Bakir. There was nothing on Li Sen. No one in an intelligence capacity had ever heard of him before.

Omar Padang's file was unremarkable. His education: none beyond public school. A few police seminars. Rose steadily through the ranks to become the country's chief law-enforcement officer. He was well-regarded by the Sultan and his family. Nothing about his trustworthiness, but Drieser guessed that had been established.

Colonel Shamin Bakir was similar. He had a university degree, and he had once participated in the U.S. Army's Ranger training at Fort Benning, Georgia, but otherwise, his career had been almost lackluster. Decent comments from fellow officers. Someone—an embassy source?—had once questioned his standard of living. His house was too big, his car too exotic—a Jaguar—for his military pay and allowances.

The royal land forces were supposed to have two generals in charge, but Drieser suspected they were now former generals. Maybe Bakir's payoff would be a promotion. Some colonels just couldn't wait to be called general.

And maybe Padang was enthralled with the title of Minister of Security.

Koehler's report also detailed the evacuation of foreign

workers, confirmed by NSA satellite pictures that were stacked on Drieser's desk. The high-resolution shots bespoke a royal screwup. At the time of the shots, just after midnight, all of the marine craft were clear of the field, but the land routes were confused with gridlocked or mired-down convoys. That was how the analysts interpreted the infrared pictures, anyway. And the rebels had closed off the border. There were dozens of vehicles and thousands of people still confined to the residential areas of Kuala Belait. It would be several hours before he received a later set of pictures, but Drieser figured this was one hell of a large hostage situation. The one on the *Maru Hokkaido* paled by comparison.

Of importance, Drieser thought, was Koehler's description of breaking the naval blockade. He didn't say so, but the perspective suggested that Koehler was present, or damned close, when it happened. Two things to be learned here: Li Sen likely had some policy against harming foreigners, and Koehler might be useful.

Drieser had missed the sun going down, and he didn't even look at his watch until Judy Blalock barged through his door carrying a pizza box.

"Oh, God! You missed your dinner."

"So did you," she said.

"I hope it's a large."

"With about ten toppings."

She opened the box on his desk, and the aroma made him feel faint. Pepperoni, sausage, Canadian bacon, pineapple, onions, green peppers, olives. All his favorites in one place at the same time.

"I missed lunch, too," he said.

She pulled up a chair, tossed a sheaf of papers in front of him, then levered a wedge of pizza for herself.

He did the same. "What's the list?"

"What I've been working on all day."

"Already?"

"I'm a project person, Chris."

"What'd you find?" He bit into his slice. Heaven!

"We had something over thirty-seven thousand Americans in Brunei. Of those, DOD showed an amazing fifty-one hundred with previous active duty in the armed forces."

"Five thousand!"

"Right. These are all rough-and-tough oilmen, so it's not so surprising. Then I asked them to run the list again, weeding out the names of anyone who had served at less than E-5 pay grade. I thought you'd want someone who had been an NCO or officer."

"Good girl."

"Woman."

She sure was.

"Woman. Good."

"That's what you've got there. Sixteen officers and forty-seven enlisted. All the services represented. Nine are still in the active reserves."

Chewing, he picked up the listing. Alphabetical, with a short synopsis of each man's service. He flipped a couple pages and found it.

"Koehler, Kelly Michael. Lieutenant Commander, ONI. Hot damn! He's with Intelligence."

"The one with the radio report," she said.

"Right."

The synopsis suggested Drieser might have been a little too optimistic. Koehler was a hotshit chopper pilot. His assignment to ONI came after an intelligence course, but he'd never been operational in that occupational specialty.

But he liked what he'd seen of Koehler's thinking.

He grabbed the secure phone and punched the button for the Chief of Naval Operations in the Pentagon. Saturday, but the military always had a duty man on board.

"CNO's office, Lieutenant Magnuson."

"Drieser at State. Who's OD?"

"Captain Works."

"Let me talk to him."

A few heartbeats. "Captain Works, Mr. Drieser. What can I do for you?"

"Make a couple calls. Verify who I am, then call me back."

"Yes, sir."

He hung up.

Fifteen minutes went by, in which he was careful to allow Blalock half of the pizza. She went out and found Cokes for them.

The phone rang and he got it before it stopped buzzing.

"Drieser."

"Got a reading on you, Mr. Undersecretary. Checked with the CNO and the DCI's office. What can I do for you?"

"I think I've got an intelligence asset in Brunei, if he's still there. He's one of yours." Drieser read off the name, rank, and serial number. "I'd like to talk to whoever is in charge of that task force you've got steaming to the south."

"We secure?"

"I am."

"That's Admiral Harold Harned. Task Force Seven-One. The *Eisenhower* is the centerpiece."

"How far are they from Brunei?"

"Hmm. I haven't checked on it in quite a while, but probably thirty, thirty-six hours."

"If he got a plane in the air, he could reach Koehler by radio, right?"

"Maybe. Depends on conditions. But given the blackout down there, you've got a nice lead. You want to activate this Koehler?"

"Maybe he doesn't want to be activated."

"All it takes is a nod from the CNO."

"Let's see if we can reach him first."

"I'll contact Harned, Mr. Drieser, then have him call you."

He put the phone down. "Love those satellites, Judy."

"One of those ten-thousand-mile calls, huh?"

"Somewhere around there."

Another fifteen minutes went by. The phone buzzed.

"Nighttime, your time, Mr. Undersecretary."

"Chris is easier, Admiral."

"Some people call me Hap. The rest of 'em call me an SOB."

"I'll stick with Hap."

"Sounds like you've found someone who is about to become a member of my command."

"If he's still there. Do you think you can contact him?"

"We're getting ready to launch an E-2 Hawkeye. If he's listening, or if he's broadcasting, we'll find him. You mind my asking your role in this?"

"I advise the Secretary, and he's working with the UN ambassador."

"This going to become a UN issue, Chris?"

"This morning, I'd have said no. With some of the reports we're getting now, I'd say maybe. If it does, because of your location, Hap, you're likely to be in the middle of it."

"Are we trying to beat the Japanese? From a diplomatic point of view, of course?"

"Have they got a presence?"

Harned waited a couple moments before responding. "The *Akagi* and her escorts are about two hundred nautical miles away. They're steering for the *Maru Hokkaido*."

"Interesting. Maybe they don't need us."

"I'd hate to see a war get started. Over a tanker of oil. Do you know what's happening in Brunei?"

Drieser read Koehler's report verbatim, including the indecipherable. "I can send you a copy."

"That's okay. I'm taping this. I think you're right, though. Koehler might be useful."

"I'd like to stay in touch, Hap."

"I'll see that you get anything Koehler supplies us. My thanks for the help, Chris."

Drieser hung up, feeling as if he'd finally accomplished something worthwhile for the day.

"You look smug," Blalock said.

"I feel smug, but it took your help."

Nine

When Padang stepped from the Aèrospatiale Gazelle he had commandeered from Conoco's fleet, Shamin Bakir was wearing stars.

Surrounded by seven of his staff officers, Bakir stood in the dust of the field near the docks and saluted as Padang approached him. The slightly built man was almost ludicrous in his spit-shined paratrooper boots—dust spattered—with the pant legs bloused over them. The Colt .45 in its polished holster jutted from his slim hips like an unnecessary growth.

Padang did not return the salute. He said, "Take them off."

Bakir's rigid arm sagged back to his side. "What? I was promised—"

"Now, Colonel! When the primary committee takes

action, you will be notified. But you will not promote yourself."

Padang watched Bakir's hostile eyes as the man reached up to unclip the insignia pins under his collar. It was just like this oaf to take initiative on things that did not matter.

He and his junior officers had stood in the field for forty minutes when Padang's helicopter did not land as scheduled and instead took a leisurely tour of Kuala Belait from the air. Padang was not pleased by what he had seen, particularly of the men lounging on the grass and the patios of the residential housing. They appeared to be relaxed now that they were not threatened by armed troops, but Padang sensed their underlying tension. Quite obviously, none had returned to their jobs on the platforms.

"These men are not working," he told Bakir.

"Minister, certainly you saw that there is no transport. The helicopters are gone, and only a few very small boats are at the dock."

"I also do not count as high as you count, Colonel. You told me there were forty thousand workers."

"I have not touched each nose," Bakir said.

"Then you had better. If we have half the number you reported, I will be amazed."

"But—"

"I counted six helicopters parked in various compounds. You will see that they are requisitioned for your use."

"Sir, I have already armed two Bell JetRangers belonging to one of the companies and assigned them to patrolling the border. Others are being retrofitted as we speak."

"Well! Commendable, Colonel. And I will order ships moored in Muara to assist you in transport. Now, tell me about your minor battle."

"Minor? My men distinguished themselves."

"I can also count destroyed helicopters and personnel

carriers. I assume you have a casualty count that goes beyond 'a few.' "

Bakir's face did not change expression. He had little compassion for the men serving him, but that was one of his traits that Padang found acceptable. He was the same.

"Seventy-four were killed. One hundred and nineteen were wounded. That is the count from both Tutong and here."

"Major Shaikh was more formidable than you anticipated."

"They ran like the dogs they are."

"Ran where?"

"To Sarawak."

"All of them?"

"I did not see—"

"Then you had better find out. If any of those Gurkhas are in the country, they can cause trouble. By tonight, I will ask your guarantee that they are gone."

Padang spun around and climbed back into his helicopter.

Sunday, March 9, 10:12 A.M.

One of the Black Hawks had taken a low-flying reconnaissance run early in the morning and located a couple of Bell JetRangers patrolling the border. The pilot reported on the radio that the small Bells had their rear doors removed and M-60s mounted.

The Gurkha pilot was also eager to engage the Bells and eliminate them as nuisances.

Koehler had listened to the radio dialogue as Shaikh had denied the request. The major didn't want to give notice to Bakir that Gurkha choppers were still operating in Brunei. Not yet, anyway.

Koehler agreed with Shaikh, though he desperately wanted to get his women to Miri Marudi.

Shaikh promised to check the route periodically and get the GlobeTech crew out of the country as soon as he could.

In the meantime, Morris had moved the Explorer and everyone else to the larger clearing. With the three helicopters taking up most of the room, two of Irra's captured personnel carriers were left on the road, but their camouflage colors blended well with the jungle around them, and the Gurkha soldiers had further disguised the vehicles with branches and leaves cut from the forest.

Shaikh had set up his headquarters in the back of a personnel carrier parked at the edge of the clearing, but it was already too hot to sit inside the metal container. Morris, Avery, and Koehler squatted or sat on the ground near the lowered rear ramp of the APC with Shaikh, his captain, and the sergeant major. Koehler kept an eye on the Explorer where Sherry and Monica were ensconced with all the doors open. Every once in a while, Monica waved the door back and forth, as if that would get a breeze going.

They kept their eyes open for snakes, also, and Kelly was certain this group would have an early warning of any encroachment by snakes.

Radios had been set up in the personnel carrier, and the irritating jump-and-stop-and-jump-again of a radio frequency scanner added to the background chatter of birds and monkeys in the jungle. The domed canopy overhead gave them protection from eyes passing by in search aircraft. A helicopter would have to be almost directly overhead to spot them. A low-flying plane with radar might get some minor feedback off the vehicles and choppers. The likelihood seemed remote, though.

Twenty-some troopers were catching up on their rest, stretched out beneath helicopters or alongside the vehicles. The jungle wildlife didn't seem to bother them, and no one took an interest in the bright oranges, yellows, and blues of the birds and parrots flitting around the edge of the clearing.

Sergeant Major Suraj Irra was reporting on the status of the Gurkha supplies, which didn't sound too impressive to Koehler. Most of their inventory had gone west, and while they had captured some canned goods and water, along with the M-60s on the APCs, the rest of the captured ammunition was useful only for the nine M-16s they had also taken. It was difficult to ram 7.62-millimeter bullets into Armalites accustomed to .223 rounds.

"When we take off," Koehler said, gesturing toward the Ford, "you're welcome to the food, water, and gas on the truck. Hell, you can have the truck, too."

Shaikh smiled. "It is well-used."

"At the time, I'd have paid good money for an APC."

"With some scrounging, and making use of the native food supply," Irra said, "we could last ten days."

The *native food supply* sounded suspiciously like monkeys and parrots to Koehler.

"Very good," Shaikh said. "That should be ample. I hope to have some direction from London shortly."

Shaikh had followed Koehler's example, sending an urgent message to a passing ship and hoping it was routed through the British Embassy in Singapore to his superiors.

A corporal emerged from the APC, his face dripping with moisture.

"Mr. Koehler, sir! You are wanted on the radio."

"What? How in hell?—"

"The scanner, sir. I heard your name and locked on the frequency."

Koehler clambered to his feet and walked up the ramp. Inside the APC, he was hit immediately with the heat. Very much of that, and he'd dehydrate in minutes, he thought.

He sat down on the canvas camp stool in front of a folding table and picked up the microphone.

"Someone trying to reach Koehler?"

There was a minute of static, then: "Kelly Michael Koehler?"

"Got me."

"We've been searching a number of bands and freqs for you. Can you go to two-six-one-point-five-five?"

"Gone."

He reached over and switched the frequency. Shaikh came inside and squatted next to him.

"Who've I got?" he asked.

"Bird Dog Oh-Four, Commander."

Uh-oh.

"We're an airborne E-2, and we've been trying to reach you for quite a while. First, let me tell you the frequency is not secure, but that it is not in active use by Brunei military or government forces at this time. We may ask you to change again if someone tries to come up on it. Second, you are now code Eagle Eye. Third, stand by for a relay."

"Roger that."

He waited four minutes before the radio squawked again and the sweat poured down his face. He looked at Shaikh, who shrugged.

"Eagle Eye, this is Sledgehammer."

Koehler felt as if something heavy was coming down on him. This voice was deeper in tone, and it carried conviction. He could recognize the command tone in it. "Hammer, Eagle."

"What is your location, Eagle?"

"Ah, we're back in the jungle, exact coordinates unknown at the moment."

"Still in Brunei?"

"Roger."

"You said we. Itemize, please."

"We're not secure."

"In general terms."

"My wife and some GT personnel."

"That's all?"

With his thumb off the transmit button, he said, "Benjamin?"

Shaikh pursed his lips, then said, "This sounds legitimate, Kelly. You may tell him we are here, but please be vague."

He mashed the transmit stud. "I need some reassurance about who I'm talking to."

"You know we're transmitting through an E-2. Use your imagination, Eagle. I carry my own flag."

An admiral. "Yes, sir. My friend here authorizes me to tell you that we have Gurkhas present. In some force. We have adequate but not extensive ordnance and supply."

"Excellent. Can you stay out of the hands of the revolutionaries? Until the situation clarifies itself?"

Shaikh nodded vigorously.

"Yes, sir. We can. However, my wife and personnel are a concern."

"I'm sure they are. We will see what can be done. For the moment I am notifying you that, per the order of the CNO, you are returned to active duty effective immediately. You report to me."

Koehler sighed. Sherry was going to love this.

"Reporting as ordered, sir."

"You'll want to know what is going on internationally, but on an unsecured channel, I can tell you very little. At this moment there is debate at the big buildings in New York. Do you understand?"

"Affirmative."

"Until something shakes out there, I simply need you as my eyes, Eagle."

Koehler looked at his watch, noted the time on the air,

then gave a concise report of the confrontation at Kuala Belait the previous evening, garnered from his and Shaikh's accounts. "At this moment, without confirmation, the city appears to be under the control of the rebels, with approximately twenty thousand foreign workers quarantined. The air, ground, and marine transport capability, outside of what's in rebel hands, should be depleted to a large extent."

"Very good," the admiral said. "Do you have any information at all about the Sultan and his family?"

He looked to Shaikh, who repeated what he had learned from his soldiers.

"They were last seen—not by me—being escorted aboard a destroyer at Muara. That was two days ago, and I don't have more recent information."

"All right. Your task is to learn as much as you can about conditions in the country, especially the fate or location of the Sultan."

"Aye, aye, sir. One other thing. My friend here has had no contact with his headquarters in Foggy Town. Can you make contact for him?"

"Affirmative. I'll do that immediately. Give me a code name."

"Lion One," Shaikh said.

Koehler repeated it over the air. He was certain London would know who Lion One was.

"When we get close enough, we may airdrop a secure radio for you, but until then, you report on this freq. We'll tell you to change, if necessary."

"Yes, sir."

"Sledgehammer out."

Koehler signed off, dropped the mike on the table, and said, "Let's get out of this roaster."

The humid, funky smell of the jungle didn't help much. There wasn't a breeze in sight.

Shaikh said, "This contact makes me feel better. This man is an American admiral?"

"Yes. At least, I'm assuming he's American. The SOB activated me. There may be a task force somewhere in the area." He glanced at the Explorer. The women were still in it, fanning themselves with papers they'd found somewhere.

"You didn't tell him about the mined platforms."

"We know of only one, but you're right. I want a secure channel before I mention it."

"You are probably correct. And thank you for the message to my headquarters."

Koehler grinned. "You may not thank me when they call you to active duty, Benjamin."

The Nepalese grinned. "Gurkhas fear nothing."

"Then *you* can tell Sherry I've joined the Navy."

Sunday, March 9, 10:37 A.M.

Koehler went off to tell his wife of his new status, and Shaikh signalled Irra and they walked over to a helicopter where Shrestha had been using the radio.

Leaning against the doorjamb, he asked, "Captain?"

"I reached Captain Singh in Miri Marudi. The log jam is beginning to clear away, but from the village westward, the convoys are long and frequently brought to a standstill. He has elected to carry the wounded men along the river to the coast and load them on a trawler. He has already contracted with a ship returning from Kuching."

"I am relieved."

"Then they will remain in Miri Marudi, assisting the convoys and awaiting your orders, Major. If the need arises, we can shoot down the JetRangers and go there for resupply or reinforcement."

Given the dialogue Koehler had had with his admiral, Shaikh thought he would attempt to remain hidden for the moment.

He told Shrestha of the radio conversation. "It seems likely we will receive some instruction from regiment via that link. And quite possibly, the United Nations will make their position known. For the time being, we will not show ourselves to the patrolling helicopters. This afternoon, perhaps we will perform a reconnaissance mission. Also, we will stay off the air, so that we will not be pinpointed by radio direction finders. We will wait and see what Sledgehammer has to tell us."

"What of Koehler's mission?" Irra asked.

"Yes. We will consider him a friendly force of one. If he needs assistance, we will render it."

"I will volunteer, Major."

"I had rather thought that I would, Sergeant Major."

"The price of command," Irra said, "is that you must remain in command, Major."

Sunday, March 9, 7:21 A.M.

Christian Drieser had flown to La Guardia at five o'clock, climbed into a waiting limousine, and been whisked into the city. Since then, he had been waiting.

He used a phone in an anteroom of the Ambassador's office to stay in contact with Blalock in his own office while the so-called decision-makers huddled behind closed doors up and down the corridor. He listened to a tape of the Harned-Koehler conversation, which Judy Blalock played to him over the phone, and he passed that information on to the Ambassador when she came back to the office during a break in the negotiations.

Which seemed to be moving along.

At six-thirty, the Japanese transferred almost two hundred million dollars electronically to United Nations accounts. Along with a note of apology for their tardiness in following up on their pledge of assistance for the Gulf War.

At six-fifty-five, the Japanese agreed to underwrite half the cost of a UN-sponsored task force sent to secure the freedom of their tanker. The situation in Brunei and the definition of "peace" in that country was not resolved. Drieser thought that if the tanker problem and the Brunei revolution proved to be linked, the UN would eventually find itself working two fronts.

Drieser had called the Secretary with those developments.

"Well, Chris, hell. They're getting the lion's share of Brunei oil, and Japanese industry doesn't work very well on unlubricated wheels. They'd damned well better pick up the lion's share of the cost. What are they talking about now?"

"The makeup of the task force, I think. The Ambassador knows the location of Hap Harned, so I suspect we're going to be in it."

"Stick close to it, Chris. We still want a diplomatic resolution. It sounds to me as if there's been enough blood flowing."

"I'll do my best, Mr. Secretary."

"In fact, right now, I'm going to call the National Security Advisor and formalize your arrangements with DOD and Harned. I want you in the loop."

"Whatever works."

At seven-oh-five, the deaths and casualties among the Gurkha troops were confirmed by U.S. State Department personnel out of Kuching, and for the purposes of the Security Council, the Gurkhas were considered to be non-native Bruneians.

At seven-fifteen, the Ambassador returned and called her staff into a conference room. Drieser trailed along.

She took the podium and announced, "At eight o'clock, the Security Council will convene and entertain a motion by the Japanese ambassador for intervention in the Brunei situation on two rationales: the *Maru Hokkaido* hijacking incident and the murders of foreign nationals who were under the protection of the Sultan of Brunei. Britain and Nepal are also submitting letters of condemnation. I expect the motion to be adopted unanimously.

"Shortly after the motion is adopted, a United Nations task force will be assembled. It will be composed of a United States carrier task force now in the area, a Japanese carrier task force nearby, and a French cruiser with four escort vessels, which is currently en route to New Zealand. Two thousand United States Marines from Okinawa will be flown to join the force, as will a detachment of U.S. Navy SEALs from San Diego."

Drieser raised his hand.

"Mr. Undersecretary."

"Are we relying on a show of force?"

"We hope that is all that will be necessary," she said.

Somebody on the Council hoped.

Drieser wasn't as optimistic.

Sunday, March 9, 8:19 P.M.

Meoshi Kyoto was appalled.

His convictions and his preferences in regard to his departure from the *Akagi* had not been consulted, and now he was again in a pressure suit and helmet in the backseat of a navalized F1-X fighter aircraft.

"Press your head against the headrest, Colonel."

He did not have to be told. The elements of his preflight

briefing were forefront in his mind, and he forced his head back with all of the power in his neck muscles.

The shriek of the aircraft's motive power reached crescendo, and Kyoto hoped it was enough.

He closed his eyes.

Then he was slammed back into the seat with unbelievable pressure. He felt the skin of his face sag, and his eyes nearly opened.

They did open, in alarm, when he felt the airplane leave the deck, then immediately sag. They popped open to see nothing but stars above the canopy, nothing but darkness beyond the outline of the pilot's helmet.

And then the airplane clutched at the air and was climbing.

The gravitational forces eased. He could breathe again.

"Wonderful, is it not, Colonel?"

"Absolutely," he managed to say on the intercom.

It was a short flight, 180 nautical miles through the darkened skies, and soon the pilot was talking to an air controller from the American carrier *Eisenhower*. After his first experience with a night carrier-landing, Kyoto knew what to expect, and he was even encouraged when the pilot told him: "It is such a huge ship. We could probably land without the arresting gear."

"Let us do so."

"Well, Colonel, I exaggerated a little."

The trap aboard the carrier did not seem to be as violent as his first landing, but the pilot complained because he had missed the first two wires, catching the third.

Kyoto would as soon *not* have known.

He climbed down from the cockpit on legs more stable than the first time—hoping he was not becoming accustomed to this form of transport, and stood in the heavy breeze holding his carryall and looking at the flight deck. He had thought the *Akagi* huge, but this was a monster, with aircraft of many types parked in every conceivable spot.

The ensign who met him let him watch as the Japanese airplane was moved forward and connected to the catapult on the waist launch. Kyoto did not think many Japanese aircraft had landed on American carriers. This one was not present for long, and only a few minutes later, it was rammed into the sky.

Again, he was given a short tour of the superstructure's maze and assigned to VIP quarters. They were much larger than his cabin on the *Akagi*, but quite functional, with exposed conduits and piping across the ceiling and down one wall. It contained a bunk, a desk, a wall locker, and a chair.

When he felt somewhat presentable in his dress uniform, he was escorted up several decks and shown into the flag plot.

"Admiral Hap Harned, Colonel."

The man was as big as his ship. Almost seven feet tall, and with shoulders as broad as the doorways, his waist was so trim, he looked like an oversized tent peg. He had a large head with close-shaven hair the color of fresh concrete. His features were square and blunt—nose, chin, ears. The eyes could penetrate tempered steel. His duty khakis must have been tailored from two uniforms.

"Meoshi Kyoto, sir, at your service."

The man offered his hand, and Kyoto was relieved that he didn't demonstrate the power in his large hands.

"You have seen the communiqué?" Harned asked.

"I have, sir. You are to command the force in the name of the United Nations. I will serve as the liaison to Admiral Saburo Yakama and to the Japanese Ministry of Foreign Affairs."

"And we've got someone coming from the French, as soon as they get close enough for a helicopter lift."

Harned offered coffee, which Kyoto accepted, and then turned him toward a wall where three large screens were fastened. A large map of the southern South China Sea was displayed on one. This would be a copy of similar information displayed in the Combat Information Center. The northern coast of Borneo and the enclave of Brunei were outlined clearly, and the *Maru Hokkaido* was identified. She was 224 nautical miles from Brunei.

The admiral pointed at a cluster of blue dots. "That's us. And over here, dressed in yellow, is Admiral Yakama's group. We'll join up at about three in the morning, and we'll all reach the *Hokkaido* just after noon tomorrow."

"And then, sir?"

"And then, if I'm reading my instructions correctly, we'll scare the hell out of them. They'll throw their hands in the air and beg us for mercy."

"Do you think so?" Kyoto asked.

"Not for one damned minute."

Sunday, March 9, 9:36 P.M.

Sherry Koehler was frightened.

The last twenty-four hours had been filled with adrenaline-producing moments of terror, and she was fatigued by them. Then, to learn that Kelly had been activated, that the country might be on the verge of war—with them caught in the middle of it, had been almost too much to bear.

She and Kelly sat in the open doorway of one of the helicopters, and he had his arm wrapped around her shoulders. It was totally dark, and insects buzzed around her head.

Her heart felt heavy, beating as if it might be visible, given enough light. She was certain he could feel it.

"I don't know if I can stand it, Kelly. It's a repeat of the Gulf."

"Not exactly, hon," his arm tightened a moment, then relaxed. "We'll just take a quick run into the capital, look around, and come back. That's all there is to it."

"Don't try to snow me, please."

"Believe me when I say I'll keep my head down. I'd stand out too clearly as a foreigner, right?"

"I feel like I should be doing something. I'll go with you."

"Ah, hell, Sherry! That's what I need, to worry about you."

"You don't worry about me, back in the jungle, with the snakes?"

"Not with Major Shaikh around."

She couldn't see his face, so she raised her hand and traced his cheeks, his nose, his lips with her fingertips.

"I don't want to lose you, Kelly."

"You're not going to. And I'm not losing you, either. But you've got—"

"I'm going with you."

"Damn it, no!"

She shoved his arm aside and slid off the compartment floor. Nearly tripped and went clear to the ground.

"Where are you going?" he called.

"For reinforcements."

Sunday, March 9, 10:03 P.M.

Azman Saim, who was a watchman on the docks at Muara, slid out of his seat, and stood by the open door of the Nissan pickup.

"Thank you for the ride."

"I should take you all the way home, Azman. It is after the curfew."

"Nonsense. It is only a few blocks. I will see you in the morning."

The driver shook his head, but Saim closed the door, and the pickup pulled away.

Saim stepped up to the sidewalk and began walking toward his house. It was a dark part of Muara, with the streetlights spaced widely, but it was also a familiar and comfortable part of the town. He had lived there all his thirty-six years.

He was a block from his house when he became aware of headlights coming up the street behind him. He almost dashed to a space between the houses nearby, but recalled that this was his home, that he was legitimate—coming home from work, and that he carried with him his credentials as a watchman.

If it were police, he could explain his situation.

He was a half block from home when the car rolled up to the curb beside him.

"Stop there!"

Saim stopped and turned to face the car.

It was a police car. With a face in the window. The door opened and the uniformed man got out.

"What are you doing out? There is a curfew."

"I am but returning from my work, Sergeant. I will show you my papers."

He reached for his wallet.

As the policeman reached for the gun in his holster.

"Now, wait!" he yelled.

But the man drew the pistol, raised it, and fired.

Saim knew one brief moment of pain.

Sunday, March 9, 10:17 P.M.

Koehler hated letting other people drive. Sometimes he'd grit his teeth and allow Sherry to take the wheel. She was a good driver, but he thought she let herself be distracted too easily by conversation and landscape. And he was relatively comfortable with Frank Morris at the controls of an aircraft. Generally, though, he detested giving control of his fate into the hands of another.

Sergeant Major Suraj Irra slipped behind the wheel of the Explorer and moved the seat as far forward as he could get it. Irra wasn't a big man, but he was probably as tough as anyone Kelly'd ever met. The dark eyes, quiet voice, and rock-steady attitude bespoke wisdom and experience.

More important, he'd driven many of these jungle trails, and he knew where he was going.

In the backseat Sherry and Monica spoke of snakes and things that growl in the night, and neither mentioned their victory over Kelly. When Sherry had gotten Monica into the argument, he knew he'd lost. Yet, he might have won, also, for he'd achieved a compromise Sherry didn't like, but said she'd take.

In the passenger bucket seat, Koehler had an Armalite for a companion. He'd never worked with the 18 before, but Shaikh had given him a quick and competent lesson.

Morris, Avery, and the two supply techs had adamantly refused to bail out, said they'd take their chances with the Nepalese, so they were teaching their brand of poker to Gurkhas they thought might be gullible.

Irra approved of Koehler's lighting arrangements—the single parking lamp, and he turned it on as he pulled out of the clearing, dodging an APC. The encampment was under Shaikh's strict order of no light emissions, and Koehler could barely tell they were leaving it.

Three times in the late afternoon, helicopters had overflown the site, or close to it, so they assumed that Bakir or Padang were looking for them.

Both Koehler and Shaikh were under orders now. In the afternoon Sledgehammer had called, and Shaikh and Koehler sat in the APC and listened to their orders.

"Eagle Eye, I want you to infiltrate more populated areas. You're not doing me much good on R&R in the jungle."

"Aye, aye, sir. I'll see what I can do."

"Just do it. Is Lion One there?"

"Hammer, I need a secure channel. I've got some crucial data."

A moment went by, before the admiral said, "I'll get someone on it right away. Lion One?"

"Yes, sir." Kelly handed the mike to Benjamin Shaikh.

"Lion One, Her Majesty's government has officially attached you to Operation Eden. I am commanding."

The major immediately pressed the transmit button. "Green Arrow."

"Very good, sir. I am to tell you, 'Polar Bear.' "

Koehler understood that Shaikh had issued a coded demand for authentication, and judging by the look on his face, had received it.

"Do I have instructions, sir?"

"At the moment your mission is suspended, and your current objective is to support Eagle Eye. As the situation develops, we will likely have more work for you to do."

"Yes, sir. I understand."

Koehler took the microphone back. "Hammer, Eagle. Can you tell me more about Eden?"

"Negative."

"This has accelerated very quickly, sir."

"I understand your lack of information, Eagle. Let me just say that a crisis external to the country precipitated some political moves."

So neither of them had more than a vague notion of what Operation Eden entailed, but Shaikh was happy to have direction, and that was to support Koehler in his thirst for knowledge of the rebel government and the whereabouts of the Sultan.

Therefore, they were off to the big city, Suraj Irra commanding the Explorer.

The only glitch in the admiral's plan—and Kelly didn't think of it as a glitch—was the presence of the women. Sledgehammer didn't know he had passengers. If the admiral didn't approve, well, Koehler could deal with it later.

"Kelly?"

He felt Sherry's hand come around his seat back and grip his upper arm. He let go of the assault rifle and covered it with his own.

"Yeah, hon?"

"You think we're doing the right thing, don't you?"

"Hard to know," he told her. "This revolt is two-and-a-half days old, and there's still nothing on the commercial radio stations except soothing music." And an occasional taped reminder from Provisional President Li Sen that all was harmonious. Every other form of communication in Brunei seemed to be blacked out. "But, yeah, I think it's the only choice open to us right now."

"You're sure you don't know this son of a bitch who activated you?"

"Never heard his voice before, love. I never had much of a chance to buddy up to admirals."

She was ticked off about his call to active duty, and especially about her inability to do anything about it, to compete with Sledgehammer. Koehler wasn't exactly happy with it, either, but then his emotions were mixed. As with his choice of drivers, he liked to have a greater voting edge when it came to dealing with his assigned fates.

Conversely, and perhaps perversely, he was flattered to

be wanted, to be needed for some special chore. He had stayed in the Navy, not only for the flying, but also because he liked the feeling of contributing to a cause more worthy than digging dead fossils out of the ground to pour into the gas tanks of Lincolns and Saabs. Call it public service.

The special angle here, as had been true in the Gulf, was that his service didn't seem to be in defense of *his* country. It was a quirk of the New World. He'd have bet his bottom dollar the UN was in charge, which wasn't always satisfying or reliable. Not that anyone was going to offer him options.

Still, the speed with which Operation Eden had been created suggested two things to Kelly. Sledgehammer was ramrodding a carrier force—carrier because he had an E-2 airborne warning and control aircraft available—somewhere close, and was therefore already on the scene when Hammer got his own call from an admiral with more stars. Secondly, some incident outside Brunei's borders, but connected to events in Brunei, had precipitated quick action. There were probably lives at stake.

So maybe what he was doing was worthwhile.

Besides, the many rehashings he'd heard of the firefight in Kuala Belait boosted his anger level. He hoped the GlobeTech people were all right, and he was mad as hell at a Colonel Bakir he'd never met because Gurkha soldiers had given their lives. Three days ago, he'd never met a Nepalese. Now, he called Gurkhas his friends.

"Commander Koehler . . ."

"If I promise to call you Suraj, will you call me Kelly?"

He felt Sherry squeeze his arm.

The sergeant major's teeth flashed white in the darkness. "Yes, sir. That will be fine. I know what this admiral has said, but what do you think is happening with the United Nations?"

The weak illumination from the parking lamp barely

penetrated the road ahead and made the rain forest feel as if it was moving, closing in. Koehler began to feel what claustrophobia was all about. Irra was doing a commendable job of maintaining twenty miles an hour, anticipating the unexpected turns the road followed.

"As pure speculation, Suraj, I'd guess the Security Council has made a decision about this other incident that Sledgehammer mentioned. The fact that you guys are attached to Eden tells me it's an international effort. They still don't know what to make of what's taking place in Brunei. If it's simply an internal struggle, they may just try to arrange a cease-fire and a talk around a table somewhere. They don't know where the Sultan is, and if he's been taken out, it makes peaceful discussions one-sided."

"Do you think future decisions of the Council depend upon what we can learn of the Sultan?"

Koehler noted how Irra had included himself in Koehler's mission. That was all right with him.

"Could be. But if that destroyer is in the harbor, I'm damned if I know how we're going to get aboard her."

"We will find a way."

Sherry squeezed his arm again, and a hell of a lot harder. She dug her nails in. She didn't like the conversation.

The whole interior of the country was hilly, wrapped in jungle, and the Ford had been climbing, then descending grades for an hour when the road abruptly disappeared, and Irra braked to a stop.

"This a problem, Suraj?"

"I do not think so. I will check." He took the flashlight and got out.

Koehler could hear water moving, but it was beyond the limits of the parking light.

"What is this?" Monica Davis asked.

"I think it's a tributary of the Belait River, Monica."

"Whoever cut this road wouldn't have been kind enough to leave a bridge for us, would they?"

"Doubt it."

There probably never was a bridge.

The Gurkha came back and got behind the wheel. "It is only half a meter deep. It will not be a barrier."

The Ford slid down a steep depression in four-wheel drive, and the light caught the surface of black water slithering out of the jungle to the right, disappearing into dense foliage on the left. The front wheels went sideways when the water current caught them on the muddy bottom, but Irra gunned the engine, and all four wheels churned. The truck lurched to the side twice, found a grip, then charged up the other side.

A few minutes later, they reached another T-intersection, but Irra continued along the top of the T.

"Where's that go?" Kelly asked.

"To Labi. It is a village where the rivers join."

"I should have studied my geography better," Koehler said.

"Why change now?" Sherry asked from the back. "You've only been interested in what's below the surface."

He didn't know whether she was being sarcastic, or demonstrating her anger, or both.

Fifteen minutes before one in the morning, without having encountered another human being, they were driving through less dense forest, and Koehler sensed the coastal plain was close.

He was wrong.

Irra pulled to the side of the track and parked. "I will be back shortly."

"Before you go, Suraj, give me a hint about where we are."

"It is about a kilometer to Kludang."

That was an inland village, maybe four or five miles from the coast. He'd flown over it a couple times.

Irra took a flashlight and his own Armalite and disappeared.

"I think I want to go back and stay with the major," Davis said. "Can we turn around now?"

"We passed that point, I think."

"More important," Monica said, "when do we get to the next gas station? This girl has to find the potty."

"You can step behind a tree," Kelly said. "I won't look."

"Not on your life. These aren't friendly trees."

Sherry crawled over the console and sat down beside him, wrapped her arm around his neck.

"I don't want to do this."

"Got to."

"Don't tell me, 'got to.' "

"For me, 'cause I love you?"

"Better." She kissed him.

Irra came back a half hour later, driving a 1974 Chevrolet Chevelle station wagon that had lost its tailgate and rear window somehow. He thought it was being utilized as a pickup.

Koehler got out to admire it. "I hope you didn't steal it, Suraj."

Again, the flash of teeth in the dark. "Of course not. I traded your truck for it. I hope you do not mind."

"Not in the least."

They transferred to the less battered and better lighted vehicle, and Irra took them slowly through the village, then east on a lightly travelled road toward Bandar Seri Begawan.

"There is a curfew," Irra said. "The man told me no one is to be out after nine o'clock. This car may not help us."

As it worked out, though, they seemed to be the only

ones breaking curfew, and Koehler didn't see another car until after they turned south and reached the Sarawak border. The two border guards there were on the other side, which was in the enclave of the Limbang River valley between Brunei proper and the eastern Brunei province. The guards only shrugged when they crossed into Sarawak.

There was a refugee village set up here, too, a ragtag collection of tents, trucks, and automobiles. Most of it was asleep, though, and they passed right on through and reached the village of Limbang at two in the morning.

"Sherry . . ."

"No! You're not leaving us here."

Irra parked the car, soon to become the property of some proud Sarawakian, and Koehler slung both Armalites over one shoulder, then picked up the two suitcases. Irra disappeared again.

Koehler led his women through the sleeping village down toward the shore of the Limbang River, and by the time they reached it, Irra intercepted them and changed their course.

"Do you have fifty dollars American?"

"God, no, Suraj. I converted all my money."

"I've got it," Monica Davis said. "Happy to contribute to the cause."

She found bills in her purse and gave them to the Gurkha.

"Put it on your expense voucher," Koehler said.

"This is going to be a whopper of a voucher, boss."

They dodged between thin-walled shacks down to the water's edge, and Irra paid off the driver of a water taxi. The boat was narrow, with a long, pointed prow, and it threatened several times to capsize while they were getting in it, clambering aboard from the muddy shore. Its outboard motor was vintage 1950s Evinrude, but came to a roaring purr at the first pull of the cord, and the driver angled them out into the river.

By three in the morning, they had cleared the Limbang and entered Brunei Bay. Skirting the mouth of the Brunei River and the capital city, they went flying up the northern shore of the bay toward Muara. The driver idled down when they reached the moorings and coasted almost silently among the boats and ships at rest.

The lights of a patrol boat were visible to the east, then disappeared behind the bulk of the island sited in the bay opposite the port of Muara.

Koehler thought the vessel population was depleted. In the darkness it was difficult to make out the silhouettes, but he didn't see several of the naval ships he was accustomed to seeing. The junk was there, lights showing in her stern windows. She was the residence of the Chinese envoy to Brunei, and he lived aboard with a crew large enough to get the huge ship under sail.

He leaned over to Suraj and said, "The *Bulkiah* isn't here."

"Then we will not worry about boarding her, Kelly."

Sherry told the Gurkha, "You don't know how happy that makes me."

The *Serendipity* was secure at her buoy, bobbing lightly in the chop of the bay, and Koehler was both happy and relieved to see her. He had feared that she would be gone, stolen or scuttled.

Koehler pointed her out to the taxi driver, and he coasted alongside, stopping long enough to see them all aboard, then disappearing on a southerly course into the bay.

They didn't waste time. Koehler unlocked the top and door to the companionway down to the cabin, then went to the cockpit and blew the bilges. Monica had been aboard before, and she went below to stow the suitcases and make certain everything was shipshape. And probably to check out the operation of the head.

Sherry went forward with Irra, showing him how to unbag the sails, and when she called back to him, Kelly was ready.

"Now?"

"Let her go," he called back.

Freed of her mooring line, the ketch drifted slowly to the south, but the auxiliary engine coughed twice, then fired, and Koehler slipped it into gear. The exhaust burbled below the waterline, and he eased into a wide circle, avoiding a power cruiser moored to a buoy on the east, and lined up to pass south of the island. He didn't want to be caught in the channel between the island and the port. He thought that patrol boat was circling the island and would be coming down the channel toward them.

By the time they were directly south of the island, moving without running lights, Sherry reported all rigging taut and sheets in place and unfouled.

"Let's bend on sail," he said, cutting the engine.

There wasn't much of a breeze, but it was enough. As the sails were hoisted, they caught wind and billowed, and *Serendipity* was in her element. He had wind off his left shoulder, so it was going to be a straight run down the bay, then out into the South China Sea.

Monica emerged from the cabin with opened cans of beans and peaches, and she passed them out, then doled out spoons.

"This is breakfast?" Koehler complained.

"This is good for you."

"As is this," Sherry said as she climbed the few steps into the cockpit. "Guess what I found hidden in the forward chain locker?"

She knew where to look.

"We aren't out of Bruneian waters," Kelly told her.

"We don't know what the current law is."

"True. I'll take one."

She popped the top on a can of Michelob and handed it to him. Irra made certain the Armalites were safe on the port settee, then accepted a can. "My thanks, Mrs. Koehler."

It was warm, but tasted good going down. Koehler rinsed his mouth with the first swallow and spit it overboard. He thought he'd like to go straight north until he hit the Philippines or something.

He was coming around on a broad reach, picking up speed and more wind, when Irra said, "Kelly."

No alarm in his voice, but Koehler detected the concern anyway.

He looked over his shoulder and saw the patrol boat. It was coming on hard from the northern shoulder of the island, all lights and action. It was several miles behind, but he could already hear the siren.

Shit.

He looked up. At the top of the mast was his radar deflector, intended to increase the image of the fiberglass and wood boat on a radar screen. He'd meant to remove it before getting under way.

"Sherry, take the helm, please."

"Kelly, what are you going to do?" Her voice quavered.

"Suraj and I will go aboard and talk to these guys. I want you to keep a heading of zero-three-zero. Flank Labuan Island on the south, then head out into the sea. You go west and put in at Beaufort."

That was in Sabah, the Malaysian state on the northern tip of Borneo.

"Not without you," she insisted.

"We went over this, hon. We have an agreement, and I have to do my thing for some admiral. Please do it my way."

"I'm worried about you."

"I'm worried about both of us. But I've got Suraj, right?"

Sherry settled behind the helm and maintained the speed, about twelve knots, glancing up at the telltales floating from the upper shrouds occasionally to check the wind. The white streamers were barely visible in the dark.

Koehler sat on the port seat with Irra, the Armalites concealed behind them. He reached back and flicked the safety off his weapon. He heard the snick as Irra did the same thing.

When it was a mile away, the patrol cut off the damned siren, anyway. They probably couldn't stand the warble any more than Koehler could.

But it came on at speed, directly at them, a floodlight blooming into being, and they didn't wait to talk it over.

Three hundred yards off, the fifty-calibers opened up.

Ten

"This Lieutenant Commander Koehler, he is reliable?"

"I have only his personnel file to go by, Meoshi," Hap Harned said. "His evaluations are excellent, he has a couple citations for his service in the Gulf, and he fast-tracked on promotions until he left active service. I'd guess he's a capable helo pilot, but for all I know, that's all he is. What it comes down to, he's available. And some guy in the State Department figured that out."

Kyoto sipped the last of his coffee, then dabbed his lips with the linen napkin. The steward started forward with the coffeepot, but Kyoto smiled and waved him off.

An early-morning breakfast in the admiral's quarters had a touch of elegance about it, despite the hour and the American tradition of scrambled eggs, bacon, hash browns, and pancakes, all of which were excellent.

Harned finished his own coffee and said, "Ready?"

"Yes, sir."

"Let's go over to the plot. If no one screwed up, we should have increased our size in the last hour."

Kyoto was accustomed to leading superior officers, but the huge Harned charged ahead, startling an enlisted man in the narrow corridor—he slapped his back up to a bulkhead to allow the big man passage.

"Mornin', Hawkins," Harned bellowed as he went by.

"Good morning, sir!"

There were over five thousand men and women on the aircraft carrier, but so far as Kyoto had observed, Harned appeared to know each one he had encountered by name.

Distantly he heard the sound of helicopter turbines. It was probably the standby rescue helicopter, preparing for morning flight operations. Kyoto was learning entirely too much about naval operations.

In the flag plot, already populated by three junior officers, Harned went directly to the wall with the display screens. Kyoto assumed that the data gathered from radar and sonar sensors was processed through a computer and converted to the iconic symbols on the map.

In addition to the eight blue symbols of the American ships he had seen yesterday, there were now eight yellow symbols, each identified in a small box next to the symbol. He saw the *Akagi* in the rear center of the group, steaming about fifteen kilometers behind the *Eisenhower*. Her defensive screen had been interspersed among the ships supporting the American carrier, and the blue and yellow symbols on the screen were integrated. He was surprised to see one yellow symbol fifteen thousand meters to the west identified as the *Yuushio*.

The *Yuushio* was a submarine and supposedly a very silent one. When Kyoto had talked to Admiral Yakama last night, the admiral told him he was keeping the submarine in reserve and would not mention it to the Americans. The symbol on the plotting board confirmed Kyoto's original estimate of American electronic sophistication.

Standing with his feet planted, studying the board, Harned asked, "Is your Admiral Yakama a sly dog, Meoshi?"

Certainly, Harned would have pored over every word the Central Intelligence Agency and the Defense Intelligence Agency had ever collected about Saburo Yakama. He would have done the same for Kyoto.

Harned wanted reassurances that his Japanese colleague would not do something unpredictable.

"I have only known him for a few hours, Admiral."

Harned turned and grinned. "Not what I asked."

Kyoto felt as if he were looking far up toward the tip of Mount Fuji when he talked to Harned.

"My impression is that he is a solid man." Kyoto pointed to the symbol for the submarine. "He may be overconfident and less the fox than you are. He would want to have, as your poker players say, an ace up the sleeve."

"Nothing wrong with that, I guess, except we're supposed to be working out of the same shirt."

Harned stepped over to his chair and pressed a button on the arm console. He spoke to someone in the next compartment. "Let me have the live-action, Lieutenant Meadows."

The middle screen came to life with a slightly shaky view of a supertanker. It was barely discernible against the sea in the predawn light.

"There's your *Maru Hokkaido*, Meoshi. Pretty decent shot from my E-2, if I do say so."

Kyoto stepped back several paces and let his eyes adjust to the luminosity of the screen. It was difficult to judge the size of the supertanker from the single image. The attitude of the ship kept changing as the Grumman E-2 airborne warning and control aircraft circled it, and he soon saw another vessel astern, one that appeared to be a rowboat in comparison to the ULCC.

"The gunboat is in tow, Admiral."

"Looks that way. Conserving their fuel, I suppose. The tanker herself is barely making two knots. Just enough to maintain steerage."

"I know very little of tankers, or their layout," Kyoto said, "but I should think the hijackers must have at least ten members, to control a crew of one hundred and twenty."

"You're trying to think ahead of me, Colonel."

"Yes. I wish to be with the boarding party."

Harned smiled. "You're supposed to be in dual roles, Meoshi—liaison to Admiral Yakama and representative of the foreign affairs ministry. Now, you want a third job?"

"My countrymen—"

"I understand. But I may need you here. After all, you talked Admiral Yakama into merging his force with mine. And you got us the plans for the *Hokkaido.*"

Saburo Yakama had resisted Harned's suggestion to blend the fleets, and Kyoto had had to call upon every power of persuasion he could think of to accomplish Yakama's submission. As for the other, it had only taken a call to Deputy Minister Asume to create a search for the construction plans of the tanker and have them transmitted to the *Eisenhower.*

"It seems so little, Admiral. I look at your picture here, and I think of what may be taking place on the tanker."

"Well, you let the boys in intel work over those plans. They may come up with an idea or two."

"Then?"

"Then, we'll see. First, we've got to take on some Marines and SEALs who are coming to us through the Philippines. They'll have some commanders with ideas of their own, and we may come up with a course of action before noon. We're also supposed to make contact with the *Los Angeles,* a U.S. attack sub. First thing we've got to remember, though, is that all good plans are usually trashed by unexpected events."

Kyoto had envisioned some dark, perhaps storm-tossed, night with rubber-suited men climbing the flanks of the tanker. He would be among them. His vision, since he had no naval and very little amphibious training, was likely a scenario from some adventure movie. Arnold Schwartzwhatever. Or perhaps they could rappel from helicopters to the tanker's deck. That was his preference, his training, but he realized that it was noisy, serving to alert the pirates. And to jeopardize the lives of the hostages.

He looked again at the live image, but it was not light enough to see whether there were men on the deck, much less on the bridge.

"I hope they are all right."

"So do I, Meoshi. So do I."

Monday, March 10, 4:19 A.M.

With the first burst from the heavy gun, Koehler had launched himself off the settee and on top of Sherry, driving her from her seat to the deck of the cockpit. Monica yelled.

Suraj Irra went to the deck also, snaking a hand out to grab Davis's ankle and pull her feet from under her.

The slugs tore up some fiberglass along the gunwale and punched several holes in the main sails.

When he forced Sherry to release the helm, the ketch fell off her reach and began to wallow. The sails flapped.

There was no follow-up burst.

Koehler called, "Anyone hurt?"

Everyone replied in the negative.

"Stay down."

Sherry squirmed under him, and he shifted onto his left side to give her room.

God, how did I get her into this!

"What in the hell are they doing?" Sherry gasped.

"May have been a warning shot that got too close."

He eased up on his left arm and peered over the stern toward the gunboat. She was still coming on, two hundred yards off, her bright floodlight held tightly on the ketch. It was difficult to see beyond the glare of the light.

"Suraj?"

"I am in uniform, and I do not wish to surrender, Commander. I will go over the side."

Irra had refused civilian clothing, not wanting to appear a spy.

The boat's engines lost some of their roar as she came closer, bleeding off speed.

The machine gun opened up again, a long burst aimed at water level. Kelly prayed the gunner was bad enough, firing low, that the bullets lost force in the water before striking the hull.

"Retaliation time, Suraj."

"As you say."

Suraj released his grip on Monica's ankle, rolled across the cockpit sole to the settee, and reached up for the assault rifles. He tossed one toward Koehler, who snagged it in midair.

"Stay down, now!"

"Kelly!" Sherry yelped.

"You hear me?"

When the patrol boat was sixty yards off, slewing to come alongside, Koehler yelled, "Now, Suraj!"

The two of them rose to their knees and opened up with the Armalites on automatic fire.

Both of them had the same idea, and the rebel manning

the fifty-caliber caught a half dozen slugs, slammed against the cabin behind him, then tumbled over the side.

The floodlight shattered, and the blessed darkness gave them some protection. They were aided by the lack of preparation of the boat's captain. Only the one mounted gun was manned, and the boat commander was caught completely by surprise. How many sailboats shot back?

A sailor on the stern returned fire with an assault rifle, and Irra mowed him down with one burst.

On the flying bridge, Koehler picked out three silhouettes and switched his aim. The tracers guided him, and his three-round bursts poured through the windshield, shattering glass, and caught one or two of them. Yells burned the night, and the gunboat's engines roared.

As the bow began to lift to plane, Koehler shifted his fire to where he thought the fuel cells were located, aft at about the waterline. He emptied his magazine, ejected it, and flipped it over for the full magazine taped upside down to it. He rammed the fresh clip home.

Irra followed his lead, firing at the stern.

Koehler was too late on his reloading.

The patrol boat was gaining speed, turning her stern toward them.

When a small explosion thumped across the water.

Nothing visible. Gas fumes reaching a hot engine, maybe.

And then an eruption of bright orange and blue.

The detonation ripped the entire stern from the boat, and secondary explosions told him an ammo locker had been breached.

Koehler lowered his Armalite and watched.

The fire raced forward on gas-drenched decks, and the midships section flared brightly. He saw several men diving overboard.

The deck shifted under his feet, and he looked behind

him to see that Sherry, still on the deck, had reached up and grabbed the wheel, forcing the ketch back on her track.

"Good girl!"

"I don't want to see," she said.

"Just keep going."

The *Serendipity* righted herself, heeled to just the right pitch, and picked up speed.

The flaming wreckage fell away behind them, and in four minutes, slipped beneath the surface.

"Nice shot, Sergeant Major."

"I think they are not suited for service in their navy."

"Do you think they got off a radio call?"

"I sincerely doubt it. My thought is that they were bent on looting. This was not to be an official act."

"Maybe you're right." He turned back and helped Sherry to her feet, then to her seat behind the helm. "You're doing fine, hon."

"Just get it over with, Kelly."

"Still love me?"

She looked up, and in the binnacle light, he saw the tears on her cheeks. He leaned down and wiped them away with his thumbs, then leaned farther and kissed her.

"Be careful, you lout."

"Can you handle any holes in the boat?"

"We're fine."

It only required a few minutes to wrap the M-18s and their magazines in plastic, and don life preservers.

Kelly kissed Sherry again and noted the tear tracks on her cheeks had increased. Her eyes held his own as if memorizing for all time what she saw.

"Nothing to worry about, hon."

"Go."

He stepped up on the settee, sat on the narrow ledge of deck, leaned back, and tumbled overboard.

Monday, March 10, 4:31 A.M.

As soon as Kelly and Irra had disappeared into the darkness beyond the wake, Sherry Koehler scanned the seas around her. The running lights of several vessels had appeared near the port. They were probably a response to some alarm created by the explosion of the patrol boat.

She couldn't worry about that now, couldn't worry about Kelly, though she was filled with a sinister dread that told her she'd never see him again. She wanted to bawl.

"I suddenly feel damned alone," Davis said. "I wish Frank were here."

"We've got darkness for company for a few more minutes, Monica. We've got to take advantage of it." Sherry engaged the self-steering.

"Is there anything in front of us?" Davis asked.

"An island, but it's twelve miles away."

Monica had already lifted the cushion on the starboard settee and was searching through the tool locker beneath it. She came up with a roll of sail repair tape.

"This is what we need, right?"

"Right. You remember how to do it?"

"Yup. I'll have to bring the booms in, though. I'm not acrobatic enough to play monkey."

"One at a time."

While Davis started patching punctures in the sails—it wouldn't do for a gust of wind to come up and expand a few bullet holes into shredded sails—Sherry slipped down the companionway into the cabin and found a flashlight clipped to a bulkhead. The deck was tilted to the starboard, and she went to her knees and felt the carpet.

It was wet, though only on the starboard side. They were taking water somewhere.

The automatic bilge pump could handle a few leaks, but

if the decking was damp, there was a fair amount of water in the bilges.

She crawled to the left side and began opening cabinets. Under the galley, with the beam from the flashlight, she found two holes. They were large, the size of quarters, and with the heel of the boat now, they were above water level. Pulling the cushion from the seats on either side of the dinette, she probed with the light and found three more. Again, they were currently above water level.

In the forward cabin and the master's cabin, she found another four, two of them low enough to be sucking water in. With caulking compound and duct tape, she went from one to the next, packed the holes with caulk, then slapped a square of tape over each. She thought they would hold for long enough to make port.

But still, there weren't enough bullet holes to account for the amount of water she thought was running beneath the cabin deck. There might be a couple holes below the cabin deck that she couldn't reach.

And now she detected the smell of diesel fuel.

She went aft to the cabin's rear bulkhead and pulled open the hatch leading down to the engine compartment. The stench of fuel nearly made her gag. Reaching around the bulkhead, she found the light switch and flicked it on.

No!

The little diesel engine at the bottom of the compartment was almost submerged.

The sheen of oil on the dark water told her the fuel tank had been punctured.

And the water level was coming up fast.

Monday, March 10, 7:22 A.M.

After they had eaten their breakfasts, Li Sen dismissed his wife and sons—all of whom were quite proud of him—and poured more of the aromatic tea for Omar Padang and himself.

His sons were disheartened at his order to reopen the store. They were still caught up in what they described as the excitement of the revolution, but Li intended to set an example, and so the store must resume its daily schedule. Soon, his neighboring shopkeepers would follow suit.

The example he was setting included his remaining in the modest house in which he had resided for thirty years. There would be no palaces for this democratic president.

"I want to release the diplomatic community today, Omar."

"It is not a good idea."

"And why not? The sooner we reestablish the international connections, the sooner we will gain recognition and legitimacy."

"Perhaps tomorrow, Sen. Today, there are other priorities."

"Name them."

"For one, you must send another message to Japan. We will not accept their ultimatum regarding our oil."

"You have seen the telecasts, Omar. World opinion is mounting against us, and we cannot allow that to happen."

Selected channels from the satellite feeds had been made available to the primary committee, so Li was not unaware of United Nations proclamations and international media reporting.

"We should let ourselves be seen as weaklings?" Padang said, arching his back and stretching his arms. His white jacket fell open, revealing the holster tucked in his armpit. The butt of the gun was obscene.

He yawned. "I think not, Sen. Here is a place we must hold our ground firmly. It will be to our benefit in future negotiations."

Li was not as certain as Padang appeared to be. Every time Li wanted to do something, Padang had a million reasons why it must be put off.

"Then, too," Padang said, "there are the funerals."

"Funerals." Li did not want to think of funerals.

"For those killed in action. There are some seventy funerals scheduled for today, and the families will necessarily be upset. Should there be some unrest as a result, we do not want the diplomats aware of it. Correct?"

"I suppose so."

"As a prelude to our reentrance into the world community, I think that we should rebroadcast today your message to the people, this time as a feed to, say, CNN. How would that be, Sen?"

"That is a start."

"Good. That is what we will do. Then, perhaps on Wednesday, we will release the diplomats. The oil people, let us say, on Friday."

"Wednesday. You are putting me off another day, Omar. Why?"

"Funerals. There will be more funerals."

Monday, March 10, 8:57 A.M.

With Li Sen appeased for a while more, Padang returned to his office at the palace, once the office of Mohammed Hassanal.

Awg Nazir, now the acting police chief, was waiting for him, sitting at the table with the telephones.

Padang pulled a chair away from the table and sat down. "The city?"

Nazir smiled his reassurance. He was quite comfortable in his new role. "Very quiet, Omar. We will see when the funerals begin."

"And the oil field?"

"Also quiet, except for the fires at Albatross and Mirador. The navy tells me that Albatross may be contained within another ten days, but the other continues to rage."

"What of Lieutenant Kwee?"

"I talked to him half an hour ago. By midafternoon, all of the charges will be in place."

Kwee was the demolitions expert with the rapid response team. His task was to lower the prepared boxes of explosives into the water from a boat, then move them toward the platform legs until the magnetic plates locked them in place.

"And Hashim reports that the control panels are set up. He will arm the charges as soon as Kwee is done."

"Our intensive planning proves itself worthwhile. Are we distributing the contents of the Muara warehouse?"

"As we speak, Omar," Nazir said.

Weaponry stockpiled in that warehouse over the past months would come as a surprise to anyone who attempted to interfere with Padang's scheme.

Still, Nazir did not appear entirely happy, and Padang asked, "You disapprove of something?"

The man sighed and said, "Dyg Thambipillai. He is not entirely reliable, Omar, and taking the tanker was not part of our plans. It is a diversion we do not need, and we should abandon that course."

"Never! It is a million barrels of our oil!"

"Well spent if we avoid a confrontation."

Confrontation did not frighten Padang in the least.

"I will control Thambipillai. And in fact, we will utilize him as our messenger should the Japanese attempt a foolhardy stunt. I will compose the message and send it to him."

Nazir did not look happier, but nodded and said, "Very well."

"Excellent. Is there anything we are forgetting, Awg?"

"I don't know where Ali Haji has gone. Colonel Bakir said that Haji and his men were near Lumut, but they haven't been seen for some time."

Padang whisked away Haji with a swipe of his hand. "They have run into the jungle like the spineless snakes they are. Without Hassanal to guide him, Haji cannot find his own buttocks."

"Colonel Bakir also reported that there may be a Gurkha helicopter still in the country."

"What!"

"He has been interviewing citizens in Kuala Belait, and some said that a helicopter flew south, rather than west, after the battle."

"Damn the man! If he reports one, there are more. Find him for me."

It took nearly twenty minutes to locate Bakir, and when he was finally at a telephone, Padang picked up his own.

"How many helicopters, Colonel?"

"At least one, Minister."

"Tell me the range of possibility, Shamin."

"There may have been two . . . possibly three."

"What else?"

"An armored personnel carrier or two appear to have been captured. Nothing of consequence."

The man was a babbling idiot.

"Can you tell me positively that they are no longer in Brunei?"

A hesitation, then, "Our border patrols have not seen them leave."

"They are Gurkhas?"

Another hesitation. "It is likely."

"What is your air strength?"

"I now have eleven commandeered helicopters, though many of the pilots lack extensive experience."

"All of them, Shamin! I want all of them searching for Major Shaikh."

"If we find him?"

"Destroy him."

Sunday, March 9, 10:12 P.M.

"Task Force Seventy-One is two hours away from contact with the *Maru Hokkaido*."

The way his armpits were drenched, Chris Drieser might have been in Hap Harned's place, having to make crucial decisions. He looked around his office to reassure himself that someone else was going to be in charge of life-and-death decisions.

Judy Blalock sat at the small conference table. She had gone off somewhere to wash her face and change to jeans and sweatshirt, and she appeared a hell of a lot fresher than Drieser felt.

The three TV sets emitted color images, but no sound. There hadn't been a breaking news story in hours, but that might not last for much longer. Every major newspaper in the country was carrying the high-seas drama on the front page, and the situation in Brunei had achieved at least second-page status. That would change as the international media flocked to Kuching to interview the mounting horde of refugees.

"We've got the Marines and SEALs aboard," Harned said, "but they're part of Plan Two."

Plan One, Drieser knew, was show-of-force and negotiation, the order issued by the Security Council.

"Wannabe dictators tend to not have a realistic view of international relations, Hap."

"I'm all too aware of that, Chris."

"So what's your expectation?"

"We'll sail into view, and someone is going to tell us to back off, or they'll sink the tanker."

"And you'll go to Plan Two."

"Want to know about it?"

"No. You're the man on the scene. You can run that part of the show. In fact, I prefer it."

"You and I get along just fine, Chris. I wish there were more like you over at the building with five sides. We've got a couple ways we can go, contingent on what we find. My only problem's my Japanese liaison officer."

"How's that?"

"He wants to lead the charge. Army mentality."

Drieser laughed. "Have you got anything more from Koehler?"

"Not yet. We've got a photo recon sortie under way along the coast. When I get the pictures, I'll send 'em along to you. Along with everyone else in the damned world. CIA, DIA, and the National Security Council are all demanding a constant stream of intelligence."

"You're not going to be negotiating with pirates, Hap." Drieser was certain of that.

"You're probably correct. Whoever's in charge in Brunei will be calling the shots."

"You got the files on Bakir and Padang?"

"I did, but who in hell's this Li Sen?"

"I'm still looking for him, Hap. He's a brand-new face."

"Maybe only a face," Harned said. "He could represent the clean-cut image of democracy while someone else pulls the trigger."

"Possible. I'll look at that angle."

In fact, Drieser thought that what was taking place in

Brunei was going to be more important than what was happening with the tanker, though it was the tanker that had captured the world's attention. The media certainly hadn't let up—page one with the print guys, and lead item for the nightly anchors.

If these guys in Bandar Seri Begawan had ignored the tanker, they'd probably have gotten away with their little revolution. His study of Padang's dossier hadn't been extremely fruitful on the surface, but he had a feeling the man was as treacherous as they came.

And he desperately needed more information.

"Any idea when Koehler will get back to you, Hap?"

"None. My F-18 Hornet is going to drop a secure radio to the Gurkhas after it shoots the pictures. We may learn more then."

"Let me know."

"I'll do that. Here's the deal. You keep the diplomats at bay, Chris, and I'll get the job done."

Monday, March 10, 2:36 P.M.

The Black Hawk remained low, its shadow on the emerald canopy of the jungle below seemingly within touch. Benjamin Shaikh glanced back at the shadow behind them from his perch next to the gunner in the open side doorway, then returned his attention to that which was in front of them.

Only more jungle. Hills rising. The helicopter followed the terrain, banking left and right around the hilltops as it pursued a wandering course more or less to the west.

In the copilot's seat, Frank Morris had been allowed to assume the controls. Morris was in the seat as a result of his winnings at some exotic version of poker. Shaikh had allowed the copilot's payoff of the bet—an hour of flight time—in good humor, but his own pilot had signalled him of Morris's competence.

"Love it!" Morris called over the intercom. "It's been a few years since I had my hands on one of these babies."

"You have a nice touch," the pilot told him.

Shaikh let their chatter move to the back of his mind as he studied the forbidding landscape. This was to be a short reconnaissance trip, not more than twenty minutes, to evaluate the possibility of bringing some of Captain Singh's platoons and an augmentation of supply in from Miri Marudi. If they did not encounter the Bell helicopters under Bakir's command, he might well go directly into Sarawak and retrieve the first load himself.

Now that he had orders from his regimental commander, no matter how circuitous those orders, he wanted his command together. He fully expected to be told in the near future that he would be expected to maintain a guerillalike pressure on Shamin Bakir and Omar Padang.

The jungle below was almost hypnotic. The unending greenness at this low level of flight tried to capture the mind and entrance it. He forced his eyes to scan left and right, to avoid the trap.

The Black Hawk rode its pillar of air softly around a rocky peak protruding from the canopy and . . .

"There!" the other door gunner yelled. "Ten o'clock high!"

Shaikh had to duck his head and look through the windscreen. A Bell JetRanger was several miles away to the southwest, but it had spotted them and was turning toward them.

"Your aircraft," Morris said.

"My aircraft," his pilot said, assuming control.

"We will evade," Shaikh ordered.

"Yes, sir."

The pilot continued the turn on around the peak, soaring even lower, closer to the jungle, to hide himself behind the peak.

And as they completed the circle, the peak high on Shaikh's right . . .

Two more helicopters appeared from nowhere.

One rose above a shallow hill on the left and immediately opened fire.

The second dove from a vantage point above the cliff.

And they were caught in a murderous cross fire.

Thunder filled the interior of the Black Hawk as the door gunners opened up without command, and as the skin of the helicopter reverberated with hits from the two enemy aircraft.

His pilot tried to pull up the nose of the helo even as he was hit. Pieces of shattered plexiglass and blood spattered backward.

And Shaikh felt an incredible pain in his hip, was spun around, and crashed into the rear bulkhead. The cord of his headset nearly pulled the earphones from his head.

Morris yelled, "Hold on! I've got it!"

The Black Hawk sideslipped to the right, diving within inches of the jungle as it shot beneath the attacker on the right. Fighting the tilt of the craft, the left-door gunner pulled his trigger to the stop, the muzzle raised to the stop that kept it from firing into the rotors, and a hailstorm of lead ripped open the belly of the JetRanger as it shot over them.

The Brunei helicopter from the north zigzagged to avoid its disintegrating companion and fell in behind them, still firing.

Morris reversed controls, ripping leaves, scraping the jungle top with the fuselage, and accelerated.

Over the open intercom, Shaikh could hear the labored breathing and groans coming from his pilot as Shaikh pushed himself to his feet.

And instantly collapsed. His right hip and right leg were numb. No pain. Blood coated his pelvic area.

"Major?" Morris called.

"We can outrun him, Mr. Morris?" Shaikh hoped his voice was much stronger than his leg.

"Damn sure. It's a two-twelve, and we've got at least seventy miles an hour on him."

"Do so. Do not lead them in the direction of the camp."

"Ten-four."

In seconds, Morris had taken them out of range of the enemy guns, and he kept the Black Hawk low, skimming the canopy, dodging around the hills, hiding them from the pursuit.

One of the door gunners dropped beside Shaikh, withdrew his *kukri*, and cut away the utilities. The flesh of his hip was ripped open, the wound gaping widely, the blood flowing freely. The man applied a bandage, urged him upward enough to wrap the long tails of the bandage around his hip, and tied it in place.

"I cannot tell if it hit the bone, Major."

"I can," Shaikh assured him.

"I see Labi," Morris said. "I'm cutting southeast."

"The other helos?"

"Can't see 'em, and we're staying low enough to avoid their radar. How you doing, Major?"

Not well. The other door gunner, who had gone to the aid of the pilot, looked back at him and shook his head. He could still hear the breathing in his headset, but the groans had subsided, and it would not be long before the man who had served him so well would serve him no more.

"As soon as you find a clearing of some kind, please land, Mr. Morris."

The American took his time about it. When he found a tiny opening in the jungle, he first established his coordinates in relation to the village of Labi, then made a wide circle to be certain the Brunei helicopters had been truly left behind. Approaching slowly, he settled them into the jungle.

Through the open doors, Shaikh could see that the rotors had the barest of clearance. They sliced and cut the branches and leaves, creating a hurricane of green that swirled around them.

Then the gear touched down and Morris immediately shut down the engines.

"We've got a hydraulic leak, and a loss of oil pressure on the starboard turboshaft," he said. "Repairable."

While Shaikh watched, Morris clambered over the pilot, unfastening his harness, and the two door gunners slid out of the compartment and went to help the man out of his seat.

He glanced out the left door in time to see the uniformed men emerge from the jungle.

From all sides.

Eleven

Captain Dyg Thambipillai was proud to be such an instrumental force in the revolution. The new minister, Omar Padang, had told him as much.

Thambipillai had never met the minister, and had only talked to him twice, but found him to be a true inspiration. He was bringing to Brunei the leadership it had long been lacking.

And Thambipillai was to be one of the leaders.

The responsibility made him feel faint.

Padang had told him the citizens would revere his name, though only if he followed Padang's instructions to the letter.

Which was not necessarily so. A true leader followed the vision of his superiors, but was also innovative. Thambipillai had read that somewhere, and he did not intend to forget it.

For the time being, however, he had his task to perform.

He had learned to read the *Maru Hokkaido*'s radar set very well. It was so much more powerful than any he had ever encountered that he distrusted it in the beginning. Now, however, he thought that the symbols that appeared on it were reflective of the situation. This had been borne out in the last few hours.

The blips on the screen—and so many, many of them!—had evolved into the ships he could now see through his binoculars. There were six of them at the moment, but if the radar were to be believed, many more would appear soon.

As he scanned the seas ahead, he was amazed at the rapidity of the response. The gray ships seemed puny, but he was a realist. He knew of their size.

And there was the aircraft carrier. He steadied the glasses on it, finally seeing the source of the airplanes that had flown over many times. No, the aircraft carrier was not a surprise.

Any other man would have been fully intimidated, he knew, but not he. He had a weapon much more powerful than any the aircraft carrier would throw at him.

Thambipillai lowered the glasses so they hung on the strap around his neck and turned to look over the bridge. Two of his men stood near the wing doors. The man standing watch, a Japanese who was the second officer, leaned lightly against the immobile helm. He had nothing to do.

The captain, Hirosiuta, cowered in one corner, his eyes following Thambipillai's movements. Such a weakling!

Hirosiuta's humble demeanor was one reason Thambipillai allowed the man a limited freedom of movement—it would give him a false sense of his own importance and, paramount, help to keep the tanker's crew in line.

He strode to the communications panel and lifted the microphone from its clip. It would not matter which frequency he was on; he was certain the naval ships would monitor all frequencies.

"This is Captain Dyg Thambipillai of the Republic of Brunei Navy. I wish to speak to the captain of the aircraft carrier."

It took them several minutes to respond.

"Captain Thambipillai, this is Captain Grant Norris of the United States. I command the *Eisenhower.*"

"Captain Norris, on behalf of my government, I will read the following statement to you."

He unfolded the paper that had been telexed to him from Omar Padang and began to read: "The Republic of Brunei will not tolerate interference by any nation in its internal affairs or international commerce. The Republic intends to aggressively protect its interests.

"The tanker *Maru Hokkaido* is currently under quarantine and will remain so until the Japanese government responds with full payment for its cargo under the terms dictated by the Republic. The tanker will be released upon compliance with this condition.

"Should overt hostile action be directed toward the tanker, the Republic of Brunei is prepared to destroy the oil platforms of the fields under its ownership. The platforms have already been prepared for destruction. It should be obvious that a consequence of that action will be toxic contamination of the seas.

"Further, the Republic demands that any international interference in its rightful business cease immediately. If military ships or aircraft of other nations are present anywhere in the vicinity of Brunei on March twelfth, at one o'clock in the afternoon, the systematic destruction of the platforms will begin.

"The environmental consequences will rest with those who do not comply with these instructions."

As he read, Thambipillai's chest filled with his pride and his power. The world would bow to his will.

"Additionally, the task force I now see will adhere strictly to the following stipulations. First, no ship of the task force will approach within . . ."

Monday, March 10, 3:12 P.M.

The *Maru Hokkaido* seemed to be as large as the aircraft carrier on which Meoshi Kyoto was embarked. With his borrowed binoculars, he studied the tanker as she rode the swells nearly eight kilometers away. She was a calm and sturdy presence, with no activity on her decks, and seemingly no concern for the oppressive force gathered around her.

The French task force under the command of Admiral Marc Jardin was arrayed to the west of the tanker, and Hap Harned had formed his fleet into a shallow arc blockading the north. Almost twenty kilometers to the east, Admiral Yakama and the *Akagi* stood sentinel on the left flank. Twenty-one ships-of-war, not counting the two submarines, wherever they were, with enough firepower to create a world war faced the tanker. A dozen Japanese, American, and French aircraft circled the area high above.

The three mighty carriers and their escorts had not disheartened the pirate in the least. The message received from a man who called himself Captain Dyg Thambipillai had demanded that the fleet stand off from the tanker by five kilometers. Hap Harned had tested that demand by placing his defensive screen of destroyers four-and-a-half kilometers from the supertanker. So far, Thambipillai had not complained about the intrusion, illustrating either his inability to read the radars aboard the *Hokkaido* or his supreme confidence in his communiqué.

That was now under debate in New York, Washington, Tokyo, and other capitals.

Kyoto lowered the binoculars and turned from the window as a junior officer called out, "Admiral, Undersecretary Drieser wishes to speak with you."

"Put it on the speaker phone, Lieutenant."

Drieser's voice filled the compartment. "Admiral Harned, I'm in the Situation Room with representatives of the intelligence community and the UN Ambassador. The National Security Advisor is present."

"I have my staff here, Mr. Undersecretary, along with Colonel Kyoto and Captain Edouard Margolin of the French Navy."

Kyoto looked across the room at the French liaison. He was a fine-featured man, slight of stature, but with wisdom shining in his eyes.

"Have you reached any conclusions?" Admiral Harned asked, speaking into the air.

"At the moment," Drieser said, "Plan A looks weak, and Plans B-1, B-2, and B-3 should probably be suspended."

After all the work of the assault commanders, Harned did not even scowl, but merely asked, "Rationale?"

"Thambipillai's threat has not been confirmed. We still can't get through to the diplomatic posts, and we've tried to contact Li Sen or Omar Padang, but neither is responding. There was an earlier international broadcast of a . . . manifesto of sorts by Li Sen, but it didn't mention mining the oil field or the drilling platforms. DIA and NSA have photo interpretation experts going over all of the satellite film we can find of the oil fields. The problem, of course, is that there were so many marine craft traversing the field during the evacuation that it's difficult to pinpoint any mining activities."

"It may have been subsurface," Harned pointed out.

"True. Until we know more, though, the UN Security

Council doesn't want to force the issue. We do have an open line to our ambassador in New York."

Kyoto did not want to force the issue, either. At least, Kato Asume, with whom he had spoken an hour before, did not want to do it. Asume and the Foreign Ministry feared that the Brunei fields might well be sabotaged as Thambipillai claimed. Japan did not want to lose its 70% share of the crude oil exports. And of the total production, with liquified natural gas a prime component, the United Kingdom, South Korea, Thailand, and Singapore—all of whom imported substantial percentages—were also sending frantic messages to the United Nations Security Council.

"Have you heard from Koehler?" Drieser asked.

"Not yet. We've got a radio on the ground at the Gurkha encampment, and we've talked to a Captain Shrestha, but Koehler is out of touch, and the commanding officer hasn't returned from a recon mission. Shrestha seems to think he may have been shot down."

"This thing is going to hell fast, Admiral. March twelfth isn't that far off, and we don't know what the hell 'in the vicinity of' means."

"You keep plugging for information, and I'll do the same," Harned said.

The connection was broken, and Kyoto crossed to stand next to the chair where Harned sat. Margolin joined them.

"I'm open to suggestions, gentlemen," the admiral said.

"I do not think," Kyoto said, "that the revolutionaries would risk their deterrent—and their source of revenue— if we proceeded to board the tanker."

"You doing a little wishful thinking, Meoshi?"

"Perhaps."

"Edouard?"

"The colonel is probably correct, Admiral. However, we do not know enough about these men Li and Padang to

judge their probable reactions. If one or the other is . . .
not of sound mind, we could initiate an action that would
pollute the seas for many years."

"That's what Chris Drieser's thinking, I suspect,"
Harned said. "Plus, there's two platforms burning. Our
signal of their determination."

Kyoto turned to look toward the tanker. "So we wait
and stare across the waters at one another?"

"That's what we do, Meoshi."

Monday, March 10, 9:20 P.M.

The Brunei destroyer *Bulkiah* had reentered the bay in
midafternoon and taken up her mooring off Muara, posing
a problem.

When he walked to the end of the rickety dock to which
his house was attached, Koehler could see the destroyer,
but he couldn't figure out how he was going to learn who
was aboard her.

After a two-hour swim, skirting the remains of the patrol
boat and the vessels that responded to her distress, Kelly
and Suraj Irra had made their way ashore at the early-
morning, deserted piers of Muara. They sat in an empty
security shack and dried and cleaned their weapons, then
scouted around until they located a pair of well-used ponchos. By the time they left the shack, their damp clothing
and weapons concealed beneath the rain gear, workers
were beginning to arrive, cranes to move, and forklifts to
shuttle about.

The port still had several dozen ships to offload, and
the inconvenience of a revolution wouldn't interfere with
that, until there were no more laden freighters in the
bay. Almost all of Brunei's sustenance relied on imports—
agriculture was constrained by the jungle with only 1% of

the land arable, and Kelly suspected that foreign interests would shut off the flow of goods soon, if they hadn't already.

Until someone got thirsty for oil.

Taking two separate routes through the port city, Koehler and Irra each collected a set of observations, then met at the western outskirts on the bay. After determining that their intelligence gathering left a great deal to be desired, they found a water taxi, which delivered them to the ladder at the foot of Koehler's veranda in Kampong Ayer. His dinghy and outboard motor were still tethered to the post of the veranda.

During the day, they holed up in the house, depleted the supplies of Coca-Cola and roast beef, and made several forays into Bandar Seri Begawan. As the only foreigners at large, they had kept to the back streets, but they had determined that life appeared to be returning to normal. Most of the shops were open, and the streets contained about half the normal flow of foot and vehicle traffic. The palace was still surrounded by military and police vehicles, and the frequency of patrols on the streets was higher than usual. The hotels were well-attended by both police and army guardians, and Koehler had seen a few of his oil industry counterparts relaxing in the sun outside two of the hotels. Irra reported the same conditions for a few of the diplomatic community housed in other hotels. No one appeared to be in danger, but they weren't free to roam.

The telephones were working, though Kelly didn't want to press his luck by trying to call someone who wouldn't answer, anyway. The radio and television broadcasts had resumed in full, but relevant news was scant.

Between recon outings, Kelly worried about Sherry. By now, she should be in Beaufort, and he longed to make a call to find out. He was relatively certain, though, that out-of-country calls wouldn't be going through.

They waited until dark, taking advantage of the shower. Koehler donned fresh clothing, but Irra wouldn't accept a loan of jeans and a sport shirt. He would stay in the uniform he had washed out in the kitchen sink.

By six o'clock, they had decided jointly that they weren't going to get aboard the *Bulkiah*. By seven o'clock, they had a fair idea of how they were leaving the capital.

When darkness had settled firmly on the city, they left the house with two small duffel bags containing their weapons and walked for almost six blocks. They were alone on the streets.

"You know, Suraj, they might actually be enforcing this curfew."

"I do not think we will find a taxi, Commander."

He hadn't been able to train Irra to use his first name.

"Then it's going to be a long walk."

"We could steal a car."

"Good idea."

In a pitch-black alley off the next street, they located an old Fiat sedan. It was locked.

Irra ripped open the Velcro closure on his duffel, extracted the Armalite, and used the butt to break the side window.

It was a sharp, sudden explosion of sound, and Koehler stood stock-still, listening for a reaction.

The lights in the house across the alley came on.

Tires screeched, and a Jeep whipped off the street behind them, plowing into the alley, its headlights eradicating Kelly's night vision. Just their luck for a passing patrol to hear the break-in.

He dove behind the Fiat, landing on his side in the dirt, fighting to get the travel bag open.

Two pistol shots cracked.

More glass shattered—the rear window.

From behind the hood of the car, Irra fired two shots in return.

"Save the Jeep!" Koehler called out.

"As you say."

He rolled to the right, moving rapidly, and found himself behind an overly full trash can.

Two more shots thunked into the trunk of the car.

Irra fired once more.

Koehler looked around the can, saw two figures crouched to either side of the Jeep, barely discernible behind the glare of light. Irra wasn't shooting out these headlights.

Kelly rolled again, to his left, rose to his knees and crawled madly for the protection of shrubbery flanking the house behind him. Lights had come on there, too, but then went dark at the sound of shots.

He reached the bushes, dived under them to the base of the house, which was mounted on short stilts. Crawling beneath the house, he listened as a few more shots were exchanged.

Near the front of the house, which faced on the street, he slithered back toward the alley.

Now he was behind the Jeep, and he could clearly make out the policeman on this side of the vehicle.

Selecting single fire, he raised the Armalite to his shoulder, sighted, and squeezed off one shot.

The slug took the man's legs out from under him.

He issued a scream that would curdle cream, and his partner decided to abandon ship. He spun around and sprinted for the head of the alley.

Koehler couldn't see him well in the darkness, but he estimated the man's speed from the sound of shoe leather, and fired three shots, keeping them low.

And was rewarded with the sound of heavy meat hitting the ground accompanied by a yelp.

Koehler hoped he had gotten both of them in the legs. He didn't want to kill anyone.

He scrambled to his feet, raced toward the second man, and found him cowering at the side of the alley, his arms raised to protect his face from the next round headed his way.

He had dropped his semiautomatic, and Koehler couldn't see it in the darkness. He reached down, groped the belt, found the portable radio, and ripped it from its clip. The man's left leg was cocked at an acute and awkward angle.

"No, no! Spare me, sir! I beg you!"

Ignoring him, Koehler ran back toward the Jeep. Irra was bent over the first cop, also retrieving the radio. Kelly was surprised that he and Irra seemed to think along the same lines.

He reached the Jeep and slid behind the wheel.

"Suraj?"

"I should shoot him."

"Maybe he's just following the best orders he's got."

Irra stepped over the groaning man and settled into the seat.

Koehler released the handbrake, slapped the shift into first, and came off the clutch. He dodged around the bullet-riddled trunk of the Fiat and headed for the opposite end of the alley.

He came out of the alley burning rubber and changing gears, and a block later, he slowed to a patrolling pace.

"With luck, the people in those houses won't go to their aid for a few minutes," Koehler said.

"And it is unlikely there will be a telephone close, Commander. We have perhaps a five-minute head start."

Nearly eight minutes went by before they heard the first of the sirens, and by then, they were on the far western side of the city. Irra fiddled with controls of the police radio, but the language was Malay, and neither of them got much out of the transmissions.

Six minutes after the sirens began, they reached the airport. It was darkened, and it was guarded by two policemen at the main entrance. The sentinels waved at the police Jeep as it went by.

Kelly parked near the general aviation section and shut off the lights and engine. They got out and walked toward the chain-link fence. The gate was locked, but they helped each other scramble over it.

There were a dozen aircraft parked on the ramp, ranging from light twins to the Sultan's gigantic Boeing 747.

"I see a problem right off, Suraj."

"There are no helicopters."

"That's the problem."

"Then we will take another."

"I haven't flown fixed wing in years."

"It is time for you to refresh your skills, Commander."

"There's no place to land where we're going."

"We will hope for the best, then. What is your choice?"

"Shit. Let's try the Piper Aztec."

Monday, March 10, 10:18 P.M.

The *Serendipity* lay canted on her starboard side on the fine white sand of the cove.

Sherry Koehler had beached her on the seaward side of the island just after five in the morning. With her sails lowered and her keel driven firmly into the sand, the ketch was at the mercy of the surging sea, and she rocked from side to side as Sherry and Monica inflated the dinghy, mounted the seven-horsepower outboard motor, then moved supplies from the sailboat to the dinghy.

They used the oars to row the hundred yards to shore,

then covered the dinghy with foliage and spent most of the day hidden back in the tree line, watching the cove. The mosquitoes were lively, the heat oppressive, and the outlook grim.

It wasn't until midafternoon that full low tide laid the ketch over, and Sherry winced with every scraping sound that floated over the water. The wave action rocked the hull against the bottom, and she pictured the smooth fiberglass serrated by rocks and sand.

She loved that ketch, and she ached with every motion of the sea. All that kept her from crying was her worry about Kelly. He could be caught, tortured, and killed by now.

At four o'clock in the afternoon, under a sun that beat mercilessly down on them, she and Monica stripped to panties and T-shirts and waded out to the boat. The sand beneath her feet felt firm, and it was warmed by the heat penetrating the shallow depth of the water.

"I hope we find the beer," Monica said. "I'm damned if I can figure out how I forgot it."

"You're taking this pretty well."

"Ten years from now, Sherry, we'll look back on this day and laugh ourselves silly."

She hoped so. She was afraid Kelly and Irra would do something foolish, all in the name of some macho man-and-warfare philosophy.

When she reached the boat, she was relieved that the level of the water was below the edge of the cockpit. Diesel fuel coated the surface and she splashed it away as she moved. She'd probably come out of this with some kind of chemical burns on her legs.

Scrambling, she pulled herself into the cockpit, then used the cabin rails, the aft boom and mast, and the cabin side to climb to the upper side, which was about ten feet above water. Monica tossed the canvas bag to her, then followed her route upward.

Sherry slipped through the lifeline and levered herself onto the hull. It was slippery, and she slid over it on her buttocks until she neared the stern.

It was a monstrous hole from her perspective. Some burst of bullets had created a ragged cavern about eight inches wide by eighteen inches long. Through the hole, she could see the perforated fuel tank.

"No wonder we were going down," Monica said as she crawled into place alongside Sherry.

"Find the sheet. This damned hull is hot."

Davis dug a sheet out of the bag, and they draped it over themselves to shield them from the sun. It didn't help much, trapping heat, but kept them out of the direct rays.

"Sunblock 10 or 12, I think," Davis said.

"Start mixing," Sherry said as she roughened the edges of the hole with sandpaper.

Davis found a paper plate, squeezed equal amounts of epoxy and catalyst from the large tubes onto the plate, then blended them together with a clothespin. Sherry told her how to coat the edges of the hole while she cut a piece of fiberglass mat to size. The two of them pressed it into place and held it while the epoxy hardened and bonded the mat to the hull. It was going to be ugly, she thought.

Then they worked their way forward, staying under the sheet, and treated the other smaller holes in the same way. By the time the last bullet hole was patched with the porous mat, the epoxy around the large hole had hardened. She used a screwdriver to pop the lids off a quart can of resin and a smaller can of hardener.

She didn't have any measuring tools, so Koehler made an estimate and poured half of the quart of fiberglass resin into a cereal bowl, then added a portion of the catalyst. She also didn't have a brush, so she used a towel from the galley to dip into the mixture and coat the fiberglass matting. The resin dripped through the matting in places. She went forward, with Monica carrying the bowl, and coated the other holes. Then back to the major hole to pour the rest of the resin over the solidifying gel.

"This is going to be so lumpy we'll lose five miles an hour of speed."

"Five knots," Sherry corrected.

"Damned proper sailors."

They spent the next two hours perched on the lower side of the cockpit, taking turns with the manual pump, and squirting dirty, fuel-laden water back into the sea. She knew she wouldn't have an engine—the diesel fuel was contaminated beyond recovery.

At six o'clock, they mixed the last of the resin and catalyst and put another coat on the patches. It was all they had, and the patches were thin, but she thought they would last until Beaufort.

Sherry waded around the boat into breast-high water and saw that the keel skeg was free of the sand. Without an engine, she wouldn't be able to rock the ketch free, so she had to hope that when the tide came in, the boat would slide herself toward deeper water. When she came upright, the keel would have to be free of the sand, otherwise they'd need a Force Three gale to break her loose.

They splashed back to shore—with the beer—and drank two cans apiece while consuming peaches and beans directly from the cans.

After dark, she restlessly left the protection of the trees and walked down the beach to check on the water level about every half hour. Monica came with her every time. It was preferable to staying alone in the jungle, listening to the eerie sounds. The insects were out in force, and they had liberally coated themselves with repellent.

Around ten-twenty by Monica's watch, the water had

reached the level of the dinghy, and they pulled it farther up the beach and re-covered it with weeds and shrubs. There was a quarter-moon, but it was blocked by a patch of clouds, and Koehler could barely make out the pale blob of the ketch a hundred yards away. A breeze was coming offshore, and she took that as a good omen. From the other direction, the wind wouldn't help a bit.

"I'm going to walk out and check on her."

"Not without me, you aren't."

The two of them waded into the swirling water and moved off into the darkness. The pale whiteness of the cabin roof gave her a bearing, and she aimed for it.

In moments they were waist deep. Some kind of fish brushed against her leg, and horrifying images of blowfish or sharks flashed through her mind. She didn't mention it to Monica. Between the two of them, they could work the sight of a snake into nightmares.

When they reached the *Serendipity*, she was gratified to find that the boat was bobbing on the surface, the water level lapping just below the edge of the cockpit coaming. It was much higher than at three o'clock.

"Oh, this is promising!"

"When we put her ashore," Koehler said, "she was carrying the weight of the water inside the hull. The displacement should be better now."

"How long?"

"I don't have the tables, but high tide should be around one or two in the morning. The wind's right."

"Maybe we should stay here."

In fact, Sherry thought the bobbing cockpit considerably more inviting than the jungle.

"Let's do it."

"What about the dinghy?"

"We'll leave it. I'd rather catch the wind when we can."

They had to help each other into the higher cockpit,

and Sherry was grateful to sit on the riser of the settee, her back against the cockpit sole. Each rise and settle of the boat gave her hope.

"We left our jeans back there," Monica reminded her.

"I'll sail into Beaufort stark naked before I go back into that jungle."

"I'll join you. We'll create quite a scene for the Islamic authorities."

By eleven o'clock, the cant of the deck under her back was about sixty degrees from horizontal. Ten minutes later, she felt the boat shift under them, sliding down the slope of the bottom.

And a few minutes later, Sherry nearly leaped out of the cockpit when the ketch began sliding, jerking, bumping against the bottom.

Then stopped.

"This flight's leaving ahead of schedule, Monica."

"God, I hope so."

"We've got to be ready. I think we slid bow first, so we may be coming around. As soon as we get some more movement, we want to get the foresail up."

"Hell, let's do it now."

Considering that the breeze under the sail might help push them off, even though they'd probably get it wet, Sherry agreed, and they made their way forward, walking like tightrope walkers, holding onto the cabin rail, on the lifeline that was now above water.

The boat lurched and she nearly lost her balance, and though she cringed at the likely damage to the hull side, she was also elated.

Working together, they cranked out the foresail, and though it dipped into the sea several times, it slowly began to fill. Mainly, it provided a little lift, urging the *Serendipity* to right herself.

And she was. The deck was about fifty degrees from horizontal.

"Let's do the next one."

The aft sail was about half-deployed when the ketch abruptly slid off a shelf, and Monica went diving over the side. The boom, which had been lashed along the center-line, came loose and splashed into the water.

Sherry slid down the cabin to the rails, then to the lifeline, and reached a hand over the side toward the arm that waved in the darkness. She found Monica's wrist and pulled.

Monica was laughing as she came aboard.

"We're actually going to do this!"

Sherry laughed with her. "Of course we are."

"I feel like Robinson Crusoe. Or the female version thereof."

The keel was bouncing on the bottom, but the ketch was nearly upright, and the two of them went into action, securing lines, forcing the aft boom to the left, centering the helm.

And then she was free, picking up speed, moving out of the cove.

And Sherry heard the powerful engines of a gunboat coming around the point from the port side.

"Oh, shit!" Monica yelped.

"Drop sails!"

One after another, they released the lines and the sails plummeted downward to collapse haphazardly on the booms and deck.

Too late.

The gunboat had spotted them.

A bright blink of light from its foredeck alerted her, and Sherry dropped to the deck.

A missile of some kind whistled as it passed overhead, then hit the water two hundred yards ahead of the boat.

She felt the concussion under the deck as it exploded. A giant geyser of water reached for the sky.

She peeked over the side deck, saw another blink.

"Come on!"

"Sherry!"

"Let's go!"

She went over the starboard side and hit the water on her face, flailing her arms, as the second round exploded off the port side. A second later, she felt herself lifted out of the water as the shock wave passed under. The detonation pounded her ears.

When she shook her head to clear it, she saw that Monica was alongside her, swimming like an Olympian.

They were sixty yards from the boat when the marksman on the gunboat finally found his target.

The *Serendipity* erupted into tiny pieces of fiberglass, wood, nylon, and some of her favorite possessions.

Monday, March 10, 11:52 P.M.

Colonel Shamin Bakir called *him* for a change.

Padang was having a very late dinner at his desk in the minister's offices when he picked up the phone. He brushed bread crumbs from his lips with the back of his hand and said, "Padang."

"Minister, this is Colonel Bakir."

"Well, Shamin, I thought you would be in bed by now."

"I do not sleep until my tasks are done."

Padang did not believe that for an instant, but intended to give him hope. "I am certain the committee members will recognize your diligence."

"I am calling with three reports."

"Proceed."

"The sailboat that sank the patrol boat this morning has been located and destroyed."

The naval commander had already reported as much, and just moments before. Bakir might have been wiling away his time listening to naval radio channels, so boring was his job.

"Yes."

"There were no survivors."

"Yes."

"The riot in Lumut was quelled without problem."

It was hardly a riot. A funeral procession had become very emotional, and a number of mourners mounted soapboxes. Two had been killed.

When Padang did not react to that report, Bakir continued, "And we shot down a Black Hawk."

Now, that was news. "Where?"

"The aircraft was seventeen kilometers east of the border and eleven kilometers south of Ladi."

"So. There are Gurkhas in the country."

"Not now, I think."

"One Black Hawk. How many did you lose?"

"Only one."

"And what else have you learned, Shamin, that I should know?"

After a moment's pondering of his response, the army commander said, "Our inventory suggests that five armored personnel carriers are missing."

"Suggests! What a quaint suggestion you make, Colonel. What are you doing about it?"

"Searching for them, naturally. But it is difficult, for they will likely be in the jungle."

"Along with the Gurkhas who are not there. Do this quickly, Shamin. We cannot have disruptions in the days ahead."

Padang replaced the telephone without bidding a goodbye. He forked a large piece of the gravy-drenched beef into his mouth—the Sultan's kitchens were well-stocked—and chewed contentedly.

His position of power was entrenched. Or for the moment, Li's position of power. Thambipillai's announcement this afternoon had quelled the entire world. No one dared move against him.

It was entirely a satisfying feeling. The United Nations, with all of its pomp and circumstance and barking authority, had immediately caved in to the tiny enclave of the Republic of Brunei.

Because Omar Padang knew how to plan ahead.

Li Sen had been incensed when he learned of the mined platforms through the televised reports, but Li Sen had also been ready to cede his authority to the world when it was unnecessary.

The hearty condemnation of the international media threatened to undermine what little backbone the President had.

The Provisional President had much to learn about effective leadership.

Then again, Li had so very little time in which to learn.

Monday, March 10, 12:06 A.M.

Hamzah bin Suliaman's fever raged. His face was slick with the sheen of his perspiration, and his eyes were bright and hot. In the weak light of the bulb over his bunk, his skin appeared sallow, green-tinged.

The Sultan had roused himself enough to come and check on Hassanal's cousin twice, and to condemn the revolutionaries in terms not as strong as he might once have used. The Sultan was in as much shock as Suliaman.

Mohammed Hassanal paced his cage like a sleepless

tiger. The bunk room contained twenty beds and a round table with four chairs. There was little else but the belongings of evacuated oilmen still hanging in the steel lockers. Hassanal was the only one awake, though his cousin slipped into and out of consciousness or sleep. Sometimes, he could not tell which.

The heavy-duty commercial grade of carpeting laid on the deck muffled his footsteps as he circled the table, walked to the bathroom, turned, walked back. Though the sun was long gone, the heat remained, trapped by the steel walls. Lieutenant—damned—Tan Hashim had refused every plea to turn on the air-conditioning. Very likely, neither he nor his stooges knew how to do it.

Hassanal looked up with some yearning at the large vent over the table. Not even warm air recirculated through the closed room, and it was ripe with the aroma of unwashed bodies.

He looked again at the grating.

It was large enough, certainly.

He looked at the door, locked solidly. No doubt, his captor of the night was sound asleep. Hassanal began to prowl through the wall lockers, a pair of them dividing each set of bunks.

In the fourth, he found several tools, one of which was a screwdriver, and he climbed upon the table and very swiftly removed the screws holding the grate in place. When he placed a chair on the table and stood on it, he could insert his head into the opening and peer into utter blackness. With his hands, he measured the vent and decided he would have a few centimeters of width greater than his shoulders.

Climbing down from his perch, he went to the closest bunk and awakened another cousin. The young man came alert with a start, and it took a few seconds to calm him and explain his responsibilities.

"You want me to replace the grill and take down the chair? That is all?"

"Absolutely."

"Of course, Minister. I will do it."

"Then you will go back to bed. You know nothing of this."

"Yes, sir."

A few minutes later, with a screwdriver and a pair of pliers stuck in his shirt pocket where he could reach them, Hassanal was inching his way along the duct, pulling himself along with his elbows. He could not raise his back high enough to get his knees under him.

At the junctures of the sheet-metal vent, with jagged screws holding the sections together, his shoulders did not have any clearance whatsoever, and he had to work his shoulders on an angle to get past. He had not gone more than twenty feet before the screws had ripped his shirt and skin to shreds. The tang of his own blood was strong in his nostrils.

Fine. The scars would match that inflicted on his nose by Hashim's pistol. They would constantly remind him of his mission in this world—to avenge the honor of his family. Padang and Hashim would rue these days during their long suffering and throughout their afterlife.

He passed a T-fitting, much too small for him to turn into, but there was a dim light coming from it, reflected from some lighted compartment. He wondered if it was the women's prison.

Within fifteen minutes, Hassanal was completely lost. He had made two turns, and he had no idea in the world where he was located, or how far he had come.

That knowledge was relatively important for he had come to the end of the line. His head had bumped into a metal wall. To the left was a secure grate, and to the right another vent, but again, it was too small for him.

He carefully ran his hand over the panel in front of him, and his fingers located a number of screws. The heads were all on the outside, of course, so he used the pliers to grip the threads and turn them from inside.

He wondered what was on the other side, and if it would shoot as soon as he could lever an opening for himself.

Monday, March 10, 12:41 P.M.

"It would be the supreme bluff," the National Security Advisor said.

The men sitting listlessly around the table in the basement of the White House weren't much interested in the poker analogy, Drieser thought. He eyed the last half of the pastrami sandwich that the general from Defense Intelligence hadn't finished, but decided he didn't really want to ask for it. Twelve, thirteen hours in the Situation Room had made him more hungry than tired. And he was much more bored than he was hungry.

On the sidewall, a large screen displayed a boring real-time view of Brunei. There wasn't much moving in the country, judging by lights on the roads, and certainly only a few boats and ships were moving in the oil fields. Except for the two fires and the pinpricks from oil rig flares, one wouldn't have identified it as an oil field. The image was captured by an NSA satellite.

The DCI—the Director of Central Intelligence—said, "If we could only get a handle on this Li Sen. . . ."

"How is it, Mr. Director," the United Nations Ambassador asked, "that the Central Intelligence Agency is completely unaware of a man who can take over a country?"

Her frustration and sarcasm dripped with about equal intensity, and the Director was saved by the chime.

He picked up one of the phones placed on the table,

listened a moment, then nodded at Drieser. "For you, Chris."

He grabbed the handset in front of his chair. "Drieser."

"This is Judy. You were right!"

"Ah, just a lucky guess."

"If we started bottling your guesses, Chris, maybe we could get Wal-Mart to market them."

"Well, Li's a Chinese name. Given the social and economic structure of Brunei, I figured the chances were better than even that we'd find him engaged in some kind of business."

The others around the table were watching him now.

"Well," she said, "I went through the manufacturing association directories, and we found the name in the electronics association. I called some sales departments for Sony, Hitachi, Sharp, and Hyundai, and they got me right down to the guys—the salesmen—who've met Li."

Drieser listened carefully to her report, then said, "Go home, Jude. Take tomorrow off."

"Not on your life."

"Well, then, 'great job!' is the best I can do at the moment."

"I'll take that."

He replaced the phone, and said, "Anyone want to hear about Li Sen?"

They all did. The DCI looked most unhappy.

"Older Chinese man, and a Brunei citizen. Maybe in his mid-fifties. Married with three kids. He runs an electronics store in Bandar Seri Begawan. My world-class secretary has talked to four men who've had contact with Li, spent some time with him. All agree on this profile: moderate politics, a timid and peaceful man, very interested in one issue, and that's citizenship for disenfranchised Chinese. Not aggressive in the least."

"It's a bluff, then," the Security Advisor said.

"Not necessarily," Drieser countered. "Don't forget Padang."

"But Li's the ... whatever, Provisional President. He's the man at the helm, and he thinks he's shaking a big stick at the world. Empty stick."

The Ambassador looked at the advisor, then at Drieser. She asked, "How about CIA and DIA?"

The DCI said, "Let's call him on it."

The general nodded.

"I'll call the Secretary General," she said. "Someone get hold of Admiral Harned and tell him to get ready to go."

"When?" the Advisor asked.

"Give me a few hours. Make it four in the morning, their time."

"I don't think it's the Front for Democratic Reform," Drieser said. "I think it's the Front for Omar Padang. Li's a pawn."

"Facts?" the Ambassador asked.

"Nary a one."

"Tell Harned to erase a few pirates."

Tuesday, March 11, 1:11 A.M.

Suraj Irra disappeared around twelve-thirty, and when he came back, Koehler didn't ask any questions, but he knew the two police guards were either incapacitated or in-*something*.

After breaking into the Piper light-twin and discovering it was also light on fuel, they had waited around a deserted hangar for the two cops on duty at the gate to be relieved. The exchange came at midnight. Irra had cautioned against taking action when a new shift of guards might come at any moment and discover what he and Kelly were trying to hide: grand theft aircraft.

When the sergeant major materialized again out of the dark, the two of them threw their accumulated gear into the back of the plane, released the tie-downs, and pushed it across the tarmac to the fuel pumps. The breaker box controlling the electricity for the pumps was in the hangar, and after they found it, they topped off the tanks quickly.

While Irra recoiled the fuel hose, Kelly disconnected the grounding strap, then crawled up on the wing. He pulled open the door, found the parachutes, and placed one on the trailing edge for Irra while he strapped into the other.

Cinching his harness tight, Irra said, "I confess to having less confidence in your flying ability, Commander."

Koehler tapped the wing with his foot. "Only in these birds, Suraj. But, hell, we may make it."

He ducked his head and climbed inside, sliding across to the left seat. Irra followed him, then closed and dogged the door.

Twisting together the bared ends of the wires with which Irra had bypassed the key lock, Koehler powered up the panels, switched on the magnetos, and checked his fuel flow.

The engines cranked right away, sounding loud in the super silence of the airport. He didn't allow them to adequately warm up, but released the brakes and began taxiing toward the end of the runway.

"We will not ask for clearance, I suppose," Irra called over the rumble of the engines, grinning.

Koehler grinned back, happy to find a bit of humor in the man.

Toeing the left brake, he swung onto the centerline, then braked to a stop. Watching the temperatures and manifold pressures, he urged the Lycoming six-cylinder engines to operating specs, and when they reached something close, he ran the throttles up, released the brakes, and started rolling. He didn't use his landing light, navigation lights, or warning strobe.

Without runway lights, and with the moon hidden, it was an eerie takeoff run. He probably held it on the ground longer than necessary, a result of the span of time since he'd flown a twin. When he finally let the lift take over, she came off smoothly, and he retracted the gear and flaps.

He banked immediately toward the sea, and a few minutes later, they were making 160 knots at five hundred feet, flashing across the beaches.

A mile offshore, he swung gently onto a western heading, still feeling out the controls, afraid of overcompensation, becoming accustomed to the responses. He trimmed the elevator and rudder.

Irra retrieved his pack from the rear seat and found binoculars. He began scanning the sea ahead of them, but twenty minutes went by before the twinkling lights of the pumping station clarified. Koehler wasn't going to fly anywhere near it, but Irra would be able to check for activity from five miles away.

He wished he could talk to Sherry. She'd be relaxing in a Beaufort hotel by now, and he was relieved at that prospect.

"Up there." Irra pointed skyward through the windscreen.

Two sets of running lights, headed south in formation. Maybe twelve or thirteen thousand feet above them.

"I'll bet the admiral's got a few more eyes out looking over the neighborhood," Kelly said.

"More eyes than our own, yes. I do not think we have discovered much of use for him, Commander."

"They'll probably dock our pay, Suraj."

Coming up on the oil field, Koehler increased his altitude. No one was around to turn on the warning beacons, and the flaring towers provided a slightly inadequate warning.

Irra had the binoculars trained on the pumping station.

"There is no activity, Commander. I see a number of tankers and several naval vessels, but nothing is moving."

"That's strange," Koehler said. "We know the port of Muara is still operating, and I know damned well the storage tanks feeding the pipeline are probably near capacity. There should be enough crude down there to load out ten or eleven supertankers."

"But the wells are shut down."

"Doesn't stop them from shipping what's already on the shelf."

"Perhaps there are no buyers?"

"Or the UN has imposed an embargo."

As the lights of the pumping station fell behind, Koehler eased into a right bank. He was going to fly the perimeter of the field. Far away to the left, and near the middle of the field, he saw the running lights of some naval craft and figured it was a patrol boat.

They came up quickly on the fire at Mirador, and once again, he stayed clear of it, steering a course to the north. The winking, wavering flames reflected off the surface with red-yellow urgency. Irra used his binoculars.

"I think the fire is less intense. There are ships pumping water on the platform, and the containment booms cover several acres."

"I'll bet they got some divers off the *Malay Princess* and cut off fuel flow below the surface, Suraj."

"Let us hope so."

Koehler levelled the wings and continued to the west. The sliver of moon had emerged from the cloud cover, and it helped his vision a little, though not much. The skeletal framework of a platform, stark and dim against the surface of the sea, came up on the left. One of Conoco's.

He was most interested in the condition of his three charges.

A few seconds later, closer to the sea, he passed Charlie. No lights, no action, no nothing.

But it was standing, and that was something to cheer about.

As GT Bravo appeared in the windscreen, and since he was relatively assured that most of the oil field was deserted, Koehler slowed his speed and lost altitude to six hundred feet off the surface.

"There are lights on the ... fourth deck," Irra announced.

Kelly immediately changed his mind about a close-in look and dipped the right wing.

"Damn it! I told those guys to shut off the lights and put out the cat."

"What is on that deck?"

"Machinery spaces. Some dormitories."

He levelled out again, then searched the darkness. A few dim lights midway down the platform. Absentminded me, he thought.

And then a blinking light. Somewhere higher. Maybe the fifth deck.

"See that, Suraj?"

Irra was leaning back now, training the binoculars across the cabin behind Koehler's head.

"I see it. A flashlight, I think."

"Morse code?"

"No. Just blinking. It is, I think, aimed at us. He has heard our engines."

"You see any boats around? Near the legs? There's an elevator cage."

"I see no vessels."

Koehler searched his memory. Surely, they had left no one behind.

"What do we do, Suraj? I could go around and get us a closer look."

"It has stopped blinking."

"Still. . . ."

"I think, Commander, that we have another mission."

Kelly wanted badly to go back, but Suraj was right, and there was no way he'd put the Aztec down anywhere near the platform. And logically, if someone was aboard, they'd have access to the radios.

Of course, Koehler wasn't using the radios he had available, either.

"You're correct, Sergeant Major. Let's do our job."

In the next twenty minutes, they completed their circuit of the field, noting that the fire at Albatross was also dying down. The MSV *Malay Princess* was still pumping a wall of water on it. They spotted a dozen small boats scurrying about through the field.

Headed inland, they crossed over Kuala Belait at a thousand feet of altitude and at a maximum velocity of 215 miles an hour. There were a few lights on near the center of the residential compounds, but they didn't see anyone out and about at that time of the morning.

Irra said, "There are many more ships at the docks."

"They've probably brought them around from Muara. Ten bucks say Li Sen's going to force these guys back to work."

"Fortunately, I do not have American bucks."

Kuala Belait was barely behind them when Irra got on the radio and made contact with his command center in the personnel carrier. The man on the ground initiated a carrier wave on Kelly's preset direction finder frequency, and he lined up his course on it, then switched on the autopilot. He used the thumbwheel to dial in a gradual climb, to account for the terrain.

"I believe you're manning the door, Suraj."

"I am, sir."

Releasing his harness, Koehler levered himself upward to get his right knee on the seat. He avoided contact with the control yoke.

Irra assumed the same position, released the locks on the door, and held onto the handle.

When the direction finder started wavering, suggesting that the receiver was getting close to passing over the transmitter, Kelly said, "Any time, Suraj."

"Please do not forget your weapon, Commander."

Koehler reached over the seat back and hooked the duffel bag, then snapped its handles to the web gear of the parachute.

His entire log of jumps amounted to three—some basic training in emergency procedures. He distinctly remembered having a reserve chute on those jumps, but the front pack was missing from this harness. One shot, with a chute packed by someone he'd never met. The prospects weren't as rosy as they might have been.

Someone had once insisted he use a helmet, too.

And he'd had about six thousand additional feet of ground clearance in his training jumps.

Irra leaned into the door, pushing it into the slipstream, pushed one of his combat boots out onto the wing, then stood . . . and was gone.

Koehler immediately slid across to the seat just vacated, shoved hard on the door, and levered himself out onto the wing. The wind whipped at his hair and stung his eyes; his left leg just about slid from under him as he forced himself away from the fuselage. He had a momentary glimpse of a shadow of white blossoming far behind the airplane—Irra!—as he released his grip on the door.

He didn't even hear it slam shut. The tail plane slashed overhead, and he didn't bother with any silly counting system. He tore at the rip cord and heard the pilot chute swishing from its casing.

Heard it, realized the Aztec was already far away, the sound of its engines diminishing as it climbed slowly into the darkened sky. It might even make five or six hundred miles before the engines sputtered out and it made a long and fatal dive into the jungles of Borneo.

The pilot chute pulled the main canopy from the pack. He crossed his fingers mentally, trusting that someone hadn't tangled the risers. Fought to get himself flipped over and in a froggy position—arms spread, knees slightly bent, riding the current.

The jungle top below him was almost indistinguishable in the dark, his depth perception gone. He didn't know how much space and time he had left.

The parachute popped above him, the slack went out of the harness, and he was abruptly jerked upright. Looking up, he saw that the luck of the draw had given him a sport chute. He could para-glide wherever he wanted to. . . .

And he slammed into a tree.

Twelve

"Why is it, Lieutenant Thambipillai, that you test your fates so recklessly?"

"Captain. I am a captain of my patrol boat. Do not forget that."

But not of my ship, Maki Hirosiuta thought. "You cannot answer the question?"

"The question is irrelevant. Fortune has not been tempted; destiny only plays itself out. Look at those ships out there. None dare test the power of the triumphant Republic of Brunei."

The slovenly Brunei Navy commander stood near the helm, his hands clasped behind his back, his feet braced widely, staring out into the darkness, imagining himself a giant of history. His name would be featured prominently in Bruneian historical texts.

One could not even see any of the naval ships, for they

had not illuminated their navigation lights at dusk, but they were out there. Occasionally, the overflight of aircraft could be heard. Hirosiuta had been astounded by the rapidity and the size of the response. Three aircraft carriers. Blips that covered his radar screen. From the radio discourse at midday, he knew there was an American captain on one of the carriers, and he assumed an admiral to be in charge and that the United Nations had intervened in this little drama. Or perhaps a large drama. The conflict seemed fraught with peril to Hirosiuta. A mistake, an ill-chosen word, and Thambipillai *might* go down in history—as the precipitator of the world's worst oil pollution disaster. It was a dismal view.

The only other view at the moment was of the panorama of the heavens, the skies filled with a million magnificent stars of the southern constellations. He loved it under almost any circumstances.

The darkened bridge of the tanker hid Hirosiuta's grim smile. He stood to the port side, near the broken window, tasting the sea breeze, and marvelling over the ludicrous figure of Lieutenant Thambipillai. The man was a simpleton, but Hirosiuta had been disheartened at the response to the naval fleet when Thambipillai declared the Brunei oil fields mined and at risk if the task force arrayed before them attempted a foolish rescue attempt. His eavesdropping on that radio conversation was the first true revelation Hirosiuta had had of a revolution in Brunei. His plight now seemed immensely more complicated.

"I can, in fact," the pirate said, "go anywhere I wish to go in the world. There is none who can stop me."

The man was a simpleton *and* a braggart *and* an egotist. It was a dangerous combination.

He took a couple steps forward to get a better look at the man's face, what he could see of it in the wash of starlight. As he did so, he heard the rustle of clothing behind him. The two guards sitting on the floor, slumped against the rear bulkhead, moved whenever Hirosiuta moved, though they did not overly restrict him when he paced the upper spaces checking on his officers and on Yaguchi.

There was a brave new radiance on Thambipillai's face. His mouth steadily widened in what Hirosiuta assumed was a smile as a new idea apparently dawned on him.

In an attempt to head it off, Hirosiuta said, "At 0600 hours, I am going to order my men to the deck for exercise."

"What!" The Bruneian spun to stare at him.

"They have been confined to quarters for many hours. Of what use can they be to you if—"

"Exercise is unnecessary. However, in fact, we will now exercise a few of them. I want you to notify the midnight watch . . . no, half of the midnight watch to report to their stations."

"It is not possible," Hirosiuta said. "I will not assist you in piracy and kidnapping."

Thambipillai's voice grated. "Captain! I have told you over and over again to not use the word 'piracy.' "

"What other word better describes your actions?"

"We seek only what is ours. When your country has paid for our oil, we will return your ship to you."

"And my boatswain's mate? You will return his soul?"

"Awaken your men! We are getting under way."

"Had you not better speak with your superiors in Brunei? I imagine they would not condone your steering the *Hokkaido* into the middle of a United Nations task force, simply to prove your arrogance."

"I have no superiors. At sea, my word is law."

"Your word may get us all killed, Lieutenant."

"Captain! Damn you, I am the captain!"

Tuesday, March 11, 2:20 A.M.

If Benjamin Shaikh did not feel completely frustrated, he did feel highly inconvenienced at the very least. His frustration was founded less in his lack of transportation than in the disruption of his communications. He did not know what was going on around him, at the Gurkha camps in the jungle and Miri Maruda, or in the capital.

In the center of the clearing, three flashlights danced in the darkness about four meters from the ground. That was at the top of the Black Hawk, where Frank Morris and the two door gunners had dismantled housings and removed panels. They had laced vines together for their ladders and scaffolding, and they had made specialized tools from pieces of metal shaped with files and pliers. Morris seemed to have no doubt about his ability to fashion new hydraulic and oil lines and some kind of pump from bits and pieces stolen from other regions of the helicopter.

The radios were another matter. All had been shattered by a stream of 7.62-millimeter rounds, and none were ever going to work again.

He tried to be patient, and he tried to ignore the pain, as he waited at the edge of the clearing, leaning back against a fallen tree trunk with Lieutenant Ali Haji, late of the Royal Brunei Police.

Haji and twenty-seven of his patrol force had been hiding in the clearing when the wounded Black Hawk landed. Haji had been defending the refinery at Lumut when he finally realized what was happening to his country, and he had raced for the jungle in his truck. Unfortunately, the truck was several kilometers away, resting in a ditch, its rear axle broken.

When the Gurkhas appeared, the policemen were healthy but hungry, and Shaikh's door gunners had shown them how to capture and roast birds.

Haji was, however, a man lost. He knew where he was geographically, but his spiritual and social guides were gone.

"If we could but find Minister Hassanal, he would tell us what we must do," Haji said.

He had said the same thing a dozen times, notwithstanding Shaikh's patient reiteration of the royal family's disappearance.

It was pitch black, but he knew exactly how close Haji was; the fat man's odor preceded him wherever he went. Of course, Shaikh would not complain. Some time had passed since he had bathed himself, and the jungle humidity did little for hygiene.

It did little for pain, either. Morris had offered morphine, but Shaikh had preferred a clear head.

Frank Morris was a wonder.

He had barely landed the helicopter, ignoring Haji's policemen emerging from the jungle, before he was at Shaikh's side, ripping the material of his trousers apart, examining the wound, dabbing at the blood with a fragment of cloth he ripped from his own T-shirt, probing the exposed white bone.

"I'm about to operate, Major. I'd offer you whiskey, but whiskey, we ain't got. There's a shot of morphine about, I expect."

"I will not need the morphine, Mr. Morris. How bad is it?"

"You lost a sliver . . . well, more than a sliver of hipbone. I don't see any fractures, though, and that's one for our side. The meat's torn up pretty good, but I can stitch it together if we can find some thread."

Benjamin Shaikh suspected Morris was more competent as a pilot than a surgeon, but he had washed the wound with water from a canteen, pulled the lips of skin together, and emplaced seventeen "not unbeautiful," as Morris called them, stitches across the point of Shaikh's hip. Sprinkling sulfa powder profusely, he had wrapped his repairs in gauze and tape.

"You stay off that hip for a couple days, Major, and stay away from the nurses, you'll be good as new."

By the time Morris had completed his chore, Lieutenant Ali Haji and his men, who surrounded the helicopter, watching the medical malpractice through the open side doors with interest, had explained their predicament.

And now, Shaikh had a force of thirty-two, counting himself, with no transport, and no communications. And though he had tried all afternoon and evening, he would have no sleep, either. Bone wounds tended to be intense, and the deep shriek of pain that radiated from his hip demanded most of his concentration and kept his teeth grinding together. Morris was forcing aspirin and water into him on an hourly basis. He was relatively certain that he suffered from some degree of shock, and the roasted parrot served for dinner had gone down slowly and almost refused to stay. The helicopter had contained seven Meals Ready to Eat (MREs), and the door gunners had stripped them for the chocolate and passed it all to Shaikh.

They had buried his pilot at the edge of the clearing, digging deeply to keep the predators away.

Attempting to keep his voice level, he interrupted the policeman's monologue. "Lieutenant Haji, what is your assessment of the attitude of the Bruneian people? In regard to this revolution."

"What?" Haji was apparently shocked by a request for his opinion. No doubt he had become accustomed to others turning deaf ears to his volunteered stream of conjecture.

Shaikh repeated the question.

The man took some time in consideration, then said, "We are a peaceful people, Major Shaikh. I think many would accept whatever power structure was in place, rather than face conflict."

"So, Li Sen might have a peaceful capital, but not necessarily a mandate for his presidency?"

"Yes, that is true, sir. The man will face a firing squad. And soon. And the people will embrace the return of the Sultan."

"You did not find life harsh under the Sultan?"

"Of course not. The Sultan has done much for his people in his time. He is a kind man."

"Do you know Li Sen?"

"I have been in his shop once, four months ago. To buy a thirteen-inch television set. It was made by Hitachi, and it has a warranty that lasts—"

"What did you think of Li Sen?"

"I did not think he would be a traitor to his country. He was quiet, not what I would expect of a revolutionary. I will capture him and hold him for Minister Hassanal's disposition."

"And what of Omar Padang?"

"Ah, Chief Padang! He is a crafty man; he would have to be, to rise from the people to his position. He will likely be our savior."

That assessment took Shaikh by surprise.

"Could you explain that?"

"Certainly. Chief Padang is very loyal to Mohammed Hassanal. I believe he has slyly infiltrated the organization of the revolutionaries, and when the time is correct, he will split them asunder, from within. He is, what do you say, Major? A sheep in wolf's clothing."

Shaikh would not say it that way, but he did not correct Haji.

"This is very important, Lieutenant. If I were to receive orders to attack Li Sen and return the country to the Sultan's rule, would you assist me?"

"Absolutely, Major! I would be honored."

"This would mean that you will have to stay here, to be where I know I can find you."

"Of course. It is not a problem."

"We will leave food for you."

"We may even be able to trap our own food. My men have built a cistern of leaves, to catch the rainwater." Haji was very proud of his newly acquired survival skills.

They were interrupted by the approach of a flashlight, and soon Frank Morris squatted on the ground beside them and shut off the light. He smelled of sweat and aviation fuel and hydraulic fluid.

"How you doing, Major?"

"Very well, Mr. Morris."

"Yeah. I can hear your teeth grinding, you know. Before this is over, you'll have to see your dentist."

"The helicopter?"

"We're going to give it the old college try in a few minutes. The big problem is finding the other clearing without radios and a direction finder. I hope to hell Kelly's back there with his flashlight, and I hope you can aim us in the general direction."

"I have faith," Shaikh said. "Lieutenant Haji and his men are going to wait here for us."

"I wondered about my load limits."

"Whenever you are ready then."

"Let me get the guys and we'll load you aboard."

"I believe I can walk."

"Maybe, but you're under doctor's orders, remember?"

"I have not seen these nurses you promised."

"That's another problem this country has, Major."

Monday, March 10, 3:15 P.M.

The corridors of the White House basement were alive with people and Marines, especially the Marine that had attached himself to Drieser when Drieser insisted on a walk. The escort didn't help his concentration, and he regretted his insistence in about five minutes and went back to the Situation Room.

The UN Ambassador had left to meet with the President, but the others were still hanging around, waiting for Hap Harned to mount his rescue attempt. As commander in the field, Harned's discretion about the timing and the tactics was supreme.

Doug Chambers, the Secretary of State, had arrived earlier, and he was as anxious about this course as Drieser was. As State Department people, they both preferred shaking hands to shaking weapons. Chambers's balding pate glistened with perspiration, and his washed-blue eyes, normally so steady in heated negotiations, darted from the situation maps to Drieser, seeking reassurance.

Which Drieser couldn't offer.

The situation boards were being fed from any number of sources now. Not only the NSA's satellites, but overflights of Harned's naval aircraft—now restricted by UN directive to high altitude—were providing real-time image and infrared data of both the confrontation at sea and the Bruneian territorial region. There were a few reports from ham radio operators in the country. Some of the Japanese and French naval aircraft from the task force were also contributing. The CIA was also gathering experts to analyze the possible scenarios coming out of the threats posed by the Bruneian pirate.

The Secretary leaned back in his chair, tilting his head toward Drieser in the chair next to him. He ran a handkerchief across his forehead.

"I wish this admiral would get it over with, Chris."

"My reading of Harned is that he's not going to make any precipitous moves, boss. He's probably got his hands full, getting the Japanese and the French to cooperate."

Drieser wanted to put his feet up on the table and tilt his chair back, but thought it wouldn't go over well with this group. Secretaries could tilt; assistants sat upright.

"What do *you* think is going to happen?" Chambers asked.

He had already asked the same question of the DCI and the general from DIA, both of whom reassured him of Harned's competence.

"I think Omar Padang is going to blow some drilling rigs sky-high. All the seagulls are going to be black, with singed feathers."

"Shit. All we've got is the pirate's word on that."

Drieser pointed at the screen on the wall on the far side of the table. It was an infrared image captured by a KH-11 satellite. Orange and red patterns indicated heat sources generated by lights, factories, and auto engines, heavy along the coast. The impressive aspects were the two blossoms indicating the oil platforms on fire. Albatross and Mirador, according to Kelly Koehler's report.

"You don't think that's a preliminary indication of Padang's will?"

"Padang. You really think Padang's calling the shots?"

"Not a shred of evidence, Mr. Secretary, but yeah, I do."

"He's not going to cut off his revenue sources."

"Probably not. Doesn't stop him from blowing fifteen, twenty platforms, contaminating the entire south end of the South China Sea, and still having several thousand pumping wells left over."

"Damn. We'd better stop Harned."

"You go talk to the President and the Ambassador. I tried."

From the far end of the table, the DIA chieftain called out, "Whoops! We've got a changing situation, gentlemen!"

Tuesday, March 11, 3:21 A.M.

The hangar deck of the *Eisenhower* was a cavernous, echoing, and awesome place. It was also as alive as Tokyo at the evening rush hour.

Support personnel were moving aircraft about, shoving the fighter airplanes out of the way, and moving Sikorsky Sea Kings and Sea Stallions to the elevators to be raised to the flight deck. Other helicopters waited on the deck already, borrowed from other ships in the fleet. They were necessary for the United States Marines who would be going in the second wave of the assault.

Of those brought aboard, 250 jubilant Marines had been selected for the follow-up assault, and they milled about on the far side of the hangar, near an open portal to one of the elevators, listening to their commanders brief them.

The ship was nearly at rest, and so no welcome wind came through the open portals. Meoshi Kyoto was sweltering in his borrowed battle dress utilities. The web gear hung heavy on his hips. The helmet was strapped to his belt, and the .38-caliber revolver borrowed from a pilot was an uncomfortable appendage under his left armpit.

He was standing with the detachment of thirty Japanese sailors airlifted from the *Akagi* and twelve U.S. Navy SEALs. The tanker was a Japanese ship, after all, and the negotiations with Admiral Harned had eventually arrived at a boarding party with a majority of Japanese. The SEALs, Kyoto thought, probably considered themselves the equal of thirty Japanese sailors.

The Navy lieutenant commander who led the SEAL

detachment was named Barry Jenkins, and he was normally a fair-haired, sun-bleached man of medium stature but also of tremendous physical fitness. Now he was coated with skin-darkening camouflage cream.

A sailor approached Jenkins and said, "Sir, the Zodiaks are alongside."

They would make the approach under cover of darkness in the rubber boats powered by super-muffled outboard motors.

Jenkins looked at his watch. "Five minutes, then we'll embark."

"Aye, aye, sir."

Jenkins turned to Kyoto. "Sure you don't want to go with the choppers, Colonel?"

Kyoto smiled. "I want to have a close look at SEALs at work."

"You got it, sir." He turned back to the waiting men. "All right! Attention, the boarding party!"

The conversations died away, and the Japanese and American sailors turned to face the mission commander. Kyoto was aware that the two Japanese officers, both naval lieutenants, still appeared sullen. Neither enjoyed serving an American commander.

"In four minutes, we're going to—"

"ATTENTION TO CAPTAIN'S ORDERS! ATTENTION TO CAPTAIN'S ORDERS!"

The bellowing call from the public-address system reverberated through the deck. Almost all activity came to a standstill.

"This is Captain Norris speaking. Operation Scalawag is now suspended. I repeat, Operation Scalawag is now suspended. Secure all equipment in place. The boarding party and the assault force are to remain in place. Colonel Kyoto, please report to flag plot."

As the public-address system snapped off, Jenkins turned to him. "Hurry up and wait. It's the Navy way, Colonel."

"Also that of any army, Commander."

Kyoto glanced through the elevator portal. It would not be long before the light of dawn would scuttle this mission. They could not afford to wait many minutes and still expect to be successful.

He headed for the door through which he had arrived, moving as quickly as he could without actually running.

It took him nearly eight minutes to make his way up the many ladders and along the myriad passageways to reach Harned's operations room. He was beginning to be worried; it was becoming easier to find his way around the ship.

A lieutenant opened the door for him, and he stepped inside.

"Admiral?"

"Small problem, Meoshi. The *Maru Hokkaido* is under way."

Tuesday, March 11, 3:50 A.M.

It had taken Koehler nearly half an hour to extricate himself from the trees that had snarled and trapped his parachute risers, leaving him suspended nearly sixty feet off the ground.

Not that he knew it at the time. In the pitch blackness of the jungle, he couldn't see two feet in front of him, much less what was below his feet.

I could be with Sherry, rounding the tip of Borneo in Serendipity, *beer in hand, moon lowering across the fantail, eastern islands beckoning, a pleasant wake leaving all this behind.*

The Navy called it desertion, of course.

After a few dozen tugs on the risers had convinced him

the chute wouldn't let go of the branches above, he had
released his thirty feet of coiled quarter-inch nylon line,
let one end drop, and tied the other to his parachute
harness. He got a wrap of the line around his left shoe,
then unsnapped the quick-release buckles of the harness,
letting his weight lower onto his left foot. He unsnapped
the assault rifle from the webbing and slung it over his
neck, hanging down his back. Suraj Irra wouldn't be
pleased if he lost the rifle.

Slowly, he let himself down into the darkness, fronds of
leaves slapping at his face, insects buzzing incessantly. He
slammed into branches not thick enough to hold him, but
still obstacles. He swayed back and forth on the line. He
tried to gauge the distance he lowered himself, but when
the last of the rope slipped from his shoe, it came as a
surprise, and he slipped down two feet before his hands
got a grip on the line.

His palms burned like fire.

Kelly knew damned well he wasn't going back up that
line. He also knew he wasn't going to let go. He might fall
two feet and feel silly, or he might fall fifty feet and feel
broken up. One thing for sure; he wasn't going to hang
there for long. His hands were beginning to cramp, the
thin line feeling more and more the size of a thread.

He began swinging his legs, got a pendulum action
going, increasing the length of his arc with every swing.
He hit branches, felt jagged-edged leaves cutting his face,
and forced himself to throw his legs harder.

The crashing of his body through the leaves must have
been heard for a mile, he thought.

THUD!

He hit something solid, kicked off it, swung away, and
when he came back, spread his legs, hit a tree trunk hard
enough to send shock waves through his groin, but got
his legs wrapped around it.

He let go of the rope and hugged the tree like it was his mother. After a moment of regaining his breath, Koehler let himself slide downward, found a branch with his foot, and let his weight rest on it.

He was glad he hadn't let go of the rope. By the time he reached the ground, taking a circuitous route around thick branches and intertwined vines, Kelly figured he had covered another thirty or thirty-five feet.

When his feet finally sank into the mushy undergrowth of the jungle floor, he knew he had accomplished but one task. The jungle around him was thick as molasses, completely invisible, and directionless. He had absolutely no idea where north was.

What now, Toto?

A footstep in the ink? To his right? Animal?

He reached his right hand over his shoulder, found the rifle, and started to work it free.

"Commander."

"Suraj?"

"It is I."

"Damned glad to see you. Or hear you."

"I rested while you worked your way down."

"Any idea where we are?"

"I have my compass. We will walk to the east, and we should intersect the road."

"How far?"

"It is unknown."

With that wicked bladed knife of his, Irra hacked at the jungle vines and cut a path almost too tiny for Kelly to work his way through, holding onto the back of the sergeant major's belt.

Almost two hours after they abandoned the Piper, they broke free of the jungle and found themselves in the middle of a narrow track. Koehler was relieved to find it. During the trek, they had encountered shapeless and faceless wildlife, all of which had left them alone. Several times he had heard the distinct slither of snakes racing along branches, dodging the intruders. Sherry would have loved it, he told himself. Once, they paused when the beat of helicopter rotors passed nearby. The turbine engines echoed across the jungle, then dulled as they went behind some hill. Shortly thereafter, the sound went away.

Unerringly, Irra turned and led them south, down a long incline that Kelly thought he remembered, up a longer hill, past the abandoned village, then to the intersection of roads. A few minutes later they were challenged by a Gurkha manning an outpost position, and Irra soon had a borrowed flashlight to lead them back to the clearing.

They found the command post APC, with Benjamin Shaikh stretched out on blankets laid on the tilted ramp. Frank Morris and Captain Shrestha were sitting on the ramp next to him.

"Hell," Morris said, "you guys just come waltzing in whenever you feel like it, don't you?"

"We took the long way home, Frank. The scenic black route," Koehler said. "Damn, Major!"

Irra's light had caught the pallor of Shaikh's face, the tension lines etched across his forehead and around his mouth.

They exchanged their stories while Koehler and Irra swallowed great gulps of water from canteens. Irra demanded that Shaikh drop his pants so he could check on Morris's stitchery.

After a close examination of the wound, Irra said, "You are very good, Mr. Morris."

"I've been trying to tell the major that, but he keeps asking for the nurses. And stop calling me, 'mister,' damn it."

"We will give you some morphine, Major," Irra said.

"Perhaps later, Sergeant Major. I think Commander

Koehler has to make his report, first. We have been pre-
sented with the gift of an encrypted radio, dropped by a
naval aircraft."

Duty first, Koehler reminded himself.

"I hope the admiral's home," he said and stepped
around the commander to enter the APC. The radio operator sat at his small desk, hung from the right-side bulkhead,
with the radios bathed in a soft glow of red light. He was
happy to step outside into the nonexistent breeze while
Kelly took his place.

The new radio, still half encased in an olive-green canvas
cover, was placed next to Shaikh's equipment. The face-
plate wasn't familiar to Koehler, but it was typically military
heavy-duty, and he figured out the controls quickly. He
only had ten channels, and all of them were encrypted.
He turned on the power and waited a few minutes for it
to warm up.

"Sledgehammer. Eagle Eye calling."

The reply was immediate. "Wait one minute, Eagle Eye.
We'll locate Sledgehammer for you."

The admiral was probably sleeping.

Or maybe not. It was only a two-minute wait.

"Eagle, this is Sledgehammer."

"I've got a report for you, sir."

"I've got one for you. We intercepted a return message
from your headquarters outfit. I'm quoting: 'Protect company assets at all costs.' "

Well, shit!

"I'll do that the first chance I get, sir."

"If it helps at all, Eagle, I can tell you that most of your
people have now reached Kuching, and that many are en
route to Singapore."

"That does help." He almost asked the admiral to check
on Sherry and Monica's arrival in Beaufort, but decided

he didn't want to explain the circumstances. Maybe he'd do it later.

"Intel from our last overflights tell us that no one else has gotten out of Kuala Belait."

"Big hostage situation, then?"

"Several, Eagle." The admiral, now with a secure channel, briefed him quickly about a standoff at sea and a threat to the oil fields. "The tanker is now under way through the middle of the task force, and we're giving her some leeway."

"A good idea, Sledgehammer. I've seen one of the devices." Koehler related what he had seen on the robot's video, then passed on the gist of his and Irra's reconnaissance patrol into the capital. True to his reported version of events, he didn't bother mentioning Sherry or Monica.

"No sign of the royal family?"

"None. We couldn't figure out a way to approach the destroyer."

"Back to the explosives. Describe them."

"Alleged explosives. What I've seen is a black box magnetically fixed to a support leg. Probably four hundred feet down. I think there's a long antenna, so there's probably an ultralow-frequency transceiver to accept a radioed detonation signal."

"This is on GlobeTech Alpha?"

"Correct, sir." Kelly gave him the coordinates, which he knew by heart.

"We've got good pictures; we'll find it."

"You might also locate GT-Bravo on your map." Koehler provided those coordinates, too.

"She's mined, also?"

"I don't know the extent of the mining, sir. I'd guess it's fairly widespread. No, this is something else. I do know that Bravo was supposed to be completely evacuated, but when I flew over it tonight, someone tried to signal us with a flashlight."

"Message?"

"None. The sender didn't have a code or maybe the ability to send code. He was just trying to attract our attention."

"Any ideas, Eagle?"

"None, but someone's on that rig who doesn't want to be there."

"I'll keep that in the back of my mind," the admiral said. "You said you saw four patrol boats in the oil field?"

"There could be more. There were two large navy vessels near the pumping station."

"Could you and the Gurkhas mount a raid on the oil field?"

Don't tell me this.

"Yes, sir. And we've got those twenty-eight cops, now. I sincerely doubt that we'd have the time to do a silent examination of all the platforms, though. You'd want us to go after the explosives?"

"Maybe. I don't want you to do anything yet, but I have to weigh all of the alternatives. The Gurkhas as tough as I think they are?"

"Tougher."

"The cops?"

"I don't know if they can even swim."

"All right. I'll be back to you soon, Eagle. In the meantime, you've got a problem."

"I do?"

"Satellite intel shows choppers and ground units headed in your direction. They probably got a radar track on the plane you stole."

Tuesday, March 11, 4:10 A.M.

The sun's reflected rays were turning the horizon pink.

In the far distance Mohammed Hassanal could see the hazy silhouettes of tankers moored near the pumping station. The skeleton of a drilling platform to the east was taking shape in the new light.

Perfectly serene, he thought; as it should be.

When he heard the helicopter approaching, he turned his head to study the platform he was on. Three men in uniform were gathered near a hatchway into one of the structures. They pointedly ignored him.

Hassanal's arms were stretched along the top rail of the lifeline at the edge of the deck, bound to it by duct tape at his wrists, elbows, and upper arms. The railing was only a meter high, and he was forced into an awkward position, too high to sit on the deck, too low to stand upright. The strain on his back and his legs was tremendous. Since sometime after midnight, when Lieutenant Hashim had caught him signalling the airplane, he had been strapped in place. He kept shifting his legs, trying to find some way to relieve the tension in his muscles.

The helicopter beat came closer, and he knew now that it was headed in his direction.

So what? These pigs would one day pay a heavenly price for their ill treatment of the Sultan and all of the family. He would wait them out. Hassanal assumed that he was to half stand thirsty throughout the heat of day. They would wait impatiently for his pleading to begin.

Tan Hashim would be disappointed. Hassanal had no intention of subjugating himself to the cowardly lieutenant.

The helicopter circled the platform once, then moved in slowly and settled on the landing pad high above him.

He squinted his eyes as dust was raised from the deck by the hurricane created by the rotors.

A few minutes later Omar Padang descended the ladder to Hassanal's deck. The fat man swaggered toward those waiting at the hatchway and issued some order or another. Padang turned and studied Hassanal from seventy feet away. He made no move to approach.

The three policemen went through the hatch and disappeared. When they finally reappeared, Serena and Jahan were with them.

The son of a pig!

Padang came toward him then, the policemen dragging Serena and his boy along behind them.

Serena became aware of him. "Mohammed!"

"Be calm, my love."

Padang stopped in front of him, withdrew his semiautomatic pistol from his holster, and without warning, swung it in a lazy and offhand fashion across Hassanal's face. His head whipped sideways.

The gunsight ripped a new furrow across his cheek and nose. The pain almost did not register; he was so worried about Serena and Jahan. He felt the blood gush and flow down his cheek. It dripped from his nose onto his lip, into his mouth. Both Serena and Jahan erupted into shrieks and tears.

"I understand," Padang said, "that you have difficulty obeying an order, Mohammed."

From his cramped position, Hassanal had to look up at the man. He understood that Padang was enjoying himself immensely. He also understood that he would not say what was in his heart and his mind. Not with his beautiful Serena at risk.

One man moved behind her and gripped both of her arms.

"Now," Padang said.

The other two men gripped Jahan by his arms and legs and picked him from the deck. They swung back once, then in a long, infinitely slow arc, they swung the boy forward.

And released him.

He sailed over Hassanal's head, yelling like a banshee.

Serena shrieked.

"Jahan!"

Hassanal screamed, lunging upward, tearing muscle as he strained against his bonds. He felt as if he were but inches from getting his teeth into his son's leg or arm.

But no.

Jahan howled all the way to impact with the surface of the sea, and his voice was abruptly stilled.

Serena's eyes went crazy, and she collapsed in the arms of the man who held her.

"You will pay dearly for this atrocity, Padang! I will have your body parts, one at a time!"

"I think not, Mohammed."

Padang raised the pistol, and the black bore centered in Hassanal's vision. It appeared to enlarge as he watched.

Then it turned blue.

Blue was such a magnificent color and infinite.

And suddenly gone.

FLASH FACTOR

Thirteen

Tuesday, March 11, 4:22 A.M.

The outboard motor's seven-horsepower seemed to pump out more noise than propulsion. Sherry Koehler kept the twist throttle almost fully retarded, the dinghy barely moving through the water. The turtle pace was preferable to attracting attention.

"You know what'll happen if they catch us?" Monica asked. "They'll put us in some two-star hotel and force us to drink orange juice and eat pancakes drenched in blueberry syrup."

"Do you have to talk about food, Monica?"

"We could talk about men."

"If we make it to that hotel."

"I was kidding," Davis said. "I'm with Kelly. A prison's a prison."

Sherry was able to make out Monica's face in the light of the coming dawn, and now daylight felt like an enemy.

She looked aft, searching for Labuan Island where they'd spent the night, and where her beautiful boat was now torn and split and resting on the bottom of the sea. The island was not yet visible, still wrapped in darkness, but she saw two sets of running lights.

They had tried twice, from both sides of the island, to make their way east in the dinghy, but both times they had run into patrol boats and turned back. After the abrupt and unwarranted destruction of the *Serendipity*, Sherry was not about to surrender herself to some band of Bruneian hooligans.

God, where had paradise gone? She'd never called any Bruneian a hooligan before.

So, they had turned back to Muara. She was skirting wide to the south around the anchorage, hoping to reach Kampong Ayer before full light and what she thought of as the relative safety of her home. Kelly would be disappointed, but neither she nor Monica saw another course open to them.

The bay was calm, and the voyage in the small rubber boat had been unremarkable. The dinghy rose and fell on the swells, pushed ahead by the rackety small outboard. There were lights to the north—Muara, the island, various ships in the mooring. Ahead she could see the lights of Bandar Seri Begawan, and more importantly, the lights of the water village. Home was minutes away. Well, quite a few minutes at their speed.

The breeze was chilled, and Sherry shivered occasionally. She was perched on her knees on the spongy and wet bottom of the boat. The legs of her jeans—recovered after their return to Labuan Island—were soaked, and the cotton pullover she was wearing did little to cut the wind. Monica, in the bow, was in about the same condition. If Monica was dreaming about food, Koehler was dreaming about hot water and warm clothes.

"Sherry!"

"I see it. Don't yell."

The patrol craft had nosed out of the anchorage, moving slowly to the south, about to cut their course, without running lights. There was just enough light to pick its sinister gray silhouette out of the morning.

Sherry pulled the tiller hard and twisted the throttle for more power. The motor coughed and belched a little louder, but the speed didn't seem to increase noticeably.

They were three hundred yards from the vessels lined up in the mooring, and it seemed like a mile. As they inched closer, the lines of the patrol boat became more distinct, sharpening, focusing.

The morning's wan light brightened perceptibly.

Two hundred yards?

Monica was leaning forward over the bow, attempting to add speed with body English.

The armed boat was a half mile away, now turning toward them.

She was afraid the noise of the motor would alert others in the anchorage, but then she became aware of several other small boats moving among the anchored ships. A water taxi. A supply tender. A naval captain's gig. Various tones of exhaust skittered across the water.

Sound disguise.

As they passed under the fantail of a sleeping giant of a container ship, she again relaxed the throttle.

And then the rust-streaked side of an island freighter hid them from the patrol craft. She moved slowly along its side, then nosed around its bow and turned west once again.

The throaty burble of the gunboat's engines was distinct, the exhaust notes rumbling over the water and echoing off the steel sides of the ships. She couldn't tell whether or not they had been spotted; could the naval boat now be searching specifically for them? Her blond hair was distinctively foreign and immediately noticeable.

Ahead she saw the distinctive outline of the Chinese junk, and she raced the motor once, then cut if off. The dinghy slid across the surface and slowed as it reached the junk. The rubber gunwale glanced off the hull of the junk, easing up to the landing stage lowered to water level.

Her eyes followed the open stairway from the landing stage upward to the gap in the railing high above. A bald-headed Chinese man stood there, staring down at them.

He grinned widely.

And aimed a rifle down at them.

Tuesday, March 11, 5:08 A.M.

The pain in his hip was forgotten as Benjamin Shaikh directed his men to take up defensive positions. Two of the armored personnel carriers, each with a couple antitank rockets, had been moved down to the intersection to block the offensive advance on the narrow jungle roads. He sent two patrols five hundred meters beyond them, to hide in the jungle and mount an attack from the rear if Colonel Bakir's forces came past them. The remaining ammunition and food had been distributed as evenly as possible among the men. They might well have to scatter and take their chances independently in the jungle.

The remaining APCs were lined up on the road, prepared for a hasty retreat should it become necessary.

At the moment, a dozen men were attempting to move the damaged and radioless helicopter from the center of the clearing, to allow the two remaining Black Hawks the necessary clearance to get airborne past the overhanging canopy. Though the third could still fly, it was incommuni-cado, and its hydraulic and mechanical systems were held together with Morris's American wherewithal. Not even Morris wanted to rely on their integrity under the stress of combat.

Shaikh found himself ambulatory. Despite Morris's and Irra's cautions, he had tested his balance and found he could hobble about. The soft ground caused him to take care when he placed his boots on it, but he felt better knowing he was somewhat mobile.

Morning light was filtering through the thick jungle now, bathing everything and everyone in a sickly green twilight, and trapped heat brought the perspiration to his forehead. He sat on the skid of the disabled helicopter and fished the plastic container of aspirin from his shirt pocket. Placing two tablets on his tongue, he washed them down with water from his canteen.

Koehler approached from the road, dodging around a Black Hawk being moved as he crossed the small clearing.

"Do you know about the Alamo, Major?" Koehler asked.

"I have read your history."

"This feels like the Alamo."

"You, Mr. Morris, Mr. Avery, and your two other men should take one of the helicopters for me. You could fly it to safety."

"For a guy who likes regulations, Benjamin, you sure aren't reluctant to throw away your equipment."

Shaikh smiled. "You will do this?"

"Can't. I'm under orders."

"Talk to Mr. Morris."

"I don't think it'd do much good."

Shaikh let it pass. The Americans were assets, after all. "Did you reach Beaufort on the radio?"

"Yeah, the harbormaster. He hasn't seen the *Serendipity*."

"Perhaps Mrs. Koehler and Miss Davis found a serene bay in which to wait out the hostilities."

"She's not responding to calls on the marine channels."

The creases across Koehler's forehead reflected his concern.

Shaikh was about to reply when he heard turbines. Far away yet, but coming closer.

"Company's coming," Koehler said.

"We will greet them at the door."

Koehler offered his hand, and Shaikh grabbed it. Koehler pulled him to his feet, then bent over and picked up the assault rifle for him. Together, they walked out to the road, and Shaikh thought that the American probably wanted to help him walk, but refrained. Shaikh appreciated the restraint.

The three APCs parked on the road were manned and ready to go. He went to the last in line and stumbled as he walked up the ramp. Inside he sat gratefully on a canvas stool and took the microphone the radioman handed him.

Koehler squatted next to the open ramp. Morris and Avery materialized from somewhere and joined him.

Shaikh longed to launch his two able helicopters, but would wait. The American admiral had reported seven helicopters and four fixed-wing aircraft flying a search pattern, moving slowly toward the Gurkha position. Perhaps they would overfly the clearing and miss the significance. Unfortunately, though their radars would not be specifically downward-looking, they would likely pick up at least minor returns from the grounded helicopters and the APCs, and be alerted.

And even if the aircraft missed them, the ground patrols could probe deep enough into the jungle and find them.

Shaikh would then have to send the Black Hawks against the greater force.

They had changed their radio code names, and he took a moment to recall them, then pressed the transmit button.

"Paper, Rock."

"Paper is in position."

That was Irra. He and three men were lying in ambush beyond the deserted village on the road that led to Kuala Belait.

"Scissors, Rock."

"Scissors in place."

Captain Shrestha also had three men and a bagful of grenades, and they were ensconced in the jungle alongside the road leading to Labi.

They were not observing total radio silence, since Bakir already had an idea of their location, but they would keep the transmissions short, hoping to defeat radio direction finders. Koehler had asked Shaikh's permission before attempting to locate his wife.

They waited in mounting tension, and almost twenty minutes went by before the radio speaker blurted, "Paper. Vehicles coming."

A few minutes later they could hear the sound of engines straining on a grade. The helicopters were getting closer, too.

Abruptly, a crescendo of sound raced over them.

"Light-twin, fixed-wing," Koehler called to him.

The sound of the engines died away.

"I don't think he picked up on us," Koehler said. "And I sure as hell didn't see him."

"Maybe they'll bail out," Morris suggested. "Seems to be the arrival mode around here."

From the north the sound of vehicles grew louder.

Shaikh could hear the beat and cackle of tracks now. Personnel carriers.

Three clicks, a brief pause, and then two more clicks sounded on the radio speaker.

"Sergeant Major Irra signals us," Shaikh said. "Vehicles are passing him."

"There goes my resolve to be a noncombatant," Slim Avery said. "You got another one of those fire sticks around?"

Shaikh nodded at the corporal, and the man retrieved one of the captured M-16s, along with several magazines, and handed them to Avery. The way Avery ran the bolt, checked the bore, and slapped a magazine in place told Shaikh he had not always been a noncombatant.

"Sure you want to do this, Slim?" Koehler asked.

Avery patted a bundle tucked inside his shirt. It gave him more stomach than he had probably ever had. "If I don't, Kelly, those suckers are apt to get hold of my girls. Can't have that, can I?"

Koehler grinned at him.

And Benjamin Shaikh had no idea in the world what they were talking about. Americans!

"Rock, this is Hard Place."

That was the APCs blockading the intersection.

"Rock."

"Hostiles in sight."

"Fire at your discretion."

Shaikh knew his men would wait until the last possible moment, until the approaching APCs were almost to the top of the long grade, then open up with the heavy machine guns, or possibly an antitank rocket, hopefully disabling the lead vehicle and blocking the road.

"Rock, Paper."

"A count?"

"Four APCs and a Jeep. I will go in one minute."

"Affirmative," Shaikh said.

He was aware that the Americans were listening to the dialogue with intense interest.

"Rock, Scissors. We count three APCs on our road. They will pass us in a few minutes."

Hard Place would not be able to wait much longer. The second set of vehicles might possibly evade the trap.

As soon as that thought struck him, Shaikh heard the first hammering of the M-60 machine guns. Only a hundred meters down the road, the heavy thunder was clear as a bell, and the sound echoed along the corridor of the jungle tunnel. Then the whoosh and thump-bang of a rocket. Something had been hit.

"Tigers, start your engines."

Even as he heard the turbines beginning to wind in the clearing, he also heard the *whop-whop* of approaching rotors. The hostiles under fire had alerted their aircraft. The intensity of the gunfire at the intersection increased rapidly as the rebels returned fire.

Koehler and Morris stood up.

Avery levered himself upright, also, saying, "Hey, boss, you mentioned the Alamo? I just remembered who won."

Shaikh passed the microphone back to the corporal. "Tell the drivers to start the personnel carriers."

He picked up his rifle, stepped out onto the ramp, and slid down it carefully, favoring his right hip.

"Well, Kelly. What do you think?"

"I've had better mornings."

The four of them waited with eight Gurkha soldiers, listening to the exchange of gunfire between the APCs, ready to provide themselves as reinforcements or to leap aboard the APCs and race to the south.

Almost spontaneously, turboshaft engines at high rpm sailed over them, unseen through the dense canopy of jungle. Almost as one, the twelve of them raised their rifles, clicked off the safeties, and fired blindly through the foliage, following the movement of sound.

With the Armalite's stock braced in his left hand, bucking as he fired three-round bursts, Shaikh glanced at the clearing. The first Black Hawk had just cleared the ground.

Go faster, he prayed.

And then the Black Hawk erupted in a ball of yellow and orange flame. It tumbled sideways, the rotors flashing, slashing, slamming the ground, breaking up, flinging their pieces into the helicopter idling alongside.

It, too, burst into flame.

And their air transport was suddenly nonexistent.

Tuesday, March 11, 5:42 A.M.

It had taken the *Maru Hokkaido* seemingly forever to gain any momentum, but now the supertanker was rumbling through Hap Harned's task force at about fifteen knots.

In the *Eisenhower*'s flag plot, Meoshi Kyoto thought Admiral Harned so composed as to be almost serene. He wished he felt the same sense of control. At any moment, he thought he might abandon protocol and voice his displeasure. Those fools in Washington had delayed the assault into an historical omission.

Harned studied the radar and sonar images on his large screen and calmly issued orders for this destroyer or that frigate to give way to the oncoming supertanker. The *Eisenhower* herself was in reverse, backing slowly away from the projected track of the *Hokkaido.*

On another screen, a listing of worst-case scenarios was being compiled, fed by intelligence and environmental experts from the United States, Japan, and Britain.

1) 10% of platforms demolished . . . 14.5 million tons of crude oil released in first 24 hours . . . affected areas include Balabac Strait, Palawan. . . .

2) 5% of platforms demolished . . . 7.3 million tons of crude . . . affected areas within 108 hours include Balabac Strait, Commodore Reef, western coast of Sabah. . . .

3) 3% of platforms demolished. . . .

On the overhead speaker he heard the Commander Air Group (CAG) talking to a flight of F-14 Tomcat pilots, assuring them that the carrier would soon be under way and in a position to recover them.

"Colonel Kyoto."

"Yes, Admiral."

"Would you please contact Admiral Yakama. I would like to have his units depart the task force and stay with the tanker."

"Certainly, sir."

"And if he is so disposed, I would like to send eight helicopters and two platoons of Marines, along with his special force, to the *Akagi*. Just in case an opportunity presents itself."

"Sir. I would request permission to join that force. I—"

"I believe I need you here, Meoshi. You're my persuasive force if Admiral Yakama decides to move too early."

Disappointed, Kyoto nodded his acceptance and turned to where an ensign held a radio telephone.

He was still dressed in his borrowed battle dress, but beginning to think he would never utilize the clothing.

Tuesday, March 11, 6:11 A.M.

"Four dead!"

"Yes, that is true," Captain Awg Nazir told him. He stood on the other side of the desk that Li Sen had commandeered at police headquarters. He did not bother standing at attention.

"And there are seven wounded," Li accused. He was so repulsed that his stomach hurt.

"But only three of them are seriously injured," the policeman said.

"It was a funeral procession, Captain!"

"It was not our fault, Mr. President. My men were violently attacked by unruly youth."

"Boys with rocks."

"They provoked a riot."

"I want the murderers arrested and charged."

"I will raise the issue with Minister Padang."

"Where is Padang?"

"I believe he is inspecting the naval craft."

"I want to see him as soon as he returns."

"Of course, Mr. President."

Nazir turned and left the office, leaving Li with the uneasy feeling that not one thing he had said, or ordered, had registered with the man.

The captain's departure left him with the stack of messages on the desk in front of him. A spokesman for the detained diplomats demanded their immediate release. Seven oil companies demanded the release of their executives and the men held at Kuala Belait. Nepal, Britain, Japan, and Australia demanded immediate investigations into the reported deaths of their nationals.

Yet more demands related to the *Maru Hokkaido*. Dispatches shouting indignations over the mining of the oil field. It was a terrible development over which Li himself felt both helpless and appalled.

Demands, everywhere.

And on the very top, a telex message from the United Nations Security Council.

TO: LI SEN, SPOKESMAN FOR THE
          FRONT FOR DEMOCRATIC
          REFORM
FROM: SECRETARY GENERAL, UNITED
          NATIONS
AS A CONSEQUENCE OF A UNANIMOUS VOTE IN THE SECURITY COUNCIL, THE UNITED NATIONS SERVES NOTICE THAT THE ACTIONS OF THE FRONT FOR DEMOCRATIC REFORM ARE DEEMED TO HAVE CREATED UNNECESSARY INSTABILITY IN THE REGION OF BRUNEI. YOU ARE HEREBY DIRECTED TO IMMEDIATELY RELEASE THE ULTRA LARGE CRUDE CARRIER MARU HOKKAIDO, TO INSURE THE SAFE PASSAGE OF ALL NON-BRUNEIAN OIL WORKERS FROM THE COUNTRY, TO REINSTATE COMMUNICATIONS FOR DIPLOMATIC PERSONNEL, AND TO INFORM THIS BODY OF THE WHEREABOUTS OF THE SULTAN OF BRUNEI AND HIS FAMILY. COMPLIANCE WITH THE ABOVE CONDITIONS WILL RESULT IN THE FORMATION OF AN INTERNATIONAL COMMITTEE TO HEAR THE COMPLAINTS OF THE FRONT FOR DEMOCRATIC REFORM.

The missive went on for another page, but Li had already memorized it. He had been carrying it with him everywhere he went.

Demands.

It was time, he decided, to negotiate. He was the president, after all, and he had considered the implications. To pursue the course Omar Padang had set was foolishness. Li could defuse the situation, encourage the United Nations to back away, and let Bruneian citizens decide their own government by the simple expedient of freeing the tanker. No response at all was necessary in regard to the other United Nations demands.

If the tanker were to be released, the intensity would go out of the international media and governmental indignation.

It was the heavy hand of Omar Padang that had propelled them into this untenable situation, and the lighter touch of President Li Sen would regain the momentum of the revolution.

Seizing a notepad, he quickly wrote his response to the Secretary General in a free-flowing script. Then he jotted a directive for the captain—what was his name? Thambipillai?

Ripping the pages from the notebook, he stood and strode into the outer office. He felt very presidential. He was finally making decisions, taking care of the direction of the new country.

Padang be damned!

Awg Nazir and two sergeants looked up as he entered the anteroom.

"Captain, you will send this message immediately. Then, contact Captain Thambipillai and order him to return to Bandar Seri Begawan—without the tanker. He is to release the crew unharmed."

Nazir finally came to attention.

"Then you will release the captive diplomats and foreigners detained at the hotels—"

"Pardon me, Mr. President. None of this can be done."

Li was incredulous.

"You will tell me why not!"

"Minister Padang forbids it."

"Minister Padang is not the president!"

"If you persist, Mr. President," Nazir grinned, "I am to shoot you."

"What!"

"I would just be following orders, of course."

Tuesday, March 10, 6:25 P.M.

Christian Drieser had given up on the Situation Room. Decisions—or nondecisions—were being made at the United Nations, with advice from Washington carrying a weight that was undetermined. No one in New York or in the White House was taking him seriously, anyway, and he had left Secretary Chambers to argue State's case from time to time.

He had returned to his office on 23rd Street, where he and Judy Blalock had ordered in a six-pack of Dr. Pepper and two large pizzas. Canadian bacon and pineapple on one. Italian sausage, pepperoni, mushrooms, green peppers, and onions on the other.

Both had been delicious. Blalock had mentioned something about his lack of diversity in menu selection.

He had his feet up on the desk and was levered back in his chair, holding the icy can of soda on his stomach, staring intently at a cobweb spanning the angle of two walls. It was nice and high, where the custodians wouldn't want to reach or bother to get a ladder.

"I know that look."

"What look?" he asked her, without breaking his gaze away from the intricate cobweb.

"You're staring off into the future, thinking, again. Gets us in trouble, every time."

The spider didn't seem to be anywhere around, so he dropped his eyes to where Blalock sat on the other side of the desk. She was pretty damned cute, he thought, and bright as they came. It was too bad he was such a firm believer in keeping romantic interludes far from the office. Still, in an era where combatants faced each other at high noon with blazing charges of harassment, it was by far the safest course.

"Judy, Judy, Judy."

"Forget it."

"You did such a beautiful job, tracking down those electronics people who knew Li."

"Oh, damn! What do you want to track now?"

"Explosives. Tricky electronics. Stuff like that."

"Can you be more specific."

"Probably not."

"Do you know where you're headed with this?"

"Probably not."

"Is it important?"

"Probably."

Tuesday, March 11, 6:31 A.M.

"Shit!" Morris griped. "I'm a hot Apache pilot, not a ground pounder."

"You had a chance to play hot pilot with a free Black Hawk," Koehler reminded him.

"Yeah. Fried pilot."

The two of them were belly down at the left side of the road, twenty yards from the intersection where one of the two captured APCs was still firing occasional bursts from its M-60 down the Labi road. Three hostile vehicles were down there, trapped between the intersection and Captain Shrestha's patrol. The APC was taking infrequent hits from some still active machine gun down the grade on the Kuala Belait road. Irra's group was down there somewhere.

The second defending APC at the intersection was dead, black smoke boiling from its hatches.

Avery and the two storage techs had loped off to look for survivors among the wreckage of the Black Hawks. Shaikh and a few of his Gurkhas were buried in the jungle on the right side of the road.

Every few minutes, a strafing helicopter laid down a barrage of machine-gun fire or an occasional rocket, aiming in the general direction of the intersection. Because of the jungle canopy, the intersection was difficult for them to see, and the incoming fire wasn't entirely accurate. There was no telling, however, when a stray bullet might come in his direction, so Kelly stayed low and wished he could dig deeper.

The triple canopy of the jungle was becoming ever more shredded by the thousands of rounds passing through it.

Koehler didn't have a radio, so he didn't know the condition of Irra's or Shrestha's patrols. It wasn't yet hot enough to sweat, but the sweat was running off his face. His hands were slippery on the rifle.

"This is not good, Frank."

"The odds are changing by the second, Kelly."

"Hang on here."

Koehler got a knee under himself, levered to his feet, and dove across the narrow road to roll up next to Shaikh.

The Gurkha smiled grimly at him.

"Time to retreat, Benjamin."

"You are probably correct."

"North to Labi."

Shaikh's smile broadened a trifle, but Koehler saw the pain in the man's eyes. "The retreat route is obviously south, Kelly."

"Obviously."

"Let us go."

While Shaikh told one of his soldiers to go back and have the three idling personnel carriers turn around, Koehler regained his feet and started down the road at a trot.

"Come on, Frank!"

A string of 7.62-rounds shrieked overhead as Koehler veered to the left side of the road, forcing him to duck his head involuntarily. Morris pounded up beside him, and by the time they reached the intersection, he was aware that no more fire was coming from the left, from down the Kuala Belait road. He slid to a stop behind the damaged personnel carrier, banging his fist on the rear hatch. He could see where an antitank round had penetrated the left side of the carrier.

There was no response from inside.

Down the road to the left, he saw a junkyard. The four APCs of Bakir's forces were a shambles, nosed off the road, slammed into each other. An antitank rocket had gotten one, maybe two of them. Two were burning. The Jeep had attempted to turn around, but Irra's men had overrun it, and its four occupants were dead or dying, their bodies hanging over the sides. As he watched, Sergeant Major Irra emerged from the jungle, and Kelly raised his hand high, a thumb up.

Irra waved back at him.

Morris banged the butt of his assault rifle against the upraised ramp of the second APC, and the ramp opened a couple inches, enough for a Gurkha face to peer out.

Koehler stepped over to it just as a fusillade of lead screamed through the canopy, ricocheting slugs spattering off both APCs. He and Morris both went to the ground. A long burst of machine-gun fire raked both vehicles from the personnel carriers besieged on the Labi road.

He had a momentary flash of precognition—those massive tracks backing over him, flattening him into Bruneian soil. Quickly he rolled away from the track and stood up. The Gurkha was still eyeing him through the gap between the ramp and the APC body.

"Back up and shove this thing off the road!" he yelled above the chatter of a machine gun. He pointed at the burning vehicle.

The man nodded rapidly, then closed the ramp. Koehler ran for the side of the road, hit his knees, and crawled forward—beyond the APC which was now grinding into reverse—until he could see down the slight incline. Shrestha's team was keeping the three Bruneian combat vehicles pinned down from behind with a steady, though slow, stream of gunfire and an occasional hand grenade. They'd be running low on ammunition.

Morris hit the ground beside him.

"I want a raise, boss!"

"We can talk about overtime, maybe," he called back as he pulled his M-18 to his shoulder and sent a burst of three down the road.

Not that they'd do much damage against armor plate.

Overhead a helicopter screamed past, its machine guns chattering.

Staying as close to the jungle edge as he could, Kelly crawled rapidly along the road, Morris falling in behind him. His concentration on the lead APC, with the driver's head poked up through a hatch, and the vehicle commander manning the M-60 partially visible through another hatch, was such that he didn't notice he had company until Irra yelled, "Commander!"

He looked to his left and saw the sergeant major with another soldier crawling along on the other side of the road.

Behind him steel smashed steel with a horrendous crash, and he glanced back to see the APC attempting to shove the defunct machine off the road, down the hill of the Kuala Belait road.

The Brunei APC commander spotted Irra, and his M-60 stuttered. An advancing row of erupting geysers marched up the road. Morris and Koehler both fired three-round bursts, the M-60 suddenly directed its fire upward, and the commander slumped over, then slid back through his hatch.

The personnel carrier's engine roared, the tracks churned dirt into clouds, and it lurched forward, advancing on them quickly. With its gunner dead or wounded, though, the driver was most interested in running over his foes. Behind him the second carrier startled into motion. The third was slewed sideways, one of its tracks fatally splintered by Shrestha's grenades.

Koehler went flat onto his stomach, brought the rifle to his shoulder, and aimed.

He never got to pull the trigger.

A waterfall of 2.75-rockets from an unseen aircraft poured through the jungle canopy and found the APC. In Koehler's sights the driver's head erupted. The personnel carrier, peppered with rocket damage, veered off the road, tangled itself in the thick jungle, and came to a halt, its tracks still turning.

Beside him, Morris muttered, "Friendly fire."

Then they were up and running again, Irra and his soldier charging down the left side of the road, keeping pace with them.

They kept the roaring, track-spinning, useless personnel carrier between them and the second vehicle, which had now opened up in their direction with its machine gun. Bullets whanged off the flanks of the first APC as the gunner tried to keep them in sight.

Koehler performed a second-base-stealing slide as he reached the protection of the combat vehicle, almost skidding into the moving track. He went onto his side and squirmed to the right, sticking his head out to where he could get a view of the oncoming APC.

And saw Captain Shrestha leap aboard it from the rear. The gunner had his attention riveted forward, and he didn't see Shrestha scrambling over the top of the carrier, coming up behind him. In the subdued light of the jungle tunnel, the flash of the Gurkha's *kukri* was only momentary, and then the gunner's throat gushed bloody red. Shrestha immediately slid sideways, produced a grenade, pulled the pin with his teeth, and dropped it through the hatchway.

Three seconds.

A dull thud.

And the APC visibly shuddered before veering right and crashing into the personnel carrier Koehler was hiding behind.

He rolled backward madly, tangling with someone.

When he looked up, he saw Irra's face.

"That is one hell of an adjutant, Suraj."

"Fortunately, Commander, he is my adjutant."

The firing on the ground died away. Helicopters were still circling overhead, but they were now apparently without radioed directions from the ground. Kelly noted the absence of jungle sound. The parrots and birds had fled, and he didn't blame them.

The Gurkha who had accompanied Irra lobbed a grenade through the driver's hatch of the still-struggling APC next to him, and Koehler covered his head with his hands.

The detonation came a few seconds later, and the track suddenly stopped moving.

He clambered to his feet, saw Morris grinning at him, and Irra surveying the carnage.

Then came the rumble of more tracks, and the four APCs still under Shaikh's control rolled past the intersection toward them.

"Private," Irra growled, "find some chains. We will need to tow these machines out of the way."

"At once, Sergeant Major."

Irra turned to him. "I suspect, Commander, that we are retreating into the face of the enemy."

"Got a better way, Suraj?"

"Of course not."

Morris lifted a finger toward the unseen aircraft. "We won't be able to hide from those radars up there."

"But, Frank," Kelly said, "they don't know whether we're friendlies or not."

"If someone doesn't respond on a radio pretty damned soon, they'll take an educated guess."

With the help of a dozen Gurkhas and the strength of an armored personnel carrier, they soon had the damaged vehicles shoved far enough to the side to allow passage. Then they headed northward, Koehler, Morris, and Irra riding the top of the lead vehicle with Shaikh commanding from inside.

And someone above them took an educated guess.

Fourteen

Meoshi Kyoto's military service had taught him to live with frustration and to endure it—witness his time in the Foreign Ministry. His cultural upbringing had also convinced him that courtesy often went further in achieving ends than did confrontation.

He was getting close, however, to abandoning his polite facade in order to deal with his repressed desire to have the ordeal with the *Maru Hokkaido* come to an end. He almost longed to return to his desk in the ministry and to his arguments with Kim. He sat in the flag plot, studying the screen displays, and occasionally glancing at Admiral Harned. He was waiting a chance—when Harned put down the telephone—to once again press his case for joining the *Akagi*.

A built-in credenza against the aft wall was littered with the remnants of breakfast, which had been brought in to them, and a steward was attempting to collect the cups, saucers, and plates without disturbing the relative silence of the compartment. On the telephone Harned listened patiently to the United States Ambassador to the United Nations. Kyoto noted that the admiral was not being allowed many moments in which to speak.

A lieutenant with a headset began to signal Harned rather emphatically with his hand.

"One moment, please, Ambassador," Harned said, then turned toward the lieutenant.

"Eagle Eye, sir. Urgent."

Kyoto looked to the third of the three plotting boards, which displayed an infrared satellite image of Brunei. A naval commander had been tracking the progress of the battle in the jungle, but the lack of detail was disturbing. Kyoto could not tell what was happening by following the moving blips of light.

The first display held the radar-detected positions of the task force, with the focus on the supertanker's progress. The Japanese ships were also changing position, coming to speed and beginning to parallel the course of the *Hokkaido*. The second plot was a real-time image of the tanker, captured by the camera on an E-2 Hawkeye airborne early-warning aircraft. He wished he could go to the Combat Information Center, where the instructions were being given, rather than stare at the screens, watching the aftermath of decisions.

"On the overhead, Lieutenant," Harned ordered.

There was a crackle of static, then the American Koehler's voice on the ceiling speakers. "Sledgehammer, damn it!"

Holding the phone with the open line to the Ambassador in his left hand, Harned unclipped a microphone from his chair arm with his right. "Hammer here, Eagle."

"We need a little assistance, Admiral."

"Sitrep."

Kyoto could hear a straining engine in the background whenever Koehler pressed his transmission button.

" "We've lost our remaining aircraft. Eleven Gurkhas dead, three wounded. Strength four APCs and thirty-eight able-bodied. Weapons adequate, ammo, food, water, and gas low. Under attack by unknown number of aircraft. We could use help, goddamn it!"

"Stand by, Eagle."

Harned hit a button on the chair's control panel, and the telephone connection was transferred to the speaker system.

"Did you hear that report, Madame Ambassador?" Harned asked.

"I heard it," came over the speakers. The Ambassador's voice was stern, and Kyoto thought, perhaps somewhat unconcerned.

"I want to send aircraft."

"I am sympathetic, but not yet, Admiral. I'll have to clear any intervention with the Security Council. Violation of Brunei airspace has not even been considered. We'll—"

"Please do," Harned said and hung up on her.

He looked to his liaisons. "Well, Captain Margolin? Colonel Kyoto?"

The Frenchman said, "I suspect she is correct, Admiral."

Kyoto thought about the strain in Koehler's voice, the stress under which men in battle lived. It was a place he should be.

He said, "Commander Koehler and Major Shaikh have been assigned to you, Admiral, and they attempt to follow your orders. In your place I would provide whatever help I could."

"Ah, Meoshi. You are impulsive." Flipping a rotary dial on the armrest, he spoke into the microphone, "CAG?"

A moment went by before the air group commander responded. "CAG, Admiral."

"You have Tomcats aloft?"

"I do, sir. Getting low on fuel, however."

"KA-6?"

"The tanker is up, sir."

"How are the Tomcats armed?"

"Air-to-air defense, sir."

"Refuel two 14s and send them south. Instructions to follow."

Tuesday, March 11, 6:41 A.M.

"Where are you, Colonel?"

Omar Padang waited while Colonel Shamin Bakir determined where he was located.

"In Kuala Belait, Minister."

Padang could not understand a commander who would not desire to be where the action was taking place. He himself had spent most of his waking hours—which were many—visiting the military and police units under his command to reassure them of his support. And just as important, to let them know that he was watching them closely.

"The report of first contact with the Gurkhas is an hour old, Colonel. Why are you in Kuala Belait?"

"There are many logistical and command problems," Bakir said. "The civilian aircraft we have commandeered require frequent refuelling. They do not adapt well to the weapons we—"

"Colonel! I am asking about the Gurkhas!"

"Reports from the area are positive. Even now, the helicopters have pinpointed the hostile—"

"Numbers! For the love of Allah, give me numbers!"

"Ah . . . a moment, Minister. Here we are. A pilot confirms that three Black Hawk helicopters have been destroyed on the ground. The Gurkhas no longer have aircraft."

"Wonderful! Casualties?"

"We do not yet know how many were aboard the helicopters. Certainly, there were many."

"And your own losses?"

"Uh . . . the aircraft are accounted for, and we are still attempting to make contact with the patrol commanders. They are not responding."

"Not responding. How many are not responding?"

"There were seven armored personnel carriers."

Padang noted the past tense. "But the Gurkhas have been defeated?"

"Well, Minister, the pilots are reporting the movement of vehicles along the road. We suspect that several vehicles are attempting to escape with the last of the Gurkhas."

"You are certain of this?"

"You must understand that we cannot see them through the jungle cover. They are firing on our aircraft."

"Shamin, get out of your chair and go kill them! Do it personally!"

Tuesday, March 11, 6:44 A.M.

The jungle along here was spotty, and there were bare spots, where the road was visible to the aircraft tracking them, and the APCs dashed across them, seeking the safety of the jungle tunnel. Koehler tried to assess the enemy in those instances, but he only saw a twin Beech King Air orbiting to the north of the trail, a Bell JetRanger and a Huey.

The Huey had a rocket pod mounted, but it was apparently depleted of ammunition. When it attacked it was from door-mounted M-60s, and the pilot quickly altered course when the APC gunners opened up on him.

He could hear the engines of other aircraft, but they were out of sight, and Kelly suspected they were mostly civilian aircraft jerry-rigged with minimal firepower. Some of them may have turned back for refuelling and rearming. Worst case, they might have another Huey show up, sporting rockets.

Forward progress was also minimal. They had abandoned the Labi road, expecting additional ground units coming from the north, and taken an eastward track that only Irra seemed to know. The road left behind was a high-speed autobahn compared to the vine- and tree-choked path they had chosen.

Whoever had cut through the jungle here had planned only to move carts through it. The personnel carriers were too wide and too high, and the trees grasped at them, scraping painfully over the men riding the tops of the vehicles, as Kelly was. Branches and vines caught, then were ripped away as the lead APC struggled forward. He figured they were making all of two miles an hour.

And frequently, a barrage of lead poured through the canopy, unaimed, but nonetheless lethal. Koehler had never been phobic about anything, but the jungle seemed to be closing in on him with relentless intent.

He was on his stomach between Irra and Morris, half protected from the foliage coming over the front end by the raised hatch coaming and the M-60 mount at the gunner's hatchway. A Gurkha trooper had his head poked through the hatch, ready to reach up and man the M-60. Farther forward, the driver's head extended through a hatch, also. The vehicle lurched and bounced, threatening to break Koehler's hold on a grab bar. The engine roared and ebbed, roared again, as the road dipped, swung around boulders, hairpinned backward to work up a rise barely envisioned in the thickness of the forest.

Koehler didn't have a clue about which direction they were going, or where in the southern hemisphere they might be.

A burst of fire erupted through the canopy, hot trails of tracers visible in the semidarkness of the jungle. The rainfall of lead was behind them, and he heard the zinging ricochets as they struck the armor of the second or third APC.

One of the gunners behind ripped off a short burst of return fire. Shaikh, who was inside the carrier, had cautioned his soldiers to conserve ammunition.

"If those assholes had decent radar," Morris called over the bellow of the engine, "we'd be toast."

"I have observed," Irra said, "that probability tends to even itself after the passage of time. The more they miss now, the more likely they will hit what they wish to hit later."

"Damn, Suraj," Kelly said. "Don't be so optimistic."

"I hope your admiral responds soon."

"He said he'd send something our way."

The APC suddenly nosed downward into a sinkhole, and Koehler slid forward. He reached out with both hands to grab the coaming of the hatchway and stop his slide, then the nose jerked upward, and he was sliding backward.

CHUP-CHUP-CHUP!

A series of small eruptions chattered to their left, tearing up jungle.

"Shit!" Morris yelped. "They found more rockets!"

"Corporal! Give me that mike again," Koehler yelled.

The gunner ducked through the hatch, came back with the microphone on a coiled cord, and handed it to Koehler. He pulled himself forward so he could hear responses on the radio's speaker through the hatch.

"Sledgehammer! Eagle Eye!"

"Hammer here." He could barely hear the reply over the engine's song.

"Where are those planes?"

"ETA twenty minutes, Eagle. Hang on."

"They loaded for bear?"

"Roger that," the admiral told him.

"Can they shoot?"

"Well, we may have a problem there."

"Your United Nations at work," Morris said.

Koehler depressed the transmit stud. "Try to figure that one out, will you? And pronto!"

"Wilco."

"One more, Sledgehammer. I sent my wife out of Muara on a ketch named *Serendipity.* Monday, 0400 hours. See what you can find out."

A pause, then: "Wilco. Hammer out."

Koehler handed the microphone back to the corporal.

He had no more than settled back, shaking his head to free it of a hanging vine, when the APC burst out of the narrow track onto another road. The driver hit the brakes, and Koehler slid into Morris. Brakes squealed behind them, and the second APC nearly drove into their rear.

"See?" Irra said. "We have completed the shortcut."

"This was a shortcut? I wish I'd known."

"To the right!" Irra called to the driver.

The left track chattered, and the carrier swung right, then accelerated on the new trail. Kelly guessed it was a couple feet wider and had been travelled at least ten times in the past year.

A dozen 2.75-rockets slashed through the overhead canopy, erupting, concussing eardrums, tearing up the road ahead of them.

And the APC drove right into the stream.

Monday, March 10, 7:10 P.M.

"Admiral, Chris Drieser. Am I calling at a bad time?"

"Could you define 'good time,' Chris?"

"Last week?"

"That was better, yes."

Drieser paced back and forth around the right end of his desk, tethered by the telephone cord.

"You heard from Koehler?"

"As a matter of fact, I have."

Drieser stopped pacing as he listened to the cryptic report.

"Jesus! Is he going to be all right?"

"We'll know shortly. I've sent a couple F-14s to mix it up with the hostiles, though the UN won't let me release weapons."

"Damn, Hap! We're going to have to move a hell of a lot faster and harder. The twelfth is coming up fast."

"I was assured you were working on that aspect, Chris."

"Ah, damn! Hey, the reason I called is I have some info for you."

"I assume it's not encouraging," Harned said.

"No. My hotshot intel operative"—he pointed a finger at Judy Blalock, who was sitting at the conference table— "just learned that Padang probably has three thousand Grails."

The SA-7 Grail was a portable, shoulder-fired surface-to-air missile produced in the thousands by the Soviets. The black markets in weapons always seemed to have plenty of them in inventory. While they were not particularly accurate, if enough of the infrared-seeking missiles were fired at an airborne target, one was bound to find its way home.

"Source?"

"Hell, the damned CIA had the data, Hap. They've been

tracking weapons-dealer sales out of the Middle East, but they didn't have this shipment logged on their computer yet. Judy stumbled into it while looking for something else."

"Was there an end-user certificate?"

"Hell, no. These went in on a Boeing 747 cargo jet, consigned as electronics components. The shipping address was a warehouse in Muara."

"What else are you looking for?"

"I've been thinking about those mined platforms. Padang and Li had to buy their munitions somewhere, so we're looking for explosives and electronics shipped into Brunei. It might give us an advantage if we know what's in use."

"I like the way you think," Harned said. "Let me know the minute you find anything."

"Roger that."

"And thanks for the Grails. I need to make a call."

Tuesday, March 11, 7:12 A.M.

Lieutenant Anthony DePalma's concentration was divided between the readouts on his panel and the right wingtip of his flight leader.

The readouts told him he was one thousand feet off the surface of the sea, at a heading of 187 degrees, and holding a speed of Mach 1.1, translated to 872 miles an hour at this altitude. The F-14 Tomcat maxed out at Mach 2.3, or 1,500 miles an hour, at altitude, and he was one-tenth off the max at sea level.

Using up fuel like it was a butterscotch malted on a hot July day. He hoped that KA-6 was following along behind.

He didn't pay any attention to the magnificent blue sky or the shining tropical waters that were a blur under the wingtips. More important was his position relative to Commander Jefferson Dray in the Tomcat a quarter mile ahead and slightly to DePalma's left.

He didn't want to hit either his flight leader or the sea.

The swing-wing fighter was designed primarily for long-range air defense of the fleet, and both his and Dray's craft were armed with Phoenix, Sparrow, and Sidewinder missiles for long, medium, and short-range engagements. He didn't know what the hell he'd use them for on this hastily fabricated mission. The General Electric M-61A-1 Vulcan cannon—a multibarreled Gatling-type weapon that spit out 20-millimeter shells—might be useful against ground targets. If one wanted to level a village in about twenty seconds.

DePalma was mildly disturbed by the mission. The entire focus of his training had been on combat, of course, but he'd never been in combat. He was quite willing to prove himself, but he was a little worried about how well his performance might measure up to Dray's expectations.

"You hanging in there, Dip?" his NFO asked over the intercom.

The naval flight officer in the backseat, Lieutenant (jg) Cale Walker, known as High Wire, never let him forget his nickname. Though "Magic Man" was stenciled on DePalma's helmet, there were a few in the mess who had shortened his name to Dip, also short for Dipshit. After he squashed an F-14 into the flight deck.

"I'm eager, Wire. When's landfall?"

The NFO checked his radar. "Call it seventy seconds."

DePalma glanced up at the lead aircraft, then let his eyes sweep the horizon. The landmass of Borneo was a fuzzy green emerald dead ahead, lying in a shallow curve. He didn't see anything else remarkable.

"Coral Blue Flight, Breadbasket."

Dray responded for the flight. "Blue One."

"Heads up. You may have an SA-7 greeting."

"Roger the Grail. Appreciate that, Basket. Anything new on rules of engagement."

"Negative. Fire if fired upon. Attempt to scatter the hostiles. Breadbasket out."

DePalma fingered the transmit button. "Two copies."

A Grail's gonna faze a Tomcat at Mach 1? Gimme a break.

"Two, this is One."

"Two."

"We don't want to overfly this whole damned country in thirty seconds. Bring it back to five hundred knots."

"Wilco."

With one eye on the vertical display indicator group and the other on Dray, he eased off on the throttles. As the aircraft slowed, and he moved a little closer to his flight leader, he began to see oil platforms appearing on the right oblique. Hundreds of them. A few ships at anchor. The shoreline began to define itself.

Dray banked easily to the right and turned the heading westward a few degrees. DePalma automatically followed, then levelled the wings as they headed directly for the oil field.

The CAG had told them the mission goal was to hit the coast low and hard, scaring the shit out of a few people, letting them know the U.S. Navy had a presence, then scooting inland to frighten off a flock of Cessnas and Bells that were harassing some friendlies. In and out. Piece of cake.

Perhaps in defiance of some rule about high-altitude flying, which had been pushed at an earlier briefing. Someone might get in trouble, but DePalma didn't think it would be himself.

He checked aft. The wings were in their full sweep, 68 degrees. If he slowed much further, the automatic flight control would adjust the sweep to the appropriate angle.

"Stay with me, Two."

"Coming up."

DePalma clicked the throttles, and the F-14 closed up on Dray.

Then they were over the oil field, platforms like nasty fingers pointing up at them. Flaring towers spitting flame.

Streaking past.

There, then gone.

Shoreline coming up. More wells inland. Paradise for greedy oil companies. DePalma's first view of the country. Green, green, green. Rolling hills and choking jungle.

Couple miles to go.

Scan the panel.

"Mile from feet dry," Walker intoned. "You're about to enter friendly downtown Kuala Belait."

"Stick with me, Wire."

"Wouldn't think of leaving."

Half mile.

And suddenly the sky filled with smoky streaks.

Ten, twelve, twenty of them, rising from the buildings along the shore.

"Shit!" DePalma hit the transmit. "Break, One!"

"Going le—"

He had a momentary view of the white streaks, two of them, centering on the F-14, then impacting.

Dray's Tomcat blossomed in a rose of yellow, blue, and white, a wing shearing away, pieces of the airframe peeling off.

Directly into his flight path.

DePalma whipped the stick right, went knife-edge, and hauled the stick back into his crotch.

The G-forces climbed immediately—the readout went to 6.5. He felt the skin pull away from eyeballs.

Something clanged against the fuselage.

Stick centered.

Left.

Level.

Back and left. Climbing steeply as the fighter angled back over the city.

A missile shot past the right wing.

"Kee-rist!" Walker yelped.

And the city was behind them.

"Breadbasket, Blue Two. One's down!"

"Now, I'm thinking of leaving," High Wire said on the intercom.

"Complete the mission," CAG ordered.

"But One's down!"

"Complete the mission."

Tuesday, March 11, 7:14 A.M.

The APC's driver seat was elevated, allowing the man's head to poke upward through the hatch above the seat. The view was much better than the one offered through the viewing slits ahead of the driving position.

One of the rocket rounds decapitated the driver, evaporated his head. The corpse was blown down and backward. Blood erupted and spewed throughout the interior, spraying Shaikh, the radio operator, and the six soldiers gripping their canvas seats.

The left track was hit, and the personnel carrier lurched left and drove into the jungle, tilting upward to the right. Shaikh slid off his seat and banged his hip on the steel floor. A massive crescendo of pain arced through his leg and up his torso, making him think of heart attacks.

He nearly screamed, but managed to grit his teeth and hold it back.

The red interior lighting flickered and died, as did the engine.

Grabbing the steel conduit of the seat, Shaikh pulled himself upright. His men scrambled to find their weapons. Light seeping through the open gunner's hatch showed him that the gunner, too, was dead. His legs dangled, swayed.

Those riding on top had probably not survived, he thought.

"Open the ramp!" he called out.

Two Gurkhas leaped to their feet, sliding on the tilted deck, and attempted to use the power assist, but it was dead. They pulled the emergency pins, and the ramp fell away, crashed to the earth. Light spilled inside.

They were angled off the road, though not far enough for the second APC to get by, and it had ground to a halt right behind them.

The third personnel carrier was burning fiercely, black smoke boiling out of its hatches. The interior heat had reached the ammunition storage, and 7.62-rounds were cooking off, banging around the inside.

The fourth vehicle was blocked by the wreckage. Men began to climb out of it. He saw Captain Shrestha.

Shaikh slid down the cockeyed ramp and looked upward. The smoke from the burning APC climbed almost straight upward, sifting through the canopy.

Pinpointing them.

He could hear the Huey helicopter circling, coming back for another run with its deadly rockets. He turned to look, but there was no one on top of his personnel carrier.

"Abandon the APCs!" he yelled, then turned back to tell a sergeant, "Bring the radios."

Tuesday, March 11, 7:15 A.M.

"Come two points to the left, Dip."

"Two points, wilco."

Tony DePalma slid the Tomcat onto a heading of 156, trusting his NFO's directions. Their target had been identified for them by the NSA's satellite, and the constellation of satellites in the Global Positioning System (GPS) fed them the correct coordinates of the target area, as well as their own position. Finding the target was not the problem.

His retinas still burned with the image of those Grails closing on Blue Coral One. His throat felt constricted, and his eyes burned.

The oxygen mask hanging to one side of his jaw irritated him, and he reached up and ripped it free.

He hadn't known Commander Dray or his backseater well, but damn it, they were fellow aviators and squadron mates.

Bastards!

Checked the readouts. They were down to 260 knots; the wings had swept forward a few degrees to compensate and increase the lift.

The hilly jungle was a crumpled carpet stretched to the horizon. He scanned left and right, but didn't see other aircraft. A few peaks stuck through the jungle in places. Downright damned inhospitable.

"You have targets, High Wire?"

"Sure do, buddy. Three-six miles. Four choppers and two fixed-wing."

"They must be low."

"They are. How we going to handle this?"

"I want those suckers to shoot at us."

"Me too."

He kept the Tomcat as low as he could, rising and dropping with the terrain, sliding easily left and right to clear the higher hills.

Closing.

"Two-one miles, Dip."

Hell, he had these nice, high-tech missiles slung from the pylons. His Hughes AWG-9 radar could count up to eight aircraft a hundred miles away, lock on, and target the AIM 54 Phoenix missiles on each. He could fire Phoenix and Sparrow missiles from here, be confident that all six hostiles were doomed, turn around, and go look for the KA-6 for go-juice.

But he was supposed to let them shoot first.

And he knew damned well that NSA satellite was watching him. If he lit off something too soon, CAG would have both his ass and his career.

"One-four miles."

DePalma went into a left bank.

"What the hell, Dip?"

"I'm going to get that low morning-sun behind us."

"Yeah. A point for the aviator."

One minute later he rolled back onto a heading for the targets, checked his fuel state, pulled the nose up, and rammed the throttles to their stops.

"This train's rolling," he told Walker.

"Bear in mind that we are twelve hundred AGL and some of these peaks won't dodge us."

"They better."

The F-14 accelerated like a Titan missile, the wings folding back, and seconds later they were breaking Mach 1, trailing a sonic boom that would alarm every living jungle creature behind them.

Those in front wouldn't know they were coming.

He played the stick with tenderness, anticipating the rise of the terrain, and seven miles out, he saw the hostiles. Two light-twins were orbiting and four helicopters were taking turns racing in on a spiral of smoke rising from the jungle roof.

"Shit. We might be too late, High Wire."

"Don't matter. Shatter 'em."

They closed rapidly, and as they did, DePalma angled the fighter into a shallow dive.

"One-point-six miles."

He didn't actually want to create a midair, and he watched the flight patterns closely. There was one 'Namera Huey and three utility helos.

"The UH-1," Walker said.

"My thought, too, buddy."

Careful, now. The closure rate was tremendous.

A few seconds.

None of the hostile pilots saw him until he went through the center of the formation at eight hundred miles an hour, damned near clipping the Huey, which was his intent.

They probably *never* saw him, the speed was so great.

But as he pulled out of his dive, climbing almost straight up, pouring on the Gs, dragging the throttles back, he checked the mirror. The concussion and the turbulence created by the Tomcat's Mach 1 passage threw the Huey inverted, and she dove into the jungle. One other chopper farther away, a Bell, was rocking and fighting for stability.

Cale Walker also noted it. "Hell, guy, who needs guns?"

"Let's arm 'em up, just in case."

"Sparrows and Sidewinders?"

"Good by me."

He rolled out at the top, kicked the nose over, and started back down.

"You watch for hostile fire, Cale."

"Gotcha."

The two twin-engined craft were in tight turns, having decided to head for home.

The three remaining helos were scrambling for a defensive posture, not knowing what it was.

This time he made the pass toward the north at less than three hundred knots, aiming the fighter right through the center of the smoke. An Aèrospatiale Alouette with a machine gun rigged in the doorway flew a high-speed retreat a quarter mile to the right as he went by.

DePalma concentrated on the jungle and the hills, and he didn't see the tracers when they came.

Walker giggled. "Son of a bitch did it!"

"Fired on us?"

"Damned right. Couldn't hit a tin can at ten paces."

He rolled left into a wide circle, heading out about eight miles before turning back. Walker reported the Alouette's attack on them to Breadbasket.

"Weapons free, Blue Two."

Hot damn!

"We've only got three Sidewinders, Dip."

"Better use 'em up."

"Might as well."

The Sidewinders had an eleven-mile range, so he was in good shape when he found the three helos on the target acquisition radar, locked one missile on each, and pressed the "COMMIT" stud. The AIM 9L Super Sidewinders thought about it for a half second, then leaped away.

At Mach 3, the missiles covered the distance in mind-blowing rapidity, and by the time he had almost reached the smoke, all three choppers were puffs of blue/gray smoke tumbling into the jungle.

"Had a thought, Magic Man."

"Tell me."

"We've got four, though I think the first one won't count. We get the two planes, and we're aces."

The tactical frequency sounded in his earphones, "Blue Coral Two, Breadbasket."

"Two."

"That's enough. State your fuel load."

"Ah . . . fuel twelve hundred."

Damn! I should have paid more attention.

"Let's see if we can't connect you up with Filling Station."

"Roger, Basket."

He pulled up and began grabbing altitude, easing the throttles back, finally thinking about conserving fuel.

DePalma was surprised at himself. He didn't feel one damned bit of remorse. Four helos didn't seem like enough. Blue Coral One wasn't an even trade.

He hoped Commander Dray would have approved.

And was pretty certain he would have.

Tuesday, March 11, 9:51 A.M.

Sherry Koehler's stomach and heart ached for Kelly.

She wished she knew where he was, if he was still in Bandar Seri Begawan. Maybe she and Monica could find him.

She very much wanted him safely on board the junk.

Looking around the salon, Sherry was astounded that she had stumbled into such a refuge. She judged that the vessel was fifty or sixty years old, but her maintenance—or her renovation—was superb. The fitted teak planks of the deck gleamed with wax. A Persian carpet—she tried to recall the name of the knotting, but couldn't—was centered between the table where she sat and the grouping of blue leather couches at the stern bulkhead. A panoramic view of the bay was available through the large windows that spanned the stern.

The interior bulkheads were hung with Chinese and Asian art she was certain she wouldn't afford in a lifetime.

Brocaded silk was laminated to the walls, and the bloodred-on-white pattern of orchids was repeated in the draperies drawn back from the windows. The table where she sat was round, flanked by eight chairs, and its surface shone so highly that she could see her reflection in the surface of the teak. Black lacquered chests and tables were spotted around the compartment. Bronze and jade sculptures rested on them.

The tea she sipped was aromatic, hot, and strong. The warmth of it flowing down her throat gave her new resolve.

On the other side of the table was a Chinese man, dressed in a gray jumpsuit, smoothly shaved—cheeks *and* head. He grinned at her, hadn't stopped since they came aboard.

His name was Han Lo, and he was captain of the *Harmonious Spirit*. The name wasn't on the fantail, and *Harmonious Spirit* was as close as Sherry could translate Han's words and gestures. Neither Han nor the six members of his crew spoke a word of English, and Sherry's limited command of the language hadn't been entirely useful in their dialogue. The Bruneian version of Chinese wasn't exactly like the dialect these men had grown up with, wherever that was. She was pretty sure the dialect wasn't Cantonese or Mandarin.

She had learned—or thought she had learned—that the junk belonged to the family of Hua Enlai, who was head of the Chinese consulate in Brunei and who normally lived aboard the luxurious ship. He had not been seen since the uprising, and the captain and crew had been maintaining a low profile. Being Chinese, of course, helped them to blend in with the Bruneian population, though they had not risked going ashore.

Captain Han apparently understood her situation, and he seemed quite willing to help Sherry and Monica hide out, going so far as to assign them to two of the six available guest cabins, each with a private bath.

And hot water!

Sherry had stayed under a stinging spray for half an hour, and she was now dressed in a man's kimonolike dressing gown, waiting while her clothing was laundered.

She and Han had been attempting to communicate for over an hour, as various members of the crew came to and went from the salon. Koehler was very much aware that each was armed, and she wondered if the diplomatic pact allowed the consulate to bring weapons into the country. She doubted it.

Han stood and came around the table to refill her cup from a ceramic pot that she thought was an antique, hand-painted with butterflies and blossoms. As she thanked him, Monica's head appeared on the floor in the corner.

It was a circular stairwell leading to a lower deck, and Monica eventually emerged in full, wrapped like Sherry in a man's dressing gown.

Her face was freshly scrubbed, and she had been positively radiant since they had been fed breakfast.

"I thought you were trying to sleep."

"Tried, but couldn't," Davis said. "Too many what-ifs running around in my head. Frank Morris is one of them."

Han poured another cup of tea as Monica took a seat, then went back to his chair.

"Captain Han tells me that all foreign shipping has been ordered to stay in port," Koehler said. "He wouldn't leave, anyway, without his master."

"Master. You make it sound like . . . a dated concept."

"The owner is master of the vessel."

She strongly suspected, however, that Han was almost an indentured servant to the family that owned the junk.

"How come they have guns?"

"Didn't ask, and I'm not going to."

"Do we know what's going on in town?" Davis asked.

"Captain Han let me listen to the radio, but that wasn't very enlightening. I wanted to make a radio call, but he wouldn't allow it."

Han's head bobbed up and down every time he heard his name mentioned. Grinned.

"Who on earth would you call?"

"I don't know. There must be someone listening, somewhere. Maybe the Navy ship with the admiral who activated Kelly."

"I'm scared for him, Sherry."

"Me too, but he can take care of himself." She said it, but wasn't certain she believed it. The situation in the country was too volatile and too confused.

"What do we do now?"

"Wait."

"For what?"

"I don't know. If I can learn enough of the captain's language, maybe I can talk him into sailing out of here."

"Fat chance. They want us here."

Monica's eyes flicked toward the double doors leading to the main deck, and Sherry followed them.

One of the crewmen, a young man with a Fu Manchu mustache and an evil-looking assault rifle, stood near the entrance.

A guardian? Or a warden?

Suddenly she didn't know whether or not the *Harmonious Spirit* was a refuge or a jail. And what did Captain Han really think of a *gweilo*—a foreigner?

The way he took turns grinning at Monica, then at her, Sherry began to think they weren't guests as much as recreational material.

Tuesday, March 11, 1:10 P.M.

Koehler had wrapped both of his arms around Morris and Irra, and rolled the bundle of them off the side of the APC the second he saw the rockets tearing up the road.

They hit the road hard enough to crack ribs, all of them scrambling to get out of the path of deadly fire and of the personnel carrier second in line. The damage was done by the time he regained his feet, with two of the APCs badly shot up and out of duty.

He was thankful to seek Shaikh emerge and order the vehicles abandoned, then he bent over and helped Morris to his feet.

"Come on, Frank. You can sleep later."

The pilot looked up at him and said, "Navy guys always have clean sheets. Us GIs learn to sleep in the mud and dirt."

Sergeant Major Irra, also rising to his feet, said, "There is something comforting about Mother Earth." He gazed at the burning APCs and added, "I thank you for your rapid response, Commander."

Morris batted at the legs of his jeans with his hands, raising puffs of dust. "Me too, Kelly."

"You guys get to make dinner."

He flinched when another burst of fire tore through the jungle overhead, but it was thirty yards off-target. The rounds bursting inside the third carrier were of more concern.

The Gurkhas were animatedly gathering their weapons and canteens of water, checking on injured, and responding to Shaikh's commands to hurry when the sonic boom hit.

He went backward onto his butt when the concussed air

slapped him, and fifteen seconds later was shaking his head, wondering if he was deaf. Everything was dim.

Around him everyone was on the ground. The silence was overwhelming.

Then he heard something.

Aircraft crashing. Dull thud that vibrated the ground under him. Secondary explosions.

Morris climbed to his knees in front of Kelly, his mouth moving. Finally he yelled to be heard, "Your goddamned admiral got here!"

A few minutes later, back on his feet, with sound coming back to him, he heard the fighter pass overhead once again.

The Gurkhas milled around, waiting, listening. The airplane and helicopter engines began to ebb.

Benjamin Shaikh came over to the side of the road, smiling grimly. "They are running away, I think."

Then one, two, three detonations, all in close succession.

"Damn," Morris said, "this is turning into a shooting war."

"I wish I could have seen it," Koehler said. "Are we regrouping, Benjamin?"

"I believe so, yes."

It took half an hour to move the wrecked vehicles out of the way and load seven injured Gurkhas aboard the remaining two APCs, then they were racing down the road again.

An hour and a half later, Irra's uncanny sense of direction had taken them off on several trails, cutting back and forth through the jungle, losing the pursuit, if any, and losing Koehler completely, for sure.

And when they found the clearing Irra was searching for, it was already populated.

With former Bruneian police lieutenant Ali Haji and his traffic patrol officers.

The Bruneians were quick to expand their camp and to help with the Gurkha injured. Pieces of canvas and shelter halves were strung on vines to complete a rudimentary hospital. Rations were sparse, and what there was available was set aside for the wounded. The policemen then spread out into the jungle to practice skills that had apparently been taught to them by some of Shaikh's men.

Koehler slept for a couple hours, waking to the aroma of spicy food.

It turned out to be a stew for which he didn't want to know the contents, but it was thick and good. He ate all he was served and wanted more, but knew that others had priority.

He washed his canteen cup with a trickle of water the policemen had accumulated in a cistern made of leaves, then walked to the latest command vehicle, where Shaikh was resting.

"Think we can risk a radio call, Benjamin?"

Shaikh sat up on the ramp. He nodded. "I would like to know what has transpired, Kelly."

Lieutenant Haji joined them and watched with undisguised curiosity as Koehler powered up the set. Since he had first met Morris, he had been intrigued by the presence of the Americans, but too polite to ask about them.

"Sledgehammer, Eagle Eye."

A long pause, then the admiral came back to him, "Go ahead, Eagle Eye."

"Thank your flyboy for us, will you?"

"I'll do that. We've been waiting to hear from you."

"You knew we got away?"

"IR eye in the sky, Eagle. We just weren't sure of the IDs of who made the break, and we didn't want to break the radio silence in case someone else had control of the set."

Koehler gave him a rundown of the numbers and their current status, then asked for the global picture.

"That's a little confused," the admiral told him. "We're waiting on UN decisions. The tanker's long gone from here, and I'm hoping that we get steering orders for Brunei."

"The tanker's gone?"

"North. We're tracking her, but our hands are tied. New York wants to know more about the Sultan and those platforms."

Koehler was tired enough to risk impertinence. "Why are you interested in coming here, sir?"

After a hesitation the admiral said, "We sent two 14s to you, Eagle. One came back."

"Shit!" Koehler knew the anguish when one of your own didn't return. "We owe those men, sir. I'll write the letters."

"Let's figure out what we're doing, first, Eagle. Is there any way you can get more information?"

"Hold one minute, sir."

He rested the microphone on his thigh, made certain the transmit button was off, and said to Shaikh. "Benjamin, I'm going to go out on a limb."

"Will you saw us off, Kelly?"

"Maybe. Look, I doubt the UN is going to react because one Tomcat was shot down. They're too damned conservative, and they need something to push them over the edge of the decision."

"You will offer conjecture?"

Koehler grinned. "That's one way of putting it. You know where I'm headed with this?"

"I believe so, yes. If no one else will make a decision, you will make it. We will make it together."

Kelly glanced at Haji, but the man's face showed he was mystified.

He raised the microphone. "Hammer, are we facing any deadlines?"

"We are, indeed, Eagle. One o'clock on the twelfth, and the fireworks begin. Unless we pull out."

"Nice to know that, sir. That's tomorrow."

"Need to know doctrine, Commander."

"Of course." Since there seemed to be no time at all left to him, Koehler decided on his own doctrine. "Well, I know where the Sultan is located."

A long pause. "And you learned this how?"

"That blinking flashlight? I couldn't read it because it was sending Morse in Malay."

"Just a damned minute!" Another long pause, then, "GT-Bravo."

"Correct, sir."

"And how did you come to interpret it just now?"

"The police lieutenant here helped me with it." He grinned at Haji, who was still mystified.

The more Koehler thought about it, though, it *was* possible. Not likely, though. And yet, *someone* was on that platform, and a platform that far out in the field made a good hiding place.

"Got any other bright ideas, Eagle?"

"I'll take the platform, sir. As soon as I do, I signal you, and you send the Marines in. You do have Marines?"

"I have Marines."

"And we've got another bunch of Gurkhas waiting to take the western border. Kuala Belait and the oil field is our primary target. Bandar Seri Begawan can fall in its own good time."

"I could agree to the targets, Eagle, but we have another little glitch."

"The mined platforms; yes, sir. I'll take care of that, too."

"Jesus Christ, Commander! When did you take on the Superman complex?"

"I want it over with, Admiral. How about you?"

"What did that Morse signal tell you?"

"Four words is all," Koehler composed. "Command-post-slash-Sultan."

After a hesitation the admiral said, "And you're interpreting that to mean that the control for the mines is also located on GT-Bravo?"

"My best shot, sir."

"Goddamn it! I've got to talk to some others here and get some messages off. I'll get back to you, Eagle."

"I've got another problem. I need some resupply—medical kits and some other goodies." Koehler read off a list in his mind, knowing he was being recorded. Benjamin Shaikh grinned broadly as he listened.

"Okay," the admiral said. "We'll handle that right away. On this other thing, are your people up to it if I give you a go?"

He looked to Shaikh, who nodded affirmatively. Koehler didn't ask Haji, but the lieutenant chimed in, "But, of course!"

"You've got our position, Hammer?"

"Roger. We'll get a Greyhound off in a bit."

"Very good, sir. We'll be waiting. Eagle Eye out."

"Hold on, Eagle! I've got some . . . disturbing news."

Shit.

"NSA backtracked their tapes. This ketch you told me about, they think they've got it leaving the harbor, 0400 hours on Monday. It was involved in a skirmish, and a Bruneian patrol boat was sunk."

"Yes, sir. I was aboard at that time."

"Damn it, Eagle!"

"Sorry, sir."

"Anyway. They tracked it eastward. It was engaged and sunk early on Tuesday morning."

Oh, my God!

"Jesus, Admiral! Survivors?"

"None they've been able to spot. I'm sorry about this, Eagle."

"Eagle Eye out."

Koehler laid the microphone down very carefully.

Fifteen

Tan Hashim stayed close to the administrative office on Deck Five of GlobeTech Bravo. He slept on a cot in an anteroom and had his meals delivered to him there. Only on occasion did he leave his post to go check on his royal prisoners.

They were disheartened, of course, in the midst of a deep depression, which he thought only fitting. Hamzah bin Suliaman was more than depressed. He was running a high fever, and Hashim fully expected him to die within a week.

He had come to believe that it would not be his fault if Suliaman died, and he had begun to worry less about it. Hashim had started to think that the Provisional President and his cronies on the committee also would not last long. Omar Padang had a plan, and Hashim was elated to be part of it. He was not simply a warden for pampered inmates; he had been given a supreme task. His future looked very bright, indeed.

His duty NCO, a sergeant, was taking a turn sleeping on the cot, and the man's snores echoed off the steel bulkheads. Hashim was not irritated in the least.

He sat in his chair, sipping from a cold Coke obtained from the machine down the corridor, and stared through the open port at the vacant sea. His view was to the south, but the shoreline was not visible. Only a greenish-blue blur slightly to the east indicated the higher mountains of southeast Brunei. He could see three other oil platforms. There were no boats in the region.

He knew that for a fact. The radar set he had assembled had its display resting on the desk in front of him. It was a small unit, but very sophisticated. The antenna was located halfway up the derrick—no one in his squad wanted to climb higher, and he could view the area around him for twenty-four kilometers.

All he saw, however, were the returns from the pumping station ten kilometers away and the ships around it, several oil platforms, and the blur of the derrick when the antenna rotated past it. The steel of the derrick left a blind spot on the radar display, but he did not think it important.

Hashim's instructions were very clear. If he received a telephone or radio call from Omar Padang with the proper directive, or if an aircraft or boat approached within a mile without providing the code sign—apple brandy nine-two—he was to close the breakers on the three special radios. They were also on the desk, next to the radar cathode-ray tube.

All of them were ultralow-frequency transmitters. The first transmitted a signal that would detonate explosives on three Brunei Shell Oil platforms located at far reaches of the oil field. The second activated high explosives on an additional seven platforms, and the last controlled twenty-one detonators. In all, Hashim could topple thirty-three platforms.

It gave him a great sense of power.

Several times he had almost closed the switch on the first radio, just to be certain everything worked. And to feel the power.

He refrained, naturally. Omar Padang thought that, yes, they would have to destroy another three platforms before the United Nations took him, or Li Sen, at their word. Tomorrow, a week from the start, Hashim fully expected to demonstrate to the world the power of the Republic of Brunei, at least with the first radio transmitter.

But it didn't keep him from hoping that soon he would see a radar return from some helicopter within the one-mile limit that refused to give him the proper call sign.

Tuesday, March 11, 1:34 P.M.

Commander Jefferson Dray and his naval flight officer remained in Meoshi Kyoto's mind. He had never met them, but he empathized with their fates.

Those two men, who may have never seen Brunei before, and whose commitment had surely been to their own United States, had died because Japanese citizens had become hostages. It was more involved than that, of course, but certainly there was a connection.

For that matter, the American Koehler was in a similar situation, fighting a running ground battle with revolutionaries, involved in a war that was not his because of time and place.

Because of Dray, the battle of words in the Security Council had become heated. Kyoto had heard different versions through Admiral Harned and through Kato Asume. Task force overflights for purposes of reconnaissance had been approved much earlier, but the *instruction* had been that the overflights would occur at high altitudes. An American aircraft shot down over Brunei was not as cut-and-dried, in terms of the response, since no one seemed to have agreed on the earlier definition of acceptable altitude, and some in the Council appeared to think that Dray was not flying high enough.

He had still died.

Kyoto thought the reaction abominable.

If nothing else, at least the second aircraft had performed flawlessly, in Kyoto's mind.

The arguments might go on for days, while the *Maru Hokkaido* sailed out of sight, and perhaps into Japanese waters to spill her cargo. And while Koehler and the Gurkhas fought a war with no discernible goal. The lack of a clear mission statement for the United Nation's involvement and the task force's direction was sickening. Men were dying for no cause at all.

And Meoshi Kyoto had nothing to do.

He stood inside the cavernous hangar deck of the *Eisenhower* and watched while the Greyhound was loaded.

The Grumman C-2A was based on the design of the AWACS E-2 Hawkeye. Rather than carrying the massive radar dish above the fuselage, though, the Greyhound was designed as a rapid transit system for personnel and cargo for the American naval fleets. Driven by twin propellers, the aircraft could make catapult takeoffs and arrested landings with up to thirty-nine passengers.

This one was being loaded with palletized packs of supplies gathered from the Marine companies on board and from ship's stores. Food, ammunition, weapons, water, gasoline, batteries, radios, medical supplies, and other materiel ordered by Koehler were strapped to the pallets with flat metal bands. Parachutes were not attached to the pallets. Their weight and momentum had to drive them down through the jungle canopy, and so the crates and boxes were packed within shock-absorbing Styrofoam materials.

The pilots climbed aboard through the hatch just behind the cockpit as the airplane was turned and aimed for the elevator.

Impulsively, before the airstair could be raised, Kyoto stepped forward and placed a foot on the lower step.

The copilot looked down at him from inside the airplane. "Colonel?"

"I would like a ride, Lieutenant."

"Ah, sir. . . ." He looked around frantically for the aircraft commander, who was just climbing the short ladder into the cockpit. "Dick!"

The pilot, also a lieutenant, stopped and looked back.

Kyoto offered his most imploring look.

"Ah, shit!" the pilot said. "CAG'll have my butt."

"It will be my responsibility," Kyoto said. "I offer my word."

"What the hell. Come on!"

Kyoto climbed inside, and the crew chief reached around him to pull the airstair up into place.

The airplane was on the elevator, rising to the flight deck, before Kyoto remembered that he no longer left aircraft carriers by way of aircraft.

Maybe Kim was correct. He should become a civilian.

Tuesday, March 11, 2:40 A.M.

"I don't think Harned should have told Koehler about his wife," Drieser mused aloud. He didn't much like what Harned had reported about Koehler's situation, but he *really* didn't like Harned's tactics with the reserve officer. He was almost sorry they'd found Koehler in the first place.

Judy Blalock, on the other side of the conference table,

had her eyes closed and her head resting on her arms crossed on the tabletop.

She was not asleep, and she said, "You'd deny the man the truth?"

"If it keeps hope alive, yes. We need Koehler, but we don't need him in a state of depression."

"That's cold. You're heartless, Chris."

"Not really, my dear. Pragmatic."

Whoops. Let's not let any phrases that might be misinterpreted slip into this conversation.

"A heartless pragmatist. That's wonderful."

She sat up, rubbed her eyes, and scanned the stacks of documents littering the table. Her hair was in disarray, her blouse was wrinkled, there were dark circles under her eyes, and Drieser thought she looked rather enchanting.

Not that he'd ever tell her she was enchanting. Whap! Lawsuit.

The files and fax sheets stacked around them had been coming in steadily for over six hours, requested from and delivered by other agencies, by customs bureaus around the world, and by international companies very willing to cooperate with a United Nations with a crisis on its hands.

This wasn't all of it, either; there was more. In Blalock's office, in the anteroom, and in a conference room across the hall. Paper in stacks two feet high. Many more stacks than people, and twelve State people had volunteered to help as soon as Drieser had called them and told them to volunteer.

He grabbed another file.

U.S. Customs.

Opened it.

Fruit and grain.

Dropped it on the floor.

The floor was littered with discards. Walking was like skating on slick ice.

Picked up a fax sheet. From a German company shipping trucks to Brunei. Last year.

Another sheet. South African corporation dealing in gemstones. They had—

"Chris!"

He looked up at the doorway where a staffer from the personnel section stood. She was about fifty years old and looked as excited as a teenager.

"What've you got, Pam?"

"Haifa Technologies, Incorporated."

"Israeli?"

"Sort of." She crossed the floor and laid an invoice on his desk.

He ran his fingertip down the column as he read. Seventy-five cartons, 17-inch television sets. One hundred and forty-four boxes, AM-FM stereo receivers. Nineteen crates, stereo speakers. In pairs. It went on.

"I'm missing something, Pam."

"Number one. Seventeen-inch computer monitors, I've seen. How many ads in the *Washington Post* advertise seventeen-inch television sets, Chris?"

Blalock sat up straight. Drieser sat up straighter.

Tiny ones. Thirteen-inch? Nineteen? Twenty-one? And bigger. But seventeen?

"Check the shipping address."

He had to search the invoice before he found it.

"Li Sen Electronics, Bandar Seri Begawan."

"That's a red flag, right?"

"Right you are, Pam. Good eye."

"I think somebody screwed up, disguising the real thing with a title like seventeen-inch TV," Pam told him.

Judy slipped out of her chair, went around behind Drieser's desk, and jiggled the computer's mouse until the monitor came alive.

"Haifa Technologies, Pam?" she asked.

"That's it."

The search of data bases took about twelve minutes, then Blalock announced, "Haifa Tech is a front for Sam Leventhal."

"Who's Leventhal?" Pam asked.

Drieser answered. "He's a U.S. citizen, Lebanese-born. World-class arms dealer."

Blalock spun around in the swivel chair and asked, "Who do you wake up, Chris?"

"I think the Director of Central Intelligence. If he doesn't respond, I call the White House. Let's call Defense Intelligence, too, and ask them to send a dozen weapons and electronics specialists over here."

"Do you want me to dial?"

"Please."

But the telephone buzzed first, and after Blalock responded, she held it in the air.

Drieser got up and, slipping on the papers spread over the carpet, made his way to the desk to take it.

"Drieser."

"Hap Harned, Chris."

"Didn't I just talk to you?"

"Yeah, but I've got a problem and I want a second opinion."

"Hell, I'm full of opinions. Not much fact, though."

"Koehler says he knows where both the Sultan and the control center for the demolitions is located." Harned went on to detail his conversation with Koehler. Blinking flashlights, code in Malay. "What do you think, Chris?"

"GlobeTech Bravo. Christ. He tell you this before or after you dropped the bomb about his wife?"

"Before. And yes, damn it, I regret having told him."

"So you knew the location when we talked last?"

"Yes. But this is pivotal, Chris, and I took it to the Joint

Chiefs, first. Right now, the President and the National Security Advisor are on a hot line with the Ambassador.''

"But no one's buying Koehler's story? That's it?''

"We picked him out of a hat. Or rather, you did.''

"Good service record.''

"As a chopper jockey,'' Harned reminded him.

Drieser remembered that, not too many hours ago, he had been very pleased with himself because he didn't have to make the crucial decisions that fell to Harned. Now, someone—Fate?—was shoving a decision his way. Hell, he was on the side of peace and order. If he backed up Koehler, and both of them were wrong, a lot of good people could die and a lot of the flora and fauna of the sea might choke on big, black globules of dead dinosaurs. Not the dream of a good State Department man.

Standing beside his desk, with Judy and Pam staring at him, Drieser closed his eyes and tried to review every contact he'd had with Koehler, or rather, with Koehler's reports. Hell, the guy was delivering whatever he could, given the fact that he was a draftee and under fire from assholes in airplanes and personnel carriers. That first report had been concise, logical, and pretty complete. He could probably add two and three. So, was he making a guess, or did he *know*?

And what the hell difference did it make? Time was running short, and New York was running on a different chronometer.

And Koehler had just gotten the bad word on his wife. Drieser *liked* Koehler.

Base a complex, world-threatening decision on *like*?

"Chris?''

"Still here, Hap. Unhappy as hell.''

"I just want your view.''

"And you'll do what with it?''

"Nothing,'' Harned said. "You will. You'll go to the

Secretary and the Ambassador and tell them what you think."

Drieser took a deep breath and let it out slowly. "Koehler's right."

"Damn. I thought you'd take the party line, follow the President."

"I'm giving him about seventy percent odds. Tell me what you're doing, Hap."

"I think Koehler's taking a wild guess, Chris. On the off-chance that he's made some logical deduction that could be correct, I've got the task force steaming toward Brunei."

"So you're maybe sixty-forty?"

"Call it seventy."

"There's a way to verify, or partially verify, Hap."

"Don't hold back on me."

"You had NSA or someone backtrack Koehler's boat on their tapes, right?"

"Right."

"Koehler reported early on that the royal family had been seen boarding the *Bulkiah*. Where is she now?"

"In the port. Muara."

"So backtrack her. See if she left port, and where she went."

"Hot damn!"

Drieser hung up by reaching over to press the reset bar.

"You still want the DCI?" Blalock asked.

"Yeah, but after you chase down Doug Chambers."

Tuesday, March 11, 3:13 P.M.

The *Maru Hokkaido* was making twenty-seven knots in calm seas, heading almost directly north.

Captain Maki Hirosiuta had slept very little in the past

four days, but he did not feel the lack. Rather, the growing sense of his impotency weighed more heavily on his mind. Though he had steadily increased the range of his movement—walking almost anywhere he wanted to go in the far reaches of the tanker by simply staring down his opposition, it seemed the tiniest of victories.

His crew members looked to him for leadership, or salvation, or both. He did his best to provide the first, but salvation appeared out of reach. When he toured the engineering spaces and talked softly to the skeleton crew manning the engines, their eyes beseeched him, and all he could do was offer words of patience. He sensed that the words would not last much longer. There was a rage beginning to surface. Arguments erupted frequently among his own men. Twice, gunfire had erupted when their captors quelled disturbances in a forceful way.

Fortunately, no one had been killed or wounded. Except for First Officer Yaguchi who was still suffering in the bunk in his stateroom. Dyg Thambipillai adamantly refused to allow the man to be airlifted from the ship.

Hirosiuta's own patience was becoming exhausted. He frequently stood on the starboard wing, as he did now, and stared out at the ships accompanying them.

Most of the American admiral's fleet had been left behind, but seven naval ships were still in attendance. Almost at the horizon was an aircraft carrier. A frigate steamed a few kilometers directly abeam. A destroyer was off the port side. The ships he could see clearly flew the Japanese flag.

Where once he had felt a sense of impending action, he now felt nothing. It was as if the United Nations had abandoned the cause as hopeless, left them to the care of the Japanese Navy, and the Navy was doing nothing. They served merely as an escort.

Perhaps an accommodation had been reached, payments made, the *Maru Hokkaido* on her way home, where she would be released.

He was not a wishful thinker, and he did not think that was the case.

Had an agreement been reached, Hirosiuta thought that pseudo-Captain Thambipillai would have departed in his patrol boat.

The breeze ruffled the sparse hair of his head as he watched the frigate. Aboard her, sailors looked back at him. His countrymen.

The missile launchers were secured.

No action was planned.

If he was to be a freeman once again, Hirosiuta thought that he would have to accomplish it himself.

A rebellion of his own would result in deaths, he thought, and that possibility caused him great anguish. Still, it was ever more apparent to him that, to achieve his ends, he should capitalize on the unrest growing in his crew.

Abruptly he turned, pulled open the door to the bridge, and stepped inside. He smoothed his hair with his hand, then settled his uniform hat in place.

Thambipillai was asleep in the pillowed comfort of the captain's chair. Two of the armed guards maintained their watch over the helmsman and the third officer, who had been given the watch. The third officer looked at him, and Hirosiuta smiled with reassurance.

The bridge was a mess. Food wrappers and plates littered the floor and the navigation table.

Speaking loud enough to awaken Thambipillai if he cared to be awakened, Hirosiuta said, "Mr. Osuka."

"Sir?" The officer came to attention.

"Summon two men from the deck crew to come up and clean the bridge."

"Right away, sir."

The two guards looked to Thambipillai, who did not

budge, then shrugged. They did not care if others picked up after them.

He left the bridge by the aft hatch, stopped in to check on Yaguchi, who was attended by the doctor, then took an elevator to the main deck.

Methodically he tested the limits of his restricted authority, silently defying the captors as he put men to work mopping decks, vacuuming the carpets, cleaning the galleys.

Within an hour he had over seventy men doing what they were supposed to be doing.

And the Bruneians let him do it.

Tuesday, March 11, 3:52 P.M.

Omar Padang's helicopter—a Gazelle belonging to Exxon—landed in the street outside the Gurkha barracks in Kuala Belait. A few raindrops began to spatter the ground as he stepped from the aircraft.

Shamin Bakir swaggered from the orderly room to meet him. He was carrying a helmet.

"You see, Omar! You see? It is the American pilot's helmet. He never knew what hit him!"

"You are collecting trophies, now, Shamin?"

"It is a major feat, shooting down an American naval aircraft," Bakir defended. "They will think twice before attacking us again."

"Rather, they will now know that we have the missiles. They will now be incensed. You have badly miscalculated, Colonel."

Bakir's face blanched.

"You are not the only one, however. Thambipillai has taken leave of his senses, too."

Padang had talked to Thambipillai by radio earlier and

learned the man had ordered the supertanker to speed. When Padang told him to immediately stop the tanker, the errant captain had only exclaimed about his prowess and how the mighty ships of a dozen nations had cowered before him and given him his head. Thambipillai was going to steer right into Tokyo Bay, and if the United Nations did not leave Brunei alone, blow up the ship right in the harbor.

"Thambipillai? Who is Thambipillai?" Bakir demanded.

Padang suddenly realized that his ground forces did not know what his naval forces were doing. He thought surely he had briefed Bakir, but could not now remember. And he thought it unnecessary at this moment to share with Bakir the gunboat captain's bizarre behavior.

The idiot would not respond to Padang's orders, and now the fleet at sea was split, one portion following the tanker, and the American fleet left alone. Thambipillai could not tell him where they were.

Though he would not admit it to Li, Padang had been shocked at the rapid response of the United Nations, the fact that the *Maru Hokkaido* had been intercepted so quickly. Now, with the Americans sailing at will . . .

"Have you bothered to consider where that American aircraft came from, Shamin?"

The light dawned slowly in Bakir's eyes.

"Yes. Think about it. I have sent an aircraft to locate the fleet." He did not bother telling Bakir that the pilot of the Cessna Citation had easily found a fleet and that twelve American and French ships—according to the flags his pilot had reported—were 160 nautical miles away. He did not tell Bakir that he had ordered every Brunei naval vessel to sea, to set up a blockade thirty kilometers off the coast.

"Tell me, how many of the oil workers have returned to the platforms?"

"Ah . . . none."

"So I see. The ships I sent to you remain at the docks."

"They refuse to work for us. Until I can demonstrate our resolve by shooting a few of them, I do not know how to force them to work."

"We will not shoot them." In this matter, Li Sen was correct. These men had to be motivated by money, not fear. "Now, show me where the Gurkhas are."

Padang walked around Bakir and into the orderly room. The colonel followed behind.

Several officers stood around a desk, on which a map had been placed.

"Where?"

Bakir pointed in the general direction of the southeast, his finger waving in the air.

"Pinpoint it for me, Colonel."

"Ah, somewhere here, Minister. Near the mountains."

Padang was incredulous. "That is all you know? You told me you had them trapped with aircraft. And I distinctly recall telling you to go after them personally."

"Ah, the other American fighter—"

"Other! What other?"

"You see, there were two—"

"For the love of Allah! Where are your helicopters?"

"Apparently," Bakir said, "they were shot down."

For the moment Padang was speechless. He was struck by how little he knew, by how constrained his sources of information were. Dyg Thambipillai ran amok on the seas, and would not, or could not, tell him how many ships were out there. A dozen, he had said. More or less. Shamin Bakir passed on only what he pleased, and what put him in the best light, and Shaikh's Gurkhas roamed the countryside.

He had to secure the country so he could concentrate his attention on the world that oppressed him.

"Get vehicles, Colonel. Do it now!"

"But, Minister—"

"I am going to show you how to do your job."

"I must wait here, to be near my command—"

"Ridiculous! You will go with me and observe how it is done."

Tuesday, March 11, 4:10 P.M.

All in all, it was a boring flight.

The Greyhound crossed the coast at nearly twenty thousand feet, far out of the reach of SA-7 Grail missiles. It didn't begin to lose altitude until they were many kilometers inland, and it was directed to the drop zone by the GPS.

The aircraft was not blessed with many windows, and Kyoto stood near the rear of the cargo compartment, looking through the small porthole there. In many ways, he thought, Brunei was reminiscent of his homeland, at least of the lesser inhabited islands. There was much greenery, and he felt partially homesick.

He was wearing a headset on a long cord supplied by the cargo master, who was also the crew chief. It allowed him to listen to the pilot's conversations with the carrier's air controller, or to utilize the intercom without having to shout over the roar of the twin engines.

The radio dialogue was boring, as well. Primarily, it consisted of interaction with other airplanes flying near the task force.

As the plane began its descent, the cargo master offered him a belt and lifeline, which he strapped in place.

Then the ramp was lowered, and he had a panoramic view of the country, beautiful, but again boring in the sameness of the jungle cover.

The glide steepened, and he grasped an interior rib to keep from sliding forward.

"All right, chief," the pilot intoned, "let's get 'em ready."

"Soon as you're level, Lieutenant."

When the Greyhound levelled off, seemingly only a few feet above the jungle top, Kyoto helped the cargo master release the canvas straps holding the pallets in place. They were side by side on the rollers set in the floor, and Kyoto got behind one of the pallets. It was stacked about waist high with cardboard boxes.

"We're going to do this in one pass, Colonel," the chief said. "Don't go out with the package."

"I will try not to."

A set of lights was mounted on the left side of the cargo bay, and Kyoto followed the American's gaze toward them.

The red light came on.

Then went out as the amber light illuminated.

"Couple minutes, Colonel."

They dragged by, then the green light came on.

"Now!"

Kyoto was surprised by the sudden change in the aircraft's attitude. The nose went up, and he barely had to push on the pallet before it slithered away from him, crossed the ramp, and dropped off.

He grabbed his lifeline to keep from following it.

Both pallets appeared to float against the green of the canopy, then abruptly disappeared.

"That is it?"

"That's it, Colonel."

The man activated controls and the ramp closed, leaving them in semidarkness.

They were at fifteen thousand feet, headed north, crossing the coast, by the time word was radioed back from the carrier that the drop had been successful, and the Gurkhas had located the pallets.

He settled into one of the canvas seats at the fuselage side, prepared to complete the trip by perhaps nodding off.

And he did sleep for a few minutes, because the crew chief shook him awake.

"Call for you, Colonel."

He shook his head, then found the transmit button on its cord and pressed it.

"Colonel Kyoto."

"Harned here, Colonel. How's the airplane ride?"

He should not have been amazed that the admiral knew he was aboard the aircraft. The man had eyes and ears everywhere.

"Not as exciting as I might have expected, Admiral."

"I don't suppose so. Listen up, Meoshi. We've got a go."

"From New York?"

"That's a roger. We reviewed some old intel tapes and figured out that the destroyer *Bulkiah* made a round-trip. That confirms some other thinking."

"I do not understand this, Admiral."

"I'll explain it to you next time I see you."

This was wonderful news, but Kyoto was afraid that he would be omitted from doing what he should do—serve his countrymen.

"Sir, may I respectfully request detachment from your command?"

"You're still my link to your admiral, Meoshi, but I'll have the pilot make a pit stop on the *Akagi*."

Tuesday, March 11, 5:10 P.M.

"But we could have supplied you!" Captain Singh's voice on the radio almost pouted.

"You will need all of the materiel you have," Benjamin Shaikh told him. "Now, keep in mind that this is not a secure radio channel and tell me your strength."

"Yes, sir. Let me . . . oh, two-thirds."

"Very good." Around two hundred men were available. If Shaikh compared the relative capability of the Gurkhas to the Bruneians under Shamin Bakir, they equated to four hundred.

"Without providing details, Lion Two, I will tell you that I have an eye in the sky. The eye tells me that a large contingent of the hostile force in Kuala Belait is now pre-paring to leave the town. I want you to move out of Miri Maruda to within a half mile of the border. When I give you the word, you are to invade and reclaim the city. The protection of the foreigners is the primary objective."

"Sir!"

"The word may be found on the contingency order of battle plan, second page from the last; first line; third word. Do you have the plan?"

"I do, Lion One."

"All right. Now, you may encounter yet another force— and you will recognize them, and they are to be considered friendly. Brief your men well."

"I will, sir."

"Do you have any . . . cryptic questions, Lion Two?"

"None. Lion Two out."

Shaikh handed the microphone back to the corporal and said to Koehler, "Captain Singh will do his part."

"I'm sure of it, Benjamin."

The two of them were standing on the half-lowered ramp

of the personnel carrier as it inched along the road at an idle. Behind them came the second APC.

And behind the two crawling APCs, Gurkha soldiers and hastily trained policemen were burying blocks of plastic explosives and detonators in the road. Each block had to be connected to a wiring harness, and the wires and small excavations disguised with spread dirt and weeds.

The American admiral had supplied them well, Shaikh thought. His wounded, who had first priority for space in the APCs, had been treated with the medical supplies as well as they could be in the field. Shaikh himself had taken one of the pain pills, and the throbbing in his hip was much less pronounced.

Back in the clearing where Frank Morris had repaired the helicopter, and where they had first encountered Lieutenant Haji, were several heavy-duty radar reflectors and other remote-controlled apparatus. If Bakir had the strength of will to once again send aircraft over the region, they would detect a strong concentration of "equipment" on their radars. Perhaps it would be irresistible.

And the arriving force would string itself out over a half kilometer of buried explosives.

Shaikh looked at Koehler. In his jeans and black sweatshirt, he did not appear very soldierly. He had taken the time to shave, and like the Gurkhas, was more presentable. It was a morale factor. The policemen, who hadn't shaved or changed their clothes in days, looked more disreputable.

Koehler also wore a backpack and carried his Armalite slung over his shoulder. His web belt was laden with a canteen, magazine pouches, and a jungle knife.

"You are a modern-day guerilla, Kelly."

"I wish I'd had more training."

Koehler tried to be light of tongue, but since he'd learned about his wife, his mood had turned sour—more so than might have been expected of the circumstances. Shaikh tried to understand, but probably could not, the emotions that might be circulating in the man.

The APC came to a halt, hardly enough to make them sway, and Shaikh stepped off the ramp. They had arrived at the entrance to Sergeant Major Irra's "shortcut" through the jungle. Here, they would turn off the main track and seal and disguise the entrance so well, that even a trained eye would not find it. Already a team of four men should have reached the far end of the shortcut to camouflage that entrance, as well.

When his APCs and men were well hidden in the jungle on the shortcut, they should be invisible to Bakir's advancing team. If all went as planned, they would bypass each other, and Shaikh could advance to the north unmolested.

"Would you check with your intelligence source one more time, Kelly?"

"Sure thing."

The encrypted radio, with extra batteries, now resided in Koehler's backpack. One of the ten channels, already selected, connected him through a series of relays with an intelligence operation somewhere in the United States. Through the daylight hours, they had been receiving reports gleaned from real-time satellites.

Koehler reached back and unclipped the microphone from the top strap of the pack.

"Reindeer, Eagle Eye."

"Gotcha, Eye."

"Where we at?"

"I hope you know. But if you're asking about the other guys, they're in eleven APCs and two Jeeps seventeen klicks to your northwest. They lost one personnel carrier—apparently broken down, and left it behind. They're out of visual, in the jungle, but we've got an IR contact. We're estimating a force of one-four-zero men. At the current speed, intercept is predicted in five-five minutes.''

"Copy that, and thanks. Eagle Eye out.''

Koehler reclipped the mike on the shoulder strap. "That do it, Benjamin?''

"I believe so, yes. Go with God, Kelly.''

"You too, my friend.''

Shaikh remounted the ramp and signalled the driver. He gunned the engine and turned into the jungle tunnel.

Koehler waved at him from the road.

Tuesday, March 11, 5:33 P.M.

"There it is!'' Lieutenant Ali Haji cried.

And so it was. Just as the policeman had predicted.

"I take back everything I ever thought about the guy,'' Morris whispered to Koehler.

"You're just tired of walking,'' Kelly said.

"I'd like a little light, too.''

The jungle night had already moved in on them, and Koehler could make out the others only by silhouette. Besides Haji, who was there because he knew where he had left his truck with the broken axle, Slim Avery and his two supply techs had accompanied Koehler. The Gurkhas were represented by Suraj Irra and four troopers.

They had hiked about four miles before finding the vehicle.

The military truck, with tandem rear axles mounting eight wheels, was tilted almost on its side in a small chasm next to the road. The right-side wheels were still on the road, and the thicket of jungle kept it from rolling on over.

Morris unclipped a flashlight and played it over the road and the truck. A few yards down the road was a huge boulder, and it was that, Haji had earlier explained, which had broken the housing on the rear axle, startling the driver, who ran off the road.

Morris and Avery knelt next to the truck and played the beams of their lights over the axle.

"They were moving pretty good, to do that," Avery said.

Koehler could see that the right side of the housing was split, and the impact probably sheared a pin or C-ring, since the interior axle shaft had slipped out of the housing and the pair of wheels and tires on the shaft had slipped out of the housing. The wheels projected about eighteen inches from the side of the truck.

"Not a problem, though, is it, Slim?" Morris asked.

"Nah, I don't think so. The differential should be all right."

"It makes a terrible noise," Haji said.

"Something binding, no doubt, Lieutenant," Avery said. "We'll pull the other shaft."

Avery issued a few orders, and everyone gathered around, hoisted the free wheels, and pulled. The axle shaft came right out of the housing, and they discarded the set on the other side of the road.

Playing his light on the axle plate, Avery said, "Sheared all of the retaining bolts. No big deal."

Morris climbed up on the running board, levered the door open, then slid down the tilted seat until he was behind the wheel. The engine caught on the second try of the ignition, and he engaged the four-wheel drive, slapped the shift into reverse, and let out the clutch.

The truck lurched backward, a horrendous grinding and clashing issuing from the rear end. It also tried to roll on over to the left, and Koehler and the other men leaped forward to throw their weight onto the right side, hanging from the running board, the bed, the fenders.

Bucking and fighting, the truck backed out of the hole

and onto the road, levelling itself. Once it was centered on the track, Morris shut it down.

Avery and his two technicians dug tools out of their packs and went to work on the left side. In half an hour, they had the other set of dual wheels and the left axle shaft removed. The drive shaft now drove through the front rear differential to the rear axle.

"She's a six-wheeler instead of a ten, now," Avery said. "We lost most of the grease in that differential, but hell, if it dies on us, we'll just throw out the drive shaft and pull our way into town on the front axle."

Suraj Irra drove, with Morris and Koehler in the cab with him, their packs stacked at their feet. The rest of the men found places in the back. Kelly didn't even think about his preference for driving himself. Irra back-and-filled on the narrow road several times to get the truck turned around, dodged the boulder, and got it up to speed. The freewheeling differential clattered, but they were moving.

"This road leads to Lumut, right?" Morris said.

"Exactly, Mr. Morris," Irra said. "But in about twelve kilometers, we will be able to take a road leading us directly to the airport and Bandar Seri Begawan."

"That's what I'd like," Morris said. He slid down in the seat, laid his head on the backrest, and peeled the folded bandanna from his head, tossing it on the floor.

Over the roar of the truck, Koehler listened for any sounds of battle behind them. Despite Reindeer's prediction on timing, he didn't think Bakir would reach Shaikh's position in the time allotted. Bakir was coming up the Kuala Belait road, and he'd run into a roadblock of burnt and wrecked APCs. It would take him awhile to clear the obstacle.

Irra was driving under the illumination of the parking lights, and there wasn't much to be seen. The jungle walls raced by them, a greenish-black haze that hypnotized. The stiff-springed truck bounced and jolted over the uneven track.

"You still with us, Navy guy?" Morris asked softly.

"I'm here, Frank."

"Shitty thing to tell you."

"Now, later, what's the diff?"

"You know military intelligence, Kelly. Don't believe anything you hear until it's verified."

"She's pretty resilient, Frank."

"Damn right. And she's got Monica with her. The two of them together are unbeatable."

Koehler wanted to believe that. All the admiral had were images from some damned satellite. Where were the details? They might have gone over the side, be ashore somewhere. Captured. That was possible. Back in a hotel in Bandar Seri Begawan.

It was possible.

It was what he had to believe.

Sherry was waiting for him.

And he was coming to get her.

If she was hurt, people were going to die.

Sixteen

Tuesday, March 11, 10:51 A.M.

Leonard Nelson had been with the Central Intelligence Agency for seventeen years, and he was now seventeen pounds overweight. A pound a year, and he didn't think that was too bad.

The easy lifestyle of his assignment in Tel Aviv had been his downfall. He had too much free time to spend in the Mediterranean coast cafes and night spots, living up to his cover as a commerce department liaison.

In his seventeen years Nelson had never spoken directly to the Director of Central Intelligence, and when he got the call at eight-fifteen in the morning, he immediately wished he had lived up to his resolution to shed the pounds. He might need to be fit.

The DCI had been blunt, and in a matter of two minutes, told Nelson exactly what was necessary. "I don't give a damn if you're ejected from the country for being too pushy, Nelson. I want the information yesterday, if not sooner."

Rather than risk ejection, Nelson had called his friend Asher Weinbergen, who also happened to be a member of Mossad, the Israeli secret service.

"Asher, I need some information from an American citizen who happens to reside in your country. I suspect he will not want to divulge the information and that I will be unable to appeal to his nationalism or his fervent desire for world peace."

"Who is this citizen, Lee?"

"Sam Leventhal."

"Weaponry, then."

"Yes, and I've got a time line. The man told me immediately. Life and death kind of thing, I gathered."

"What is the context?"

"Asher. Do you think they'd actually tell me?"

"Probably not. How do you wish to appeal to this man?"

"Judging by his character—and I know little about his character, I thought his pocketbook. Can you help me out?"

"Give me twenty minutes to find out. I'll also find out where he is, and pick you up at your flat. We'll probably have to take a leisurely drive to Haifa."

"Not too leisurely, please."

And now, they cruised the waterfront of Haifa in Weinbergen's four-year-old battered Chevrolet Lumina, looking for the Haifa Technologies sign. The late-morning sun was bright and hot, and he soon found a tiny sign tacked to the front of a faded wooden structure.

"There we go," Nelson said. "Not a humongous operation."

"The product goes through other warehouses in other countries, I expect, Lee."

"Are we going to be able to pull this off?"

"My friends do wonderful things electronically," the Mossad operative said.

Nelson believed him.

Weinbergen pulled up and parked in front of the decrepit building, and they got out and entered a corner office through a glass door, which hadn't been cleaned in five or six years. One could barely see through it.

A woman sitting at a gray metal desk looked up at them, assessed them for what they probably were, and didn't smile.

Nelson ignored her, walked past the desk, and pushed open the door to the next office.

"Hey!" the woman said, but without enthusiasm.

Leventhal was behind a similar gray desk in the tiny office. He was about seventy pounds overweight for his five-four frame, and Nelson felt better about his own paunch.

The florid-faced, balding man stared at him a few seconds, then leaned back in his chair, threatening the law of gravity.

Nelson took the folded fax sheet from his breast pocket, a copy of the Haifa Technologies invoice the DCI was so excited about.

"Mr. Leventhal, my name is Lee Nelson, and this is Asher Weinbergen. We represent American and Israeli bureaucracies."

"Gentlemen. What can I do for you?"

This guy actually thought he was on the verge of a sale. Clandestine operations, no doubt.

Nelson flipped the sheet of paper on the desk. "I want to know all about that transaction."

Leventhal eyed the listing. "Just what it says."

"Seventeen-inch TVs?"

"Obviously a typo. Twenty-seven-inch is more like it."

"You'll guarantee that?"

The man smiled. "Naturally. All of our products are guaranteed."

Nelson returned the smile. "This morning at the Bank of Commerce in Bern, Switzerland, there was an account with a balance of . . . what was it, Asher?"

Weinbergen smiled, also. "I'm good with numbers, Mr. Leventhal. The amount was forty-one million, three hundred and sixty-five thousand, American. There were a few odds and ends of dollars on top of that."

"What was the account number? Do you remember, Asher?"

"Eleven-gee-aitch-zero-six-four-one."

Leventhal's face paled.

"Why don't you call the bank and ask about that account number, Sam. I can call you Sam, can't I?"

Leventhal's hand was shaking when he picked up the phone.

When he put it down, Nelson would have sworn he'd picked up a bad case of palsy.

"Account balance about zero, is that what they said?"

"Who in the hell are you?"

"I'm quite willing to give you your money back, Sam, but not until I have a detailed list of what was actually in that shipment."

Leventhal's fat hands gripped the edge of his desk. "I have a reputation to uphold—"

"That's fine. You choose between your rep and your money."

It didn't take long for a choice to be made. "It'll take me—"

Nelson looked at his watch. "About five minutes, Sam. That's all the time we have."

The fat man spun around in his chair and leaned toward an old-fashioned, chest-high safe standing in the corner.

"It must be a real luxury to have two sets of books," Weinbergen said.

"You know the computer age," Nelson told him. "Always back up your data."

Tuesday, March 11, 6:31 P.M.

By five o'clock, every naval vessel belonging to the Brunei Navy—Royal or Republic of, whichever—had left the harbor. The *Bulkiah* was among the first to depart.

By six o'clock, a large number of commercial vessels had slipped their moorings and were steaming for the entrance to Brunei Bay. There were no explanations made on the marine radio frequencies, but Sherry Koehler was certain that the ships' captains were taking advantage of the naval absence to scoot for safer waters. Some crisis somewhere—which made her think longingly of Kelly—was allowing the rats to escape the maze created by the Front for Democratic Reform.

She and Monica ganged up on Captain Han Lo.

At the table in the salon, with Koehler on one side of him and Davis on the other, using every possible gesture and configuration of sign language, English, Pidgin English, and Sherry's smattering of Chinese, they attempted to communicate the situation to him.

"There's obviously going to be a major naval battle . . . the port will come under siege . . . others are escaping! You can see them leaving! We can wait for Envoy Hua in Beaufort. . . ."

Captain Han grinned.

But Monica finally got to him, with great booms from her pursed lips and swooping, capsizing hands. "They will sink your junk! Right here! The *Harmonious Spirit* will be no more!"

His eyes went round as the concept crossed the language border, and he jumped up and ran for the deck. Sherry moved to follow him, but the guard at the double doors stepped in front of her and shook his head negatively.

"Did I say something to offend Captain Han?" Monica asked.

"Well, he's excited about *something*."

A few minutes later Han came back, gazed appreciatively at Davis, and went to the spiral staircase leading up one deck. The navigation, communications, and conn stations were up there, though Sherry had only been to the radio compartment.

Koehler went to the sofa at the stern and sat down. She and Monica were both back in their freshly laundered, but still tattered, jeans and pullovers. She felt a little safer than in the guest dressing gown, but realized that Davis was the recipient of most of the admiring glances from the crew. Monica was built along more voluptuous lines than Sherry.

Twenty minutes went by.

Han appeared, feet first, on the staircase and descended to tell them, "Night . . . time. Dark, yes?"

It wasn't dark yet, so she figured something would happen at nightfall. And she hoped she knew what it was.

Tuesday, March 11, 6:44 P.M.

It had rained for about forty minutes earlier in the afternoon, but under the jungle canopy, Padang would not have known. It was dank and humid, with almost no light at all. The headlights of his Jeep shone on the rear end of a personnel carrier as it banged up and down over the rough road. To either side was only the interminable growth.

After clearing the trail near the deserted village of

wrecked personnel carriers, they were making better time, and Padang was hopeful of finding the renegade Gurkhas soon.

He rode in the right seat of the Jeep, with a radio microphone resting in his lap. He frequently checked with Shamin Bakir, who was in the lead personnel carrier, to prod him to move faster. He had also called the pilot of the business jet—coded Moonstone, and told him to reconnoiter the area ahead of the convoy before he stopped to refuel and head out to sea to check once again on the fleet.

He had called Awg Nazir at police headquarters and told him to have Li Sen issue an ultimatum to the approaching United Nations task force. If they came within one hundred kilometers of Brunei, oil platforms would go down. Li Sen complained, but also complied. The man was becoming more malleable than ever.

Changing the radio frequency, he picked up the microphone and called Tan Hashim.

"Crimson Sea, this is Father Time."

Hashim must have been right next to his radio, for the response was immediate. "Yes, Father Time."

"Report."

"All is quiet. Two patrol boats came close, and I almost had to require a code verification, but they veered off and went to sea."

"Yes. We are setting a blockade."

"A blockade. May I ask for what purpose?"

"In case someone attempts to probe our forces. It is nothing for you to worry yourself about. You have your instructions."

"Of course, Father Time."

He was about to change frequencies and call Bakir again when the speaker blurted, "Father Time! Moonstone."

"Go ahead, Moonstone."

He had not heard the jet over the rattle of the APC ahead of them.

"I can see your column on my radar, and I also see a target a kilometer ahead of you. It may be several vehicles."

"Thank you, Moonstone. You may go on with your primary mission."

He switched to Bakir's frequency. "Did you hear that, Colonel?"

"Yes, Minister. I propose that we halt here and form a defensive line. We will force Shaikh to come to us."

"I propose that you increase speed, Colonel. Drive in on them before they have time to react. Do it now!"

Padang wished he had elected to ride at the front. He wanted to see Shaikh's face as he died.

Tuesday, March 11, 6:53 P.M.

Benjamin Shaikh did not breathe.

He held his breath even though the moving convoy made so much noise, it was not required for purposes of silence. He and Captain Shrestha were flat on the soft ground, three meters from the road, but the foliage was so thick, they could not see the road. They could hear, however.

The last of the vehicles went by in a rush, and he was finally assured that his men had adequately concealed the entrance to the side trail. They had left evidence of APC tracks on the road, but had disguised the point where they exited the main road. Bakir's force was moving so quickly that they wouldn't have noted a neon sign pointing the direction to where he and Shrestha were hidden.

He began counting to himself. It was nearly a kilometer to the clearing where the dummies were set up.

Behind him, nearly a kilometer down the winding track,

his remaining vehicles and his force of Gurkhas and Bruneian policemen waited to burst out of the side road and
race for Kuala Belait.

Shrestha was counting, too.

"I think now, Major."

The rumble of tracks had died to some extent as the
convoy went around a curve and climbed over a hill.

"Proceed."

The adjutant turned on a small penlight and focused it
on one of the two small radio transmitters. It was marked
with a large numeral "1" with red paint. He flicked a
switch at the side of the case and a red light came on.

As soon as the light came on, he pushed aside a protective cover with his thumb and pressed a black button.

They could distinctly hear the response over the distant
reverberations from the APCs—a building chatter of small-
arms fire and grenade explosions.

The remote control device had set off a block of plastic
explosive in the middle of a small munitions dump of
7.62-rounds and grenades. Frank Morris had relished the
construction when he was building it.

It sounded as if the supposed force of men in the clearing
had jumped the gun, opening up on the approaching
Bruneians.

At least, Shaikh hoped it sounded as such. He couldn't
tell if the APCs had accelerated or ground to a halt.

"Would you care to use the second device, Major?"

"I would, but you go ahead, Captain."

"Thank you, sir."

Shrestha moved the second transmitter closer, armed
it, and pressed the button.

A dull flat boom, then another and another, like rolling
thunder. The ground beneath them rocked. The concussion wave curled down the tunnel of the road like
uncapped champagne. It stung his ears when it hit.

Secondary explosions followed, booming and pealing.

"It seems that the shaped charges and armor-piercing warheads have had some effect," Shrestha said. "At least with some of the carriers."

"Yes. I think we will leave now, Captain."

"After you, sir."

Shaikh scrambled to his feet, and pointing the small flashlight ahead of him, began trotting down the trail.

Tuesday, March 11, 7:04 P.M.

As soon as he heard the Gurkhas open fire on the front of the column, Padang had slapped his driver's arm. "Stop, you fool!"

The Jeep slid to the side of the road as the brakes locked up.

The convoy continued, moving away from them.

For about one minute.

Omar Padang saw a premonition of hell.

A tremendous and reverberating concussion began near the front of the convoy, and seconds later the APC ahead of them leaped about a meter in the air, the rear ramp burst open, and bodies were hurled out, chased by fingers of fire.

Flames shot everywhere along the line of vehicles, heat ignited ammunition and fuel cells, and the thunderclaps continued, echoing back on each other, slamming into the jungle walls. Men screamed, running for the protection of the jungle, but were unable to penetrate it. Other men writhed on the ground, rolling madly to smother the flames that clung to their clothing.

"For the love of Allah!" intoned the driver.

Padang grabbed the microphone. "Bakir!"

After a pause a timid voice came back to him. "Minister, this is the driver. Colonel Bakir is gravely wounded."

"Driver, get as many men as you can and rush the Gurkha position!"

"Sir . . . uh, yes, sir."

As the explosions died away, Padang got out of the Jeep and began walking. The fire in the first APC he came to was so fierce and hot, he could not get by it. The vines and leaves overhead were singed and burnt, but they would not catch fire and spread it.

A half hour passed before he could get around the destroyed personnel carrier and march toward the front of the column. By the time he reached it, he had a count.

Six of the vehicles were destroyed, the others trapped by the wreckage. At least forty men had been killed, and as many more had suffered burns or wounds from exploding cartridges. Bakir had succumbed, but Padang did not consider his passing a momentous occasion.

And when he passed the last APC and found Bakir's driver and ten other men coming toward him, he learned the worst news of all.

"Minister, sir, there are no Gurkhas."

Tuesday, March 11, 7:46 P.M.

"That is correct, Sen," the radio crackled, "it was a short skirmish."

"And the Gurkhas are gone, Omar?" Li Sen asked.

"As far as I can tell. I am on my way back to Bandar Seri Begawan."

"Bakir? Where is he?"

"He, ah, died in the battle. It is too bad he never made general."

"But that is terrible, Omar."

"These things happen, Sen. There are other wounded, and we are taking them to the hospital at Lumut. I will talk to you later."

"Omar! I must tell you. The ships are leaving Muara."

"Ships? What ships?"

"The commercial interests. They have been leaving for two hours."

"But I have quarantined the port! They cannot leave!"

"There is no one to stop them," Li said.

"We will see about that."

Li tried to respond, but Padang was no longer listening.

He sighed and sat back in his chair. Near the door Captain Awg Nazir stood watching him. The man did not let him use a radio or telephone without being nearby.

Li felt as if he were in a prison. And he the Provisional President of the Republic of Brunei.

Everything was closing in on him. The pilot of the corporate jet that Padang utilized as surveillance reported the United Nations task force 120 nautical miles from the coast. Padang ran around the country like a madman, involved in skirmishes Bakir should have been attending to. Padang ordered the navy to leave the port and set up some kind of line, as if the warships of the United Nations could not run over them with impunity. The foreign workers refused to work. The goods necessary for survival turned around and fled Muara.

And Padang only promised that the UN ships would stop a hundred kilometers away.

Li did not know where the royal family was located. They were supposed to be on the *Bulkiah*, but he had learned they were not aboard when the destroyer put to sea. Had Padang already executed them?

It was unthinkable!

Padang, Padang, Padang!

The man made decisions without consulting with him or the committee. It was intolerable.

"Will you make another call, President?" Nazir asked. "Or perhaps you will go to your home now."

Li stood up and strode past the man in the doorway. "Find me a cot. I will stay in the office until this situation is resolved."

Nazir smiled. "It sounds to me, President, as if it is already resolved."

"Like Padang, Captain Nazir, you understand very little of international diplomacy."

He wished he could find a way to send a message of hope and compromise to the Secretary General.

Until Padang and Nazir were out of the way, however, that desire would remain an empty one.

"And, Captain, call Peng Ziyang and Lim Siddiqui. I want them here tonight, also."

"Of course, President Li."

As he walked back to his office, Li was cognizant of the eyes that followed him. He was also aware of the rack of weapons on the far wall of the squad room. The glass door was unlocked, as if the policemen expected to be invaded at any moment. They wanted to be prepared, no doubt.

As for Li, the police seemed more concerned about his access to communications than to weapons. When the other committee members arrived, he thought they must discuss alternate means of achieving their ends. If it required guns, then Li would have to make a new resolution.

He thought he could do it.

Tuesday, March 11, 9:14 P.M.

"Sledgehammer, Eagle Eye."

"Hammer, here. Reindeer's got you pinpointed on the western end of the airport."

Slim Avery was carrying a powerful infrared emitter that issued a coded set of flashes every time he aimed it at the sky and pressed a button. Shaikh had a similar device with him. Reindeer—some guy at NSA—could pick them out of the ground clutter of heat radiations with his satellite-borne sensors. If worse came to worse, and he lost the radio, Kelly could also send a Morse-coded message to Sledgehammer via the emitter. He just couldn't get replies. He supposed the admiral had a copy of the NSA's display on one of the screens in the carrier's CIC or the flag plot.

When he thought about the technology available to Sledgehammer, he wondered why in the world some idiot like Li Sen thought he could compete.

"Affirmative, sir. Could I have a sitrep?"

"Roger, Eye. Situation as follows: Lion One evaded the rebels and is now in position nine klicks to the south of Kuala Belait. Lion Two has a large force massed just over the western border. You'll want to know about the rebels. Judging by the emissions, they were hit hard. It took them awhile to recover and get organized, and now five vehicles are making their way toward Lumut. They'll be there in another half hour, but I suspect they're pretty demoralized.

"On the marine front, we're observing Li Sen's dividing line and have taken up station outside the one-hundred-kilometer marker."

Koehler wondered if Li Sen or Omar Padang knew how fast a fighter at Mach speeds could cover that distance. One hundred was just a number someone had picked out of a hat.

"Interestingly," the admiral went on, "they've sent a

couple dozen ragtag vessels out to set up a blockade twenty-five miles off the coast. Or maybe just to make sure we don't sneak some commandos in on them.''

That wasn't the brightest tactic, Koehler thought. The admiral would just hop over them with aviation assets.

''Apparently, they left the port unguarded, because we've seen about twenty ships depart. They're all making speed due north.''

''Good, Hammer. Are you ready to go?''

''The Marines are standing by, and they're getting itchy. We're only waiting on your signal, Eye. No one is going anywhere until you tell us we can.''

Koehler had been thinking, when he could get around his stored images of Sherry, about the rashness of his so-called logical deduction. At the time he hadn't thought he'd be putting so many lives on the line.

''One thing I ought to tell you, Eye. The *Bulkiah* did make a short round-trip to GlobeTech Bravo. That confirmation got us the go sign from New York. Another thing I ought to tell you. The Secretary General—and I suppose the Security Council—have set priorities for you. The demolition equipment comes first. If you have to choose between the royal family and the munitions . . . well, we don't want polluted seas.''

Or lost petroleum.

Unfortunately, Koehler understood the priorities nations set up. He was also relieved to hear about the *Bulkiah*. The chances of the Sultan being on the platform were much better.

''Yes, sir, copied. I have a request. Could you send a high flyer over the target site? We don't want to alert them, but I'd like to know if they've got ships or aircraft in the area.''

''We'll do that, Eye. Anything else?''

''I don't believe so, sir.''

"All right. What's your situation?"

Koehler had scanned the grounds of the airport with the night vision glasses dropped from the Greyhound.

"I don't much like what's available, Hammer. We've spotted two choppers, but they're small, and I suspect they're inoperable. There's a 747, two 727s and a few DC-9s. No one in this group is jet-qualified. The only possibles I can get my whole group aboard are a couple Hercs, a Provider, and a Beech King Air. We're going with the King."

Koehler thought this particular plane was probably the one that had been chasing them earlier.

"Good choice, Eye. A 747 is pretty much overkill, anyway. You *can* fly the Beechcraft?"

"I've got an Army Apache jockey with me. Between us, we'll get it off the ground. If we can find enough chutes, we'll jump. If not, I'll put her down in the water."

A long, long pause, then, "Your call. You're commander on the scene."

"That's it, then," Kelly said. "We plan to be wheels-up around midnight."

"What's the security around the airport?"

"They've beefed it up since I was here last. Probably a couple dozen roving guards."

"Can you take them out silently?"

"Without question, sir. I have Gurkhas."

"Yes. That's right."

"Sir. Have you learned anything new on my own situation?"

"Negative, Eye. But we're still looking."

"Thank you, Hammer. Eagle Eye out."

Koehler dropped the microphone and rolled over on his back. He was lying in a drainage ditch at the far western end of the runway, on the outside of the fence. The rest of the team were spread around the ditch, resting. Kelly studied the stars, which were bright and magnificent. He saw the shadow of Sherry's face in them.

"You're counting on me to get a *fixed*-wing in the air?" Morris said.

"You get to play with the throttles, Army dude."

"I sure wish you hadn't mentioned me. Sure as hell, somebody will draft me, too."

"I held back on your name."

"Good man."

Sergeant Major Suraj Irra's teeth gleamed in the night. "Shall we proceed, Commander?"

"It's your show, Suraj. How long will it take?"

"Not long at all."

Koehler sat up and looked around. "Okay, soon as we get the all-clear from you, we'll join up at the King Air. Everyone got that?"

The light was poor, but he counted heads and came up one short.

"Where's Ali?"

Everyone looked around. A few climbed to the edge of the ditch and scanned the fields around them.

Haji was gone.

"Shit!" Morris said.

"I think," the sergeant major said, "that he would not betray us. I also believe he did not want to take this particular airplane trip."

"He's not alone," Slim Avery said.

Tuesday, March 11, 10:34 P.M.

On the *Akagi*, Meoshi Kyoto was in the CIC with Admiral Saburo Yakama, several Japanese officers, Lieutenant Commander Barry Jenkins of the Navy SEALs, and a United States Marine captain, named Goodfellow, who commanded the contingent detached from the main Marine force.

Kyoto had just recited their plan of attack on the radio to Admiral Harned.

"Sounds good to me, boys and girls. Admiral Yakama, I applaud your planning team."

"It was a joint effort, Admiral Harned."

"Well, it has a good chance of succeeding, I think. Just remember that we don't make the final push until we hear the code from Koehler."

"Space Mountain," Kyoto said.

"Yeah. Koehler came up with it himself. Good day, gentlemen."

After Harned signed off, they excused themselves and went down several decks to a ready room just off the hangar deck.

The Marine, Navy, and Japanese naval unit noncommissioned officers were waiting for them, and Kyoto briefed them, then allowed them to leave to prepare their men for the assault.

Barry Jenkins went to an urn in the corner and drew mugs of coffee for them. As he passed them around, he said, "I'm damned glad I thought to bring a can of coffee with me. Your guys drink too much tea, Meoshi."

Kyoto accepted the mug with a smile. "And your guys drink too much coffee. At least, I've come to like it."

"Along the same line, between you and me," Jenkins said, "we could use a little less rice in our diet."

"It is good for you."

Captain Goodfellow swigged from his cup and said, "I wish I were going with you."

"You will reach us in good time, Captain," Kyoto told him.

"Yeah, but all the fun will be over."

Kyoto did not think it would be fun.

But he had made his own resolution. If ninety percent of the crew survived, the operation would be a success.

Now, they must wait on an American named Koehler.

Otherwise, the world would be mad at Japan.

The intercom buzzed, and Kyoto got up and went to the bulkhead to depress the button. "Tactical briefing, Kyoto."

"Colonel, there has been a change," Yakama told him.

"Sir?"

"Tell Commander Jenkins that his SEALs are going back to the *Eisenhower*. He is to report on the flight deck in ten minutes. You will have to take a platoon of the Marines with you."

Captain Goodfellow was to get his wish.

And Kyoto thought he knew why.

Japanese sailors were more expendable than oil.

Tuesday, March 11, 11:01 A.M.

Chris Drieser had gotten about five hours' sleep while waiting for the CIA to do its thing. Judy Blalock had also gotten a few winks, stretched out on the sofa in his office.

Drieser had slept on the floor.

And now his back ached.

He walked around and around the perimeter of the office, trying to work the kinks out, sucking down coffee, and slipping once in a while on the paper that still littered the floor. Blalock had sent out for pastrami sandwiches, but they weren't here yet.

She'd ordered a bunch of them. Everyone on his floor of the State Department building seemed to be hanging around now that the word had gotten around that State was involved in the Pacific crisis. The twelve people who'd helped scan paper were in the conference room. The corridors were full.

The Defense Department experts had taken over Blalock's office.

"Fourteen hours," he said aloud.

"Yep," Blalock said. "Can't do anything about it, Chris."

If that schizo named Omar Padang thought something was amiss around one o'clock in the morning, Washington time, then there was going to be a great big messy bang.

Come on, Koehler!

"I'm going down the hall to wash my face, Chris."

"Your face looks just fine."

"But feels gritty."

She didn't leave because the army colonel from DOD came bouncing in. He walked on his toes, as if his heels were superfluous. Drieser hated him and his vibrancy.

"I think we've got it, Mr. Undersecretary."

"How bad?"

"Not good. From the manifest Leventhal provided, we estimate that not more than forty charges could have been prepared. That is, charges strong enough to cut the platform legs."

"Forty."

"Yes, sir. And there were fifty receivers in the shipment, but we don't think all could be utilized. We could perhaps hope that the Bruneians built fifty bombs, and then none of them will be effective."

"But we shouldn't count on it?"

"No, sir. However many they built, some are probably

going to work. All of them operate on ULF, and all of them have a range of about ten miles."

"Ten? That's all?"

"Yes, sir. The transmitters will have to be within that range, or nothing is going to happen."

"How many transmitters?"

"There were three in the shipment. They are quite specialized and expensive. The antennas are four hundred and twenty feet long."

"You think they have three separate circuits, Colonel?"

"Possibly. It would allow them to provide a demonstration or two, without blowing the whole thing at once."

"They already did two demos," Drieser said.

"Yes, I've gone over those details. However, the explosions at Albatross and Mirador were above surface, somewhere on the platforms. I don't think they utilized their primary weapon."

"So, three circuits, then. What do you think of GT-Bravo as a control site?"

The colonel unfolded a map and spread it on the table. Drieser leaned over to look at it. It was obviously a satellite shot, blown up. GlobeTech Bravo was marked with an orange circle around it. A larger red circle had been scribed, with Bravo as the locus. Small red numbers had been printed next to thirty-nine platforms.

"I like it," the colonel said. "A ten-mile radius encompasses enough platforms, as well as the pumping station."

"The pumping station."

"That would be spectacular, and it would probably engulf the tankers anchored near it. If they're empty, they're full of fumes, Mr. Undersecretary. That's far more dangerous."

"Thank you, Colonel. Would you see that that map is faxed to Admiral Harned?"

"I will, sir. There is one more item, though."

"Which is?"

"There was also a small radar set in that shipment from Haifa. I think that is significant."

"Shit. I do, too."

As soon as the colonel departed, Drieser turned to his desk, where Blalock was already dialling the phone.

It took a few minutes to route the call to Harned, who was probably tucked away in his bunk, or should have been.

"Hello, Chris."

"Hap. Got some info for you." He relayed the colonel's estimates.

"That's excellent, Chris. For a State do-gooder, you're all right."

"What about that radar?"

"I think Koehler's ahead of us. He asked for a recon, and I should have the results in a little while."

"If they've got radar on that platform, we're sunk."

"Don't say 'sunk' to a Navy man, Chris."

"Sorry."

"Weak joke. No, you're right. If they see Koehler homing in on them in his Beech, we're going to have a whole flock of eruptions."

"Beech?"

Harned brought him up to date on Koehler's plan.

"Jesus Christ! You've got a good man there, Admiral."

"Only a part-timer, I'm afraid. I'm also afraid he's right in the middle of a go-to-hell, who-gives-a-shit attitude."

Which you gave him, Hap, old boy.

"Should we straighten him out?" Drieser asked.

"No. We should use every asset we've got, and he's it, right now."

Jesus. Wearing stars was a tough damned job.

"Not that we're relying entirely on Koehler, Chris."

"Oh?"

"I'm running a sub in there with a detachment of SEALs. They're backup, in case Koehler doesn't come through."

Drieser didn't like it.

"That's risky, isn't it, Hap? Those Bruneian ships—some of them—will have sonar. That sub could be spotted."

"Everything's a risk. If Koehler blows it, we probably won't be in time, but I have to give it a shot."

Tuesday, March 11, 11:51 P.M.

The turboprops ticked like a pair of fine watches, and Koehler watched as the temperatures came up. Everything green.

Glancing through the open cockpit doorway, he saw that seven of the eight passenger seats were occupied. Irra gave him a thumbs-up. Slim Avery was checking his treasure chests of foldouts. He had found some plastic wrap and was using it to protect his life savings.

Two of the Gurkha soldiers had bloodstains on their uniforms, so Koehler understood that the task of removing the airport guard contingent, while silent, had also been fatal.

They had located only one parachute, and it leaned against the rear bulkhead, though he couldn't determine how it was going to be utilized. This was going to be a wet arrival.

He and Morris—in the right seat—had headsets on, so they could use the intercom, and Morris said, "Wanna roll?"

"Let's see if it will."

He came off the brakes as Morris advanced the power levers, and the King Air moved out of the line of parked aircraft. He turned to follow the taxiway.

Except for a few floodlights near the hangars, the airport

was dark, and the yellow line of the taxiway was difficult to discern. He concentrated on it.

"Uh-oh," Morris said.

"Don't go 'uh-oh.' "

"The night shift has arrived, Kelly."

He glanced out the left window and saw the truck near the gate. It was beginning a tour of exchanging guards, and as he watched, it found the first guard, probably in a sad condition.

"Little more power, Frank."

Morris goosed the power levers, and the Beech picked up speed. The end of the runway was still a half mile away.

Koehler worked the unfamiliar controls, trying to get a feel for them as he kept an eye on the truck at the gate. Flurry of activity, there.

"We're going to have to come back toward them," Morris observed.

"Not a happy prospect."

Quarter mile.

Men scrambled back into the truck, and it started moving.

"You suppose we need the whole damned runway, Army?"

"Well, the Navy might. The Army doesn't."

"Going right." Through the doorway, he yelled, "Everyone hang on!"

He veered the airplane, which was moving at about thirty miles an hour, off the taxiway, and onto the weedy patch of ground that separated the taxiway from the runway. The ground was still soft from the afternoon rain, and the wheels threatened to bog down.

Morris ran in more power.

The Beech bounced and joggled, the wing seesawing up and down.

Then they hit the hard surface of the runway, and

Koehler immediately swung into a right turn, the left wing going down and the right gear raising as he made the turn at too high a speed. He couldn't see the centerline.

Truck headlights ahead, racing for the runway.

He eased off the turn; the right gear banged down.

"Full power. Full flaps."

"You got both, chief."

As the power came on, he straightened the King Air out of the turn, saw the centerline.

He was parallel to it, to the left, and decided to let it be. He'd fly off the left side of the runway.

Speed coming up.

"Fifty-five knots . . . sixty," Morris called off.

The truck came banging across the median, slowing as it fought the soft soil. The men in the back were tossed about haphazardly.

The Beech zoomed past it. There was a fusillade of muzzle flashes. Clunks as rounds hit the fuselage.

"Seven-five."

The truck swung in behind them, showing up in his rearview mirror, accelerating, men leaning over the cab, firing at them, but the gap between them was widening.

"Big one-zero-zero," Morris said.

"What do we need?"

"Hell, who knows? When it feels right, you leave the ground."

He focused on keeping the control yoke and rudders steady.

Noticed he was on a slight angle to the runway and was running off toward the left edge.

And at 125 knots, as the left gear was headed for soft earth, the King Air flew itself off the ground.

"Love this airplane," Kelly said.

"While you're doing that, please remember we have to clear a few buildings ahead."

"Roger."

Morris called back to see if anyone had been hit by wild gunfire, and Irra reported everyone unharmed.

As he gained altitude, Koehler banked slowly to the right. He was going around Bandar Seri Begawan to the south, right down Brunei Bay, then north above the entrance to the bay.

"Altitude two-five-hundred, air speed one-nine-zero knots. Can we lose the flaps and gear?"

"Do that, Frank."

Morris retracted both, and the plane picked up speed.

The city lights twinkled on the left, but not many of them were on. Koehler picked out several of the hotels, the palace, the mosque. And then they were over the bay, still climbing. He saw Muara ahead on the left.

"See the ships?" Morris asked.

It took some doing because none of them were running with navigation lights, but he picked out five or six headed up the bay.

"Everyone wants to leave town, Frank." He thought for a minute, then added, "Maybe we don't want to draw attention to them."

"There's a chopper on our left oblique. He's coming around toward us."

Koehler found the strobe light. It was angling toward them from Muara, maybe a thousand feet below. The King Air would be hard to see without navigation lights, but the helo had probably been alerted.

"Cut across the city?" he asked.

"Okay by me."

Continuing to climb, and now making 240 knots, Koehler went into a left turn, then straightened out. He would cross directly over Muara, and he wasn't too worried about the helicopter.

They passed right over it.

Then they were over Muara at 4,500 feet, and the gleam of the open sea beyond was as inviting as anything he'd ever seen. He wished Sherry could savor it with him.

"Shit!" Morris yelled.

Short streaks of light erupting from the city streets, followed by white vapor trails.

"Missiles!" Kelly realized.

"Go left! Left!"

Seventeen

God, Kelly would love this!

Sherry and Monica stood by the railing on the open deck of the junk, their hair blowing in the warm breeze. Above, the stars shone like Hollywood would have them be.

The junk was heeled to port by ten degrees, and overhead, the sails cracked and whipped in the steady breeze. What was amazing to her was that the sails were black. Captain Han's crew had spent a considerable amount of time exchanging sails as darkness fell in the port. It made her feel certain that the junk had once been a privateer. Piracy on the high seas. Opium trader.

More amazing, the junk did not have auxiliary power. She depended entirely upon the wind. Kelly would appreciate that aspect, too. There was only the whisper of the seas passing under the hull. Crewmen moved silently on rubber soles around the deck, tending to lines, coiling excess rope.

The two of them had had to remain in the salon when Han finally released the mooring and allowed the junk to drift backward in the bay. The silent passage was reassuring, and Han's crew were able sailors, steering to avoid a freighter on an escape route.

It was full dark, after eleven, when the sails were hoisted, and the junk began moving down the bay. As soon as they reached the entrance to the bay, Captain Han came himself to show them out onto the deck, apparently finally satisfied they couldn't escape or be seen by some Bruneian fanatic. One or the other. She noted first that her rubber dinghy was lashed to the deck.

Off the port side, she saw the point of land, the lights of Muara beyond it. Several ships were running near them, all without lights. It was difficult to tell in the night with such a large ship under sail, but she thought they were making at least fifteen knots.

"I wish Kelly and Frank were here," she mused aloud.

"Frank gets seasick," Monica said. "He hates boats."

She wondered where they were, wished she could tell him they were finally free of Brunei.

"This will be over soon," Davis said. "Something's come loose with this revolution."

"You think so?"

"I don't know why else all these boats would be allowed to escape."

"Ships. Most of them are ships."

"Proper sailor."

Then, out of the dark, Han Lo appeared, gesturing frantically at them.

"Back to confinement," Monica said.

"Let's humor him. He humored us."

They followed him across the immaculate main deck,

into the dimly lit salon, and when he continued gesturing, up the spiral staircase to the deck above. He ushered them into the radio room, where she had listened to commercial broadcasts.

Despite the antiquity of the junk, no expense had been spared in bringing her electronics into the most recent century. The compartment was small, but one wall was stacked with various types of transceivers, tape decks, and other gear. There was a computer. One crewman sat in a chair at the console.

Sherry would have bet money that the steering position was outfitted with radar, sonar, depth finders, and GPS navigation aids. She had seen the radar antenna mounted on the aft mast. But the purist Hua Enlai wouldn't spring for a diesel engine.

There was a jumble of static and voices issuing from a speaker, and when Captain Han pointed at it, she forced herself to concentrate, pick out certain voices, try to understand what was being said.

Han couldn't understand the English.

She could, though, and in two minutes, she knew.

"There are Bruneian naval vessels out there, trying to turn back the escaping ships!"

"Oh, no!" Davis said.

"They're threatening to sink a container ship, and she's agreed to return to Muara."

"How far away?"

"I don't know."

Together, they tried to explain the situation to Han, but Sherry wasn't sure he fully understood.

She turned to the console, studied the sets mounted there. All of the labels were in Chinese characters.

But the digital readouts were in numerals she recognized. She pointed to one display and asked the technician, "UHF?"

He smiled and nodded vigorously.

She twirled the knob between her thumb and forefinger until the readout read: 243.0.

The operator looked up at Han, who was still grinning. He nodded his acquiescence, and the operator flipped a couple switches, then moved the table microphone her way.

Sherry went to her knees on the deck, depressed the transmit button in the base, and spoke. "Looking for a U.S. Navy contact on Guard. My name is Sheryl Koehler."

Static, and she repeated herself.

Finally a deep voice came back to her. "This is the United State Navy replying to Sheryl Koehler. What is the nature of your emergency?"

"I am not in immediate danger, but I need to speak to the admiral commanding."

"Ah, Ms. Koehler, that is not possible. Go to two-five-seven-point-one."

"Going two-five-seven-point-one."

She changed the frequency quickly.

"Navy here."

"Koehler. I'm on a junk called the *Harmonious Spirit,* just out of Muara. We've learned that Bruneian naval ships are attempting to stop commercial shipping at sea."

"We are aware of the situation, Ms. Koehler. We thank you for your report."

She was going to be brushed off by some hack in a uniform.

"I want to speak to Sledgehammer. Call me Eagle Eye Two."

A hesitation, then: "Back in one minute, Two."

It was less than a minute. "Sledgehammer here. Do I have who I think I have?"

"That's correct, Admiral."

"Tell me about your last few days."

She did.

"I know a gentleman who's going to be happy. He's been worried about you."

"And I've worried about him. Where is he?"

"Let me assure you that's he's all right, but we don't have a secure radio channel. What is your position?"

Sherry was so relieved about Kelly that she felt faint, but she managed to say, "I don't know, and the captain and crew don't speak English, just Chinese."

"I'll find a Chinese speaker," the admiral told her. "And I'm going to tell him to stay about ten miles offshore and away from those patrol boats. We'll monitor you from here and give you directions."

"Thank you, Admiral."

"I'm also going to tell him to get rid of his radar reflectors. I think we've got you on our scan, and we see you pretty clearly. Without them, you'll be all but invisible."

"Again, thanks."

"Thank me when all this is over."

She handed the microphone to Han, and soon he was babbling away with someone in Chinese.

Davis said, "See, it's going to be all right."

"Only when I see Kelly again."

Wednesday, March 12, 12:17 A.M.

Ali Haji had gone home to the small house he shared with his mother. He slipped inside without waking her, and went to his room to shed the remnants of the uniform of which he was so proud.

His time in the jungle, the lack of solid food, and the hiking had forced him to lose perhaps ten pounds. He felt much the better for it. Padding down the short hallway to the bathroom, he quietly drew a hot bath and languished in it for what seemed a long time. When the water turned cool, he got out, found his razor, and shaved very carefully. He went back to his room and selected his best uniform and dressed in it. The waistband was a little loose.

Haji felt like a new man.

Turning on the radio for news, he spent time disassembling, cleaning, and reassembling the M-16 rifle Major Shaikh had given him. It was so much better a weapon than the riot guns issued by the police force. This one had the selector for fully automatic fire.

There was no news on the radio, only soothing music intended to quiet the populace.

Haji was a little disgusted with the populace. They allowed men like Li Sen to rule their lives, forgetting forever all that the Sultan and his family had done for them. He missed Mohammed Hassanal, and hoped he would return soon.

For lack of guidance from his cousin, however, Ali Haji knew that he had a task to perform, one that Hassanal would approve.

Slinging the assault rifle over his shoulder, he let himself out the front door, and began the long walk to police headquarters. He had done it every day for many years, and the quiet streets were very familiar to him.

He did not know what he would find at the police station. Perhaps Omar Padang would be there, in his undercover guise. Together, the two of them could make a plan to free the Sultan and return the country to proper rule.

When he reached the station, he found only two police cars, but several civilian cars in the parking lot. There was also a helicopter. The force had been reduced, or perhaps more patrols were on the street.

He marched right in the side door, went down the hallway, and into the squad room.

He was surprised to find Li Sen and two other civilian

men there. It did not seem right that the usurper should be in his police station.

Two policemen stood near the door to the communications room, and Captain Nazir was speaking to them. He looked over their shoulders, saw Haji, and barked, "Arrest that man!"

Haji did not know quite what happened. He took a step backward into the corridor, his shoulder slumped, and the rifle sling slipped off it. Frantically he grabbed the rifle and raised the muzzle even as his thumb found the safety, then the fire selector.

Automatic.

He held the barrel down against its tendency to rise as he squeezed the trigger. In the squad room, the civilian men yelled as the rifle bucked and spit chunks of death. The staccato roar of the weapon echoed off the walls and hurt his ears.

Both of the policemen went down in the doorway, six rounds penetrating their chests, blood flying. Awg Nazir's eyes went opaque as four holes appeared in his stomach. Haji turned toward the civilians, forgetting to release the trigger, and a line of bullet holes chattered across the wall, then across the three men. All went down screaming.

And the rifle bolt snapped open and stayed.

The magazine was empty.

He shook his head, trying to clear his ears. They were numb.

Looked up to see Omar Padang standing in the door to the communications room, looking down at the dead men.

"Chief Padang!"

The man looked up at him, his eyes red with rage. He withdrew his semiautomatic, aimed it at Haji.

"Chief! It is me!"

And fired.

He fired at least four times because Haji counted them as he was hurled backward into the hallway. After four, he lost track.

Or something.

Wednesday, March 12, 12:21 A.M.

Koehler had barrel-rolled the King Air.

Without intending to do so.

As soon as Morris yelled, Koehler reacted, and the plane rolled, raising a few yelps from the passenger compartment.

A missile whished past the right wing.

And Koehler, who wasn't entirely up on his acrobatics—he didn't normally roll choppers—nearly lost his orientation. He did, in fact, lose about a thousand feet of altitude before he regained control.

In time for Morris to call out, "Try right this time. Now!"

He brought the left wing up and pulled back on the yoke. The Beech responded, and two missiles shot by on the left side.

"Level!"

"Pretty soon, guy. I want to breathe again, first."

He levelled off, found himself heading due east at 3,000 feet, and immediately began a left turn, climbing.

The coast fell off behind them.

"Jesus, Frank. Where'd the missiles come from?"

"Damned if I know, but they were tiny ones. Shoulder-fired."

"Just as lethal as big ones."

"I've got a puddle in my seat."

"How're the guys in back?"

Morris turned to look. "I think there're a few more puddles. Nobody hurt, though."

He finally got on track for the west and figured he was about fifteen minutes away from GT-Bravo.

"You often roll twins?" Morris asked.

"Always wanted to. Seemed like the thing to do at the time."

"Yeah, like you planned it."

"We could probably use some intelligence up here."

"My thought, exactly," Morris said.

"I meant the radio."

"Oh. Well, hell."

Morris called to the back, and Irra brought the radio up, trailing the antenna.

"Metal skin," Morris said, "but we should be high enough to get a good signal."

He was at 6,500 feet now, holding 220 knots. The airplane felt pretty good, though he could hear some high-pitched whistles when he shoved his headset off his ears. That would be the holes in the fuselage from a few ill-placed bullets.

"You can have her for a while, Army."

"Gee, thanks. After you've tired her out."

Irra handed him the microphone and held the radio so they could all hear the speaker. "That was very nice flying, Commander."

"That was lucky flying, Suraj."

He flipped the switch on the radio.

"Sledgehammer, Eagle Eye."

"Hammer here. Reindeer tells me you had a close call."

"Just flight-testing the controls. You have a position on us?"

"Roger. We show you twelve minutes off target at present course and speed. There is a problem, though."

"Tell me."

"Our overflight detected radar emissions. The platform's equipped with radar. We think if you penetrate some preselected range, we're going to set off Armageddon."

"Shit! Sorry, sir!"

"Understandable. We want you to orbit for a few minutes while we review some alternatives."

"Tell me just one, sir."

"We've embarked SEALs on a sub. We can sneak her through the blockade."

"Not without activating a few sonars, I think."

"We may have to take the chance. Are you orbiting?"

"Going now."

Morris went into a slight bank to the right and set up a right turn. Koehler locked in the autopilot.

Morris said, "All the best-laid plans, etcetera, etcetera."

"Have you ever considered landing a King Air on an aircraft carrier, Frank?"

"The thought and the image boggle my mind, Army. I think I'll use that chute back there."

Irra said, "I could jump from altitude and steer myself right onto the platform, Commander."

Kelly thought about it. "That's a possible, Suraj."

He pressed the transmit stud, "Hammer, I've got one parachute and a Gurkha sergeant major who says he can jump on the rig from any altitude. I believe him."

"That is a thought, Eagle. I'll put it on my list. While we're thinking about this, let me update you on the explosives."

The admiral recited some list that he said had been collected by a guy in the State Department and evaluated by Defense analysts.

"Three transmitters? Four-hundred-foot antennas?"

"Four-twenty."

Which wasn't surprising. ULF antennas were always long. Some submarines deployed antennas over a mile in length, just to get a long, drawn-out command from headquarters.

The length of the antennas was probably what limited the range of these transmitters. Which is what the experts from Defense were paid to figure out.

"But only three, and all on Bravo?"

"That's what they estimate. We'll have to get to them quickly and quietly."

"Yes, sir. Good to know."

For all the good it would do him.

"One other thing, Eagle. I've had a conversation with Eagle Eye Two."

"Two?"

"Says her name is Sheryl."

"Hot damn! Is she all right?" It was a good thing he wasn't flying the airplane. The relief that coursed through him made him giddy.

"Yes, and she'll have a story to tell you. She says don't worry about her."

"Monica?" Morris asked on the intercom.

"Is Monica Davis with her?" he asked the admiral.

"Roger. Also safe."

"Where is she?"

"You won't believe this." Sledgehammer told them about the Chinese junk. "We've got them positioned inside the embargo line, and we had them drop the radar reflectors. We no longer see them on our radars."

It took Kelly only a moment to see the possibility. He looked at Morris, who shrugged.

"Suraj?"

"Absolutely, Commander."

Hit the transmit. "You realize what you just said, Hammer?"

A full two minutes went by, and Koehler waited impatiently.

"I'll put it on my list of alternatives, Eagle. Damned dangerous to put that plane in the water."

"I'd have to do it at the platform, and probably not very quietly."

"Let's think it over."

"While we're thinking, give me a last position on the junk, and I'll see if I can find her."

Kelly thought the admiral's response somewhat reluctant. "Seven miles, your bearing two-seven-four."

"Eagle out." He dropped the mike. "You find it, Frank?"

"No sweat."

Morris put it right on the deck, flying half-blind in the darkness five hundred feet off the water. Fortunately, there were no platforms in the area.

They didn't see a thing on the first pass, and turned back for another try.

Irra, who probably had the best eyes, saw it first. "There!"

It was a blocky silhouette, a bare blackness darker than the water, and they went by fast, banking into a turn to circle her.

"Black sails," Morris said.

"Beautiful," Koehler told him.

"How we going to do this?"

"With you and Suraj strapped in, in back. We'll probably bounce three times. As soon as she begins to settle, you pop the door and get everyone out."

"If she bounces four times, I'm going to be pissed."

"I'll buy you a beer."

"You'll do that, anyway. Keep the wings level, or we're going to corkscrew, and I won't like it."

The radio blurted, "Eagle! Go two-five-seven-point-one on standard UHF."

Koehler dialled it in.

"Eagle here."

"Kelly!"

"Hey, hon! I'm coming to see you."

"Kelly, don't do this! We can meet somewhere else."

"It'll be a breeze, Sher. Just stand by for us, will you?"

"Oh, God! Be careful!"

"See you in a few minutes."

Morris said, "Wings level, Navy," and shed his headset. He slid out of his seat and followed Irra to the back.

As soon as he was gone, Koehler felt alone and wished the Beech had more emergency exits.

This time, as he flew past the junk, her navigation lights came on giving him a decent orientation. He flew on westward for several miles, then turned back into the eastern wind.

As he came out of the turn, he eased the power levers back, and shortly thereafter, dropped his flaps to full extension. He needed all the lift he could get for extremely slow flight.

As normal in the area, the seas were running smooth, and he worried less about the first contact with the sea than actually figuring out when he was going to touch down. In the darkness, he had very little depth perception.

The speed drained off quickly, and his altimeter kept spinning backward.

Four hundred feet.

Ahead he saw the distant lights of the junk and aimed to the right side of her. If things went wrong, he didn't want the airplane spinning into her.

Two-fifty feet.

Speed 110 knots.

Closer.

One-twenty-five. He couldn't tell by looking.

Trust the instruments. That's what the instructors always say.

Speed 90 knots.

The plane felt as if she were sagging, the tail dropping.

He eased the yoke forward.

Navigation lights coming up fast now.

Fifty feet?

She was stalling out.

Nose down.

Tension from the passenger compartment seemed to roll forward on him.

Twenty?

Star gleam on the wave tops. He thought he was in imminent danger.

Eighty knots.

The muscles in his left arm bunched up as he fought to keep the wings level. He reached out with his right hand for the pedestal. Killed the turboprops. Feathered the props.

She came off power skittishly.

The left wing dipped.

He brought it back.

The tail went down.

Hit the surface.

Hauled back on the yoke to keep the tail down.

Wham!

The fuselage slammed into the sea. Loud banging.

Then the airplane went airborne again.

Down. Skipped on a wave top, slewed sideways.

He couldn't control that.

Rose.

Down.

Slammed hard. He was shoved against the straps as the Beech went sideways. The right wing went down, caught a wave top, and she spun the other way.

And slowed, settled.

Koehler was half-dazed, but slapped the harness releases, and climbed out of his seat. There was still forward momentum, but she was slowing fast.

And sinking fast.

He stuck his head through the cockpit doorway and saw a sea of smiles. Irra had his thumb up again. Morris was out of his seat, undogging the airstair.

"Pretty decent, Navy," he called.

"I don't know how many times we skipped."

"I don't, either, and I don't give a damn." Morris shoved the door open, and water began to pour inside.

"Everybody out!" Irra yelled.

Wednesday, March 12, 1:47 A.M.

The two Zodiaks bounded along, skipping across the wave tops at thirty knots, forced along by their two-hundred-horsepower outboard motors.

They were amazingly quiet for all of the power they exuded, Kyoto thought.

He clutched a rope fixed to the top of the rubber bladder near the bow to keep himself from falling overboard and watched the huge stern of the ULCC coming up on them. It stood high against the sky, blocking out the stars.

In his boat were ten Japanese sailors. In the boat alongside, Captain Goodfellow led ten American Marines. Goodfellow waved at him, and Kyoto could barely make out the gesture. When he did, he returned it.

They closed more rapidly than he had thought they would, and he was soon able to make out the phosphorescence in the bow wave coming off the patrol boat. The white numerals "122" on the stern soon appeared, seeming to dance by themselves above the surface of the sea.

The patrol boat was the target.

As hoped for, but not anticipated, there seemed to be no sentinel aboard. The Zodiaks spread apart as they came upon her and moved up on either side, Kyoto's boat on the left.

He reached up and grabbed at a lifeline stanchion. The deck was about a meter-and-a-half above the surface, and he had to let go of his death grip on the Zodiak's own lifeline.

He found it, gripped tight.

The Zodiak bounded up and down, changing her vertical position in relation to the patrol craft, and as it rose, he leaped upward, found a line with his left hand, and pulled himself aboard.

He was not the first. Other sailors clambered aboard along with him, and in less than a minute, they had heaved their canvas bags of equipment aboard, transferred to the boat, and allowed the Zodiak to fall off behind.

He found himself on a narrow side deck, just aft of amidships, leaning up against a low cabin roof. Toward the stern, he could see the rear gun mount. Across the top of the cabin, he saw Goodfellow's Marines.

Forward, the superstructure was elevated, with an enclosed flying bridge, machine gun mounts to either side. There appeared to be no one on the bridge, an oversight caused by days of being in tow behind the tanker.

Still, the assigned Marine padded quickly forward, disappearing behind the superstructure. He would work his way up to the bridge and subdue any hostile located there.

Kyoto quickly advanced up the deck, followed by three sailors. He found the side hatchway into the cabin, looked back at the sailors, and when they nodded, gripped the handle, twisted, and pulled the hatch open.

The sailors slipped inside.

He followed and saw Goodfellow entering from the other side. They were in a narrow corridor spanning the breadth of the boat. Supposedly, there were storage spaces aft, bunk and mess rooms forward.

Two sailors went aft, and Kyoto went forward with the Marines.

They found three sleeping Bruneians, and the boat was theirs two minutes later.

Now, they had only to wait for Space Mountain.

Wednesday, March 12, 1:58 A.M.

Maki Hirosiuta watched it all.

He thought it fortunate that he was probably the only person on the tanker who looked aft, and he did so through the large port in his stateroom. Unable to sleep, he had been sitting in his easy chair, staring at the sea, when he saw changes in his view.

Thambipillai always remained on the bridge, where he thought he was in control, staring ahead at where he thought he was going. The man could not even plot a decent navigational course, and he had no grasp on the concepts of the Global Positioning System. He was steaming a course toward the north, hoping he would hit something.

Hirosiuta felt reenergized. Something was going to happen yet; though he had no idea quite what it would be. He envisioned the next step as he tightened his necktie and prepared to leave the cabin.

In the last ten hours, Thambipillai had become complacent, allowing Hirosiuta to keep his crews busy in the engineering and other spaces, cleaning and maintaining equipment. Hirosiuta advocated these duties as necessary to operating a ship the size of the *Hokkaido*. Thambipillai grinned his disdain.

And allowed it to happen.

Now, the true captain of the ULCC must make his rounds among the night watch and inform them of what was about to happen. He must have them keep the Bruneians looking forward, or downward, or upward.

He hoped the fatalities would be few.

Wednesday, March 12, 2:14 A.M.

As soon as he had determined that Li Sen and the others were dead, Omar Padang declared himself the President of the Republic of Brunei.

He stepped over the body of Awg Nazir into the communications room and told one of the cowering sergeants, "Call the radio stations and tell them that Provisional President Li has been killed by an assassin and that I, Omar Padang, am now the President. Do not give other information. Then, get a detail in here to remove the bodies."

"Certainly, Min . . . uh, President Padang."

This has certainly worked out well, Padang thought.

Everything was moving ahead splendidly. The Gurkhas were gone from the country. Yes, they had left a booby trap behind that proved unfortunate for Shamin Bakir, but that was to be expected in the course of a revolution. The flight of the Gurkhas resolved the problem of armed resistance internally.

Externally, his last report from Moonstone confirmed that the United Nations force was observing his line of demarcation. The navy was turning back the deserting commerce privateers. It was all being accomplished in the week he had set for himself.

He was the President. Again, on his own timetable.

He had only one irritant, and that was Dyg Thambipillai.

Padang had worked that one out, however. It seemed the Japanese were resolute in denying him payment for the oil on board the *Maru Hokkaido*. Very well. Then, no one should have it. He would tell Thambipillai to scuttle the ship at one o'clock today, then return to Brunei with the patrol craft. Thambipillai would find this action very dramatic, and to his liking. He would follow orders, this time.

"Sir!" one of the sergeants said. "The *Bulkiah* calls you."

Padang stepped around a splotch of still bright blood on the linoleum and took the microphone.

"Padang."

"*Bulkiah*, Minister. . . ."

He almost corrected the captain, then remembered he wouldn't have heard yet.

". . . we have just had a sonar contact."

"Well?"

"A submarine, sir. It is inbound for the coast."

Those charlatans!

"Kill it, Captain."

"Ah, sir, we have lost the contact now."

"Then find it and do your duty."

Padang threw the microphone against the wall.

He didn't know what the task force thought it could accomplish with a submarine, but he certainly was offended by the thought of having it in *his* waters.

Without announcing his destination, Padang spun on his heel, stepped over the bodies in the doorway, and went down the side corridor. He also had to step over the body of Ali Haji.

The fool.

In the parking lot, he strode directly for his helicopter, roused the sleeping pilot, and told him, "We will go to the platform."

If that submarine was not sunk or out of his area of influence by six o'clock this morning, he would give that task force commander something to think about.

Fortunately, Nepal was right next door to China, and two of the Gurkha soldiers spoke fluent Chinese. With their help and his assurances to Captain Han Lo that the United States Navy would be Han's protector and underwriter, the junk had soon been set on a course for the oil field.

Slim Avery and his techs scoured the ship for anything that might provide an unnecessary radar return. They locked down the navigation, sonar, and radar equipment that, if activated, would provide recognizable emissions.

"And tell him that I owe him the largest favor of my life for rescuing my wife."

The soldier made the interpretation, and Han grinned even wider and bowed his head several times.

Koehler was sodden, dripping on the salon's fine carpet, and he hadn't let go of Sherry since he'd climbed out of the dinghy and up the landing stage of the junk. She didn't seem to mind, stood with her back against his chest, clasping his right hand in both of hers, tugging his arm tightly against her body. He didn't mind, either; she felt good to him.

Morris had disappeared somewhere with Monica Davis. He said he was seasick and looking for a railing to lean over.

Irra entered the salon and said, "Commander, we have lost some of the equipment."

"Weapons?"

"No, sir. My men are fieldstripping them now, to clean them. The bag with the plastic explosive and grenades was lost, as was the encrypted radio."

"I was tired of talking to Sledgehammer, anyway, Suraj. We'll make do."

He had already explained to Sherry what they were going

to attempt to do, and she was dead set against it. Dead set, but acquiescent.

"You won't need them?" she asked.

"No, hon. We're going to be very quiet, go in, and come out. Then you and I will go sailing somewhere."

She turned to him and her eyes misted. "We don't have a boat."

"We'll find one. The only thing is, I'd like to put you and Monica in the dinghy and send you ashore."

"Bullshit! We're not going through that again! You said this wasn't going to be particularly dangerous."

"For me. But, just in case—"

"Forget it. You're staying in my sight." Her eyes bored into his, as if she meant every word. There was also a red tinge of anger in them.

Koehler sighed. He didn't really think the peril level was high for those on the junk. She'd just sail right by the platform.

"Commander, sir," the interpreter said. "Captain Han asks if you'd like to have dry clothing."

He had broken the spell, and Sherry's stare, and Kelly said, "Thank him, but no. We don't have much time."

And by now, as they closed on GT-Bravo, he was almost dried by the warm breeze coming over the gunwale. She had let go of his hand, but not without a whispered threat. "If you kill yourself, I'll hate you."

"Then, I won't." He kissed her briefly, not caring that a dozen eyes watched, then turned and went down the steps of the landing stage.

Sherry and Monica stood at the rail and watched him go.

The supply techs, Morris, and the five Gurkhas were gathered on the stage or on the lower steps. Kelly had vetoed Slim Avery's volunteerism. The man was getting up there in age, and this would be a strenuous climb.

The stage was lowered to about two feet above the water, allowing for the starboard heel of the junk when she had to tack onto another course beyond the platform.

Kelly hadn't seen much of the ship, but he loved her. There were creaks and groans in the rigging and the hull, but in the great scheme of things, she was almost totally muted. The rush of the water along the hull was the most alarming sound.

But they wouldn't hear it on the platform, where the main decks were fifty feet above the surface.

"Damned ironic, don't you think?" Morris asked. He didn't bother whispering since anyone on the platform wouldn't hear him, anyway.

"What's that, Army guy?"

He patted the hull. "Takes technology a century old to defeat today's high-tech systems. Your admiral has a whole arsenal of multimillion-dollar choppers, fighters, and missiles out there at sea, and he can't reach us."

"I like it, Frank. This is stealth without a half-billion-dollar price tag."

"Yeah, I do, too."

"You didn't get seasick?"

"Nah. This baby's more stable than those corks you ride."

Han himself was at the helm, and his crew were spotted all over the ship, ready to do his bidding with lines and sails. She glided through the night, long past the pumping station, which was lighted well enough for them to discern the tankers gathered around it.

Ahead, emerging from the night, he saw his platform. He'd know the silhouette anywhere.

"Coming up, guys. Don't forget: The admin office is on this side, the elevator side."

The towering structure came closer, rising high into the

sky. There were some dim lights on the fourth and fifth decks. He could hear the wind moan in some of the rigging.

Despite the size of the junk, the platform dwarfed her. Kelly would like to have seen an aerial view of the junk passing the rig. Kind of like scenes he'd seen in Hong Kong, junks with a skyscraper background.

He slung his Armalite, wrapped in plastic wrapper, over his chest and checked the pouches hanging on the web belt.

The junk heeled a little farther to port as Han changed his steering, giving the platform a bit more leeway.

No one said anything. Sergeant Major Irra sat on the edge of the landing, then let himself off into the water. The rest of them followed.

It was warm, almost silky. Buoyant.

Koehler looked up and watched the junk glide by. In a minute she disappeared into the western night. He set up a steady dog paddle, and it didn't take long to reach the closest pier.

At surface level, only the drilling conductors and legs entered the sea. On this leg, however, the elevator guides and skeletal framework were mounted. Naturally, the elevator was not waiting for them. It was always raised, in case of storms or high seas.

The latticework grid of girders and reinforcing bars was all they needed, though. He grabbed a cross beam and pulled himself high enough to get a toehold on a lower bar, then pushed himself up out of the water. The others did the same, all around the perimeter of the cage that contained the elevator. They waited a few minutes to let most of the water drain from their clothing. Kelly tore the plastic wrap from the M-18.

Then it was a steady climb, not overly arduous, but he didn't look down. Forty, fifty feet, was a long way, even if one couldn't see the surface.

He could hear the others grunting from time to time, muffling a curse as they skinned a knuckle or banged a shin against steel.

When he reached the bottom side of the first deck, the drilling deck, he wrapped his arm around a vertical girder and reconnoitered. The elevator shaft continued up through the decks, and he was a trifle reluctant to move around to the inside of it. What if some jerk decided to bring the car down?

The others also rested, hanging to the outside of the shaft cage.

Koehler wrestled with the button on his shirt flap, finally popped it off, and got two fingers inside the wet pocket to retrieve his penlight. After checking up the shaft and seeing no one, he turned on the light and aimed it toward the sea.

Swinging the beam slightly to the left, approximately under the location of the administration office on the fourth deck, he found what he was looking for.

"Right there, Suraj."

"Yes, Commander. I see them."

Wednesday, March 12, 3:36 A.M.

"This is the *Bulkiah.* I am calling Father Time."

"Father Time," Padang said.

He had commandeered Tan Hashim's chair at the desk, and Hashim paced back and forth in the small office, a malevolent look on his face. Hashim wanted to be the one to do the button-pushing.

The destroyer's captain said, "We have located the submarine."

"And where is she?"

"Ah, sir, nine kilometers directly north of the oil field."

"You are to begin dropping depth charges on them, Captain."

"As you order, sir."

Padang said to Hashim, "We warned them, did we not?"

"We did."

"Lieutenant, you may have the honor of activating the first detonation."

Hashim's face brightened immediately. "Sir! The first one?"

"Yes. We will give them a couple spills to reinforce our resolve. Do it now."

Hashim leaned over the desk, touched the first radio reverently, and pushed down the small toggle switch that armed the system. Then he raised the clear plastic cover over another toggle switch, and pushed down on it.

He smiled at Padang.

Padang smiled back.

But nothing else happened.

Wednesday, March 12, 3:38 A.M.

Frank Morris had taken a piece of quarter-inch nylon line with a small hammer tied to the end, swung it wide and outboard of the platform, and when it came back, it had snared all three of the antennas hanging from the port of the admin office and trailing into the sea.

Koehler had figured that four-hundred-foot antennas had to go somewhere, and if they weren't hanging from the derrick, they'd be hanging into the water.

As soon as Morris had drawn them in, Suraj Irra had brandished his *kukri* and neatly severed all three.

"Now, we go up," Kelly said.

Quickly they scrambled to the inner side of the elevator cage, climbed the few feet to the first deck, then clambered through the grid work onto the deck. It felt good to have a solid deck under his feet, Kelly thought.

Unslinging his rifle, Koehler led the charge toward the stairwell. They raced up the stairs, some men peeling off at predetermined decks to begin their searches.

Koehler and Irra had the fourth deck. He was breathing hard when they reached it.

He stopped to look around the darkened deck. There was so much equipment welded and bolted in the oddest places that one had to be careful or risk shins and hips.

Light seeped from beneath the door to the admin shack.

He snapped on his penlight and quickly shone it around the deck.

"There!" Irra whispered.

He brought the light back. A body was hanging from the perimeter lifeline. Judging by the condition of the skin, it had been hanging there for some time.

"Minister Mohammed Hassanal," Irra said.

"Damn. We're too late."

"Not for everything, Commander."

Koehler killed the light and they started for the admin shack, just as the door burst open.

A fat man in a white suit, and a skinny man in a uniform, rushed out.

"Omar Padang!" Irra called out. "I arrest you on behalf of the Sultan!"

"What in the name of Allah!" the fat man yelled, knowing he was backlit by the doorway.

Three shots rang out on another deck, and that galvanized the skinny man into action. His hand darted toward a semiautomatic holstered at his waist.

Irra shot him.

One bullet hole appeared above his left eye, and the force of the impact slammed his head back. He tumbled backward into the shack.

Padang rushed out of the light and started running across the deck, his fat body rolling as he ran.

He was headed for the ladder to the helicopter pad, and Koehler looked up to see a rotor projecting over the edge of the pad. He hadn't expected a chopper on the platform.

Irra swung his Armalite to line up on Padang.

"Suraj. I'd like this guy alive."

Irra lowered the assault rifle. "Very well, Commander."

"Death might be too easy on him."

"As you wish."

Padang reached the bottom of the ladder and started up, yelling at his pilot to start the helicopter.

Koehler ran to the southside crane and quickly climbed the short ladder to the operator's cab. There was electricity available on the platform, so he wasn't surprised when he released the safety switch and found he had power on the controls.

The chopper's turbines were winding up as he rotated the cab and switched on the floodlights. Padang was halfway up the ladder, and he looked back when the lights hit him. His face was tightened in a rictus of anger and fear.

He kept climbing.

Koehler looked up the boom, which was almost vertical, and shoved the control rod. The boom began to lower. He stopped it when it was almost directly over the helicopter, thirty feet above it.

The rotors had begun to turn.

Padang ran around the nose and pulled open the passenger-side door. He pulled his bulky body inside.

Koehler released the brake on the lift cable. The heavy block came down fast.

Right within the arc of the rotors.

Snapping and gnashing, the rotors came apart, flying in all directions. The helicopter reacted by jumping and spinning on the pad.

But it didn't go anywhere, and the half-bright pilot immediately killed the overrevving turbines.

Koehler secured the safety switch and climbed down from the crane cab.

He and Irra stood there, looking up at the landing pad, until Morris came down from the fifth deck in the elevator.

He had a large gaggle of happy royals with him.

Sergeant Major Suraj Irra asked, "Now, Commander?"

"I believe so."

Irra went to the admin shack to use the radio for a brief message: Space Mountain.

Wednesday, March 12, 3:43 A.M.

The patrol boat bobbed on the surface about forty meters behind the tanker, tethered to her by a thick steel cable. Through the forward ports in the mess compartment, Kyoto could only see a massive steel wall, and high above him, the meter-high lettering *Maru Hokkaido.* Below and aft, he could hear the diesel generator chugging.

The hour and a half the boarding party had spent loitering in the darkened cabin was nerve-wracking. The only real diversion was when one of the sailors or Marines went aft to check on the three prisoners bound and gagged in one of the staterooms. For the most part, they spent their time examining and reexamining their equipment. They adjusted their black clothing and their web gear.

The radio they had brought with them rested on the galley table and did nothing.

Meoshi Kyoto was on the verge of declaring himself retired from the Army and taking Kato Asume's offer to be a diplomat. Kim would be happy, and Kyoto would no longer find himself waiting interminably on others.

Diplomats expected to wait. Soldiers expected to act. He was—

"Space Mountain," the radio squawked.

"That's it," Goodfellow said. "Let's go, gyrenes and tars."

They had not actually rehearsed, but the phases of the operation had been burned in by constant repetition, and Kyoto thought they performed flawlessly. Standing, they each grabbed the equipment they were responsible for, and filed out of the side hatchways.

To the forward deck, past the bow gun mount.

Six men squatted on the deck, lifted the rope guns from their packs, aimed, and fired. The wind whipped the dull explosions away. The dark lines arced from the barrels, chasing the grappling hooks, climbing, fighting the wind, and reaching for the antenna deck, seven stories above them. Five of the grappling hooks found a purchase, on an antenna, a cable, something. They had only planned on four connecting.

"Great!" shouted Goodfellow. "Let's go, go, go!"

The near ends of four lines were secured to bitts and stanchions, whatever was closest to hand, and the four strongest men stepped forward, clipped the hook from the web gear crossing their chests to the line, and without apparent thought, stepped over the lifeline and off the bow. Like monkeys, they scrambled up the lines, tugging with their arms, clamping the feet to the line and pushing. Behind them trailed additional nylon ropes connected to their belts.

On the bow deck, four other men slowly paid out the lines the climbers were carrying upward. It seemed to take forever, and it was a long climb. As they neared the top, their efforts were obviously a struggle. They not only had to contend with the climb, but with the bobbing of the patrol boat, which caused the lines to go taut, then slack.

But they made it.

Kyoto snapped the clips on the wrists of his gloves, patted the Uzi submachine gun strapped to his side, then stepped forward. He unclipped the coil of rope from his belt and handed it to a sailor, then stepped over the lifeline and clipped his web hook to the suspended line. The sailor took the end of the line the first climber had towed upward, cut off the excess length with a K-bar combat knife, and quickly tied it to Kyoto's harness.

"Good luck, sir!"

"Thank you, seaman. You, also."

Kyoto tugged on the second line, felt a responding pull, and stepped off the bow. The line sagged, and he nearly hit the sea in front of the bow, but then felt himself being pulled upward. He swung until he got an ankle over the anchor line, then got a firm grip on it and started pulling himself upward. With the assistance of the man at the top, his ordeal was soon over. He had trouble getting a leg up and over the edge of the deck, but then the Marine grabbed his webbing and hauled him up.

"Welcome aboard, Colonel."

"I am glad to be here." He found he was gasping, trying to recover his breathing.

The two of them then bent to the task of pulling the next man aboard, and the operation was completed in seventeen minutes.

When they were all aboard, Captain Goodfellow immediately organized his party on the forward edge of the antenna deck. They refastened lines and prepared to rappel to the main deck.

Kyoto and one sailor went to the port side, secured their lines, and when he saw the starboard team was in place, he waved, then slipped over the side.

The wind was strong, tugging at his clothing, but he had only to lower himself a dozen feet, until he found himself on the port wing of the bridge. His assistant landed beside him, and he freed his weapon as he peered through a broken window.

There were seven men on the bridge, and he immediately picked out the aggressors from their bedraggled naval uniforms and unshaven appearance. A trim Japanese in a white uniform was apparently the captain of the tanker. He would be Maki Hirosiuta. Another officer in whites stood at the helm. Two men in denims were polishing instruments, and they had mops and pails of water nearby.

Hirosiuta first noticed the two Marines on the starboard wing, crouching outside the window, only their black watch caps and eyes showing, but swept his gaze on past them, stared through the forward windscreen for a moment, then lazily brought his attention to the port wing. His eyes caught Kyoto's, and he gave a brief smile.

Hirosiuta spoke a soft order in Japanese to the two seamen, and they finished with their polishing, grabbed their pails and mops, and started toward the back of the bridge.

Kyoto had a premonition that it would be this way all over the ship. The boarding party was to have much help.

As the two men passed the guards stationed at the back of the bridge, the pails came flying up, water spilling forward, dashing the men in their faces. Curses in Malay erupted.

Kyoto immediately grabbed the handle of the door and yanked it open. He stepped inside as the other Bruneian spun toward the commotion at the back of the bridge.

One of the guards raised his rifle with one hand, wiping soapy water from his face with the other.

And a Marine coming in from the other side shot him.

The single report echoed in the bridge, but didn't seem to faze Hirosiuta.

He looked down at the fallen man, then said to Kyoto, "I am pleased to welcome you aboard my ship."

Kyoto stepped forward and offered a slight bow from

the waist. "I am happy to be here, Captain. I am Colonel Kyoto."

Hirosiuta returned the bow, then said, "May I present Lieutenant Thambipillai. He believes he is a captain, but I think of him as a pirate."

Thambipillai seemed out of his depth. He gazed stupidly at Kyoto, then turned as he heard the turbines swarming alongside the tanker. Four helicopters appeared out of the darkness, flashing on their landing lights.

The Marines had arrived, but Kyoto did not think they would be necessary.

One of the Marines on the bridge stuck his Uzi in Thambipillai's face. "Would you like to go to the main deck, pirate? Or would you like to taste this?"

A defeated Thambipillai elected to lead the Marine to the main deck.

"You are not in the Navy, Colonel Kyoto?" Hirosiuta asked.

"No. I am in the Army, Captain."

He rather thought he would stay there.

On more days than not, he felt very good about himself. Especially on a day like today.

PARADISE
REVISITED

Eighteen

Wednesday, March 12, 4:07 A.M.

The two personnel carriers entered Kuala Belait side by side, Gurkhas and policemen clinging to precarious positions on the tops of both.

Resistance was minimal, and only a few shots were exchanged with rebel forces before the revolutionaries dropped their weapons and fled.

Benjamin Shaikh rode in the commander's position on one APC, and Captain Shrestha was in the same position on the other vehicle.

They drove past the hospital waving at oil workers lounging on the front lawn, and when they reached the residence compound, found that Captain Singh was already there with his troops deployed around the compound. The foreign workers were out and about, conversing with the soldiers, sharing soft drinks and snacks.

Shaikh called down to his driver, "We will go to the barracks."

"Sir."

The APC wheeled to the right and drove toward the barracks. There was a great deal of debris to be cleaned from the streets. His crashed Black Hawk still blocked the first street in the compound. The apartment building where the Huey had gone in was completely destroyed.

When they reached the barracks, and Shaikh entered his orderly room, he found that the occupation of Shamin Bakir had left it the worst for wear. The radio still worked, however, and he used it to call Sledgehammer.

"This is Lion One."

"Good to hear from you, Lion. The Bruneian naval forces are showing white flags everywhere, so we're under way again. I've got ten helicopter loads of Marines on the way."

"They won't be necessary here, sir. Kuala Belait is secure. I would recommend that they be diverted to the capital. I am uncertain of conditions there."

"We'll do just that. Tomorrow or the next day, I would like to have you and your officers join me for dinner aboard the carrier."

"I look forward to that, sir. Good day to you."

"It is that, Lion. Sledgehammer out."

He turned to Shrestha. "Do you think it will ever be the same again?"

"No, Major. The world now knows where Brunei is. Some will think that democracy is necessary in this country."

"You are probably correct, Captain. It will not be the same paradise."

Tuesday, March 11, 4:20 P.M.

Drieser's back ached fiercely, but he couldn't stop himself from pacing around his office. He kept waiting for another call from Hap Harned, but suspected that he wouldn't get one.

It was all over now, and Harned would be engaged in the cleanup activities.

It was hard, being so far from the action, but Drieser was just as glad he was. Real guns were not his forte.

"Chris, you look like hell."

"Thank you for sharing that with me, Judy."

"You haven't been out of the office in a week. What you need is about two days in a hot tub."

"Bliss," he said. "Maybe not the paradise of Brunei, but awfully damned close."

"I've got a hot tub," she said.

"What? I don't believe it!"

"That I have a hot tub?"

"No, that you . . . well, I just don't believe it."

"Try," she said.

Wednesday, March 12, 9:40 A.M.

The *Harmonious Spirit* was on a broad reach, slicing the sea in a joyous mood.

Kelly Koehler had the conn.

He stood behind the huge mahogany wheel on the high afterdeck, his feet braced against the pitch of the deck, and his right arm wrapped around Sherry's waist. Her hair flew in the wind.

God, he felt good.

"I told you I'd take you sailing. You just didn't expect such a grand boat."

"I wish you'd taken a shower first."

"Complaining?"

"Not in the least, my dear."

"I could do this for weeks," he said.

"Envoy Hua wants his residence back."

"We promised it by five. He'll get it."

"And Captain Han is very nervous."

Han Lo sat on the edge of a settee on the starboard side, carefully watching Koehler. He grinned.

On the port-side settee, Frank Morris nuzzled Monica Davis's neck. Morris had decided he liked sailing, as long as it was a huge, huge sailing ship.

"I owe Captain Han a large Chinese dinner," Koehler said.

"He might like something other than Chinese, for a change," Sherry told him.

"We'll send out for pizza."

She elbowed him in the side, then winced. "What's that?"

"Present from a damned good friend."

She stepped away from him, raised the flap of his shirt, and extracted the sheath from his belt.

"What *is* it?"

"It's called a *kukri*, hon. Only the best guys get to carry it."

THE AUTHOR

William H. Lovejoy is the best-selling author of many novels, including *Dark Morning, Shanghai Star, Back\Slash, Red Rain, China Dome,* and *White Night.* A Vietnam veteran, former college president, and former college system chief fiscal officer, he is the fiscal officer for the Wyoming Community College Commission and lives in Cheyenne, Wyoming, where he is at work on his next novel.

FLY THE DANGEROUS SKIES OF TOMORROW
THE WINGMAN SERIES BY MACK MALONEY

WINGMAN	(0-7860-0310-3, $4.99)
THE CIRCLE WAR	(0-7860-0346-4, $4.99)
THE LUCIFER CRUSADE	(0-7860-0388-X, $4.99)
THUNDER IN THE EAST	(0-7860-0428-2, $4.99)
THE TWISTED CROSS	(0-7860-0467-3, $4.99)
THE FINAL STORM	(0-7860-0505-X, $4.99)
FREEDOM EXPRESS	(0-7860-4022-9, $3.99)
TARGET: POINT ZERO	(0-7860-0299-9, $4.99)
DEATH ORBIT	(0-7860-0357-X, $4.99)
THE SKY GHOST	(0-7860-0452-5, $4.99)